A Light Deficiency

Andrew Lewis

To Amanda for all your love and support and imagination.
Without you, Luke would have never gone to Rome.

Cover by Samuel Cotterall

Thank you Chris for all your support.

This is a work of fiction. Names, characters, organizations, places, events, and incidents are either products of the author's imagination or used fictitiously. Any resemblance to actual persons, living or dead, or actual events is purely coincidental.

PART ONE

CHAPTER 1: THE HANGING MAN.

Luke didn't take his normal route through the woods that morning. Of course, Luke, being Luke, replayed this arbitrary change over and over, finally convincing himself that fate had somehow led him on that seemingly insignificant Tuesday morning. A morning that would change his life forever.

In fact, if the agency had rung, as they often did at 7.30am, he would have probably been sitting in front of his usual group of disengaged teens sensing fresh meat and a typical supply lesson of doing 'fuck all', with the added bonus of a few laughs at the expense of 'Stand-In-Sir'. Luke's heart sank when his appearance in class was greeted with a sporadic cheer. To an outsider this might suggest approval - but after 3 years on the supply circuit Luke knew different.

Luke hated teaching. He hated the fact that these children - complete strangers - sensed what he knew himself: he was a weak and vulnerable man. And he hated most of all recalling the man he used to be when Sarah would send him off in the morning with a kiss and an encouraging word if she sensed Luke needed it. She was good at that. Now Luke was very alone in the world and thoroughly beaten, living his very own version of quiet desperation. His version, though, was a far more prosaic version than the one he read about at university. That had always seemed quite heroic. Luke couldn't even do desperation properly!

But, if pushed, Luke would have admitted at this point in his life he was better than he *had* been - certainly better than the months after Sarah died. He cycled a bit now and went to the pub on Sundays to watch the football, instead of retreating from the world completely. And every day he ran with Noah, Sarah's Golden Retriever, through Sunnyhurst Woods. In fact, this is what Luke was doing when he found Richard's body on the top path that Tuesday morning.

Luke found a fleeting sense of security in routine and repeated actions. The path most taken was his path in every sense - and that was the path that followed the stream through woods and took a right at the bandstand before meandering uphill towards the kissing gate and the top road that dissected the reservoir and eventually ran back down to The Sunnyhurst Pub. And, anyway, Luke really didn't like the idea of running up the steep scar of a path that lay immediately in front of him as he crossed the bridge before the bandstand.

Yet for some strange reason on that unremarkable morning Luke *did* take the steep path. It might have been that Noah had led, and he, in his usual reverie, followed instinctively. It might have been that Luke was feeling uncharacteristically strong that morning. He had thought about it a lot but whatever led him *up* instead of *across* on that cold Tuesday, he really did not know. But up he went. The path snaked left then right then left again before it met the higher path - a much quieter and uncertain route that had become overgrown through lack of regular use.

As he got closer to the top where the higher path intersected, Luke became conscious of Noah's sudden change in behaviour. Luke snapped out of his reverie and into the moment. The dog stopped on the path and lay down like he would when another, fiercer dog approached. Yet there was no sign of another dog. More strange, however, was the dog's mood - Noah whined and suddenly panted hard. Luke had never seen him behave like this before.

But the dog's strange behaviour was instantly forgotten when Luke turned to follow Noah's gaze. A man was hanging from the tree straight in front of him, a mere six feet from where Noah had stopped. Both looked up, frozen in the moment. Luke had only seen one dead person in his life, Sarah in the hospice. Her face in death had been beautiful - he had been impressed at *how* beautiful - almost childlike - Sarah had looked in death. Not just asleep, at total peace. The face that confronted Luke now was very different. Try as he may, he could not avert his gaze. The face was tilted back and the mouth hung open like a gate on a broken hinge and a red tongue protruded out of the dark chasm. Below the jaw was a thin rope that ran around the neck, fastened to a thick branch above the bench. The rope had eaten into the flesh and separated it, it had pulled the flesh above the rope tight under the jaw like a rolled-up stocking, revealing a gaping wound underneath of dried blood, sinew and bone. This was a terrible sight - something of nightmares. And yet it was the eyes of the man that frightened Luke most. It was these he would never forget. They were open and seemed to be staring into the distance at some horror too dreadful to imagine. What, thought Luke, had this man been thinking at the moment of death!

Luke suddenly became aware of Noah's bark. How long he had been barking, he did not know. But the bark was insistent and it diverted Luke's attention away from the corpse for long enough for him to become aware of himself. He felt as though all the air had been sucked from his body as he stood there barely breathing. Luke's instinct was to run but he could not move. He looked again at the hanging man. The face slowly evolved from abstract into something more familiar. Richard!

'Richard!' My God, Richard!' Luke shouted out, involuntarily. *'Oh, My God, Richard!'* he cried. The sound of Luke's own voice shocked him and Noah immediately stopped barking, mistakenly believing his master was shouting at him.

The dog turned tail and raced down the path – and fearful of being left alone with the gargoyled head, Luke summoned all his will and followed the dog. Luke nearly ran into Noah in his gathering speed; he only had one thought - to get down the hill and out of the woods as quickly as possible to a place where he hoped he would be able to draw breath. He felt like a drowning man deep underwater and desperately clawing for the surface and air and daylight. Luke ran and ran, he was usually so mindful of Noah but now his dog trailed behind as he reached the edge of the woods and the sanctuary of civilisation and roads and houses. At this point a more rational mind would have stopped the first person he saw but this option did not occur to Luke's frenzied mind. He ran on. And he ran until he reached his own doorstep.

Retrieving his house key from the zip pocket in the back of his jogging pants, Luke stabbed at the Yale lock of the front door of the small terraced house he once shared with Sarah. The second attempt found the aperture and Luke twisted the key violently with his right hand and pushed the door open. He'd quite forgotten about Noah at this point and was startled when the dog pushed past him. Luke threw himself onto his couch face down, gasping for air. A surplus of adrenaline shot into every muscle and cavity of his body, delivering its poisonous cocktail of chemicals. Luke had experienced this many times, but he'd never been able to explain quite how wretched and frightening it felt – the closest, he thought, was being dropped into the deepest, darkest depths, your body slowly squeezed by the most unimaginable pressure, leaving you gasping for breath.

Luke became slowly aware of a gentle tap on the window. He turned in terror. It was Frank from next door. He was cupping his hand and leaning on the window clearly trying to catch some sight of Luke. He knocked again.

"Luke, are you ok? Luke, are you in there?" he shouted.

Luke rose like an automaton, opened the latch and returned to the couch. This time he sat to one side tacitly giving the old man space to sit beside him, but he did not. Frank was a tall man and he appeared awkward standing over Luke and staring down on him. Luke leaned forward and put his head in his hands. Frank could see Luke was shaking but continue to hover, a woman or a younger man would probably have sat down at this point, maybe put an arm round a neighbour so clearly in distress but Frank was old-school and really not the tactile type. Instead he lamely repeated the question he had asked through the window.

"Are you ok, Luke?" he said.

Of course, it was a stupid question - Luke was clearly not *ok*! But it was enough to get Luke's attention this time.

"I've just seen a body in the woods." His eyes met Frank's eyes momentarily. "I've just seen Richard hanging in the woods," Luke said, like a confession. His whole body shook violently as if in spasm and Frank put out his arm and placed his hand on Luke's head. To an outsider this would have looked a bizarre tableau, like a priest at communion, but

Luke found the human touch strangely comforting. He became a little more composed. Frank took his opportunity.

"Should I call the police, Luke?" he asked quietly.

Luke nodded.

"I'll nip back then," he said. "Would you like to come with me ... or do you want to stay here?" Frank answered his own question. "I'll get Brenda to make you a hot drink," he said. "Two sugars?"

Luke nodded. His head was still in his hands as Frank backed towards the door.

"You'll be ok for a minute then?" Frank asked.

Luke nodded again. "Thank you," he said, as Frank edged round the front door and disappeared.

Luke lay back on the coach and closed his eyes and Richard's dead face was there again - as vivid as it was earlier. He shuddered at the thought and opened his eyes immediately. He suddenly felt sick, very sick. He ran to the door but threw up before he reached it onto the laminate floor. He wretched again and again, bent double by the violent motion. And then the feeling of nausea subsided just as quickly as it had come. The dog lazily got to its feet and sniffed inquisitively at the steaming mass. Luke ushered him away with a scolding. Now Luke felt ashamed and embarrassed - Frank would be returning shortly with a cup of tea and he would have to navigate this steaming moat. Luke went into the kitchen behind the front living room and snatched a towel. He ran some hot water, soaked the towel and ran back into the front room and placed the wet towel over the vomit. He scooped it up and returned to the Belfast sink, rinsing the towel before repeating the action.

When he was satisfied he had cleaned the floor as best he could, Luke put the dirty towel in the flip-top bin, washed his hands and resumed his position on the couch. As he did, Frank returned, accompanied by Benda carrying a tray of tea cups. To Luke's relief, they seemed not to notice the wet patch they walked over. Brenda sat next to Luke and placed her ample arm around his shoulder and patted him.

"Frank's phoned the police, they'll be here in a minute, dear," she said. Her voice was warm. "Now don't you worry, dear, it will all be sorted." Luke nodded to show he had understood. "Are you feeling a little better now?" she asked looking momentarily at the wet patch on the floor and then back into Luke's face. "Here, drink this, I've put in an extra sugar."

"Thank you, I'm sorry," said Luke.

"Don't be silly," said Brenda, patting Luke's back vigorously, as if trying to wind a new baby.

All this time Frank stood by the open door in the centre of the wet circle and stared out in silence, regularly lifting his right arm, pulling back his jacket sleeve and staring at his watch. Luke sensed his awkwardness and it made him more anxious.

After around five minutes and a few half-hearted sips of sweet tea, Luke heard a car park up outside. Frank became uncharacteristically excited and announced to Brenda and Luke: "The police have arrived!"

"Hello, are you looking for Mr Adams? In here, please?" Frank shouted out of the door. "Luke, they're here!" he shouted over his shoulder.

A man and woman police officer were ushered into the front room. Brenda stood up deferentially and then pointed to Luke, "This is Luke, er, Mr Adams. Do you want us to leave you alone?"

The lady officer smiled, "No, it's fine. In fact, we won't be here long," she said to Brenda. "I believe you saw a body hanging in the woods?" she continued, now addressing Luke. "Is that right, Luke?" She paused. "Is it ok if I call you Luke?" She smiled again. "Sorry, I should have introduced myself. I'm PC Ronson and this is PC Dwyer," she said, motioning towards the other officer.

"Yes." Luke paused again. "Yes, I did see a body - he's called Richard Harrington. I know him." And then he rephrased the sentence, "I knew him!"

"Ok, Luke, I'm sorry, I'm sure this must be horrible for you," the female officer said, "what is your friend's surname again, Luke?"

"Harrington, Richard Harrington." Luke anticipated the next question. "He lived on Harwood Road .... 21, I think."

"Thank you, we better pass this on to the inspector," she said. "Could you, John?"

PC Dwyer nodded and went out to the car.

"Now would it be ok if we took you straight back to the woods so you could show us where you found this man?" PC Ronson continued. "There are a few coppers down there already sealing off the woods but we like to get the exact position of the body as quickly as possible. We don't want anyone else stumbling over it if we can help."

Luke nodded.

"Of course, we shall need a full statement from you later today but if you could, Luke...." PC Ronson gestured towards the door.

Luke obeyed - he got up and led the officer out of his house. The male officer who had just finished on the radio got into the back and Luke sat in the front of the car next to the female officer. Frank waved Luke's keys to indicate that they would be next door when he arrived back. Luke waved tamely back.

On the way to the woods, the officers were very quiet - no further questions. Their radios jabbered incessantly as they had done since entering the house. Luke always wondered in his rare dealings with the police and other emergency services how they knew when a message required their intervention and when they were to be ignored. It all seemed like a low-level drone to the uneducated ear.

As they approached the woods, Luke noticed an officer patrolling the entrance that led down to The Kiosk, a small cafe where the woods were most open. The police car drove straight down the steep hill and parked at the bottom next to the café. Two police cars and a white van were already parked-up and various officers milled around, clearly waiting for instruction. Luke suddenly felt at the centre of all this as all eyes looked to him. He was the only person in civilian clothes, the police had clearly acted quickly in removing the general public and securing the area. A more senior officer approached Luke's side of the car and opened the door for him.

"Hello, I'm Inspector Philips. You are Mr Adams?" The inspector read the name off a mobile device then glanced up into Luke's face and shook his hand. He was brusque and business-like. "I believe you've seen a body ......a Richard Harrington?" Again, he looked at his device.

"Yes, over there," said Luke, vaguely pointing in the direction of the highest part of the wood.

"Well I think it's best you show us then. Ok?"

With that, the inspector set off at a brisk pace in the direction Luke had pointed, followed by Luke who was, in turn, followed by four officers. Luke noted how his extraordinary day was just another working day for the rest of his party. Conversation was lively amongst the officers as they exchanged pleasantries and their experiences of walking in Sunnyhurst Woods: the woods in snow, the state of the paths, etc.

It was clear to Luke that Inspector Philips had walked the woods before - he strode out purposefully with little interest in the trailing party. As they got close to the bottom of the path he had run up that morning, Luke was filled with new feelings of dread. He had suffered from anxiety for as long as he could remember and he knew how to read the signs of an impending panic attack. He suddenly wished he'd had the foresight to take a valium at home. He took them rarely – but they were always his safety net, his quick fix in emergencies. 'And if ever a quick fix was needed, it was now!' Luke said to himself. His thoughts turned once again to that face, and those eyes, those desperate eyes he knew would never leave him.

As the inspector approached the intersection, he turned to Luke.

"Are we up here, then?" he enquired, lifting his head in the general direction.

Luke nodded. Without stopping, the inspector attacked the steep slope with added vigour and the party of constables followed. All conversation now stopped. Luke wasn't sure whether he was expected to follow too but he knew he could not see that sight again. He sat on a bench close to the intersection and waited. Luke involuntary shuddered when he thought once more of the sight that was about to confront Inspector Philips. Luke stood up - he could not sit still for long. He felt ill. His body ached, and the muscles around his abdomen squeezed hard on his guts. Luke attempted to massage the muscles in the back of his neck to release their tenseness but there was little he could do, pain was now travelling up his neck and already developing into one of Luke's mega-headaches. He felt the pressure in his skull slowly build to the point of bursting. Luke's breathing became more laboured. If only he'd remembered the bloody valium!

Luke's thoughts were suddenly diverted by a single police officer returning down the steep path and he consciously embraced the distraction as he'd been taught to do in therapy. He noticed how composed he was – so very different to the way Luke had raced down the same path less than an hour earlier! The PC was carrying a roll of the blue and white tape and proceeded to wrap it around two trees either side of the path, closing off access to the top path. With a nodded acknowledgement in Luke's direction, the PC walked further down the lower path in the direction of the reservoir.

Luke could hear the sound of officers quietly talking and the continuous babble of radios. He sensed the scene above was calm, business-like and suitably sombre. Sadly, a sudden death was very much part of the police routine. 'Surely even police officers must feel the horror at a sight like *that*!' thought Luke, 'and take it home with them and wake up in the middle of the night, their minds invaded by God knows what! Surely, you *never* get used to it!' Luke sat on the bench again, putting his head in his hands, trying desperately not to think about the scene above him.

"Hello, Luke, I've come to take you home," a voice said, suddenly.

Luke visibly jumped at the sound and sight of the lady PC who had collected him earlier from home. She had seemed to appear from nowhere like some guardian angel. She was on her own this time and she smiled sweetly at Luke and helped him to his feet. Her voice and her manner were so gentle and kind, it brought a tear to Luke's eye. He wanted her to put her arms around him and let him cry into her shoulder, but he forced a smile. He noticed the officer for the first time now, she was a pretty, dark-haired girl. Early thirties, he guessed. He wondered if *she* had seen the hanging man. No, Luke was sure she wasn't in the party that went up the path. He was relieved.

Luke walked with the PC in silence as they retraced their steps through the woods. He wasn't used to seeing them so deserted.

"Do you live with anyone, Luke?" the girl asked.

"No." Luke immediately regretted his curt, monosyllabic response - the girl was trying to be kind, but Luke was desperate just to get out of the woods and back to the sanctuary of his small home. And he wanted to be alone.

"I really think you need to be with someone today. Are there any family or friends you could call?" she asked.

"I'm ok. Really. I'll call someone when I'm ready." Luke knew that he sounded sharp too. The PC was just doing her job - it was probably standard practice and she would no doubt be in big trouble if she just left him alone and he then did something stupid.

"I'm sorry, I didn't mean to be short. I suffer from anxiety and I'm not feeling great." Luke said. He paused and sensing the officer's genuine concern he added, "I feel shit, actually. I've not felt like this for a while - the drugs usually seem to help but ...."

"Well, it's totally understandable at the moment," said the officer kindly, "you've just had a hell of a shock."

They reached the car and she opened the door for him. Luke got in.

"My brother suffers from depression," the officer volunteered as she put on her seat-belt.

"It's not the same," Luke said.

"He had Cognitive Therapy," the PC went on, seemingly ignoring Luke's comment, "it seemed to help him. Whenever he gets bad he goes back for more."

"I didn't work for me," said Luke, curtly.

There was an awkward silence.

"Richard suffered from anxiety, too," said Luke, attempting to break the silence. "That's something we had in common." Luke didn't know why he had offered *that* and he regretted it immediately.

“Did he?” Luke could see by her response that the girl had gone into PC mode. Metaphorically, she got out her notebook and made an entry.

“It was under control, though. He was in great spirits, actually,” said Luke, trying to repair the situation.

Both parties decided to leave the subject.

They pulled up outside Luke's house. Frank, who had been watching for Luke, hobbled out, brandishing the key. Clearly, he'd been networking since Luke left in a police car. The whole road seemed on high alert, Luke really couldn't remember the last time his neighbours had been so conscientious in cleaning cars and washing windows.... one was even sweeping the pavement outside their house! It wasn't every day on Avondale Road that someone was taken away and then returned in a police car!

Frank opened the door for him and stepped back to allow Luke into his house, followed by PC Ronson.

“I'll leave you in peace then. But if you need anything ....” Frank left the offer dangling. He was stiff and awkward, but Luke appreciated his kindness.

“Thank you, Frank, and please thank Brenda too. Thank you.”

Luke shut the door as Frank turned towards his house. Noah greeted them enthusiastically and Luke approved of the way PC Ronson gave time and attention to his dog.

“What a lovely dog. We used to have a retriever, best dogs in the world!” she said.

Luke forced a smile. "Are you going to take a statement now?" he asked.

The officer laughed gently, "No, I'm just checking you are ok. Guess my old man will be round later for a statement if you feel you are up to it today. They like to get statements as soon as possible."

"Your old man?"

The girl laughed again. "Sorry, that's most unprofessional, isn't it! My father is Inspector Philips: you know, the man who introduced himself to you down in the woods. He's the main man for Sudden Deaths." She smiled. "The coroner is a fussy old bugger and if my old man isn't the investigating officer he really gives the local plod a hard time. They work well together."

"I'd prefer to give *you* my statement. Would that rock the boat?" Luke said.

"I don't know. I can ask him, though. Would it be easier for you?"

"Well, yes."

"Would you mind if I went back to the car and made a call?"

"No," said Luke. "I'll just nip upstairs. I need to take something for my head."

With that, PC Ronson left. It occurred to Luke that, except for the nagging headache, he was feeling a little less anxious. The PC's company was a pleasant distraction - it stopped him thinking too much.

She returned promptly. "Yeah, that's fine," she said, smiling.

"It's an open and shut case then!" Luke said, flippantly.

The PC looked hurt: "So, I guess you now assume if my father thought it was anything more than a suicide he'd be here right now." Her warm eyes were cold for the first time.

"No, I'm sorry, it just occurred to me." Luke was embarrassed now. "It was a stupid thing to say. I'm sorry."

She had stepped out of role, but she was back within a breath.

"Inspector Philips says I need to wait until PC Dwyer arrives before I take your statement."

"Ok, listen, I'm really sorry, that was absolutely no criticism of you." Luke sighed. "But you must admit it's a bit rushed, isn't it? Your father seems to have already made up his mind that this is an unfortunate suicide .... within the hour!"

"He's usually got an instinct. All good coppers have."

"What!" Luke made one of those open hand gestures. "Is he Dixon of Dock Green!"

"He's bloody good at what he does - he's seen hundreds of sudden deaths," the PC said, defensively.

"Well, in my mind that makes him the very worst person to investigate a sudden death. You've already told me, he's got this cosy relationship with the coroner .... *'Let's clear this up quickly and go home to a nice glass of Shiraz and an evening in front of the telly with the missus.'*

"My mother's dead!" PC Ronson said, angrily.

Luke had been standing in his excited state but he fell back into the couch when the young officer spoke. He lent forward and put his head in his hands. He felt wretched. He knew he was being unfair.

PC Ronson broke the silence: "My father is a good man and he's very thorough and very conscientious. I know you're angry at the moment but please believe you've got the very best man to investigate this ...this......." she struggled to find the words. "......well, what seems to be a tragic case of someone taking their own life." PC Ronson paused and stared at Luke, there was pity not anger in her eyes now. "PC Dwyer will be here shortly, should I make us a drink?" The officer did not wait for an answer but walked to the door at the back of the room. "In here?" she asked, as she pointed at the closed door.

Luke nodded. He could soon hear her opening doors and he sensed she was having trouble finding things. He went to help her.

"Where do you keep your mugs?" she asked.

"In this one." Luke opened a large cupboard containing two mugs.

"You don't cater for large parties, then!" she said with a smile.

Luke smiled back. "To be honest, I had some more but I binned them last week, they were all chipped."

The exchange had relaxed them both a little. She complimented him on his kitchen, something Sarah had chosen not long before she died, and they drank coffee at the breakfast bar.

"How long have you been married, then?" Luke asked

"I'm not. Why did you assume?" the girl said.

"Well, you haven't got the same surname as your father."

"Oh, I see, amateur detective, eh! Actually, he's my step-father." She smiled. "Long story!"

There was a knock at the door. Noah, who had been dozing on a chair in the front room, suddenly became animated and barked. Luke returned with PC Dwyer, carrying a small leather folder. He crouched down and stroked the dog affectionately. "I've got a Setter at home," he said.

"Should we do the statement in the kitchen, Luke?" PC Ronson asked. "It would be easier on the flat surface."

"Yeah, wherever," said Luke leading the way whilst Noah followed them all and drank from his bowl in the kitchen.

PC Dwyer spoke for the first time: "Inspector Philips asked me to tell you that he will come and see you in the morning, if that would be OK? But for now we are to take a statement from you. Ok?"

"Ok," Luke said, noticing the young, fresh-faced second officer for the first time. He was flushed and his shoes were now dirty. 'Poor boy!' he thought. "Can I get you a drink? Tea? Coffee? Or I've got some coke in the fridge, I think," Luke offered.

"Yes, thanks, a coke would be great. I've done a lot of walking today." PC Dwyer sat down, unzipped the folder and arranged the paperwork.

PC Ronson, who Luke assumed had briefly left the room to make another call, returned and took over.

"Ok, let's get on with this, then," she said in her business-like tone.

The statement took about forty-five minutes to complete. Luke told them about his usual routine of running with Noah through the woods. He tried to remember who else he had seen that morning. It was hard for Luke to recall - he tended to remember the dogs more than the people. He was able to say for certain that he had passed Karen who lived in Byron Street – he'd nodded at her when Noah had stopped to have a sniff at her old black Labrador. Luke found it hard to explain why he took the right turn up to the high path that morning and he felt tense and defensive as PC Ronson gently quizzed him on this. She clearly didn't believe in fate!

Luke went on to recall the dog barking. He found it painful describing the scene that confronted him at the top of the path - the seat, the rope, Richard's lifeless body. PC Ronson asked him if he saw anyone else on the top path or on his way down the path or on the lower path on his way back home. Luke wasn't much help - he remembered walkers on the bottom path but they were a blur to him. He promised he'd let the officers know if he remembered anything more.

Luke and PC Ronson both signed the statement and it was returned to the folder.

"Have they removed the body yet?" Luke asked, suddenly. He wanted to satisfy himself that his friend was not still hanging there in the woods.

PC Dwyer was cautious in his response, weighing every word, unsure how much he could say. "When I left around an hour ago they were just taking the body down. Forensics were still there. I think the area will be still cordoned off overnight."

"There won't be much to see after all those coppers have been tramping around," said Luke.

The PC smiled, "Oh don't worry about that. It's my first time at one of these but the inspector runs a tight ship. Straight off, he grabbed the tape and made a big no-go area. And if anyone even breaths near it he gets bollocked. Just the doc and forensics allowed in."

PC Ronson glanced meaningfully at Luke but he pretended not to notice. PC Dwyer said goodbye and left with his wallet to wait in the car.

"So, what are you going to do for the rest of the day?" PC Ronson asked once they were both alone in the kitchen.

"I'm ok," Luke said. "I know Darwen, I'm sure Frank and Brenda will drop round later. And probably half the street the minute your car leaves!" Luke wasn't really expecting this influx but he wanted PC Ronson to feel she could leave him.

"Well, as long as you're sure. I'll drop round in the morning to check on you. And if you remember anything else overnight...?"

"Ok, thanks, but I thought your father was coming," Luke said, a little surprised.

"Sorry, meant to say, I rang him earlier. He says there's no point until Thursday, after the autopsy."

PC Ronson could see the mention of an autopsy had upset Luke. "Were you and Richard very close? I mean had you known him long?" she asked.

"Around three years, I guess. I joined the cycle club after my wife died. Yeah, about three years ago."

"I'm sorry, I didn't know .... about your wife."

"How could you!" Luke paused. "You've been very kind and really helped - you know I was desperate for a Valium when I left the woods and I haven't had one. Thank you, I'm feeling calmer now."

PC Ronson smiled again and clearly appreciated the compliment. "Ok, see you tomorrow. I won't come before 10 o'clock. You'll need a lie-in!"

And then, just as an after-thought: "Please don't tell anyone Richard's name yet," she said, "I'm not sure when he will be formally identified. And I don't know whether the family have been informed."

Luke nodded and showed PC Ronson to the door. He waited and waved while the car pulled away. He went back into the house and piled the cushions at one end of the couch and lay down across the length of it. He suddenly felt very tired.

When Luke awoke it was dark outside. He looked at his watch, it was only 6 o'clock. He hadn't slept long. He became aware of a gentle tap on the front door - maybe *that* had wakened him. It was Brenda with a tray.

"I'm sorry, I haven't disturbed you, have I?" she half-whispered, "I was doing tea and I thought you might like some. You've had a couple of visitors since the police left but I told Frank to intercept them and let you have a bit of a rest."

"Thank you, that's very thoughtful. And thank you too for mopping the floor. I saw it was still wet when I came back from the woods with the PC."

Brenda looked embarrassed for Luke. She smiled kindly and left.

Luke lifted the cover from the plate and viewed the contents: a pork chop, mash, gravy and cabbage! He smiled - Luke wondered whether you suddenly reach an age when you eat nothing but chops and gravy! He laid aside the plate, but then he immediately felt guilty. Frank and Brenda lived on a meagre state pension, they had probably shared one chop for tea so they could give one to him in a genuine act of kindness. He sat with the plate on his knee. He wasn't hungry but he forced himself to eat the food and to his surprise he was quite enjoying it when the phone rang.

"Hey, what's happening, pal? I'm in The Sunnyhurst, they're saying you found a body in the woods. Is that right, yeah?" It was Josh from the cycle club and a regular member of the 'Serious Drinkers Club' to be found most nights in the snug. Luke could hear the typical bustle in the background. "Come down mate, I bet you need a drink!"

Luke had no intention of going to The Sunnyhurst. First and foremost, he couldn't trust himself not to say something about Richard after a drink.

"I'm feeling knackered, Josh, I'll see you around, mate. But thanks for ringing."

Josh was not to be put off so easily. "Well, we'll come to you, alright? Bring some cans..."

"No, no, *really*!" Luke tried to be emphatic. "It's been a difficult day, I just need to be alone."

Luke could picture the scene, Josh and the lads wanted 'The Update' so they could disseminate it - no doubt, with a touch of poetic license - before last orders and at work the next day. The man in Darwen with fresh gossip was 'King for a Day!' Surprisingly, Josh relented - was it simply the fact that a body in Sunnyhurst Woods had become tragically unremarkable of late...or had something in Luke's tone made even Josh realise that their mate needed to be left alone.

"Ok, no probs, pal. Maybe see you tomorrow, yeah?" he said.

Luke was relieved. The message that he didn't want to be disturbed seemed to have got round. He was conscious of Frank's patrols, quietly chatting with folk. Luke imagined the conversations and Frank's gentle insistence that his neighbour should be left alone, at least for one night.

He made himself some coffee, took his daily 100mg Sertraline, locked the front door, turned off the lights and went to bed.

Luke intended to sleep but without the distractions of PC Ronson, Luke started to muse on things and as he did his muscles started to tense once again, his breaths became short and laboured, his stomach knotted and his head felt light and giddy. He got out of bed and paced the bedroom, he went to the toilet and then back to bed, then out again and downstairs for coffee - not the most sensible drink under the circumstances, he knew! He took it to bed.

At first his mind was like a butterfly settling on nothing for long. It started with the moment when he first saw the body hanging from the tree. Then other images came to mind, random images: a scene from The Exorcist, something he watched as a young boy and had wished, ever since, he had not; then a scene from Mississippi Burning where black men were being hung by White Supremacists; then his thoughts turned to Inspector Philips and his brisk manner. He decided he really didn't like Inspector Philips, he was glad it was his daughter that was coming in the morning. Luke realised he was perspiring - he was on top of the bed in just his boxers and sweat was seeping from him. He needed a Valium. Luke reached for the box of Diazepam 2mg and he took one with the remains of his coffee. Then once again he went downstairs into the kitchen and filled half a glass with a cheap whiskey he'd had in the house for as long as he could remember. He retreated into the security of his bedroom again and necked the whisky in two large gulps. He put his phone on silent, turned off the light and got back into bed and lay on his back. The drugs and alcohol worked quickly - the tension seemed to drain down and out of his body: first his head, then his neck, and shoulders, and chest, and stomach and finally out through the flats of his feet.

Luke was asleep.

CHAPTER 2: RICHARD

Apparently, you only remember the last dream before you wake. Most of our dreams remain in the subconscious which is probably as well. But Luke woke from a lovely dream - he was in a hotel room in Paris with PC Ronson and they were lovers. The room had seen better days with cracks in the ceiling and peeling wallpaper. In front of them, through the long, uncurtained window, was the classic sight of The Eiffel Tower and Notre Dame and The Seine, made geographically plausible by the dream. And PC Ronson was beside him, his arms around her warm, naked body. He could feel her breath on his face ....

Luke awoke. As is often the case on first waking, it took him a few seconds to acclimatise. How quickly tender love turns to wretched guilt. How quickly a confident erection retreats into its usual flaccid state ...and how quickly the dreadful events of the previous day invaded Luke's conscious mind.

He jumped out of bed in panic, his heart racing. "Fuck!" Guilt and Fear, Fear and Guilt: the two emotions that rule our lives - stronger than love! Lovers die; fear never dies. Lovers leave; guilt *never* leaves you. Luke felt wretched: he wished he was still asleep, he wished he had gone to sleep and never woken up. At that moment all the hurt and loneliness, all the little disappointments, all the guilt that Sarah and not *he* had got cancer, all the intangible fears of 51 years of existence advanced upon him, like noisy battalions.

Luke had never felt like this before - he'd had anxiety attacks, of course, he'd also felt desperately unhappy, like the day they told Sarah there was nothing more they could do for her. But he'd never - even in his darkest day - wished he was dead before.

He lay back down on the bed and put his hand behind his neck in an effort to calm down. What had brought this on? Was it the trauma of the previous day ...... or was it the guilt that he had now slept with PC Ronson. PC Ronson, who he would have to face later! PC Ronson who had been so kind to him.

Luke decided when he had calmed a little that it was probably all the above. But there was something more eating into Luke. Something that had troubled him yesterday from the very moment he had recognised in that grotesque face, the face of his dead friend: Richard had *not* taken his own life, it was impossible! He knew it instinctively straight away, but it had not formed into a conscious thought until that moment. Yet Luke also knew that Richard's death would eventually be found to be another sad and unexplainable suicide by Inspector Philips and the coroner, the 'Morcambe and Wise' of sudden deaths in the Darwen and Blackburn Borough! It was this that was making Luke feel so wretched the morning after the day that would change his life forever.

Luke felt annoyed that he could not really find any tangible evidence for this sudden conviction. He couldn't just stand up to the police, the coroner's office, or Richard's family and say: *"It is my belief that Richard did not - could not - take his own life. It is my belief that he has been murdered by persons unknown!"* They would righty ask: *"And how do you know this, Mr Adams?"* And then Luke would say: *"Because I do!"* Genius! He'd have to do better than that, that's one thing he *did* know!

Luke tried to form a rational case in his own mind but at this point all he had was the absolute belief that Richard, when he last saw him, was in fine fettle. He'd just booked Majorca in April for a week of cycling in the spring sun. Would someone contemplating suicide book a holiday, for God's sake!

Luke made up his mind that he would broach this subject with PC Ronson when she came later. He decided he would tell her about Richard so she could start to understand the man like *he* did. If he could get her on-side, she might have some influence with the main man!

Luke was beginning to feel a little better. He flicked the switch on his iPhone off silent - no calls or texts: he was relieved and disappointed in equal measure. He sat on the bed and reasoned with himself that his head was all over the place and his irrational thoughts were probably very normal after what he had been through. As his doctor had said: *'You don't suffer from depression, you suffer anxiety, Luke. They are not the same.'* What he was feeling was not depression - it was a serious case of self-pity and he must snap out of it. And Quickly!

Luke cleaned his teeth and as he did his reflection looked back at him in the bathroom mirror. He was looking old: his beard was long and greying, his hair was unkept and his skin looked yellowy and marked and lines had appeared across his cheeks, seemingly overnight. Yes, he looked old, old and ill.

He went downstairs. Noah got lazily to his feet and greeted him, tail wagging. He let him out into the yard for his morning ablutions and then refilled his water and food bowl. Luke made coffee and a bowl of muesli and sat at the bar. He winced momentarily as he recalled PC Ronson sitting opposite him the day before. Noah sauntered in, had a drink and then started pawing Luke. He wanted a run, but Luke would certainly not be running in the woods. In fact, he couldn't ever imagine going in there again!

After breakfast Luke decided Noah needed a short walk at the very least. He got dressed and prepared for a circuit round the block with a few minutes on the old school playing fields where Noah could run and chew sticks, his favourite past-time. Just as he was leaving the phone rang, it was the agency - could he go to St Hilda's in Blackburn today? A timetable of English. Luke lied that he'd been up all night with a tummy upset. It was easier to tell a little lie than give a long explanation about finding a body. He certainly didn't want to mention he was stressed - he'd heard the agency put a big black line through your name if the 'S word' was uttered. He thought this quite ironic because stress was the main reason most of the teachers ended up on the supply register in the first place. The irony was compounded by the fact that supply was the very last job *anyone* prone to anxiety should be considering for a moment.

It was a beautiful morning but very cold and there was ice on the paths. Luke set off down the street. At the intersection with Earnsdale, a dirty white van hooted and Josh stuck his head out of the window.

"Bloody Hell!" Luke said to himself, but he spoke in as bright a tone as he could muster: "Ok, Josh," he said, "where you off to today?" Josh would drive *anywhere* is his rusty shit-heap, with his partner in crime, Lee. But only if the price was right. They made good money from a contract with the NHS sprucing up old hospitals the government couldn't afford to pull down and build again.

"Feeling better, mate?" he asked. "You should've come down last night. We had a lock-in. Greg fuckin' got off with that girl who goes around with Jen." When Luke showed no sense of recognition, he elaborated, "You know, the one with the tits!"

Luke hadn't any idea who Josh was talking about. He just wanted to move on.

"So, was the guy you found in the woods from round here then? Did you recognise him?" Josh asked suddenly. Luke knew the conversation had been leading to this.

"Sorry mate, I can't talk about it," Luke said.

Josh laughed and warmed to the task. Something in Luke's uneasy manner intrigued him. "So, you *did* recognise him! Bloody Hell! Give us a clue then - has he been in the pub?"

"Really, I can't say, I've got to go ...." Luke moved away

"Listen mate, just tell me, it'll go no further. Come on whisper, I won't even tell Lee!" said Josh, now excited. He laughed and leaned further out of the van window.

"Fuck off Josh, I might as well call The Telegraph directly! You've got the biggest gob in Darwen!" Luke walked away with a smirk. He felt he'd navigated the situation quite well, but he really hoped the police would release details soon and take the pressure off him.

Luke was detained twice more. It was awkward and he was feeling anxious by the time he got home. He showered and changed.

PC Ronson arrived prompt at 10am. He was surprised to see her in jeans and a jumper and a slim-fit quilted jacket and blue wellies. She looked younger out of uniform and without make-up.

"Hi, come in. Are you not working today?" he asked.

"I'm on a late today. How are you? Did you sleep ok?"

"Not so bad .... on both counts," Luke replied. "You really didn't need to come on your day off, you know. I didn't realise ...."

"Don't be daft, it's fine," PC Ronson interrupted, "I was coming to the stables at the top of Sunnyhurst anyway. I need a coffee, though."

She led the way and Luke followed her into his kitchen.

"I've just realised I don't know your name ... "Luke said, as he sat down at the breakfast bar.

"Sophie," she said. There was a momentary and slightly awkward silence. "So, you slept well, yeah?" she asked, revisiting the previous conversation. "What are you doing today?"

Luke hadn't given a thought. He would normally be working or he'd be out and about with the dog and perhaps a pint. But until he had the green light from the police about Richard he felt a prisoner in his own home.

"Do you know whether Richard's family has been informed yet?" he asked.

"No, sorry, maybe I'll hear something later."

"Didn't your father ......?"

"I wasn't home last night," Sophie said.

"Can you ask him to let me know when it's OK to talk about it?" Luke asked. "I know it sounds silly but I'm frightened of letting it slip!"

"Of course I will. In fact, I'll text him now." As she texted, Luke noticed how proficient she was at holding her phone in her palm and using her thumb to stab at her touch screen. Texts and the process of texting revealed more about the generation gap than nearly any other thing, Luke realised. He suddenly felt guilty again.

"So, did you call anyone last night?" Sophie asked, as she sent her message and looked up from her screen.

"No," Luke said.

"Why?"

"I don't know, I just didn't feel like talking." Luke felt a little embarrassed. "And, as I said, I've got to be careful what I say!"

"Isn't there anyone *outside* Darwen you could talk to?" Sophie seemed concerned.

"There's Jon and Emily, I guess. They live in Chester, in Hoole. I go over to see them every year just after Christmas."

"How do you know them - living quite far away and that?"

"Emily was Sarah's best friend at uni and the four of us used to go on holiday quite a bit when Sarah was alive."

"When did she die? Did you say three years ago?"

"Yeah, three years two months - just before Christmas," said Luke.

"Oh, no, Luke!" Sophie's face was suddenly a study in pain. Luke could feel Sophie's compassion towards him and he needed to avert his eyes and preoccupy himself with making coffee just to stop making a fool of himself. He manufactured an upbeat tone: "I've got this clever machine, what do you fancy - Cappuccino, Mocha, American, Hot Chocolate ......?" He named each container as he took it out.

"Cappuccino is fine," said Sophie with a smile.

"You might wear wellies but I can tell you're a girlie girl. And your favourite tipple is Prosecco right!"

They laughed.

"I bloody love it!" she said. "Mind, if it's wet and gets you pissed I'll drink it!" She paused. "To be honest, I'm feeling quite fragile today, I was on lager last night - went out into Preston with my mate. It was supposed to be just one and then drive back to Darwen but we had a right session. I ended up sleeping on the sofa."

"On a Tuesday's night!" Luke deliberately exaggerated a shocked tone.

"Yeah, not much talent out there but I needed a blowout... I hate my job sometimes."

"Was that Richard, then?" Luke asked.

"More *you* really - I felt so sorry for you, you looked so absolutely devastated ... and then you told me about your wife dying." Sophie paused. "*Then* I got back to the station and my old man had to go to the mortuary on the way home. He decided it was time that I saw my first body so he insisted I come in with him. I think he felt he couldn't shield me from it forever!"

"Was it Richard?" Luke asked, tentatively.

"Yes, Richard popped my cherry! I've only been a copper for a year."

Luke handed her the cappuccino. He put another pod into the machine for himself and placed a cup under. "Well, I honestly thought you'd been in the job for a while. You are really good," he said.

"Thanks - I don't know if I'll be in it much longer, though. I'm not tough enough, I can't just walk away and switch off."

"So, you saw Richard?" Luke asked.

"Yes." Sophie paused but didn't elaborate. "Was he your best mate, then?"

"Do you have best mates at my age!" Luke smiled at the concept. "Yes, I guess he was." His tone became more decisive. "I'm not the gregarious type, I don't have a full address book!"

"What was he like?"

"Is this PC Ronson asking or Sophie?" Luke became suddenly serious.

"Sophie," she said, smiling.

Luke collected his black coffee and sat down across from Sophie.

"He was a genuinely nice man. I know that word 'nice' is a bit woolly but that's what he was. He was nice to everyone. And nice *about* everyone too – never critical, always tried to see the good in people. You know, I never heard him say a negative thing about anyone. That's rare, I'm not like that."

"Bloody hell, I'm not either. I love a good gossip!" Sophie interjected.

"He was totally without ego as well - just comfortable in his own skin, you know? Like he had this quiet confidence in himself and he gave me confidence somehow. He was so honest about everything and so anti-bullshit. And very honest with himself too." Luke stopped. He could easily have gone on listing Richard's qualities but he looked directly across at Sophie, catching her eye, "He didn't kill himself, you know!"

"People *do*, Luke. Good people do," she said gently.

"Not Richard ...."

There was now a tension between them. Luke got up and busied himself cleaning the coffee machine.

After a pause, Sophie spoke, slowly: "What are you saying, Luke? Your friend was murdered?"

"It's the only explanation," Luke said with a sigh.

There was another longer pause. Sophie stared hard at Luke as if trying to weigh him up, deciding whether Luke was serious or whether this was just the typical reaction of a friend in denial. "Can you think of anyone who would want to kill him?" she asked, finally.

"No-one! I can't imagine *anyone* wanting to kill him," Luke replied, emphatically. "He got on with everyone, as I said."

"I know he wasn't married but did he have a girlfriend or boyfriend?" Sophie paused. "You and he weren't ...."

"No, of course not!" Luke interrupted. He was immediately ashamed of being embarrassed by the question. After all, he and Richard could so easily have been lovers as well as friends. Luke went on, he wanted to give Sophie more of a picture: "He'd had a few little flings but nothing serious and not for a while. Least I don't think so."

"My father will look into all that. It's standard practice to ask whether anyone had a motive to kill the deceased in a case like this. We must discount murder before we can confidently state that suicide was the cause of death." Sophie paused again, and then she adopted a tone Luke had used himself so often at school when talking to an emotional teenager: "But you do know, Luke, if something looks like an egg, tastes like an egg, smells like an egg .... then it's very probably an egg!"

"Is that one of your old man's?" Luke asked with the trace of a smile.

Sophie nodded sheepishly.

"Did he text back?" Luke asked.

"No, he's probably speaking to relatives so I better not ring. He's usually good at texting straight back." Sophie looked at her watch. "Listen, I've got to go and muck out a horse. Are you going to be ok today?" she asked. "I can come back later….."

"No, I'll be fine," said Luke interrupting, "I think I'll drive somewhere and have a walk with Noah. He didn't get much of one this morning. But thanks. And thanks for coming round and giving up your morning."

"My father's coming to see you tomorrow morning sometime, but why don't you get away for a couple of days after that? Could you go and stay with your friends?"

Luke hadn't thought about it, but it did seem to make sense to get away - especially when it all came out about Richard. "Yeah, maybe, I might ring them today," he said.

"What would you do about the dog?"

"Oh, that's not a problem - they've got a retriever and Noah gets on great with her."

"Well, there you go.... no brainer!"

"I'll ring them," Luke said. "Thanks."

As Sophie was heading out of the door, she paused. "Should we swap numbers?" she asked. "I can let you know when my father gets back… and if you need to talk ...." Sophie's words trailed off.

"Yeah, that would be good." Luke wondered whether Sophie gave her phone number out so readily on other jobs. He was both flattered and confused by the offer. "Thanks," he said reaching for his phone, "I'll put it straight in, then I'll call you so you've got mine. I can never remember it!"

They exchanged their numbers in silence for a moment.

"Oh, could you ask your father whether they have found Richard's glasses" Luke asked as Sophie reached the door. "He always wore his glasses. They might have dropped off at the scene …but …."

"Yes, Luke, I'll ask about the glasses!" Sophie exaggerated impatience in an effort to gently mock Luke.

Luke pottered for a while. He put the towel in the outside bin - to his embarrassment, a smell of vomit had confronted him as he disposed of the pods from the coffee machine when Sophie was in the kitchen. Then he put some dirty clothes into the washing machine and set it off. He also washed the dirty coffee cups, made himself another coffee and sat down on the couch.

His thoughts turned to Richard. Talking about him briefly with Sophie had caused him to think of his friend. Yesterday he was a grotesque abstraction - a body in the woods, something disconnected and certainly not his friend Richard. But now the fact that Richard was dead, his friend was dead, brought new feelings of grief. Salty tears soon ran down his face and into his mouth and Luke made no attempt to wipe them away. He cried for Richard and he cried for himself. Alone again!

He recalled meeting Richard the first time he went out with the cycle club about a month after Sarah had died. He had forced himself to do something – Sarah had been on and on about it in her final months. And his doctor had told him exercise would help his anxiety. Anyway, he'd let himself go since Sarah, eating take-aways and ready meals and drinking at home every day. Richard could see he was struggling to maintain the pace on his first ride and dropped back to offer some silent but much appreciated support. When they stopped for a beer Luke was relieved that Richard came to sit next to him. It wasn't as if Richard had no other options either - he was a popular member of the group and others were eager to ask about his latest Ironman, a ridiculously demanding challenge, involving cycling, swimming and running in quick and painful succession.

But Richard bought 'The New Boy' a drink and sat with him and showed interest in his old and battered Ribble bike and asked him questions about himself. They'd seen each other in the pub a few times, they decided, but had never spoken. Luke was surprised even on this first meeting how easily the conversation flowed. Richard was a good listener - a good listener in Luke's view was one that could show genuine interest in a speaker's most mundane descriptions and be able to return with a meaningful comment or a further question. So many of Luke's teacher friends had the annoying habit of glazing over when he spoke. *"Let's get back to me again!"* Luke could hear their unspoken demand and he always curtailed his conversation. And then he began to avoid starting conversations at all for fear of boring others. Sarah's death had eaten into his self-confidence.

But Richard was different. He seemed to value what Luke had to say. On that first brief beer-stop they talked about rides they had done in the area and they compared a list of top pubs. To their mutual surprise, they discovered they'd both ridden Lands End to John O'Groats in the same summer and in the same appalling weather. Richard made Luke feel a new pride in his achievement and conversation continued when they started cycling again. Luke forgot his aching legs and began to enjoy the ride.

He joined the club that day and paid his subscription and even ordered the club's distinctive green top and shorts. The club met on a Monday night at the Sunnyhurst and Luke started to go along, although he and Richard usually sat in the corner and played little part in the proceedings. They drank beer and swopped stories with relish, they discussed quite intimate things, things blokes rarely talk about, like anxiety and loneliness, and family disputes and faith and doubt. Richard told Luke he was a Catholic and went to Mass and

Confession each week. As he recalled this, Luke made a mental note for Inspector Philips - good Catholics don't kill themselves, it's a mortal sin!

Richard also helped Luke with his anxiety - he too had suffered for years, he'd been adopted as a child into an affluent family, but his mother and father later had a daughter of their own and the father had then pushed Richard away and worshiped the daughter. This had led Richard into all sorts of attention-seeking behaviour at school which only drove he and his father more apart. It was around this time that Richard started having panic attacks and he was diagnosed with Generalised Anxiety Disorder. Richard had an intelligent, enquiringly mind and he had researched the condition thoroughly. It was he who advised Luke that his dosage and mix of drugs were too strong for him, making him permanently lethargic and prone to weight gain. And it was Richard also who showed Luke that it was ok for a bloke to suffer from anxiety, it was a medical condition like any other. You had not to panic about panic attacks, he said, as that would simply prolong the anxiety and become self-perpetuating. You had to ride with them, let them do their worst, encourage them on, even, until they wore themselves out. Of course, this was at odds with all Luke's instincts because he would always try to suppress them, to fight them. When Luke had another attack, he tried to take Richard's advice. It left him totally exhausted and he finally fell asleep, but to his surprise he felt much better when he woke up.

Richard was a great role model too – he never let his anxiety stop him living a demonstrably full and active life. And although slight and unassuming, physically, he was the strongest cyclist in the club by a country mile and had the admiration and respect of everyone. And he'd befriended

Luke - the unblokiest bloke in the club - and taken him under his wing.

Luke and Sarah would sometimes call into the Sunnyhurst for a drink after their walk up to The Tower but they really didn't socialise much. Luke recognised people and could have the odd chat about the football on the big screen but nothing more. But now, with Richard's approbation, he was slowly welcomed into the inner circle.

Luke and Richard had what might be described as a honeymoon period, cycling every weekend, often Saturday and Sunday, and even going to France together. But then Richard's father got sick – he had developed cancer on top of the Alzheimer's which had been diagnosed two years earlier, so Richard went over to see him at weekends and help out. His mother, who had always doted on Richard, had died a while earlier and his father was now looked after by an old housekeeper. Richard told Luke how his father was often ungrateful and even quite nasty towards him. In his hour of need, he wanted his daughter, and not the adopted son! But the daughter had run off to London with a musician after her mother's death and had now gone off the radar completely. Richard's feelings about his relationship with his father would surface after he'd had a few drinks. It was now Luke's turn to support Richard.

But Richard had rallied recently. His father seemed to be finally starting to appreciate that his adopted son was not the complete loser he'd always assumed. Luke persuaded Richard that he must have a break and he booked a cycling holiday in Majorca that Luke found for him. Richard was keen for Luke to go too but he made the excuse he needed to work. The truth was, Luke was terrified of flying.

As he thought about Richard, Luke knew it was his time to step up to the plate and be strong for his friend in the way that Richard had been strong for him. Who else was there! A life like his could not be just snuffed out without anyone asking why?

After attending to the washing and distributing it around radiators to dry, Luke changed into some clean running gear and ushered an eager Noah into the back of the car.

But the run didn't help. Luke was too preoccupied with thoughts of poor Richard and the more he thought about his death the more convinced he was that it was not suicide. 'Maybe Inspector Philips will come to the same conclusion,' he told himself. 'Maybe he will be round in the morning to gather more evidence and make a case and find a motive.' But Luke was doubtful.

On the drive back from the reservoir, Luke noticed the billboard outside the newsagent: "BODY DISCOVERED IN WOODS." Luke stopped and bought The Darwen Telegraph, the local paper. There was a small report on the front page under the large heading and what he imagined was a stock picture of the woods. Clearly, the police had released little information. It said a walker had found a body but there was no reference to Richard. Luke was relieved to note there was no mention of cause of death either.

When Luke got back he washed and dried Noah and fed him and gave him fresh water. He checked his phone - there were a couple of missed calls and four texts.

Alex: **"Hope you ok. Give us a call, yeah?"**

Josh: **"Will drop round later. Have you seen Telegraph?"**

Abbie: **"Thinking of you. xxxx"** Abbie was landlady at The Sunnyhurst.

The final text was from a number he didn't recognize: **"Hello Mr Adams, this is Steve Finchley from The Telegraph. Could you call me back on this number please?"** One of the missed calls was from the same number. The other was from the agency.

This made Luke anxious. 'What do I say if this Steve Finchley calls again? Do I just not pick up? But then he will probably doorstep me!' Luke knew how tenacious and determined the papers were once they got you in their sights. And even as he was pondering this, Luke's mobile rang again - same number! He decided to answer, it was better than waiting anxiously for the knock on the door.

"Hello," he said, tentatively.

The voice on the other end was warm and confident: "Oh, Hi! Is that Mr Adams? This is Steve Finchley, I'm a reporter at The Telegraph."

"Yeah, I've just read your text. I've been out," said Luke, defensively. "How did you get my number?"

"My boss just handed it to me and asked me to follow it up." It was clear Steve was embarrassed and unwilling to say how he came upon the number. "Would it be ok if we had a quick chat? I believe you found the body yesterday in Sunnyhurst."

"I really can't say anything at the moment," said Luke, eager to close down the conversation as quickly as possible, "the police have told me that...."

"Oh, I quite understand," the reporter interrupted, "I wasn't expecting much. But can you just confirm a couple of details, that's all?"

"Listen, I'm not being awkward but I really don't want to say anything at all at present. I'm sorry." Luke felt genuinely sorry, the man was only doing his job… and politely.

"Yes, I understand. I'm sure you are under enough pressure and you don't want us on your back. I'll leave you alone. But could I call again?" He paused. "Maybe tomorrow?"

"Ok, but I can't promise..."

"Thank you Mr Adams, and I'm sorry to have troubled you."

Luke was relieved that the reporter had not been more pushy. He made up his mind that if he was to talk to anyone from the papers then it would be him.

Whilst he had the phone in his hand, Luke pondered whether he should ring Emily. Sophie's suggestion had been a good one - it would be good to get away from Darwen. She would probably be at work so he'd leave a voice mail. To Luke's surprise, Emily picked up immediately. From the background noise he could tell she was out shopping.

"Luke, how are you?" Emily's tone was warm.

"Hi Emily, is this a bad time?"

"No, no, it fine, but you may lose me, I'm in in the supermarket. You are not very clear."

"Hope you had nice New Year. Thanks for the card. I hope Ethan got my voucher." Luke half-shouted into the phone. "Sorry I've not been in touch since Christmas."

"It's fine. Yeah, has he not thanked you? Sorry!" she said. "We were only saying we need to get together."

"Well, actually, that's why I'm calling......"

The line went dead. Luke tried again but it was engaged. Emily must have been calling him back. He waited a couple of seconds and his phone rang.

"Sorry, we got cut off." Emily was clearer now. "I've moved nearer the doors."

"Yeah that's better, as I was saying," Luke paused, embarrassed. "…er, I know this sounds really cheeky but any chance I could come over for a couple of days?"

"Of course, of course. Were you thinking this weekend cos we're out Saturday at a wedding?"

"I was thinking tomorrow, actually." Luke suddenly felt awkward. "Please say 'no' if it's too short notice, it's just that ...." Luke's face contorted as he said it. He hated asking anyone for anything.

Emily interrupted: "No, that's fine. *Absolutely* fine. Look forward. I'll make the bed up. Be great to see you, Jon will love an excuse for a few beers - so will I! We did Dry January, it nearly ended in divorce!"

"Ok that's great. I'll see you sometime after dinner."

"We will both be at work but I'll put the key in the normal place. Good to hear from you, Luke." Emily giggled, mischievously, "Have you found a nice girl yet? No, don't tell me .... wait till tomorrow. Byeeeee."

Luke pressed his phone to end the call. He felt much happier now. Emily's voice was always bubbly and reassuring and made Luke feel for a moment that all was right in the world again. In fact, he couldn't wait to get over to Hoole, and Emily and Jon's place. He knew that Emily would assume he was bringing Noah. He always did.

Luke felt secure in the knowledge that he would be able to talk things through with his friends tomorrow. Jon was a quiet, gentle man – economical with his words but wise. Emily was loud and tactile, and always full of fun. And she could drink any man under the table. They were opposites but they loved each other to bits and had a great life together in Chester. Their son Ethan was in Paris for a year as part of his degree in French and Business.

Luke got a beer from the fridge and decided to watch *Midnight in Paris*. Thought association is strange - maybe the connection with Ethan had prompted it. But Luke had loved Woody Allen films ever since he had watched *Annie Hall*. He found them quirky and different - characters talking into the camera, subtitles, hand-held cameras that made you feel quite queasy. And he loved Woody Allen's angst, it mirrored his own. And Luke particularly loved Woody Allen's most recent films, set in various European cities - they were sexy and cool and they made you wish you were there sitting at the next table, eavesdropping. Of course, the English teacher in Luke loved the idea of recalling Hemmingway and Fitzgerald and Gertrude Stein and those impossibly romantic days of Paris in the 1920s. Woody Allen made Luke feel clever and cultured - he drank his bottled beer quickly and went for another. For the first time since his grim discovery, Luke found to his surprise that he was quite relaxed and his interest in the film had pushed all thoughts of the previous day into the background for the moment.

Suddenly, the moment was broken by an insistent knock on his front door. He hadn't heard Josh's van park up outside and he was shocked to see him standing before him with his dirty ripped jeans tucked into his cowboy boots and his trademark checked flannel shirt. He smelt of sweat and smoke.

"It was *Richard*.... was it *Richard* you found in the woods? Richard, Fucking Hell!"

Josh had hardly paused for breath and was clearly in some distress. He pushed past Luke and sat on the couch. His mate Lee followed awkwardly and stood playing with his phone.

"I'm sorry, I couldn't say. How do you know?" asked Luke.

"It's just been on Rock FM news. I fucking nearly crashed, didn't I, Lee? Fucking Hell, Richard!"

"Would you like a beer?" Luke didn't wait for an answer, he headed for the fridge and brought out three bottles. He distributed them and motioned for Lee to sit down next to Josh, then he muted the film.

"So, I guess next of kin have all been informed," Luke said. "Sorry, but you understand why I couldn't say anything," he added.

"Yeah, yeah," Josh said. Luke had never seen Josh so lost for words. He and Lee sat in silence and Lee seemed a little embarrassed by Josh's raw emotion. He didn't really know Richard himself but suddenly found himself caught up in this unfolding drama.

Luke tried to break the silence. "The inspector who's heading the investigation is coming to see me tomorrow so hopefully I'll know more then." Luke exhaled. "It was a bloody shock seeing Richard like that, I can tell you!"

"Fuck, I bet it was! Why did he do it?"

"Do you think he killed himself, then?" asked Luke.

"Well, the report said he hung himself."

"Did it say that exactly?"

"Well, no, it said he was found hanging but it's obvious!"

"Not to me!" said Luke, coldly.

"Fucking hell, Luke, course it's obvious he hung himself. What else could have happened?" said Josh, angrily.

"I don't know, Josh, I really don't know!" Luke's voice betrayed his frustration that Josh was so quick to jump to the same conclusion as Sophie. "I just don't believe he would kill himself. He'd booked Majorca for next month!"

"So, what does that prove? You never really know people," said Josh. "Can I have another beer? I'm going to ring Alex!" he said, decisively.

Luke went into the kitchen. He didn't want to hear it all again. He was angry with Josh – he *knew* Richard, didn't he!

Lee stuck his head round the kitchen door: "I'll be off now, thanks for the beer," he said.

"How you getting home? Is Josh going too?" asked Luke.

"He's on the phone. I'm fine to walk. I'll cut through the woods, it'll only take me ten minutes."

"Alright mate, I'd take you but I've had a few beers."

"No worries, I'll see you around," Lee said. With that, he was gone.

When Luke returned to the room, Josh was texting. "I was with him Sunday, we watched the Liverpool match in the pub."

"How was he?"

"He seemed fine. We didn't talk that much cos Fat Tony was there and you never get a word in edge-ways. But, yeah, he seemed fine."

"Not like a man who was about to kill himself, then!" Luke asked, pointedly.

"Bloody Hell, Luke, stop this shit. How the fuck would I know *how* a man who's about to kill himself acts!"

"Have you ever heard Richard talking about his family?" Luke asked, deciding it was time to move on. "All I know is that he's got a father with Alzheimer's and a sister he never sees who lives in Italy."

"I didn't even know he had a sister!" Josh said. He had now picked up the remote control and was flicking through the sports channels, feigning disinterest.

"I wonder who identified the body?" asked Luke.

Josh erupted. "I've no fucking idea! Bloody hell, Luke, does it matter!" Then just as quickly Josh calmed himself and smiled. "You're like a fucking old woman at times!" he said.

Luke could sense Josh shouldn't be pushed. He'd seen him angry and out of control when he had a contretemps with a motorist on a ride in the Ribble Valley. Anger was Josh's way of expressing his feeling about the news. To Luke's relief he got up after he finished texting.

"I'm meeting Alex at the pub." And then as a kind of after-thought, "Are you coming, pal?"

"No, I'm going away for a few days in the morning so I need to sort some things and do some packing."

Luke knew he could have gone for a couple and packed later but he was concerned about Josh's mood, especially after a few more beers! And Luke really wasn't ready to relive his experience with every Tom, Dick and Harry who arrived at The Sunnyhurst that evening.

"Where you off to, then?" asked Josh.

"Chester, to some friends I've known for ages. They've invited me over," Luke lied.

"Ok, have fun. You'll be back for the funeral, yeah?"

"Of course! I'm only stopping a couple of days, max."

"Ok, mate." Josh paused, "I know you must be feeling shit right now. Look after yourself, yeah!" he added, in an uncharacteristic moment of sensitivity.

Luke knew how hard it was for Josh to show genuine feelings and appreciated the acknowledgment. The two men embraced and Josh patted Luke on the back. As Josh closed the door behind him, Luke shook his head in disbelief. 'I never thought I'd see the day!' he mused with a quiet chuckle!

After watching the rest of 'Midnight in Paris' and drinking three more beers, Luke ironed and packed. He got a text from Sophie: "Sorry for not giving the heads-up about releasing Richard's name." She explained that her father had not got back to her all day. Then as a kind of post-script she said her father would be around mid-morning.

Luke felt very tired around 8pm. There was no need for Valium and whisky, he put his phone on silent and fell into a deep sleep almost as soon as he turned out the light.

*

The next morning Luke felt no awkwardness in taking Noah for his walk. Now that it was common knowledge about Richard, he had nothing more to hide and feel cautious about. He had prepared a well-rehearsed statement in his mind that he would deliver to anyone who enquired. It was quite a long walk to Bold Venture Park and he was stopped around half a dozen times. Local folk knew the full story of Luke losing his wife and were eager to express their sadness at Luke's new loss and the shock of finding his friend. "You poor boy!" one lady said, folding her arms around him. Luke had only really ever spoken to her in the queue at The Late Shop but her response was typical of goodwill towards him that morning. There were offers of meals and open doors – 'morning, noon or night'. And people spoke warmly about Richard, expressing their sadness and surprise that he had resorted to taking his own life. Luke felt very grateful for the outpouring of genuine love he experienced - it reminded him of how lucky he was to belong to such a community.

After he'd washed Noah, Luke checked his phone - he'd had three missed calls from Steve, the reporter from The Telegraph. He'd left a voice-mail asking whether he could pop round for a "chat" that morning. Luke sent a text back, **"Sorry, early night and phone on silent. Will let you know when I'm free. Inspector Philips coming sometime this morning but not sure when or for how long."** Luke kept his phone on silent.

Inspector Philips arrived soon after 11 am. "Good morning, Mr Adams, I'm sorry to keep you in all morning. Were you supposed to be in work?" The inspector had a firm, confident handshake.

"No, I'm a teacher and I do supply so it's quite flexible."

"Primary or Secondary?" the inspector asked.

"Secondary. English teacher."

"I don't know how you lot put up with all their cheek. Always answering back, no respect for authority any more. At least *we* can lock them up for a couple of hours, put the frighteners on them. Little buggers!"

"It's a small minority in my experience. Most are great," Luke said, defensively. "You probably don't get to see the 99% thoroughly decent kids in your line of work." Luke found himself indulging in this little hyperbole to make his point.

"Hmm, it seems a lot more than 1% of teenagers on the streets on a Friday night round here, making a bloody nuisance of themselves!" The inspector continued, dogmatically.

Luke could see he was never going to convince Inspector Philips. In fact, it was clear that when Inspector Philips made up his mind about *anything* there was no swaying him. "Can I get you a hot drink?" he said.

"A glass of water, if you don't mind."

"Coming right up, inspector!" Luke said, with a dash of sarcasm in his voice.

By the time Luke returned from the kitchen, Inspector Philips had removed his jacket and established a position in the centre of the couch. He had pulled the coffee table towards him and was now closely scrutinising what appeared to be the statement Luke had given to Sophie and PC Dwyer. He had put on his glasses and was leaning forward, his head over the table.

When Luke placed the water on the table, the inspector thanked him without looking up. Finally, he broke his silence: "Can I read back your statement to you, the statement you made to my officers on Tuesday?" he said, briefly raising his head.

Luke nodded and the inspector read the statement slowly. After he'd finished, the inspector leant back, peered over his glasses at Luke and asked: "Is there anything you wish to add or amend, Mr Adams?"

"No, I don't think so," Luke said.

"Good, then can I just ask you a few questions about Richard Harrington?" As he spoke the inspector produced a notepad and pen from his jacket. He didn't wait for Luke to reply. "How long have you known Mr Harrington?"

"About three years."

"What was the nature of your relationship with him?"

"We were friends - we met through the cycling club. We cycled together and we met for a drink in The Sunnyhurst."

"Did he discuss his depression with you?" The inspector was now scrutinising Luke as he spoke.

"He didn't have depression," Luke said, abruptly.

"We found prescription pills at his home." The inspector flicked back in his notes. "Yes, Serotonin. These are prescribed for depression, I understand."

"They are also prescribed for anxiety," Luke said, defensively. "Richard had anxiety – General Anxiety Disorder, so do I." He could feel his anger rising.

"Well they are anti-depressants," the Inspector said casually, again looking down at his notes. "Anxiety. Depression. It's the same condition, isn't it!"

"I think that is a common misconception," Luke began, "as I said, I too suffer from anxiety. Of course, I get depressed sometimes like everyone, but I *don't* suffer from depression - the type of condition that paralyses you like bi-polar and that can lead to suicide." Luke was warming to the subject: "And I talked to Richard about it a lot - the difference between anxiety and depression. I'm convinced that Richard did not suffer from depression and I also believe he did not kill himself, Inspector Philips." Luke was pleased with the way he had asserted himself.

"We've spoken to his family and they feel convinced he did!"

"What family?" said Luke making no attempt to hide his sarcasm. "His father has advanced Alzheimer's. He's got a sister somewhere in Italy. Have you spoken to her?"

"No, do you have her address?" asked the inspector.

"Richard had no contact with her in recent years. So, what other family are you talking about?" asked Luke, impatiently.

"He has an uncle and nephew who live close to his father in Oxford."

"I've never heard him talking about them!"

"Well, his uncle….." the inspector paused as he searched his notebook for the name - "Mr Eric Harrington," he said finally, "came over yesterday to identify the body. He came over with his son, Will. They both confirmed that Richard suffered with mental issues."

"I'm sorry, but did these people even *know* him!" Luke was becoming animated and angry and he stood over the inspector. "Richard was a really laid-back kind of man. Ok, he was concerned about his father's illness but he wouldn't have killed himself over that!"

"It's not up to me or you to make that decision, Mr Adams - I simply speak to people, collect evidence, receive reports from pathology." The inspector paused and sighed.

"*Then* I place all this before the coroner at the inquest." The inspector removed his glasses and studied Luke closely now. "It's very difficult for family and friends to accept that anyone would take their own life," he continued. His tone was patronising and his words well-rehearsed. It occurred to Luke that the inspector must have had many such meeting with relatives and friends of the deceased after a body had been found.

"And what if someone commits a murder and makes it look like suicide?" Luke asked suddenly, deliberately catching the inspector off-guard for the first time in the exchange.

"That's very hard to do and very rare," he said, dismissively.

"But it *does* happen?" Luke pressed.

The inspector's tone now became impatient. "Mr Adams, you need to trust the system that's in a place. It's a bloody good system - the police, the coroner, pathology. I can't tell you how many sudden deaths we've investigated but it must be in the hundreds." The inspector paused and sighed. "You are an English teacher - I wouldn't tell you how to teach Shakespeare, would I!"

"So why are you here?" asked Luke, abruptly.

"PC Ronson told me you had suggested your friend had been murdered. I'm here to reassure you that I very much doubt this is the case." The inspector sighed once more. "Obviously, there will be an inquest and the final verdict will be down to the coroner."

"But he will base that on what you have to say," Luke pressed.

"Partly," he repeated the word but his tone had become indignant, "yes, partly." The inspector threw his pen on the table and sat upright. "Listen, a dead body tells us a lot about the cause of death," he said, clearly frustrated that he had to explain all this to a member of the general public. "If a person is strangled they put up a desperate fight. There is bruising all over the body. There's none on Richard's body except for round the neck where the rope was! There would probably also be tissue under his fingernails - he would have grabbed at the rope around his neck, grabbed at his assailant. Again, there is nothing." During this lecture the inspector's voice and become louder and more insistent. He stood up and Luke noticed a shirt button had come undone exposing his corpulent stomach. He hitched up his trousers.

"Now listen…!" he said loudly. The inspector at this point must have suddenly realised he was half shouting because he adjusted to his default patronising tone, as if trying to reason with an annoying child: "You must leave this to the professionals, Mr Adams!"

Luke didn't like the way Inspector Philips was speaking to him. "How many times has that phrase been uttered before a cover-up!" he said.

"Are you suggesting this is a *cover up*!" Inspector Philip was shouting again.

Luke paused and took a moment to calm down. "No. No, I'm not saying that at all." Luke paused. "I'm sorry," he said, "but inspector, I've every right to express my view. I think I knew my friend and I do not think he would have killed himself. Surely my views should not be dismissed so readily!" Luke pleaded.

"Well give me something tangible then, Mr Adams?" The inspector seemed at his wits end with this amateur detective. "Evidence?"

"Firstly, he'd booked a holiday," Luke used his thumb to illustrate it was his first point. "he was really excited about going to Majorca to cycle. He was going alone but he was meeting up with some guys he knew." Luke paused then continued, emphasising each new point on his fingers: "Secondly, he was a Catholic - and a practising Catholic, he hated the idea of anyone taking their own life. He saw it as literally defying God, a mortal sin."

The inspector scoffed but didn't comment. Luke ignored him.

"Thirdly, and most importantly in my mind, Richard did not have his glasses. They were not found in the woods, were they?"

The inspector shook his head. "At his home," he said.

"Well don't you find *that* strange? He never went anywhere without his glasses – he wouldn't have been able to find his way," Luke said, triumphantly.

"I don't know, Mr Adams. I really don't know." The inspector suddenly seemed less confident and more human. "I cannot explain about the glasses at this stage but that does not mean your friend was murdered." He paused. "In my career there have been many times I have not been able to explain things. But, on the balance of probability, I am still quite sure your friend killed himself." Luke attempted to interrupt but the inspector gestured that he had not finished. "By its very nature," he said, "suicide is an irrational act – people who kill themselves often act totally out of character, often on the spur of the moment. They go against their most firmly held beliefs and principles. Remember, many leave husbands and wives and children behind." The inspector paused for breath. "And as for the glasses.... well, your friend must have left his home in such a state of distraction that he clean forgot about whether he was wearing them or not." The inspector paused again. "I'm sorry, Mr Adams, I really am!"

Luke was silent. He fell into the couch and, sensing an advantage now, Inspector Philips went to sit next to him. "Do you know what I rarely hear from friends and family of a suicide victim?" he said quietly, before pausing to add to the drama of the rhetorical question, "I saw that coming! I knew he was going to do that!" The inspector paused. "Suicides are messy, unpredictable. The victim often seems in good spirits immediately prior to his or her death, and maybe they are - but then something happens. If it's bi-polar then depression comes on suddenly. But it may not be that - a failed relationship, a sudden guilt, a belief that they have a terminal disease. Anything can trigger it. And loved ones often choose to believe any other explanation than suicide - a tragic accident, foul play. It's the way people cope with it - it's a way of dealing with their own guilt. *'I could have done more! I should have seen it coming!'* Inspector Philips had become far more human, more vulnerable, it seemed. "Of course, it's not their fault at all ......it's no-one's fault."

Luke had to admit the inspector had a point. Maybe the inspector *was* right and *he* was wrong.

The inspector, sensing he had quelled the mutiny, pressed on. "We searched the immediate area around where the body was found and there was nothing to suggest that it might have been murder that had been made to look like a hanging. Both the condition of the body and the 'crime scene' - for want of a better word - were consistent with a suicide by hanging. Furthermore, the family confirm that the deceased had a history of mental illness, his doctor also confirms he was on anti-depressants. I have investigated cases where I have had doubts .... but this is really not one of them. I'm sorry, Mr Adams."

"Will I be called for at the inquest?" asked Luke.

"Yes." The inspector paused. "And please, Mr Adams, this is not an opportunity to voice your own theories. Please remember members of his family will probably be there and we do not want to add to their distress." Inspector Philips stood again. Luke noticed for the first time how tall and imposing he was. Luke stood too but moved towards the other side of the room.

"I have a meeting back at the station in 25 minutes," the inspector said, looking at his watch. "If there are any more developments I will keep you informed. I'm sorry to rush off but ...."

"It's ok," said Luke, interrupting, "I've got to get to Chester as soon as possible."

The inspector put his coat back on, picked up his paper and made for the door which Luke had already opened for him. The inspector gave Luke a quick nod and Luke closed the door behind him.

Inspector Philips reminded Luke of teachers he had worked with who had this unassailable belief in their own opinion and could not - absolutely would not - be swayed to entertain any other opinion. And like the inspector they too would liberally use the imperative '*Listen*'. And people like that rarely listened to another voice other than their own. Luke hated how they made him feel. And now he couldn't decide whether he still profoundly believed that his friend had not killed himself or whether he just didn't want Inspector Philips to be right.

Luke knew he had to get away from Darwen and quickly. He wanted no more visits and he wanted time to think about things like why, despite everything Inspector Philip's had said, he *still* did not believe that his friend had killed himself!

He had packed already so it took Luke little time to load the car and check the house. He left his spare key with Frank and then bundled Noah into the back and headed for the M65 and Chester.

He was well on the way when he realised he had left without returning Steve Finchley's call.

CHAPTER 3: CHESTER.

Hoole is known in the city of Chester as 'Notting Hoole' on account of its café society and the money that gravitated towards this unassuming suburb early in the new millennium. The houses are elegant and Victorian and so are the parks. The Victorians knew how to design a park. And Hoole is a great place for a pub crawl too - you can start at The Suburbs - Luke's favourite - and then head for The Faulkner on the corner, which often has live music. If you fancy a session, then you might head across the road for real ale at The Bloomfield and then down Fulkner Street to The Royal Oak and then back to The Suburbs for last orders. There's another lively bar attached to a hotel on the main Chester Road if you ever fancied a change.... or staying out all night. The bar there only closes when the last resident calls it a night, which never seemed to happen in Luke's experience. Luke had woken up many times at Jon and Emily's with a mega-hangover, making deals with the drinking gods that he would never, ever, be so *stupid* again if they would just help to relieve his pounding head and the waves of nausea.

When he arrived at the house, Luke found the key round the back in the usual place. He opened the door and brought Noah in with him. Their dog Millie raced to greet Noah and then immediately ran away from him, inviting Noah to chase her around the house. It was the same routine every time. Very soon both dogs would be exhausted and lie next to each other on the beautiful tiled floor in the hallway, an original feature. This was a magnificent house full of original features. Emily had great taste and the colours and furnishings were all sympathetic to the style and period of the Victorian house yet married with some thoroughly modern touches. Luke noticed as he got further into the house that Jon and Emily had removed a wall in the back room and there was now a new and extended kitchen with an island and a large American fridge and a black AGA. Large folding doors at the end of the room had opened up the back of the house and looked out onto the courtyard. Luke imagined the doors open in summer with the courtyard becoming an extension of the house. The once dark room was now filled with light. Sarah would have approved, Luke thought to himself.

Luke brought his bags in from the car and sat down with a beer from the American fridge and waited for Emily to arrive back. It felt a long way from Darwen.

Luke wasn't a jealous man, he didn't covet what others had. But as he sat in the front room on the impressively large L shaped settee he couldn't help but compare his life with that of Jon and Emily. They had a child for a start - he and Sarah couldn't have children. Maybe he'd feel less alone in the world now if things had been different. And Jon and Emily had each other and were still very much in love - they did everything together, like he and Sarah had. And they had this amazing home and interesting, cultured friends ……and they had dinner parties and evenings under the stars in Tatton Park with classical music and fireworks.

But Jon and Emily were such lovely people it was difficult to begrudge them anything. And they had been so very kind to Luke. Because Emily had been, first and foremost, Sarah's friend, Luke wondered whether his relationship would peter out after Sarah died - but Luke was delighted that Emily continued to invite him over and Jon even started to cycle and 'the boys' went out without Emily from time to time. In fact, Jon had even come over to Darwen and cycled with Richard the previous year.

After Sarah's death, Luke had felt awkward at first when he arrived alone in Hoole but it hadn't lasted long, Emily made sure of that! She too missed Sarah terribly and she loved to sit and talk about her with Luke. Whilst some of their mutual friends found the situation unbearably awkward, Emily tackled it head-on and refused to skirt round the fact that Sarah was dead.

Luke didn't have to wait long for Emily. He'd just finished a second beer and scanned a recent edition of Empire Magazine when she clattered through the door with her carrier bags, shouting at the dogs to get out of her way and loudly greeting Luke with a "Where are yooou?"

She was dressed in her NHS blue uniform and some brightly coloured and slightly incongruous clogs.

'Typical Emily!' Luke thought to himself and smiled at her.

"Oh, come here, you?" She threw her bags down and embraced Luke warmly. "It's so good to see you!" she said.

"Thank you for having me at such short notice, but there's a story behind it," Luke said, apologetically.

"So, you have come to tell us you are getting married!" Emily said, excitedly.

"Sorry, not much chance of that! I'm afraid it's rather sad."

Emily sat down and patted the cushion next to her inviting Luke to sit down. She would have preferred to get a beer and put the shopping away, but she had recognised that

Luke needed to talk and it couldn't wait and felt it was important to give Luke her immediate attention.

"Do you remember my mate Richard from Darwen? You know, the one that went cycling with Jon last year?" Luke asked.

"Oh, yes, your Marathon Man?" Emily said.

"Well, I was out jogging in the woods on Tuesday morning with Noah and I found Richard in the woods. He'd hung himself." Luke was surprised he'd expressed it that way - maybe he was starting to believe it too.

"Oh no, Luke, Oh no! That's awful! How old was he? God!" She held Luke close as they sat next to each other. The position was awkward so she got off the sofa and knelt before him and embraced him in silence, rocking him slightly as she did. Luke's face was level with her breasts. He would always become emotional now with any affectionate touch - it was perhaps because it was such a rare occurrence in his life. He felt his tears well up and escape down his cheeks and onto Emily.

Emily decisiveness and strength soon kicked in. She stood up, suddenly. Both her hands held his and she pulled Luke up to her.

"Now, we are all going to get pissed tonight. I'm going to text Jon and tell him to leave work now - he will be home in half an hour. You put my shopping away and I'll go and have a shower and then we will walk down to The Suburbs and Jon can join us there - he will want to get changed first." Emily paused to catch her breath: "*And* we will have a takeaway from the Indian on Charles Street, like we used to. Ok? I really can't be bothered with cooking."

Luke smiled. He had known Emily would understand exactly what he needed - sympathy but not too much…. and then over a few drinks she'd gently prompt him and let him tell her as much - or as little - as he wanted to.

They sat in the window of The Suburbs and Luke told Emily the story of finding Richard in the woods. Emily knew how important Richard had been to Luke, he'd come into Luke's life at a time when he needed it most. And although she knew nothing would ever fill the enormous void left by Sarah, Richard had certainly been good for Luke. Emily had worried about Luke being lonely and she knew, living in Chester, she couldn't be there for him all the time. And, anyway, that would not have been fair on Jon. She *had* hoped Luke would quickly find someone else but he hadn't shown any interest - although that didn't really surprise her. At least Richard meant that Luke wasn't lonely. But now *he* was gone.

As usual Emily was forthright, "Poor Sarah did everything to hold onto life – the chemo, the operations, all those wacky herbal remedies, she even tried faith healing, for God's sake!" Emily was becoming angry. "I can't understand how some people just throw their lives away like a ....like a……"

Luke interrupted Emily in mid flow: "I know I said he hung himself - but I still can't really believe that. I spent the morning debating this with the investigating officer. But everyone seems so convinced he *has* killed himself!"

"Well it's not surprising.... it's not like you found him with a knife in his back, is it!"

She paused. And so did Luke.

"Fancy another?" asked Luke, holding up his empty glass to Emily. "Bloody hell, that went down fast!" he said.

She nodded. "Can I have some olives too, they're great here," she shouted across to Luke at the bar.

When he returned with the drinks it was clear that Emily had been thinking about Richard's death. "I'm sure you don't want to believe he killed himself, Luke, but people do. I was maybe a little hard on him before." She paused. "I wish you could find someone," Emily continued, touching Luke's hand. "There's this girl at work, she's really lovely, her husband left her last year, grown up children ...."

"Stop it, Emily. I'm ok. I'm going to be ok," he repeated, "it's not like I saw Richard all the time or anything. In fact, I hadn't seen that much of him recently, anyway."

Luke changed the subject by asking about Ethan and his time in Paris. He'd fallen in love with a French guy he'd met at the university and they had set up home together in a lovely apartment near Musee Dorsay. He was loving it there - Emily showed pictures of Ethan and Pierre walking next to the Seine and having coffee in the park with the Arc De Triomph in the background, and selfies of the two of them in front of famous works of art. Emily was very proud of Ethan - he was a beautiful boy with a generous, open character. He looked more like his father than his mother but he certainly had his mother's nature.

Jon finally arrived full of apologies: "Sorry, sorry, I came as soon as I could… but the traffic ...."

He kissed Emily and gave Luke a hug.

"So, what are we all drinking?" he asked. "It's really good to see you, Luke. Same again? Lager?"

Jon was a little younger than Emily, he was probably forty-five now but he looked younger. He kept his fringe long and it fell over his forehead and he pushed it back as he talked. It was something he often hid behind as he did not have the same confidence as Emily. Luke thought it was cool and made him look like a writer. Jon had a degree in English Literature from a red brick university but now worked in HR at a large factory next to the Mersey. It paid well and it gave him and Emily a comfortable life-style but Jon still hankered after a career in culture and art and always enjoyed having Luke there to discuss literature and films. Emily didn't indulge him in that way - she positively celebrated her obsession with low culture just to annoy her husband!

Jon brought the lagers - Swedish Crocodile beer, smooth and aromatic …… and expensive!

"How's life, Luke? Cheers, by the way!" said Jon when he returned. The men touched bottles.

"Luke's mate, Richard, hung himself," said Emily, interrupting. "You remember the guy you went cycling with last year?"

"No! No way!" Jon fell back into his chair. He was clearly shocked. "He was a top bloke. I really can't believe it. Bloody Hell!"

"And Luke found him ...... how *shit* is that?" said Emily.

"Oh, for fuck's sake, that's so ....". Jon seemed genuinely lost for words. He pulled back the hair from his face with both hands and held it there. "Bloody Hell, Luke, I'm so sorry. Bloody Hell," he repeated. For a moment Jon was lost in his own thoughts. "Are they sure he killed himself? I mean, he didn't seem the type?" he said.

"So, what's the type then, Jon?: Emily's voice betrayed a slight impatience.

Jon ignored his wife and went on: "Remember the talk we had at that pub in Waddington, Luke? You know, when you were in that dark mood: 'What makes life worth living?' " Jon smiled at the recollection. "You were having one of your Existentialist moments but your mate took it really seriously, didn't he?" Jon smiled again. "He gave us all a lecture on the sanctity of life, remember? *It wasn't ours to do what we liked, etc!"*

"I'd forgotten that!" said Luke, enthusiastically.

Emily interrupted, "Oh come on, Jon, Luke found him hanging from a tree, for God's sake!"

Jon recognised a rebuke from his wife when he heard one. He paused and they all drank in silence for a minute of two.

"Sorry Luke, I didn't mean to upset you even more," Jon said, after a respectable pause. "but don't *you* think it's strange?" he asked, earnestly. "I didn't know the guy well - but I still can't believe he was the type to *kill* himself!"

Luke smiled. He could have hugged Jon at that moment, "You know, you're the first person that actually agrees with me!" he said excitedly. "They all think I'm mad ....or in denial!"

"Well you knew him mate, had he changed dramatically?" Jon said. "Had anything pushed him over the edge?" Jon paused to consider the type of thing that might cause a man to take his own life. "I mean, did he have a terminal illness or something? Or was there some accusation made against him? I know people can be together one minute and then totally fall apart when something bad happens."

Luke was slow to respond, "Well, I can't honestly say. He was definitely upset by his father's decline - his father didn't recognise him sometimes and then he was quite brutal too." Luke paused momentarily to emphasise his main point: "But was he so down he was suicidal? I really don't think so!"

Emily chipped in. "He might have been bi-polar, I watched this documentary with Steven Fry. You can be high on life and then in total despair. And there's no reason, it just happens."

"He wasn't bi-polar, Emily," said Luke, adamantly. "There was this poor guy I worked with who was bi-polar. It's very different."

Emily could see that Luke was getting emotional and she gave Jon one of those wife-to-husband looks to say DROP IT! Jon backtracked on cue, "I'm sure it will all come out at the inquest - they will have had access to Richard's medical records. I know I only met him once but ......" his voice trailed off and Jon ended with one of those open-handed gestures.

Luke was relieved he finally found someone who thought like he did about Richard. "Shame that sister isn't around," he said. "I would like to know what he was like growing up, whether there was any depression in the family.

It's genetic isn't it, clinical depression?" Luke asked, looking at Emily who he imagined knew about these things.

Emily didn't take Luke on: "I'm more concerned for you, Luke," she said, "I didn't know this guy and to be honest what happened to him doesn't really concern me. I care about you, Luke. It's like life is giving you another kick in the balls - the shock of finding the body and everything!" Emily was a little tipsy by now. She grabbed at Luke's hands and searched into his eyes in a way that made Luke feel a little uncomfortable. "You must try to put these thoughts out of your mind, Luke. And if there is anything suspicious let the police deal with it."

It was apparent that Emily feared that Luke would return to one of those dark places like he did immediately after Sarah's death. He'd seemed to be getting a bit better of late and she wanted to keep it that way. She tried to change the subject: "Listen, I know I promised a take-away, but why don't we eat here and get pissed? They've got a really funky menu." She laughed. "God, did I really say *funky*!" They all laughed. Luke knew that Emily had his best interests at heart.

"Yeah, whatever," said Luke, "I'm just glad to be away from Darwen and with you two. Thank you so much for taking me in at such short notice. I love it here."

By 'here' Luke meant the whole package - the area, the house, the company. But as he looked around he thought The Suburbs must rank in his top ten best drinking places ever. The decor was eccentric and cool and as darkness fell outside, the place became more intimate and romantic. Every table had candles and water bottles which were empty bottles of Monkey Shoulder whiskey with the distinctive metal monkeys on the side of the bottle. There weren't the same spread of people in 'The Suburbs' as 'The Sunnyhurst' as it was almost exclusively middle class with bar prices to match. But it was interesting – there was a young man reading alone, and a cool couple on the settee drinking wine and totally preoccupied with each other, and there was a group of men standing at the bar and chatting in animated fashion and occasionally laughing loudly in unison as groups of men do. They were all dressed alike, Luke noted, in designer jeans and pointy leather shoes and branded tops and they made Luke feel rather underdressed in his supermarket jeans and jumper. Emily and Jon, however, were very at home - the bar staff knew them by name and the regulars nodded in recognition.

"So, what do you think, lads? Have a look at the menu? I'm bloody starving!" Emily said.

They decided on halloumi fries with sweet chilli mayo, goats cheese and red onion marmalade, boerewors with tomato relish and big bowl of mussels in white wine and cream and garlic with French bread to mop it up. Jon also ordered some chunky chips and he doubled up on the Crocodile beers. It was the eclectic mix that people choose when food becomes something of a sideshow to a good night out. Luke tried to pay but he was waved away by Jon.

"Jon's got a new bike. He's very proud!" Emily suddenly announced when Jon got back from the bar. It was her way of introducing a change of subject but it reminded Luke that he'd not just lost a friend in Richard but his cycling buddy.

"Well, we are getting serious!" Luke said. "What have you got, then?"

"It's a Colango CLX ."

"Wow!" Luke exclaimed. It didn't mean much to him as he had never been into the technology of cycling but he knew he should be impressed. Jon bought only the best.

"I took mine in for a service," Jon explained, "and the guy told me it needed new wheels and a new bottom bracket and God knows what else and he convinced me it would be cheaper to buy a new one." Jon looked slightly embarrassed. "Of course, I could have got a van load of wheels for the price I eventually paid! But I decided I'm not into expensive cars or that kind of stuff and Emily said I should treat myself."

"Well that bike you gave him was embarrassing," Emily interrupted. "Sorry, Luke but it was!"

Luke smiled. "To be honest, it was old when I had it. I bet it was twenty year's old!" Luke said, apologetically.

"Anyway, I've decided," said Jon, excitedly, "I'm going to really get into it this year when the nights get longer. I thought if I spent *that* much on a bike, I'd bloody *have* to ride it! I'm going to come over to you. I love it round Rivington, and the Ribble valley. It's flat and boring round here!

"Yeah, anytime, just let me know," said Luke, trying hard to sound enthusiastic.

Emily and Jon talked about holidays and visiting Ethan and Pierre in Paris. They'd been to The Louvre, of course, but Jon said he preferred the Musee Dorsay and The Impressionists.

"And he took me to see Hamlet with Benedict Cumberbatch - bloody 4 hours of it!" Emily raised her eyes to the heavens.

"He was amazing!" Jon said, getting excited, "I really didn't know he had that in his locker but I was pleasantly surprised. I saw Branagh do it a few years ago and I thought that could never be bettered ......"

Emily interrupted: "I liked him more in Sherlock ....mind you, he *did* look pretty fit as Hamlet."

"I bet Mark Kermode's looking over his shoulder right now!" mocked Jon, gently.

"Fuck off, Jon!" Emily stabbed her husband in the ribs, "You do take yourself so bloody seriously at times!" She addressed Luke: "Frankly, I was bored - it was far too long. Why do we watch bloody Shakespeare anymore when there are perfectly good things to watch that take half the time!" she said, smiling.

Jon was up for a fight: "Well, I love Shakespeare. The older I get the more I keep coming back to him. I love his poetry - he's the perfect antidote for this crazy text-speak world we live in today." Jon sighed. "You know, Luke, I despair when I read some of the letters of application – and for quite senior positions." He paused. "I'd bloody love to sit round a table and discuss Shakespeare all day with a group of beautiful sixth formers. That would be my perfect job."

"Yeah, it sounds idyllic but it's not, I can assure you!" said Luke, despondently, "it's like pulling teeth sometimes."

Luke knew Hamlet, he had taught it to students far brighter than he would ever be, but he'd lost his passion a long time ago. Any enthusiasm for literature now was manufactured for his class in an effort to engage them. He didn't read or go to the theatre anymore - he was a literary fraud who talked the talk in the classroom but then went home to his ready meal and an unhealthy diet of shit TV.

But Luke had enjoyed himself in Hoole. It had been a good evening and conversation had flowed easily after the early awkwardness about Richard's death. And Emily and Jon had refused to let Luke pay for anything.

They were greeted by two excited dogs when they got home. Luke could tell Noah was loving the company of Millie, he was so excited. He knew he should have really walked them around the block but he felt drunk and tired and he reasoned that they had probably both worn themselves out play-fighting and chasing each other around the ample space inside the house. He topped up their food and water whilst Emily and Jon busied themselves locking up and switching off, then he said goodnight and 'thank you' and went straight to bed.

Luke checked his phone, he'd had a couple of missed calls. One was from Sophie, she'd left a voicemail saying she'd popped round and assumed he'd gone to Chester and hoped he was able to chill out a bit. He also had messages and attachments from some of the lads down the pub keeping him up to date via The Telegraph on the latest news about Richard's death. Luke had also a couple of texts from Steve saying he'd popped round. He suddenly felt guilty - he'd promised to get back to him. He sent him a short text apologising, explaining he was in Chester for a break and that he would ring in the morning.

Emily and Jon always made a bed up in the back room for Luke. It looked out onto the small courtyard, lit by fairy lights. As with everything in Emily and Jon's world, it was tasteful but understated. The bedroom was too - elegant waxed pine furniture, polished wooden floor, an easy chair in the corner in a modern check and curtains to match. Emily had nipped in before him and left towels on the bed and switched on the lamps to make it cosy. He cleaned his teeth in the newly fitted en-suite with its chic grey tiles and got into bed.

This was the bedroom he and Sarah shared. The colour had changed - it was now a neutral mushroom and Luke seemed to recall it was darker then, but otherwise it was much the same. The room always brought back memories of when Sarah and he were happy before the cancer had started to eat away at her. Luke didn't know whether it was drink or his sensitive emotional condition but he so wished he could reach out to her like he had many times in that very bed. He remembered a time when they returned drunk from an evening in Hoole when Emily and Jon had just bought the house. It had no central heating and it was winter and the room was freezing. They undressed and jumped into bed pulling the heavy duvet over them and cuddled energetically, their teeth chattering. He could remember the warmth of her body - her supple, beautiful body - and how he couldn't quite believe she had chosen *him* with his tragic dress sense and his panic attacks.

In fact, if it hadn't been for one of his panic attacks he would have never even have met Sarah. He was still living at home at the time, working in a cafe in Lytham where he grew up. He was in his early twenties and it was around this time that the panic attacks seemed to start. He remembered that even at school he'd suddenly start sweating and feeling dizzy but the doctor had dismissed it as puberty at the time. But when the full-blown panic attacks started they were frightening. They usually started in the middle of the night - he'd wake up suddenly and sit bolt upright trying to catch his breath.

But the panic attack that led to Luke meeting Sarah for the first time was the worst. Normally he would not wake his mother and father but he did on this occasion because he was genuinely scared. Looking back now it was probably acid from his upset stomach which caused it, but he started to get a pain on the left side of his chest. Those who have panic attacks will tell you they are convinced that their symptoms are so severe that their body will be unable to take the trauma and they will die. On this occasion Luke was convinced he was having a heart attack.

He practically fell into his parent's bedroom clutching his chest. His father who had seen Luke's panic attacks before told him not to be silly and went downstairs to make him a sweet tea, his answer for everything it seemed. His mother, though, became genuinely concerned for her son. Luke was ashen and she could see a fear in his eyes that she had never seen before. She insisted that her husband drive she and Luke to Accident and Emergency to "get him checked out".

It was a typical Friday night at the hospital and Luke seemed to have to wait forever to even get seen. As he sat in the crowded waiting room surrounded by noisy drunks he was convinced that the pain was getting stronger and that he was going to die right then and there on the waiting room floor. His mother held his hand and reassured him it was 'all in his mind', although later she did admit that she, too, was scared at that time - he had looked so ill. Eventually he was seen by a triage nurse who followed the usual routine for chest pains by arranging an ECG. This showed up an anomaly and soon a doctor came into the small cubicle and took a blood sample. After another long wait he returned to say there were some enzymes in the blood that *could* suggest something and it was probably best that they kept Luke in overnight for observation. It was unusual, the doctor reassured them, for a lad in his twenties to have a heart attack but it was better safe than sorry.

Luke hated hospitals, he was a terrible hypochondriac, and the fact they were keeping him in only made him feel worse. His breathing became even more laboured and by the time a bed was ready for him he was in a wheelchair and holding an oxygen mask over his face. His father stayed in A & E reading a book but his mother accompanied him to the ward. It was the middle of the night and the other patients were asleep. Luke was quietly directed to a bed by a young nurse whom Luke, in his state of high anxiety and the half-light, really didn't notice at the time.

The nurse took Luke's blood pressure and his temperature and pulse. His pulse was racing but otherwise he seemed fine, she said. The nurse and his mother sat either side of Luke and reassured him that he was not dying as he feared. Luke didn't take much comfort from his mother - what did she really know! But the nurse's calm words and manner did start to register. She told him she'd looked after lots of heart attack patients and whatever Luke had it was definitely *not* a heart attack in her opinion. In fact, as his mother explained about Luke's history of anxiety and his panic attacks, she became totally satisfied that this was the underlying problem and she gave him a couple of anti-acid tablets to suck. The pain in his chest slowly subsided and very soon Luke fell asleep.

He was woken by a different nurse in the morning and offered a cup of tea. The panic attack had subsided; it had been replaced by a strange sense of euphoria, a pattern that was often repeated. He sat up in bed and greeted the day as a new life beginning. A doctor came around at 9 am, looked at his notes and decided because of the blood test it was probably best if Luke stayed in hospital for a couple of days so they could monitor him. The blood enzymes, he said, could well be caused by a bruised muscle but they could also be a sign of a mild heart attack. They would give Luke a chest X-ray.

Luke was surprisingly relaxed about his stay in hospital - in his mind he'd always imagined it would be like going into the lower reaches of hell itself with dead and dying all around and big machines keeping people alive and poor souls with large tumours growing out of them. Luke's ward was not like that at all - in fact the patients adjacent to him were all around his own age and they seemed remarkably well. The conversation soon turned to football. Where would blokes be without this default position!

The nice nurse who reassured Luke the previous night was back on duty late afternoon and came to tell him that his chest X-ray had showed that he had definitely *not* had a heart attack. In the light of day he could see her more clearly - she was fair with amazingly blue eyes. Eyes that danced and glistened when she talked. Whilst most people averted their gaze from him, this pretty nurse looked him straight in the eyes. It was endearing and slightly unnerving in equal measure. Unlike the other nurses, she had no official name badge for some reason - she had handwritten her name 'Sarah' on a sticky label which was peeling off her uniform top pocket.

Luke and Sarah immediately hit it off, the other nurses on the ward noticed this and the banter started:

- "I'm sorry, Sarah's not allowed to take your blood pressure anymore. The readings are far too high when she does it!"

- "Sarah, your favourite patient would like to speak to you .... Apparently, *I* don't understand him like you do!"

- "Sarah, Mr Adams would like to know if he could take you on a date if he ever gets out of here alive! You know with the hospital food and that ...!"

By the time Luke was leaving, Ward 4B's nursing staff and doctors had Luke and Sarah well and truly married off – the wedding was booked and the bridesmaids had been decided upon. It was, therefore, not surprising, as Sarah helped him pack, that Luke plucked up enough courage to ask her to go out on a date. Luke was nervous because he still wasn't sure whether she felt it was one of those intense nurse/patient relationships that cannot exist outside the hospital ward. To his delight, her face lit up, her eyed danced and she kissed him gently on the lips and said, "I'd love to, Luke. I was getting a bit nervous you'd just leave and I would never see you again."

Their first date was at Portafinos. Like Luke, Sarah lived with her mother and father in Lytham. They'd even gone to the same high school, although she was a couple of years younger than Luke so their paths had never crossed. Luke picked her up at home, met her mum and dad and then walked with her to the Italian Cafe Bar, which he'd booked in advance. Sarah always told the story later that their first date could well have been their last: Luke's dress sense turned out to be truly appalling. Whilst in hospital Sarah had let it slip that she found a man in a white shirt very sexy so Luke had pushed the boat out and bought a new one from the supermarket. It was regular fit and easy iron, really not the kind of white shirt Sarah had pictured on her sexy man. And to make matters worse, Luke was wearing a pair of those hideous cheap jeans that started just under his armpits and seemed to have a surplus of denim around the crotch. The look was completed with an ill-fitting cream jacket that Luke had found on the 'Final Reductions Rail' somewhere. (It was clearly there for good reason!) It was far too big for him and made his legs look ridiculously short. Sarah told friends that luckily she had the wisdom to see past Luke's awful dress-sense to the man underneath. And the man underneath 'had potential', she said.

On the second date Luke drove Sarah into the Ribble valley. It was a beautiful day and they went for dinner at The Inn at Whitewell, an impressive pub with rooms in the heart of the valley. Sarah had never been and she thought it romantic. The Queen had stayed there and it was a popular place for weddings. They sat outside on the terrace that overlooked the river and the hills and shared fish pie, the pub's signature dish. Luke was impressed that Sarah liked proper food. He'd also taken the hint about the clothes on the first date and had now bought a nice new jumper and a linen shirt and a pair of jeans that actually flattered his physique. Sarah watched him walk towards her carrying the drinks from the bar and decided there and then that this was *her* man. Her man for life. And at some point on that same date - although it might well have been earlier on the hospital ward - Luke decided Sarah was quite perfect.

Sarah changed Luke, she gave him a confidence. He'd wasted his time at school because he had been so desperate to impress his peers. To a young Luke, the honour of class clown brought an immediate gratification that outweighed the need for any qualification. But after he met Sarah, Luke's horizons broadened and he wanted more. He had devoured books as a child: first Enid Blyton then Agatha Christie… then just about anything. By the time Luke met Sarah he was working his way through his father's old Penguin Classics and she knew from early on in their relationship that he must get out of his dull nine-to-five and go to university to study Literature.

Of course, Luke was nervous – would he cope? But Luke more than coped, he positively flourished. Three years later Luke graduated with a First Class and decided his future course ...... to be a teacher. A high school teacher.

Luke and Sarah were married soon after he started university. They first lived at her parent's house but then Sarah had the opportunity of promotion to Clinical Nurse Leader at the newly built Blackburn Hospital. With Sarah's extra salary they were able to buy a modest house in Darwen where prices were considerably cheaper than Lytham. And so started their new life together.

It should have been easy for Luke to fall asleep after all the beer and wine he'd drunk at The Suburbs but he couldn't stop thinking about Sarah. How he missed her! And he missed her more than ever now. Luke knew he could stay longer in Hoole – as long as he wanted – but Jon's conviction that Richard had not killed himself had encouraged him. Luke felt he needed to get back to Darwen in the morning and do something. Anything he could to convince others that his friend had not killed himself. He would start with the reporter at The Telegraph.

But even as he contemplated returning home to Darwen, Luke was filled with renewed anxiety. He would have to go back into The Sunnyhurst sooner or later and face the questions. And Inspector Philips had warned him that he would be called to give evidence at the inquest .... and then there was Richard's funeral. He so wished Sarah could be there for him right now. He reached out to the cold, empty space beside him, then he turned his head into his pillow and sobbed quietly - deep, angry sobs.

CHAPTER 4: WAITING FOR AN EPIPHANY

Luke was woken by his mobile ringing at 7.45am. It was the agency asking whether he was better and available for work. The agency was always desperate for supply staff - and especially teachers of English. Luke explained that he was feeling better but he was in Chester and so he could not work *that* day. He promised the girl who coordinated the supply he would be available on Monday if they had any jobs. Luke didn't want to piss off the agency. He didn't have a mortgage because the endowment was paid in full when Sarah died and he had her Death in Service lump sum to help him a little but Luke had eaten into this already when he couldn't work at all. And he'd needed to buy a new car and he'd had the roof done. He knew Sarah's money wouldn't last forever, and, anyway, much as he disliked his job now, it was a useful distraction. And Luke knew he needed a distraction.

Emily had obviously heard him talking on the phone because she popped in with a coffee. As he drank it, he replied to his texts. Then he rang Steve and promised he'd be back after dinner if he wanted to drop round.

By the time Luke made it downstairs, Jon had set off for work. Emily was on a late shift at the hospital and she and Luke sat in the newly converted back room, looking out onto the courtyard.

"I love what you've done here," Luke said.

"Yeah, it's turned out better than I could have ever hoped," said Emily. "When my dad died last June he left me something. Not a lot because he and Ruth spent most of it on cruises, but enough to do this," said Emily, casually taking in her new surroundings. "It makes more of the courtyard, don't you think? We've not had chance to open the doors yet but it's going to be nice in the summer." She raised her eyes to the heavens, "If we *have one* this year!"

They both laughed.

"So, I guess there's no reason to go back to Lytham now?" said Luke. "Do you get on with Ruth?" Ruth was Emily's stepmother, her father had married her late in life after Emily's mother had died.

"Yeah, we get on fine. But she's got her children around her, so I don't feel I need to go over. I ring her every now and again. We spoke over Christmas, she misses dad terribly."

"I was thinking about Lytham last night when I got into bed." Luke said. "My first date with Sarah at Portafino's." Luke paused. "It's still there, you know?"

Emily laughed: "And those pants!"

"Yeah, she loved to tell that story, didn't she!" Luke laughed with Emily.

Emily and Sarah were young nurses then, working at Blackpool Victoria Hospital. They'd gone to school and university together too and were inseparable. Emily was with another guy when Luke met Sarah but he messed her around. Luke and Sarah lost track of the times there would be a knock on the door at some unearthly hour and Emily would be standing there crying. Of course, Sarah was always ready to offer a listening ear and good advice in equal measure. Unfortunately, the advice was rarely taken because Emily kept taking the bloke back. Luke recalled that even when the two of them moved to Darwen, Emily was still having problems.

But then one day she announced: "I've found my Luke!" His name was Jon and he, too, was the arty type.

"I was there quite a bit last summer visiting dad at home when he was very sick," Emily continued, "and then I was backward and forward sorting things out after that. But I've not gone back since. I still love it, though," she said. "Jon and I just love sitting outside Capri in the summer with the dog, people-watching. There's some serious money round there now - you should see the cars!" Emily paused when Luke showed no recognition. "Have you been back?" she asked meaningfully.

Luke shook his head, "No." He paused. "I think it would make me sad."

There followed a momentary awkward pause.

"You've not got to let this thing drag you down again, Luke," Emily said, suddenly changing the subject. "I know how you were after Sarah died and you can be so proud of how you've got back on your feet. You've got back into work and everything," she continued.

"Well, I've just *had* to get on with things. What's the alternative?" said Luke, sadly. "But I've accepted that my life will never be the same again. I'll *never* recover from Sarah's death. I've just learnt to live with it a bit better."

"Jon and I were talking about you in bed last night. This latest thing - Richard's death….and you finding him and everything. It must be really shit for you?"

"Yeah, well, we got on. I guess he became my 'New Best Friend'. It's funny, he was like Sarah in many ways." Luke smiled again. "I think the blokes in the pub thought we were a bit weird, talking about our anxiety and paintings."

"And now you must be feeling, here we go again," interrupted Emily. "Another one taken away from me!"

"I was last night," Luke said.

"But you can't be angry with him for doing what he did, Luke. When someone takes their life it is not a rational act. They are not thinking straight at the time."

"I'm *not* angry with him. I still don't believe he *did* kill himself."

Emily paused, she was facing Luke now and put a hand on each shoulder and scrutinised his face. "Do you think this theory thing of yours could be kind of denial on your part? Like you don't *want* to believe he would have been so selfish as to leave you ...."

"No, absolutely not," Luke interrupted angrily, "I know about mental illness, Emily. If I thought he'd killed himself I'd understand more than most, I can assure you. I wouldn't take it personally!"

And then mid-sentence Luke's indignant tone softened. He couldn't be angry with Emily. "Oh, I don't know, Emily, I don't know anything. I'm all at sea." He sighed. "Maybe psychologically that's part of it and I haven't even admitted it to myself yet. Maybe I just need a cause to distract me. Who knows!" Luke paused. "But to be honest I wasn't feeling great, even *before* this."

"I think you need to go and see your doctor and explain the situation to him. Are you still taking your Sertraline?"

"Well, to be honest I forgot to bring them here," Luke said, a little embarrassed.

"You *must* take them every day, especially at the moment. And if you want to stop here for a while then Jon and I were only saying last night you are *very* welcome. Noah and Millie get on well and it's not a problem."

Luke drew Emily towards him and hugged her. "You two are so good to me, I *so* appreciate it. And thanks for the offer but I'm off back today, I've got some things to sort out this weekend. And I need to get back to work on Monday....... if they want me!"

"You sure?" Emily asked, studying Luke closely.

"Yeah," Luke said.

"Ok, whatever. But please remember you can come over any time, even if we are not here we can leave a key. You may just need to escape Darwen at times."

Luke nodded.

"And Jon is determined to get over to you when it gets a bit warmer and lighter."

"I'd enjoy that," Luke said, with a forced enthusiasm. He could not imagine ever cycling again at that moment.

"But please, Luke, don't get obsessed with the idea that Richard's death is deeply suspicious and that there's this murderer on the loose and you have to avenge his death like Hamlet. I know how you literary types think!" Emily held onto Luke's hand. "Jon didn't really know Richard well at all and he was stupid to even offer an opinion last night. I told him so later, I can assure you!"

'Poor Jon!' thought Luke. He allowed himself a chuckle - he imagined that by the time he got to sleep Jon had wished he'd never opened his mouth!

After he'd taken Noah and Millie round the park in Hoole and had some breakfast with Emily and then driven back down the M6, it was 2 o'clock before Luke reached home.

There was a car parked in his usual spot and he assumed it must be Steve who seemed to be asleep behind the wheel. He tapped on his car window and Steve jumped to attention as if he'd been caught doing something reprehensible.

"Hi, sorry I'm late," said Luke.

"No worries." Steve got out of the car. "I've got a baby at home and she's a bloody nightmare sleeping at the moment."

"Come in, I'll get you a coffee, that should perk you up!"

"Thanks, let me help you with your stuff while you get the dog?" Steve grabbed the bags.

The two men went into the house and Luke dumped his stuff upstairs. He came down immediately and put the kettle on. Steve followed him into the kitchen.

"Did you enjoy your break, then?"

"Well, I was only really there for a little less than 24 hours but it was good to see my friends again - and have a few beers." Luke paused. "Sorry I forgot to get back to you."

"No worries. I feel guilty pursuing people at times like these when they really only want to be left alone."

"So how can I help you?" Luke asked.

Steve began with what sounded like a rehearsed speech: "Just to reassure you I'm not wanting any gratuitous descriptions of you finding the body and that grim stuff. We've already printed details about you being out on a walk - or run - with your dog and then discovering Richard's body. And we've said that it was a hanging and probable suicide, etc." Steve took a breath. "As you probably know, there have been three suicides in Sunnyhurst Woods in the past 18 months. All men of around the same age. As well as the normal reporting of Richard's death, my editor wants me to do a more discursive piece about this spate of suicides in Darwen." Steve paused. "I was hoping you could tell me something about what Richard was like. His family ignore our calls and his mates at the pub and at work just say he was a regular sort of guy, which isn't much help really."

"Well what kind of story are you after? I can't tell you we were having a passionate affair or anything!"

Steve laughed.

"He *was* a regular sort of guy," Luke said. "A thoroughly decent man. There was no bullshit with him, as I was telling the police. I mean, so many people talk and you just know they are lying to you - and lying to themselves too. All to make them seem bigger or richer or somehow more important. Richard wasn't like that at all. I guess that's why I always enjoyed being with him."

Steve could see that Luke enjoyed talking about his dead friend. He could work with this! "So how did you meet him? You'd only known him a few years, right?"

"Yeah, I met him when I joined Darwen Cycling Club," said Luke.

"Did he have a partner or a girlfriend or anything?"

"We never really talked about women in his life .... but I think he had a couple of friends. You know, 'Friends with Benefits'! He was sometimes in The Sunnyhurst with this girl and he left with her once or twice. And there was a girl he brought in from work. But I only saw her once."

"So, you don't know names…?"

"No, sorry," Luke said. There was a pause. Luke felt uncomfortable.

"Do you know what might have driven him to suicide? I know he was on prescribed drugs for depression?" Steve asked eventually.

"How did you know that?"

"Well the police don't tell you much but they let that slip."

"I wonder why!" Luke said, sarcastically.

Steve ignored Luke's acid tone and went on. "Was he depressed? His father is very ill and I know he was visiting him a lot. Do you think that might have caused him to take his own life?" asked Steve.

"Richard wasn't that close to his father - his mother died a few years back, he was a lot closer to her. I know he was down about his father - but more because it reminded him about the past and his difficult relationship with him. As I keep telling everyone, he had just booked a cycling holiday in Majorca." Luke paused, almost anticipating Steve's response. But Steve continued writing his notes. "I know that can happen." Luke went on. "I mean, people making plans then killing themselves, but it doesn't make sense to me. Not with Richard, anyway."

"Were you going with him?" Steve asked, lifting his head.

"No, I'm frightened of flying. Anyway, I need to work during school terms."

"Who was he going with?"

"No-one, he was very independent - I think he preferred it, really. And he knew some guys over there. He'd been before."

"What was he like, then? I mean, was he a talkative type?"

"He was a quiet in big company but chatty enough one to one. I found him really interesting. He was really into Religious Art, he'd even bring books of paintings to the pub sometimes and we'd talk about them. Sounds dead pretentious but it wasn't because he didn't make a big show of it. He'd explain to me about the lighting and how the picture was constructed.... but he was more interested in the stories that lay behind them." Luke was enjoying the opportunity to talk about his friend whether the journalist was interested in this aspect of Richard or not. "His favourite was *'Doubting*

Thomas' by Caravaggio. It's this dramatic and technically perfect painting – it's pure genius. The old wrinkly disciple leaning into the body of Christ, poking his bony finger into the hole in the Jesus' side. And that beautiful paradox: 'I believe, help my unbelief'." Luke paused, realising the journalist had stopped writing.

"He worked at BA, did he?" Steve asked, trying to get back to something he could use.

"Yeah, at Samlesbury, mostly, just up the road. But sometimes he was called over to Warton and he'd been to Germany and Australia. I think he was pretty much at the forefront of these new drones, he was responsible for the electrics. He didn't really socialise with his work mates but one came down to the pub on a quiz night once and he was saying Richard was a real genius."

"I need to try and talk to work mates," Steve said, eagerly, "you've not got any on your contacts have you?"

"Sorry, no."

"It's so hard getting access," Steve said with a sigh. "And he was really into fitness, yeah? You don't think he had a health scare or something?"

"Well he'd just done an Ironman and finished third!" Luke assumed the journalist knew what an Ironman was. "I think he'd have told me," he said, "we talked about health a lot, he was very proud of his physical fitness. He was always going to those Well Man check-ups. He felt there was a strong connection between physical health and mental health." Luke had deliberately introduced the topic.

"So, this mental health thing?" said Steve, seizing upon it.

"He suffered from anxiety most of his adult life, like me. It started when he was at school. He said his father put him under a lot of pressure to excel at school and he couldn't cope. And around this time he learnt that it wasn't his real father and mother, he'd been adopted." Luke was keen to explain to the journalist the real nature of his friend's anxiety. "You see, he never knew his own father and mother and I think this might have been partly to blame for his anxiety. He started failing at school and this caused more tension between his father and him. It became a vicious circle."

"Did this lead to his depression?"

"No, as I said, he suffered from anxiety not depression - I keep telling the police this. There is a difference, you know!" Luke reached out his hand to stop Steve interrupting. "And before you say it, I know he was on anti-depressants. But for his *anxiety*!"

"So that's why you made that sarcastic comment about the police before."

"I feel I need to defend him. He's being misrepresented in death. He was *absolutely not* a depressed person...... he had anxiety! It's so hard to describe what it feels like, yet he was able to articulate how you feel better than anyone. And trust me, I've read loads and sat through hours of CBT!"

"Could anxiety make you feel suicidal?" Steve gently prompted.

"I'm not saying that anxiety could *never* lead to suicide. I know how desperate it makes you feel at times when it goes on and on and you think it's never ever going to stop. Even though you've had them before, when you're in the eye of the storm you convince yourself this is the one – this is the one that's going to send you into total madness and it will never, ever stop. But that's more about me, I think Richard had learnt to deal with these attacks far better than I ever could. He was convinced that you mustn't fight it when it happens. You allow it to do its very worst and kind of wear it out. It's still horrible at the time and frightening because you honestly think you're gonna have a heart attack or a stroke or something. And you are absolutely knackered after. But I think he was right."

"So, if you *don't* think he was depressed, and you *don't* think his anxiety simply became too much to bear, and you *don't* think he had a physical illness or relationships issues ....then *why* did he kill himself?" Steve tone was impatient. He stopped and stared at Luke, he had put his notepad down on the table. "*And* he had a well-paid job and a modest lifestyle so I don't think he had money worries." He paused again and sighed. "Do people just kill themselves for no reason at all?"

"I don't know. Maybe. But I really cannot think of a reason why Richard *would* kill himself - and that's why I keep coming back to this stupid notion - which I know sounds ridiculous - I think someone must have *killed* him. I don't know why, I don't know how ...." Luke was becoming animated and emotional. He knew Steve had not come to hear all this but he had said what he wanted to anyhow.

Steve allowed a silence before he responded. "You *do* know I can't write that or even suggest it, Luke," he said pointing at his notebook. "The Darwen Telegraph depends on a good working relationship with the police and especially Inspector Philips. Clearly from what he's said to me and what you've told me today he's convinced it *is* suicide." Steve paused again. "If I rock the boat and piss him off he will never talk to me again."

"No, I understand," said Luke, "I don't know why I'm telling you this, I've got no evidence, no Prime Suspect, no motive, nothing!"

Steve was quiet for a minute, he finished what was left of his now tepid coffee. "I've got a mate who works for the dailies who might be interested in your story. I could ask him …. but you would never be able to say to anyone I put you in touch."

"No, no, I'm not stupid," Luke interrupted. "I know how I'd be presented ... I know I'd come across as some poor sad bastard who can't accept his friend's checked out on him. No, I'll only raise my head if I have something more tangible than a hunch and a few half-baked notions."

"Listen, you've been very helpful," said Steve, getting up, "and I promise you that I won't paint you as 'a nutter'. Let's agree to keep in touch, yeah? If you change your mind about the dailies because you think it might force Inspector Philips to at least consider the option of an open verdict then let me know. But I think you're right, you do need something more tangible." Steve smiled, mischievously, "Listen, mate, from a journalist point of view I'd love it to be a murder!"

There was a sudden knock on Luke's front door and Noah started barking.

"Shhh, Noah, Quiet! Sorry, I'd better answer that," Luke said to Steve.

It was Sophie at the door in uniform.

"Oh, Hi, I was just in the area......... how are you?" she said.

"I'm not too bad, come in?" said Luke.

As he ushered Sophie into the house, Steve appeared out of the kitchen, coat on and ready to go. They recognised each other.

"Ok, Steve?" Sophie smiled coyly.

"You know each other?" said Luke.

Steve smiled, "Oh, Sophie and I go back a long way!" he said.

Luke wasn't sure but it seemed that Sophie was blushing. "Should I come back later, if you two are halfway through something?" she asked.

"No, I'm just off." Steve walked quickly towards the door. "Thanks Luke, I'll be in touch. And thanks for the coffee."

Luke and Sophie watched him drive away and Steve waved.

"So how was Chester? Was it a good suggestion of mine, then?" said Sophie quickly, clearly eager for Luke not to ask any questions about Steve.

"It was, thank you. Good to see my friends again." He smiled. "We had a few beers too."

"Did it take your mind off things back here for a time?" Sophie asked.

"Not a bit!" Luke said, shaking his head.

"Oh dear, I was hoping it might."

"Thanks for trying, though. Unfortunately, I'm notorious for dwelling on things. Would you like one of your coffees?" Luke asked.

"Yes, if you don't mind."

Instead of following him into the kitchen, Sophie lingered in the front room this time. When he got back she was looking at a collection of photos on a chest of drawers at the back of the room. He handed Sophie a coffee. He had a bottle of beer.

"Sarah, looks very pretty." Sophie said, holding one of the frames.

"She was."

"And you look *so* young - I think you need to trim that beard," she said mischievously pulling on his facial hair.

"You are getting very familiar, PC Ronson!" Luke was flattered that this attractive woman took an interest in his appearance.

Her tone suddenly changed into police-speak: "I've come to tell you they are releasing the body. The family want the funeral next Thursday."

"So, all straightforward then!" Luke's tone was bitter.

"That's why I came to tell you, I knew you'd be upset," she said kindly. "Of course, there will be an inquest, you know, when the cause of death is ascertained."

"When will that be?" Luke asked.

"My father says it could be between three to six months hence."

"Well, if they're releasing the body so soon I'm sure the outcome is pretty much a given!" Luke said, sourly.

"I asked about the glasses, there were none found in the woods."

"Well he's blind without them – and he didn't wear contacts!"

"Yes, I explained to my father." Sophie said, impatiently.

"He just wouldn't go out without his glasses, it's ridiculous!" Luke was animated now.

"Please, Luke, drop it!" Sophie was shouting and the suddenness of it took Luke by surprise. "Please," she said, "you will never move on from this if you can't let go."

And then PC Ronson started to cry. Luke was confused, he stood mute for a moment.

"This sudden death has been difficult for all of us. You, me …… my father." Sophie said wiping her eyes after she had composed herself a little.

"What are you talking about?" said Luke, finding it hard to disguise his anger.

There was another pause, a long pause. Sophie sat with her head down. Luke stared at her inviting a response. "My brother Ryan tried to hang himself last month," Sophie volunteered, eventually. "Luckily, my father found him just in time! But now my brother's asking questions and my father's getting angry with him.... and *me*, it seems! Please drop it, Luke." Sophie pleaded. "Please don't cause waves." Sophie sat on the edge of the couch. "If you raise any questions in the mind of the coroner at the inquest he might go for an open verdict."

"Sophie …." Luke wanted to reassure her.

"And please Luke don't get the press to start a debate." Sophie interrupted. "What have you told Steve?"

"Don't worry about Steve, he's not going to do anything," Luke said.

"It's really not worth making a fuss, Luke. The family are satisfied Richard *did* kill himself - so let it go," Sophie pleaded. "Why are you continuing this?"

"And why is your dad acting weird……." Luke responded, coldly.

"I asked him about footprints too and he went absolutely mad." Sophie stopped herself going on. "Oh, that sounds so disloyal, I love my dad. He lost his wife and now he's got this problem with Ryan. And Ryan's been obsessed with this case. I guess *that* scares dad."

"But you didn't need to even mention the glasses today ...." Luke said.

"I was frightened you would ask dad and he would explode."

"Well, I'd already mentioned them actually. Why do you think he exploded when you mentioned footprints?"

"No idea!" Sophie said.

Luke paused for a moment before continuing. "You know, I keep telling myself to let this go and people keep convincing me I'm deluded or needy or something. But then you tell me this and I become even more convinced that Richard did *not* kill himself," he said.

"I need to go." Sophie moved towards the door.

"You don't need to. Are you still working?" Luke asked.

"No."

"Do you want a beer?"

Sophie paused for a moment. "Yeah, why not, I bloody need one!"

Luke and Sophie had a few bottles of beer and Luke cooked some food. He cut up chorizo and mixed in one of those ready-made tomato sauces and served it with pasta and grated parmesan. They ate it on the couch whilst they watched TV with Noah sat at their feet. He seemed to enjoy the new company.

Luke opened a bottle of red wine as they watched football. Liverpool were playing Chelsea in a cup replay. Sophie was a big Liverpool fan and lived every kick of the game and her enthusiasm was infectious.

Luke laughed at Sophie who lay drunk on the couch after the game was over. She'd taken off her police issue shoes and sat in an unbuttoned white shirt and her black trousers and bare feet. She looked beautiful and sexy and it made Luke feel old and a little sad. Luke made Sophie a coffee to help sober her up.

Sophie's eyes kept closing between sips of coffee. "You can't drive home," Luke said, "I'll make up the bed down here. This couch pulls out and I've got some sheets and a spare duvet upstairs."

Sophie smiled and mouthed "Thank you." Luke went upstairs and quickly returned with a bottom sheet and a double duvet he kept for Jon and Emily along with a white duvet cover and two white pillows. Luke made a pantomime of putting the cover on the duvet, at one point almost ending up inside the cover.

"You are good company, you know," Sophie said.

"And you're really good company too," Luke said, accompanied by an exaggerated bow. "I've enjoyed this evening. Thank you."

Luke gave Sophie a warm hug, and kissed her on the forehead, like a father might.

"I feel we are mates now," he said.

She smiled.

He turned out the lights in the kitchen and on the stairs, leaving Sophie with the lamp-light on the table.

"Goodnight PC Ronson," Luke said, "I feel very secure with this police protection!"

She smiled again, a tired smile.

And with that Luke climbed the stairs. He lay fully clothed on his bed, hands behind his head. He felt nicely drunk and relaxed ....and excited. He couldn't sleep and spent the next hour reliving the conversations with Sophie, picturing her sleeping just below him on his couch. Luke stripped down to his boxer shorts and got into bed. But he still could not sleep – he'd started with a headache, which wasn't surprising after all the beer and wine he had drunk that evening. But the painkillers and the glass were down in the kitchen. He put off going for them, he didn't want to wake Sophie and he really didn't want her to think he was coming on to her. But after half an hour the headache got stronger, he felt he had little choice.

Luke tiptoed down the stairs, past the dark outline of the silent couch and carefully turned the handle on the door of the kitchen. If Sophie *were* awake, then he certainly didn't want her to think he was deliberately waking her. The handle creaked a little but he pushed the door open, went into the kitchen and quietly closed the door behind him before switching on the light. Luke put two tablets into a glass and half-filled it with water, allowing the tablets to dissolve.

Whilst he waited the kitchen door opened slowly and Sophie was standing there in her long police shirt, creased along the bottom where it had been tucked into her trousers.

"Can I get a drink of water?" she said.

"Yes, of course, I really hope I didn't wake you," said Luke. "Bad head," he said, offering up the effervescent glass as evidence.

"No, I was awake anyway," Sophie said, as she walked towards the shelf that contained the glasses. She ran the tap a little, felt the water with her fingers and then filled her glass.

Sophie turned. She was now standing next to Luke who was leaning on the Belfast sink. He could smell her perfume. Luke threw back his glass of painkiller whilst Sophie gently sipped her water. The tension between them was palpable.

Sophie leaned towards Luke and kissed him on the side of the face. It was clumsy and misdirected, her lips kissed more beard than flesh. He turned towards Sophie and kissed her on the mouth and she pulled him around so he was now facing her. Luke leaned into Sophie, pushing her against the sink. Sophie's hand reached down to the back of Luke's boxer shorts and pulled him closer. Luke felt under Sophie's shirt, finding naked flesh.

In a sudden movement, Sophie pushed Luke away.

"I'm sorry, we shouldn't, we really shouldn't. I'm sorry," she said.

"Ok, it's ok..." said Luke, breathlessly. He moved back.

"What if it *is* murder. How would this look in court? I'm sorry," Sophie said again.

"It's ok, really!" said Luke making for the kitchen door. "I'll go back to bed."

"Thank you," Sophie said as she followed Luke out of the kitchen. "Thank you, Luke."

*

Sophie started her shift at 8am so when Luke heard the toilet flush and Sophie return downstairs he put on a t-shirt and followed her down. She was back in her uniform. Luke made a coffee for them both in the kitchen. He was pleased that there was no mention of what had happened in the night .... but nor was there the awkwardness that often follows such incidents. It was business as usual. They talked briefly about the day ahead – Sophie needed to go home, shower and change before her shift. Sophie thanked Luke for a lovely evening and they exchanged a warm embrace as she left.

After she had gone, Luke let the dog out and then went back to bed. He didn't sleep but lay thinking about the kiss in the middle of the night. He realised that it has been the first time he had kissed a girl since Sarah. He couldn't recall now who had started what but for the brief minute it had been exciting and tender in equal measure, and - although he could not know for certain - he sensed it had been the same for Sophie. And Luke's disappointment that it had not gone further was mitigated by Sophie's explanation that any sexual relationship would play out badly in court if Richard's death did turn out to be murder. Was he finally winning her round, he wondered? Or was that just a convenient excuse? Luke didn't even know whether Sophie had a partner. In fact, he knew very little about her really; he'd only known her for a matter of days. No, he was glad they had stopped it when they did, whatever the reason.

Noah had come upstairs, he was restless and full of energy and had clearly decided it was time for his master to get up and take him out. He stood by the side of the bed and panted excitedly then walked backwards, doggy-speak for *follow me*. Luke decided to go for the long run around Entwistle Reservoir as Noah had been rather short-changed of late.

A mist hovered over the water and the hills that enclosed and contained the reservoir. It wrapped around the large pines and seeped onto the muddy paths that led up from a large track that circumnavigated the water, meandering into the forest at times and then back to the water's edge where it was accessible. Luke had enjoyed the place in winter on cold, clear days or when there had been snow on the ground. But this was a dark day, as if dawn had stalled at 7am that morning. The darkness and the mist meant that it was impossible for Luke to see across to the other side of the reservoir. Yet sound travelled fast at this time in the morning, and in the stillness the barking of an anonymous dog across the reservoir sounded much closer than it actually was.

The valley was quiet. Noah would have much preferred a few more dogs to sniff at but Luke was relieved to be alone. He'd read about the Romantic poet William Wordsworth going for early morning strolls around his home in Rydal looking for God in nature. Of course, the poet lived in a different age: an age of faith before Darwin and Science had given us another explanation - nature was a result of chance and change and *not* the signature of a creator God. Wordsworth lived in an age that would make time to listen for that still small voice, a voice that reassured the wanderer that all was right, that there *was* a plan, a reason in everything. And that life - after all - was merely a blink of the eye compared to the endless horizon of eternity.

Luke lived in an age that saw trees and hills and water as so many molecules and atoms. He knew that Wordsworth's view of nature had no real place in the modern world and that, anyway, for every noble tree or pretty stream there was an indifferent cancer eating away at innocent flesh or another tsunami waiting to happen. But just for that hour on that dark, misty Saturday morning in February, and four days after this significant event in Luke's seemingly insignificant life, Luke felt quietly reassured by nature - that things would be ok.

After their run, Luke and Noah sat together on a seat overlooking the reservoir, it was still dark but the mist had cleared a little, allowing Luke to see a little more of the reservoir. Mist hovered close to the surface of the still water. The atmosphere was at once foreboding and strangely mystical and Luke enjoyed the peace of the moment. He sat and waited: he waited on nature, God's whisper, for answers. Why did Sarah have to die? Why was it *he* who had to find his friend in the woods? And why was he now so full of doubts about his friend's death? He wasn't expecting a burning bush or the clouds parting or some celestial light beaming down – no, not anything so dramatic. In fact, he didn't know what he expected. Just a sign, perhaps, something he could take away from that dark morning, something that told him he wasn't alone, that it wasn't all so ….so bloody meaningless.

But when Noah tugged on the lead after 20 minutes, needing his breakfast, Luke suddenly felt stupid. What the fuck was he doing there! Was he really expecting an epiphany! Maybe that momentary feeling that things would be ok was the closest he was going to get … maybe that's what he could take away with him. But as he drove home from the reservoir Luke was already having doubts.

Luke pottered around when he got home. He had a shower, washed and fed the dog and tidied away the duvet that Sophie had used. He smelt her perfume again and recalled the kiss. He really hoped she had not kissed him out of pity.

Luke decided he needed some provisions. In the local supermarket, he met Rebecca, Alex's wife. She told Luke that all the lads were asking after him ....and the girls were telling the lads to let him take his time.

"I've told them you'll come back to The Sunny when you're ready. But please just know that people care about you and are thinking about you," she said, giving Luke a warm hug. "No pressure, but if you ever want to drop round for a bite to eat or just a drink, you know where we are, yeah?"

"Thank you, Rebecca, I was hoping you didn't think I was ignoring you ... I've been away and, to be honest, I just couldn't face walking into the pub. But I will, I promise," Luke said.

"I hear we're having Richard's wake at The Sunny." Rebecca said.

"Good. Someone told me the funeral's next Thursday?" added Luke.

"Yeah, The Crem, I think."

"No church then?" Luke asked in surprise.

"No, just The Crem then back to the Sunny."

"What time?" asked Luke.

"Eleven, I think. Should be a good turnout!" Rebecca sighed deeply. "Still can't believe he's dead."

"Nor can I!" said Luke.

Luke had expected a religious funeral, a Catholic mass at St Joseph's. But it seemed that the family had made all the arrangements. Richard must not have made a will, he surmised.

"Guess the family have sorted everything then," said Luke. "Funny but I really only knew he had a dad, who's very sick, and a sister somewhere in Italy."

"Seems the uncle and his family have been arranging everything. Did you know the house is on the market already?" Rebecca said, incredulously.

"No! They haven't wasted much time, have they!" Luke said.

Luke couldn't resist driving up to Tockholes after Sainsburys. It was hardly on route but he was intrigued. He pulled up at Richard's house, he had to check for the number because he had only called at Richard's once or twice .... and that was only to hoot outside and wait for Richard to come out.

Rebecca had been right, there was a 'For Sale' sign from a local agent. He also noticed that the front door was ajar and there was a Range Rover outside with its tailgate raised. Someone was collecting Richard's possessions.

Luke parked up, intrigued and a little indignant. "Hello." He knocked gently on the open door, peering around it and smiling benignly.

"Hi, can I help?" came a voice from inside.

The door was swung open by a young man, probably in his early thirties, Luke imagined. He was wearing jeans and a t-shirt which barely covered his large, overhanging stomach. He was perspiring and he used his arms to wipe the perspiration from his brow.

Luke peered past him into the front room. Like his, the front door opened straight into the room. In fact, the house layout was the same as Luke's. The room was dotted with boxes and black bin-liners. There was a separate pile of old computers, computer games and printers and this was by far the largest island in the room. Luke realised that this was the first time he had seen inside Richard's house in the three years he had known him.

Luke offered his hand: "I'm Luke Adams, I was Richard's friend."

There was no hint of recognition.

"Ok, come in. I've got the job of clearing the house whilst my old man is down at the funeral directors........ and the pub, no doubt!" he said. "My God, your friend collected a load of crap! I'm going to have to get a skip."

Luke smiled politely.

"So how did you know Richard?" asked the cousin.

Luke couldn't bring himself to be rude to this man who was rifling through Richard's life. "We cycled together," he said.

"Ok. He was big into his cycling, wasn't he! He's got four bikes in a room upstairs. Who needs *four* bikes, for God's sake!"

"Well, they are all different..." Luke was going to explain but the question was clearly rhetorical. The sweaty relative disappeared into the kitchen and returned with a box of assorted cutlery.

"What are you going to do with Richard's bikes, then?" Luke asked when he returned.

"I'm not sure, some of this stuff's going straight to the tip, and we are taking the bits we can sell back with us. We've got a lock-up at home. I guess we will sort it and sell it on eBay or a car boot."

"Where's home then?" asked Luke.

"Oh, it's near Oxford, a little village called Kings Langley," said the cousin.

Throughout the conversation, the man was disappearing into the kitchen and reappearing with assorted paraphernalia. It was obviously the kitchen's turn to be stripped and items were placed in various parts of the front room which seemed to be the collection point. The man was distracted but cheerful and he didn't seem to mind Luke's intrusion.

Luke followed him into the kitchen on one of his raids. It was a typical 1980s kitchen with its outdated cupboards and wallpaper. Luke remembered Richard telling him how he bought the house when he moved to Darwen twenty years ago after he was transferred by British Aerospace. Luke imagined it was the kitchen he had inherited with the house. He had only seen two rooms but he'd seen enough to know that Richard was not particularly interested in interior decor.

"I was just thinking," said the man suddenly, "You'll know about bikes, will you have a look at this contraption up in the second bedroom for me? I don't know what to make of it."

"Yeah, of course." Luke was interested to see what the house was like upstairs. He followed the cousin upstairs and into a small bedroom that was completely taken over by bikes. Three were hanging from the walls on those fixtures you more usually see in garages. There was a picture of Mark Cavendish on one wall winning a stage of the tour, his face a study of concentration and pain. The 'contraption' was a trainer that Richard had attached to his second road bike. Luke explained its purpose and separated it from the bike.

"Thanks, mate. By the way, I'm Will, Will Harrington!" he wiped his hand on his jeans and offered it to Luke.

Luke shook his hand.

"So how much are they worth?" Will asked, his eyes scanning the room of bikes.

"That one on the wall," said Luke, pointing to the Bianchi C2C, "is worth about three grand. Richard bought it a month ago."

"Fucking hell!" Will said, excitedly. "And what about the rest?"

"Well, the mountain bike's worth about two grand and the trial bike with the funny bars about the same. This one," said Luke pointing to the bike he had just removed from the trainer, "is the 'cheap' bike but I bet you could get a grand for that too! I wouldn't put them on eBay personally." Luke stopped to think. "You'd be better advertising in a specialist bike magazine. I'll write a specification if you want," he offered. Luke's sudden generous offer was not totally altruistic. He felt if he had some sort of relationship with Will he could perhaps have the opportunity to talk to his father.

"Thanks mate." Luke's advice had clearly been appreciated. "I get 50% of anything we make from this." Will suddenly became more interested in Luke. "So, you and Richard went cycling a lot?"

"Yes, that's how I got to know him. He was a really good cyclist ...... and a really great guy." Luke paused. "You didn't see much of him, then?" he asked.

Will was taking the bikes off the wall - they had now become his prime interest.

"No, to be honest my father said he was a bit of a loner and a bit weird. I don't think he got on too well with Tom either."

"You mean *his* dad," Luke asked.

"Yeah, his dad."

"He loved his mum," said Luke, "he used to talk about her a lot."

"Yeah she was nice," offered Will. "Very religious."

"Did you ever meet his sister?"

"Anna? Yeah, when she was young she was at family things. But I've not seen her for years," he said.

"Does she know about Richard?" Luke asked, tentatively.

"No. No-one can contact her. Even her father hasn't got her address. I guess she wouldn't be interested anyway."

Will said, putting a bike down. "She didn't show much interest when Richard was alive!" he added, sarcastically.

Luke was too polite to say that nor did Will but here he was divvying up Richard's possessions! It reminded him of the scene in A Christmas Carol when Scrooge's maid takes the shirt off her dead employer and even the sheets on his bed where he lies and sells them for a pittance. But Richard was no Scrooge and the undue haste in which the house had been put on the market and his possessions ransacked had surprised and upset Luke.

"Did you get on with Richard, then?" Luke asked Will as he helped him lift a bike down.

"To be honest, I hardly ever saw him. Not recently, anyhow." Will seemed disinterested.

"Well, he'd been down to Oxford quite a lot recently to see his father."

"He must have stayed at his father's. I'm not sure whether my old man saw him. I'm always away - I work in Europe a lot."

"What do you do?" Luke asked, trying to sound interested.

"It's a bit of a side-line to the day job really, I go round French markets and pick up old stuff for my father's antique shop in Woodstock." Will smiled. "Most of it turns out to be shite but you can make a good profit on some things."

"Anything here, then?" said Luke, gesturing to the inside of the house.

"Nah, nothing antique here! Just clearing the house to sell it basically. If it's slow to sell, we'll rent it out unfurnished. That's my proper job," Will said.

Luke helped Will take the bikes down to the front room. He couldn't resist a quick look in the other rooms upstairs. The bathroom was very pink, not a colour Richard would have chosen for himself, Luke mused! The finish in the other bedroom, where Richard slept, was also very 1980s, with a dado rail: a pattern underneath and fleck wallpaper on top in a pink again. The colours looked washed out and insipid and clashed terribly with an incongruous orange quilt cover.

Richard had made some attempt to personalise this room. He'd put some photographs on the wall next to his bed. Luke was flattered there was a picture of he and Richard standing together in their cycle gear, arms round one another, at the top of Mount Ventoux. There were assorted pictures of Richard crossing the line on Ironman competitions and a few of Richard as a young man with a profusion of fair hair wearing those voluminous shirts and those high-waisted pleated trousers that were all the rage in the 80s. Luke was drawn to a picture of Richard standing next to an attractive young girl and an older lady at a wedding. It was probably his sister and his mother, Luke thought. The sister too had a mass of fair hair that seemed too big for her face. It was The New Romantic look, made fashionable by the likes of Duran Duran back then.

Will came into the room at that point.

"Do you think I could take this picture of me and Richard?" asked Luke, pointing to the picture on Mount Ventoux. "It meant a lot, that experience."

"Of course, please take any you want. The rest will go to the tip anyhow."

Luke didn't know why but he also took the picture of Richard and the girl.

"I better go. I've still got my shopping in the car and it needs to be in the freezer. I'd just come from Sainsburys!" Luke said, eventually.

"No problem, mate," said Will, hitching up his trousers again.

"But I will write specifications for the bikes and send them to you if you like. Have you got an email address?" asked Luke.

"Of course, I'll give you my phone number too," Will offered.

The men swapped numbers and Will thanked Luke again.

"Are you going to be at the funeral on Thursday?" Luke asked Will, almost as an after-thought.

"Yeah, it's at the pub after, isn't it?" he said.

"Yeah, The Sunnyhurst. It was Richard's local."

"I'll buy you a beer," Will said. He looked at his watch. "That reminds me, I need to pick my father up in 20 minutes!"

Luke pulled the door to.

When Richard was alive and said: 'I'd better get home', Luke had never really thought about what 'home' looked like for him. But now Luke understood why Richard had never invited him over and never arranged to meet there. Clearly, he didn't want Luke to see his home even though Richard had often been to Luke's house… perhaps he felt embarrassed, even ashamed, thought Luke. And now, in death, Luke had intruded, as people often do – sometimes because they have to and sometimes because they are curious. Suddenly, Luke felt guilty...guilty and sad.

CHAPTER 5: SUNDAY IN THE SUNNYHURST.

Luke had two favourite sayings ......aphorisms he hid behind and that closed down awkward topics. Saying One: *"I can't manage myself, let alone other people!"* a saying he used whenever anyone asked him why he had not progressed in his career as a teacher. He had used it a lot! He was asked at work before Sarah died. And his father was always finding him 'Head of Department' jobs in the TES, encouraging him to apply. But Luke knew himself, and he knew he wouldn't cope under pressure, even *before* Sarah's death. And being a Head of Department meant you got grief from above and below. The thought of managing and cajoling and supporting people like *himself* frightened him most - people like him who always did everything at the last minute and needed constant reminders about deadlines for data and the like. People like him who always cut corners and could never be found after 3pm.

Saying Two: *"I never belong to any club that would accept me as a member"* sounded spontaneous and clever, to anyone unfamiliar with Woody Allen who, in turn, stole it from The Marx Brothers. It was Luke's stock response when he was asked to join something, like being invited to church by Antony, a friend from work, or invited to join the Masons by Frank. But Luke *had* joined Darwen Cycling Club - and to his surprise, he found he actually enjoyed being part of things in Darwen. This is where Luke belonged, he decided. All his most treasured memories of Sarah were in Darwen too. Not that Luke had ever really appreciated the community then – he and Sarah were always rather too wrapped up in each other. In fact, that had been Sarah's biggest worry when she knew she was dying and she constantly harangued Luke about going out to the pub for a 'bit of a break from all this' as she put it.

Luke recalled Rebecca's kindness near the frozen aisle in the supermarket the previous day and it reminded him what he knew already: these were good people and now he needed them more than ever. He knew how he was after Sarah died and how he retreated into himself and his house and hardly saw anyone for a month and how he became fearful when he heard a knock on the door. He couldn't let that happen again - when he was alone, he would dwell on things and this only increased his anxiety. To be truthful, he didn't have any other friends or family except for Jon and Emily and they were in Chester. And doing supply work meant you were never in one school long enough to make friends. He congratulated himself that he'd coped far better than he'd first expected on Tuesday morning and this was because he'd kept himself busy and seen people. He must force himself to get out.

It was Sunday and Man United were on Sky at 4pm so he decided he would go up to The Sunnyhurst. He took Noah, he enjoyed the bustle of the place and the other dogs…and it gave Luke an excuse for leaving if needed. The usual crowd would all be there. And, according to Rebecca, they had been warned to be sensitive!

He'd had a text from Sophie that morning telling him to buy The Telegraph because he was in it and Josh and Alex texted as well. Apparently, there was a picture of him on page four (he had no idea where they had got it) with the heading *'Darwen Man Finds Friend's Body'.*

This could have been reason enough for Luke to stay home but he forced himself to walk up the hill to the pub. He paused at the door and his nerves almost failed him but he pushed the door open and walked in. The place was unusually quiet for a Sunday afternoon but Abbie was there as usual. She smiled warmly when she saw Luke and came out from behind the bar to give him a warm hug.

"Luke, it's so good to see you. How are you?" She pushed him back with both hands in a dramatic gesture so that she could inspect him and look into his eyes. Her face was serious and concerned.

"I'm ok," Luke said quietly, not wanting to draw attention. "Sorry I've not been in before, but I've been away and busy since…you know!"

"Hey, don't worry, just as long as you are ok. We've been worried about you but we didn't want to pester. Peroni?"

"Please."

Greg came over. He was separated from his wife but he had the children on a Sunday and it seemed the usual routine was a quick walk up to the tower followed by the popular homemade soup and sandwich or a burger. I'm sure his ex-wife probably complained about Greg's visiting arrangements but the children seemed to love it. They loved the food, which was simple and the type of thing young children loved. They also loved the fact that there were always other children there to talk to. And dogs. They *loved* the dogs, although it was probably fair to say the dogs did not always feel the same way about Greg's children!

It seems The English pub – along with the church - has always been at the centre of the community. But when Luke was growing up it had been a male domain where the presence of women and children was discouraged. Any man bringing women and - God forbid - his children into this environment was regarded as a "man under the thumb" and roundly ignored by the regulars for breaking an unwritten code. But things had changed in Luke's lifetime and The Sunny was a shining example of that. Men, women, dogs…even children were welcome. And single men with children to entertain on a rainy Sunday were especially grateful for this.

Men like Greg are not good at expressing serious emotions and saying something meaningful when required. "Sorry about, you know…" Greg said to Luke, touching his glass which seemed singularly inappropriate under the circumstances. But then Greg rallied a little. "Sorry, that sounded shit – but good to see you mate. By the way, you are not buying a drink today, OK?"

The two men started talking whilst Greg's children who sat on the floor and fed crisps and their left-over lettuce to Noah and various dogs in the pub. Little pieces of discarded lettuce dotted the floor.

Alex took no time in broaching the subject. He leaned into Luke's ear: "Fucking hell mate, I didn't see that coming!" he said, conspiratorially.

"Nor did I!" said Luke, not taking his eyes off the children.

"Why would you do that?" Greg continued, "I mean, I get down - you know with all the maintenance payments and with Angie living it large with that wanker from the golf club - but I'd never top myself! I really can't get my head round it." It was obvious that Greg had already drunk a few Peronis. Luke didn't want to get into a debate about suicide but he felt he couldn't just move away either. That would be rude.

Luke noticed others he knew in the bar. There was the doctor, who, when he was drunk, would always tell Luke how he could have studied literature instead of medicine. He now wished he was teaching Shakespeare instead of administering beta-blockers and sick notes. He smiled and raised his glass at Luke.

"So what time's the match on?" Luke asked Greg in an attempt to change the subject.

"I think it starts at four, but you've got all that bloody talking first!" Greg was distracted: "Katie, don't keep trying to feed the dog your lettuce, he doesn't like it any more than you do! Go and get the games box." Katie did as she was told and started rummaging through the box.

Luke was relieved when the door swung open and Alex and Rebecca walked in. The whole mood in the pub changed. These were a popular, fun couple and they allowed others to relax. Every pub needs an Alex and Rebecca, thought Luke.

"Luke!" Rebecca exclaimed as soon as she saw him at the bar. She held out her arms as she walked towards him in an extravagant gesture and wrapped them around him tightly without saying anything.

Alex patted Luke on the back as his wife started to release Luke. "Good to see you pal. Drink?"

Luke nodded.

"Greg?"

"Cheers, Alex," Greg said.

"What time did you come down?" Rebecca asked Luke.

"Just a few minutes ago. It's quiet in here, isn't it?"

"There's something on at the golf club, I think," Alex said, as he ordered the round.

They talked about the things they would usually talk about. What they had talked about the previous Sunday with Richard, no doubt. The Cycle Club went out occasionally during the winter months but it really got going again in March. New members joined in March and longer rides were usually planned. Alex had clearly been given the job of ensuring Luke was a part of things and he asked for his views on various subjects, like starting time-trials for those interested on Thursday evenings once the clocks went forward. Both men decided the main problem was finding a flat enough route around Darwen and Blackburn.

Familiar faces started appearing before the football started. It occurred to Luke that many texts had probably been sent from the pub that afternoon.

Josh came in with his wife, Dani, and their new baby. Rebecca had done a good job because even Josh didn't broach the subject. In fact, all talk was about the new baby: serious, and not so serious. Doubts about Josh's suitability as a father were expressed. Josh had been a wild lad in the past and everyone was surprised when he suddenly announced he was getting married and buying a house. And they were doubly surprised when they heard that he was going to be a father.

Rebecca led the public interrogation of poor Josh for the next thirty minutes:

"So how many times do you get up in the night, Josh?"

"So, Josh, just give us a demonstration on how to change a nappy. Here, imagine this bag was the baby's bum!"

Josh entered into the spirit. He got a nappy from under the pram and, placing Rebecca's bag on the bar, he attempted to attach the nappy whilst the newly assembled crowd roared with derision at Josh's ineptitude. Then Rebecca stepped in and showed him how to remove a full nappy before challenging Josh to have a go, it was like The Generation Game.

It was all done in good humour and Josh was laughing and returning the banter. But Luke couldn't help feeling a little sorry for him. He and Lee worked really hard and had built up a thriving business which had given Josh and Dani a good lifestyle. He'd bought an old house on Earnsdale Road and gutted it in his own time, and it was now beautiful. The new baby would want for nothing and it already had a cute little nursery overlooking the woods. Josh and Dani's parents, who were also regulars in the pub, helped Dani with the baby whenever Josh was working away.

The rounds kept on coming and so did the regulars. The match came and went and no-one paid much attention that Sunday afternoon and Noah seemed happy enough to sleep under Luke's table.

When Luke finally got to buy a round he asked Abbie about the arrangements for Thursday and the wake. "I'm bloody annoyed actually," she said, "the uncle rang me on Thursday. He asked if I could put some food on. I told him the place would be full so he'd need quite a big spread. I mean, it looks bad and reflects badly on the pub if it's like one sandwich each! Anyway, he insisted that £200 was the maximum he'd pay."

"Bloody hell, that won't go very far!" Luke said, "unless you're doing jam sarnies!"

"Well a few of us are chipping in so we will have enough, don't worry. But it's really the family's duty…"

"Yeah, especially as he's ransacking the house as we speak," said Luke, indignantly.

"No!" exclaimed Abbie in horror.

"Yes, I was over there yesterday - do you know the house is on the market…Already!"

"What! Can they do that! What about the will and that?" said Abbie, incredulously.

"Well, either Richard's left it all to them - which I doubt - or there isn't a will."

"Bloody hell, it's not right!" said Abbie. "And this guy said he'd drop in a deposit and he hasn't."

"He was around yesterday. I know that for a fact! Listen, I'll text his son, I've got his number," offered Luke.

"Thanks, if you could, I've got to order food tomorrow," Abbie looked reassured. "You know, it makes me feel so sorry for Richard. Obviously, the family don't give a fuck," she said as she handed Luke his change.

"Not everyone's as lucky as Josh and Dani. You're lucky too, being close to your family," Luke said. "But I was thinking last night after I'd seen them stripping Richard's house that I need to make a will. I'd hate it if any member of my family was coldly stripping the house and throwing my life into bin bags."

"Well, you *need* to make a will," Abbie said.

“And leave it all to you?” said Luke, smiling.

“Yes please!” Abbie said, excitedly rubbing her hands together and laughing.

As the alcohol relaxed the regulars they became less concerned about mentioning Richard. Trips to the toilet, away from the girls, were a starting point.

“Fucking hell, I was standing right here last Sunday talking to Richard! And now he's lying in the morgue,” Josh said to Luke as they stood together at the urinals, “I still can't believe he went and fucking topped himself!”

Others had theories as to why he might have done it from the almost plausible to the absolutely ridiculous. Of course, all these relied on the fact that Richard was a most marvellous actor who could spend four hours in The Sunny the previous week and ‘seem perfectly normal’, something that was unanimously agreed upon.

It was also the unanimous opinion of the pub that there would always be a Richard-shaped hole in The Sunnyhurst. But for Luke it was something more, he had lost a friend…his best friend. He was very careless, he mused, he'd lost two best friends in three years!

When Luke got home he put a ready-made Chicken Jalfrezi in the micro wave and heated up a naan bread. He texted Will asking him to tactfully remind his father about the deposit. He also mentioned that he didn't think £200 would provide enough food and could he mention this to his father too? He was pleasantly surprised when Will texted back fifteen minutes later saying his father had just paid Abbie £400 in full over the phone. Reward, Luke thought, for tipping Will off about the bikes!

Sophie had texted just to say she hoped he was ok after reading The Telegraph. She was thinking about him. Luke had completely forgotten about the newspaper story but now he wanted to read it for himself. He went on The Telegraph website:

Darwen Man Finds Friend's Body. Teacher, Luke Adams, 51, was doing his usual run through Sunnyhurst Woods in Darwen when he discovered the body of his friend and cycling partner Richard Harrington.

Mr Adams has spoken for the first time about the "horror" of discovering his friend who it is believed hung himself on the top path. "I'm still in total shock," said Luke. "It was bad enough suddenly finding a body, but then realising it was your friend makes it doubly awful."

"Richard was a thoroughly decent man," said Luke Adams, from his home in Darwen which is very close to the Sunnyhurst Woods. The deceased was a fitness fanatic who'd taken part in a number of Ironman challenges which involve swimming, running and cycling.

Luke and Richard were both members of Darwen Cycling Club and spent a number of days cycling in France last year.

Luke Adams says he has no idea why his friend would take his own life but admitted, "suicide is an irrational act and done in a moment of madness. Who knows what was going through his mind at the time! All I know is that he seemed fine when I saw him last week."

The newspaper report went on: *Mr Adams said his friend had just arranged a cycling holiday in Majorca for late March and he was really looking forward to it.*

It also mentioned Luke's own life: *Luke, who lost his wife to cancer only three years ago, regarded Richard as his closest friend.*

There was nothing in the newspaper that either particularly upset or surprised Luke. He felt Steve had been quite fair to him. Luke realised he must have been talking to a number of regulars at The Sunny because there were details he'd not given to the reporter. The report was accompanied by a picture of Luke with Richard in the Darwen Cycle Club colours. It was from a larger group picture which had been taken to promote the club. The caption underneath read: *Luke Adams (left) with his friend Richard Harrington.* There was a link to a further editorial entitled *Darwen's Suicide Curse Continues* but Luke didn't bother to read it.

*

By the time Monday came around Luke was half hoping that the agency would not ring. But they did. They asked him to go to St Helena's, apparently they were desperate as the previous supply had only lasted two days. That sounded ominous to Luke.

He'd never been to this Catholic School High School before but he knew it was on the supply black list. Since Luke started on the supply circuit he had built up a reasonable relationship with one or two other supply teachers when their paths had crossed at various schools across the North West. As the regular teachers tended to talk to one another at dinner time and breaks, usually complaining about pupils and Senior Management in equal measure, the supply teachers tended to gravitate towards one another. They shared horror stories and tipped each other off about good gigs…and more significantly, bad ones. They compared daily rates and complained about the agency cut for doing very little. After all, it wasn't they who had to stand in front of the class! Luke was quite certain that the various agencies would have loved to keep supply teachers as far apart as possible if they had their way!

As there were no other offers except for St Helena's that day, Luke felt obliged to go. He was covering for an English teacher who had been off for a while and the classes had had a succession of cover teachers. Parents had been complaining, explained the Head of Department, and the school was desperately searching for a supply teacher who would commit to a month's work. There was even the hint of a more permanent contract at the end of it if the supply could only keep the children in the classroom and in their seats!

In Luke's experience, most of his supply was covering bottom set classes with behaviour problems. He could never decide whether they were behaviour problems because they were taught by a succession of supply teachers…or that they were taught by a succession of supply teachers because of their behaviour, which had no doubt made the regular teacher sick in the first place. It was often a bit of both, Luke imagined.

Period One set the tone for the day. He was left to himself after the Head of Department had explained the work and given him his photocopied sheets. There was an air of inevitability about his expectations for the lessons: "They are supposed to be doing an essay on how time is presented in two poems in the Relationships Section of the anthology. But if you can just get them to write all they know about the poem that would be an achievement." He sighed and shook his head. "I bollocked them last week after the other supply complained so let's hope they are a bit better for you."

"What is the policy if I have any problems?" Luke asked.

The teacher sounded impatient, "Well, if it gets too bad send one of the good ones to find me. It's my free and I've got lots of marking so only do it if it's a real emergency! I'll probably be in the staff room."

"Don't you have an isolation room, then?" Luke asked, surprised.

"No, the new Head says behaviour is not the problem, it's the quality of teaching." The Head of Department sighed again. "…not that he's ever seen *how* they behave!"

As usual Luke tried to go into the lesson in a positive frame of mind. He had always tried to give every pupil the benefit of the doubt until proved otherwise and tried not to listen to the usual: "Watch out for Ryan, he's alright with me but he can be a little toe rag!"

Luke explained who he was and that he was a "proper teacher." He introduced the set question and read the poem and valiantly tried to start a discussion about time in "To His Coy Mistress".

"So is time a friend of the lover…or his enemy?" asked Luke.

"His enemy cos he can't wait to shag her," a voice shouted out.

The rest of the class laughed and the comment spawned a few more inappropriate comments.

"Ok, ok," interrupted Luke in a slightly raised voice trying not to appear to be too draconian too early. After all, they'd clearly got some grasp on the basic narrative of the poem. "Right, now can you find me a line from the poem that shows that time is the enemy of lovers?"

The class were really not interested in looking for quotes. One character had set the tone and seemingly got away with it and this had opened the floodgate.

"You've got your GCSE Lit exam in June - in a little over three months - it's really important to know how to answer an exam question and then learn to write a response." Luke said in his best teacher voice.

"We're not going to pass anyway, so what's the point!" said the same voice that had replied earlier.

"You can't just give up," said Luke.

"It's not our fault - it's Mrs Rawlinson. She was a crap teacher, she never taught us nothing," shouted another angry voice.

"But did you *let* her teach you? Be honest!" asked Luke.

This was greeted with a chorus of jeers. Luke knew it was nearly always impossible for individuals in a group to show any self-reflection. And if any did they would not dare to voice it.

Luke felt he'd lost them already. He felt his anxiety course through his body like a current. As often happened now this made Luke feel angry. How dare these children treat him with such contempt! They didn't understand for a second what he was going through!

"SHUT UP, SHUT UP! Right, the next person to shout out will be sent straight to Mr Spence."

"QUIET……!"

Luke felt defeated already. He knew that shouting at children only excited them further and led to more bad behaviour. He decided to withdraw and adopt another tack.

"Ok, if you can write four paragraphs, I mean four *proper* paragraphs about the poem, I'll stop the lesson 15 minutes early and show you a brilliant thing on YouTube that I know you'll enjoy." Luke sensed he was now getting some attention.

"What is it? Can we watch Paranormal Activity?" a voice shouted.

"No, that's an 18, you know I can't show you that," said Luke.

"Miss Rogers does," another voice shouted.

"Well *I* can't. Now is it a deal?" Luke asked. "I promise you it's worth doing some writing."

This seemed to pacify most of them but the boy who had shouted out first was obviously determined to drive a hard bargain. If you let us watch it 20 minutes before the end of the lesson!"

"No, 15 mins, my final offer!" said Luke, angrily. "Now get on with it!"

Books were opened slowly and Luke wrote the date and the task on the white-board. He then wrote an opening two sentences as a style model and three suitable quotes. Five of the class didn't have pens but Luke was ready for this and handed out five B & M Bargain pens he'd had the forethought to pack.

There was silence for 5 minutes. Result! Then a quiet lad on the front row asked Luke to read his work. The minute Luke moved from Policeman to Teacher the talking started again. And for the remainder of the lesson it was a constant battle to keep the class on task. Luke relented and put on "People are Awesome" 20 minutes before the end of the lesson. He couldn't fight them anymore.

Period Two with Year 9 followed a similar pattern. Period Three was worse because one particular girl was a nightmare. She started screaming at Luke because he had insisted that she leave the classroom and go to Mr Spence for hitting a boy. Of course, she claimed that he hit her first and that Luke was just picking on her. And just when it seemed his day couldn't get worse he ended up covering the same GCSE class…for French!

At the end of the day Mr Spence seemed quite pleased with Luke. After all, he hadn't needed to come into the classroom to restore order! He offered Luke a month's work and seemed slightly put out when Luke said he'd have to get back to him!

By the time he got home, Luke felt terrible. His anxiety never left him, it was always there like some vicious liquid simmering inside him. At times he congratulated himself it was hardly noticeable, almost inert. But then it only took a little conflict to make it boil inside him again. Although he had been worse then, he felt like he did just after he'd discovered Richard nearly a week ago now. He told himself he was in no fit state to stand in front of a class at the moment. Teaching wasn't like working for the Civil Service where you could hide away on a computer if you were feeling below par. You had to be on top form all the time: tough and quick-witted and resilient. And Luke was none of the above. He decided that even if it meant dipping into Sarah's life assurance pot he would. At least until after the funeral and things had settled down a bit. And he would *do* things, keep himself occupied, he promised himself.

Noah had not been walked at all that day so Luke let him out into the yard. He knew he really shouldn't, but Luke took two Valium and lay on the couch and closed his eyes.

Within seconds there was a knock on the door. "Bloody Hell, who's this?" he said to himself! When he was anxious he hated having to be sociable. But he couldn't just ignore it, his car was outside and the house lights were on. He went to the door.

"Hello, hope this isn't a bad time but I just saw you come in?" It was Frank.

"No, no, come in," Luke lied.

"I keep meaning to catch you and check you are ok. Brenda says you'll be thinking we are awful neighbours!"

"Oh, don't be silly, it never crossed my mind. And it's just reassuring hearing you shuffling around next door," Luke lied again. He had honestly not given them a thought since the Tuesday when he had run back from the woods.

"In fact, I feel a bit guilty because I meant to come and thank you for being there for me. And Brenda's kindness in making that meal. In fact, I must give you your plate back…" Luke was all on edge and looking for an excuse just to be on his own again, if only for a few seconds. He turned and went towards the kitchen. He became conscious his breathing was laboured and he was sweating. He had a glass of water before returning to Frank, carrying the decorative plate the chops had been served on.

"Listen Frank, I'm really sorry but I've got this dodgy tummy today...... hope you don't mind but……"

"Oh, I'm sorry, no, of course. You don't look well. I'll let myself out." Frank had taken the hint and edged towards the door. "But if you need anything…And Brenda said if you wanted her to cook your tea again please....? Well, you know?"

"Thank you, Frank. And thank Brenda…Thank you. I'm sorry…" said Luke feeling relieved.

After Frank had gone, Luke stood behind the door and closed his eyes and tried to calm himself with slow deep breaths. He went back to the couch and lay with one hand on his forehead and the other behind his neck, just at the point where neck meets the base of the skull. He'd used this technique to calm himself since he had read it was an effective way of warding off a panic attack. He didn't understand why, but it seemed to give him some release and it often sent him to sleep.

His breathing began to regulate and the tightness in the stomach slowly lessened as the valium began to work. He felt pathetic and silly. Why had those bloody children done this to him again? He felt guilty about having to lie to Frank and chase him out in the way he did. He had been only trying to help! He recalled how he and Richard agreed it was always better to use physical illness as an excuse because it was easier for people to understand and less embarrassing. Fancy, it was less embarrassing to tell Frank that he had the screaming shits than admit you were suffering anxiety! The irony of it even brought a smile to Luke's face.

Luke woke up around 2am. Noah was standing over him whimpering. The poor dog needed food and water, no doubt. Luke realised that he too had had nothing to eat and drink since dinner time and - as was often the case - he awoke with an acute headache and felt cold. He wasn't sure whether it was the result of the tension or dehydration but he rooted out his dispensable tablets which were the only thing that relieved these heads for Luke. Then he attended to the dog and shut the back door and went up to bed.

Luke fell asleep again almost instantaneously.

The alarm woke Luke at 7am. He would have to ring St Helena's at 8am and lie again about his health. He pictured Mr Spence's frustration when he received the news. *'Not again!'* Mr Spence had the hound dog look of someone who could well suffer like Luke did. It was reaching epidemic proportions in education, it really was!

Noah was restless. He needed exercise. After the phone call Luke decided to take him a walk round the block…and a longer one later. Luke was thinking about the previous day and his vulnerability at the moment: he knew he was getting all anxious about the funeral. He found himself on Sunnyhurst Road, the road that ran adjacent to the woods. He wondered whether it was a good idea under the circumstances, but he thought that he might feel better if he did confront the woods. After all, he couldn't avoid them for the rest of his life. Not with a dog!

He took the exact route he took the previous Tuesday and where the path forked sharply right he climbed up the steep hill. The path seemed a lot more worn that it had done the week before. When he reached the intersection Noah lay down and growled.

Luke walked ahead. The blue and white police tape hung randomly around the area but this was now the only evidence of the horror show that had greeted Luke seven days earlier. He didn't really know why he was there or what he had expected to see. The dog now seemed confident enough to follow Luke and sniffed around the empty bench as though, he too, was looking for some clue as to what had happened here.

Behind the tree was the path that met a road through the riding school. Luke hadn't been that way before so he explored. He was surprised to see how close Richard's body had been to the road and the riding school. How easy it would have been for one of those young girls who came down that path on their horses to have discovered what Luke has seen, he thought.

And then another thought crossed Luke's mind - Richard knew the path through the riding school. After all, it ran into Tockholes. He would have known full well that young girls rode down that path as it was a short cut to the reservoir. Surely, he would not have been in such a deranged state of mind that he would have cared nothing about who found him! Whatever Richard's desperate state of mind, Luke refused to believe that he would have been so thoughtless: so thoughtless in his choice of death and his choice of location. And then there were the glasses! Yes, the case against suicide was building. He'd entered the woods with a certain amount of trepidation but now he felt uplifted, somehow; he was going to prove his friend had not killed himself and discover who had taken his life. This is what any true friend would do, wasn't it? And he knew he could never shake off this anxiety and return to any kind of normality until he'd tried *everything* he could to get to the bottom of this mysterious death.

CHAPTER 6: THE WAKE.

Luke had not been to the Crematorium since Sarah's funeral. It had been a frosty day with blue clear skies and it was a simple and short ceremony after a church service that had been a celebration of Sarah's life. He'd arranged with the undertaker that the curtains were to be closed at the end of the service instead of watching the coffin disappear. But Luke felt he'd rather made a fool of himself: he'd planned on walking to Sarah's coffin to lay a single rose upon it, but when he got there he just couldn't leave her. The congregation stood there awkwardly until Emily finally came forward and gently ushered him back to his seat.

Despite many offers of company, Luke decided to go home alone after the funeral. He sat in his front room, lit candles and watched the snow fall. And he knew that somehow this it was a sign from Sarah, that she was with him. She loved snow and became a child again when it fell.

And now it was Richard's turn. The Crematorium was packed, his work colleagues at British Aerospace had come in large numbers. And Luke was so proud to see how many folk had turned out mid-week from The Sunny and Darwen Cycle Club. It was standing room only with some mourners outside; the uncle who had arranged the funeral has sorely underestimated what Richard meant to his community. The small confines of the Crematorium were totally inadequate......but that was all people had to mark his passing. There had been no service of celebration in his church and even the service at the crematorium was decidedly abrupt: no music, no speeches. The family had arranged for a totally non-religious send off, it was dull and impersonal and although the congregation was full of those who knew him and loved him, there was no voice to mark and celebrate the life of a friend and work colleague.

The fat uncle was on the front row with Will, who looked uneasy in his suit. An elderly lady completed the family group. Luke had heard Richard talk about his nanny and housekeeper and he imagined the old lady must be her. Luke noticed she was crying.

After the service, Luke drove back home and let the dog out before walking to The Sunnyhurst. As he walked his anger towards Richard's so-called family grew. Yet as soon as he walked into The Sunny and saw how much effort Abbie had put into preparing the pub all anger was forgotton. The snug had been turned into a buffet bar for the day. She'd decorated it with tasteful matt black balloons and coordinating tablecloths and she'd dotted pictures of Richard around the place, in little black frames. And she'd closed the curtains and lit candles so that it looked like a little shrine to Richard. Rebecca and the girl Luke had once seen with Richard were in the snug looking at the pictures. They had clearly been crying. When Rebecca saw Luke she hugged him tightly. He could feel her warm tears on the side of his face and it brought tears to his eyes. Tears came easily to Luke now.

"This is Fran," Rebecca said, turning, "do you two know each other?"

"Not really, but I've seen you around here," said Luke. "Hi, I'm Luke." Luke offered his hand.

"Yes, I know, it's really good to meet you, Luke. I didn't know Richard very well but he always spoke of you fondly."

"Oh, thank you," said Luke, a little taken back, "Yes, I was very fond of him, too."

Fran hugged an embarrassed Luke. Was that the best he could do? "Had you seen Richard recently?" he asked.

"No, I'm afraid I hadn't," Fran said, "I've been working in America for over a year now. The Boston area, I've just flown back to visit my parents and read about Richard in the paper." She paused. "It must have been horrible for you, Luke," she said.

Luke nodded. He feared that if he said anything more he would become emotional.

"I can't believe he would have killed himself, poor man," Fran continued.

Again, Luke didn't trust himself to say anything. He made one of those open hand motions to suggest Richard's suicide was somehow beyond explanation. At that point another girl came across and occupied Fran's attention. Luke continued to speak to Rebecca but made a mental note to catch Fran later when he'd had a few more drinks and felt more able to talk about Richard's death. Fran was another person who clearly found it hard to imagine that Richard had killed himself.

Alex came into the room with two beers and gave one to Luke. The girls already had drinks resting on the only bit of space on the laden tables. The spread looked beautiful. Abbie enjoyed the catering side of her job, normally the punters only wanted pies and chips and assorted paninis for bar food but occasions like this gave her the opportunity to show off her talent for preparing and presenting food.

There were big bowls of couscous with coriander and finely chopped red onions and tomatoes in them. Under heat lamps, there were spicy meat balls and a chicken dish with what looked like preserved lemons in it. The chicken was charred, the way Luke liked it and there were coriander leaves scattered over the surface of the dish like water lilies. There were home-made kebabs with peppers and red onions which looked appetising and colourful. There was a big feta cheese salad with a fragrant dressing, a rice salad where the rice had been cooked in turmeric and mixed with different types of beans and more coriander. There was a pasta in green pesto. And there were dips…dips of every flavour and colour - aubergine, tzatziki, hummus, yoghurt with mint and others that Luke could not name, but Luke knew Abbie had made them all herself. And there were home-made flatbreads too.

The snug was getting crowded as others came in to look at the pictures and drool over the food. Luke and Alex started to mingle. Josh and Dani arrived and fought their way to the bar and Luke cut across the pub to them.

"No let me, it's my round," he said.

Abbie was serving with three of the other girls.

"Bloody hell, Abbie, that spread is amazing!" said Luke, enthusiastically.

"Thank you, to be honest I was up most of the night…"

"Well, you've done Richard proud, Abbie. It looks too good to eat!" Luke gushed.

The pub was crammed and the bar was three deep and it took Luke a while to get served. There were lots of unfamiliar faces, Luke guessed they were BA colleagues because dotted amongst them were the more familiar faces of friends Richard had introduced Luke to at various times. He must have talked fondly of The Sunny and its little community because his work mates often came over on a Sunday to walk up to the tower and have a drink.

The fat uncle, Will and the old lady had ensconced themselves around a large table near the fire. Will and the lady were sitting and seemed deep in conversation. The uncle stood with a pint in his hand and another waiting. He was talking at a guy from British Aerospace and almost prodding him to emphasise a point he was making.

Luke felt a sudden rage. He wanted to walk straight over to him and prod *his* finger in emphasis and say: *"Hello, I'm Luke, I was Richard's friend. Can I just say that was undoubtedly the worst funeral I have ever attended. Do you know, Richard was a beautiful, talented man and deeply loved by all who knew him? The Crematorium was full of those who wanted to celebrate his life but you didn't give them an opportunity. You clearly never knew him! So, drink your drink and fuck off back home in your posh fucking car, groaning under the weight of everything you've plundered from his house, you fat bastard!"*

But of course, Luke being Luke, didn't say anything. And when the fat uncle looked over in his direction, Luke smiled meekly. The uncle banged on the table suddenly with the palm of his hand. The violence of the strike stopped conversation immediately.

"Hello. I'm Richard's Uncle," he announced pompously. "And this is my son, Will," he continued, waving an arm carelessly in his direction. "And erm…this is Miss McKenzie who has worked for the family for many years and wanted to come today because she remembers Richard as a child in Oxford."

The fat uncle continued: “It was hoped that Richard’s father, Mr Thomas Harrington, would be able to make it over today but he is too sick.” He paused, it was the first time the uncle had shown any emotion. “A great man tragically struck down by Alzheimer’s,” he continued.

Luke was angry: this was Richard’s funeral, not his father’s!

“Finally, thank you all for coming today. I'm sure Richard would have been pleased to see such a healthy turnout.” Then a smirk grew across the uncle’s face. “Or are you all just here for the food?” he said. The attempt at a joke was greeted with silence. “Anyway, get stuck in, it's self-service. And make sure you don't leave a crumb it cost me a bloody packet!”

Josh raised his glass and shouted out: “To Richard, a top bloke, we are all going to miss you, mate!” And in unison the whole pub raised their glasses and repeated “RICHARD.” Then there followed a spontaneous round of applause which must have lasted a full two minutes. Luke’s hands were sore after it had finished.

Luke patted Josh on the back, “Good man, we didn't want to let that dick have the last word!”

The fat uncle sat down and started on his next pint. Will signalled a “let me know when you need a beer” gesture across the room. Luke gestured back with his full pint.

Luke started chatting to a girl from BA who had worked with Richard as a purchaser. It was clear that everyone loved and respected him. As they were talking, Luke became aware that the old lady, who had come with the uncle, was standing at his side. She'd moved so close he felt he ought to introduce himself.

"Hello, I'm Luke. I was Richard's friend," he said.

"Yes, I know who you are," she said smiling at him, "fancy a cigarette?"

"I don't smoke," said Luke.

"Well, come and watch me smoke then!" she replied, playfully.

Luke recognized the clear imperative and excused himself from the girl he had been talking to and followed the mysterious lady outside.

The light was starting to fade and it was getting cold. She took out a packet of cigarettes and a lighter from her handbag and lit her cigarette. She inhaled deeply as though it were her last cigarette.

"I needed *that*, I couldn't stand another second with that silly man," she said.

"I guess you are referring to Richard's uncle…or is it Will."

"No, Will is harmless enough, just totally dominated by Uncle Fester. He must get embarrassed too but he is very loyal."

"So why did you come?" asked Luke.

"Well, I cared about Richard very much. And I was determined to be here." The old lady paused. "*And* I wanted also to speak to you."

"To me!" Luke was surprised.

She brushed Luke's comment aside. "I'm dying so I've decided I've no time to beat about the bush."

"I'm sorry," said Luke rather taken aback by the candidness of the comment.

She waved Luke's awkwardness away, "I'm 79 so I've had a good innings. But I want to try and sort out a few things - and a few people before I shuffle off."

"You've lost me completely. I've had a few drinks so take it a little slower." Luke paused and smiled a little. "Can I scab a cigarette after all?" he said.

"Of course, I knew you were a secret smoker." She pulled out a cigarette and Luke took it from the packet. She handed her lighter to Luke who lit his cigarette. The old lady stared hard at him as he did it. "I can see now why Richard liked you so much," she said. "He's been up to see his father quite a lot recently and we'd talk, you know? He didn't get much sense out of his father, after all!"

"Well we got on really well," Luke said, "we hit it off, as they say in Romantic fiction!" Luke stopped and smiled at what he had just said and then added. "No romance, of course!"

"I think a good friendship is like a romance. In fact, it's often longer lasting without the sex. That complicates things in my experience."

Luke blushed, it didn't seem right to hear an old lady alluding to her sex life. But as he looked at her he thought she had probably been in high demand in her younger days. She was petite and she still dressed stylishly with black trousers, a black turtle neck sweater and a tight fitting black coat and a grey scarf around her neck. She had well cut short hair which was straight and grey. She reminded Luke of the actress and politician Glenda Jackson for some reason and Luke has always quite fancied her angular features since Women in Love. Luke decided he liked this woman.

"Richard and I just chimed together from the moment we met," Luke continued. He never grew tired of talking about his friend.

"You did make him a better person. He wouldn't have come back to his father if it had not been for your influence," the old lady said, "and I wouldn't have got to see him again either. So, thank you," she said, squeezing Luke's wrist.

Luke could see that the old lady was close to tears. There followed an awkward pause whilst she recovered herself.

Luke jumped in: "Well I can assure you that Richard gave me more than I ever gave to him. He saved me after my wife died. I'd just lost my best friend and I was lonely and lost." It was Luke's turn now to fill up and he paused before recovering himself enough to go on. "Richard helped me get back on my feet again. I'm going to miss him very very much." Tears welled in Luke's eyes. "By the way, I don't know your name?" Luke said.

"Rachel." She paused and threw down her cigarette and immediately lit another one. "I need you to find Anna for me?"

"Anna?" said Luke, "Richard's sister?"

"Yes, she's in Italy."

"Ok, well that narrows it down, I'll set off immediately!" said Luke, playfully.

"I'm being serious!" The old lady seemed taken aback by Luke's flippant response. "I know she lives somewhere in Rome."

"But why ask me? Luke asked. "You've only just met me."

"Because I know you cared for Richard and I'm hoping you will to do it for him. If he took his life, I need to know why. Have you any idea why he killed himself?" Rachel's eyes searched Luke's face as she asked the question and it made Luke feel uncomfortable.

"No."

"Well then!"

"How would Anna know? Richard told me they hadn't spoken for years," said Luke.

"They had!" Rachel said, firmly.

"What!" Luke exclaimed.

The old lady sat down on the bench near the front door of the pub. She suddenly looked very tired and what little colour she had was now drained from her face. Luke saw for the first time that she was clearly very sick. She began to tell her story: "Richard was over last week when his father took a real turn for the worse. To be honest, we didn't think he was going to last the night. Do you know he's got kidney cancer as well as Alzheimer's?"

Luke nodded.

"Well last week he got a bladder infection and his blood pressure dropped dangerously low. As it turned out the antibiotics did their work and by the morning he'd rallied a little." She took a drag of her cigarette. "Mind, he's still a very sick man and it's only a matter of time."

"I didn't know that he'd taken a turn for the worse - I didn't see Richard after he'd returned," Luke interrupted.

"Anyway, Richard took the whole thing badly," Rachel went on, "I don't think it was so much the thought of losing his father, he was more frustrated that Anna was totally unaware of this. She'd missed her mother's death, see."

"Why?"

"Long story, but Mr Harrington put her in hospital and didn't let anyone know she was ill." Rachel paused. It seemed the telling of the story was taking what little strength she had left. "Could you light me another cigarette please?" she asked, offering her handbag to Luke. Luke opened the bag, retrieved the cigarette packet and the lighter and lit the cigarette and gave it to the old lady. She inhaled deeply once more and it seemed to sustain her. "Anyway, Richard ended up ringing his sister that night. The conversation was quite civil at first. I was trying to listen in but I'm rather deaf and to begin with it was all very quiet and there were long pauses. In fact, I thought the call had finished at one point. But then Richard started talking louder." Rachel paused and took another drag of her cigarette.

"Have you ever heard Richard raise his voice in anger, Luke?" Rachel asked, suddenly.

"Never," Luke said.

"Well nor had I, until last Friday."

"What was he saying?" Luke asked, surprised.

"I couldn't make out the words .... it was just shouting." The old lady was getting upset. She stopped for a moment and her head fell forward as if she had suddenly fallen asleep but after a moment she continued. "When he finally came off the phone he was really upset and agitated. I went into the office to speak to him but he didn't want to talk." The old lady was becoming more and more upset. "I've never seen him like that before, Luke. And he seemed angry with me too." The old lady was shaking. Luke put his hand on her shoulder. Once again she rallied. "I asked him if he was upset with me and he just kept saying, 'I don't want to discuss it,' then he went to his room. He didn't sleep, though, he was pacing about all night."

"You think he was upset because Anna refused to see her father?" Luke prompted.

"Yes, but there was more to it than that. I think Anna told him something that made him despise his father all over again." Rachel paused once more. "When he left in the morning, he hugged me – but it wasn't warm, like usual - and he just said, 'I'll see you at the funeral, Rachel.' Then he went." The old lady stopped, threw he cigarette to the ground and stepped on the butt.

"So, do you think Anna might have told him something that led to him taking his life?" Luke asked, tentatively.

"I don't know," the old lady said, "but I need to know before I go to my grave. I've always thought there were family secrets."

"Big enough to make Richard kill himself?" asked Luke.

"I don't know. I honestly never thought he was the type but......"

"Why don't you ring Anna yourself, tell her Richard's dead and then ask *her* what they discussed?" Luke suggested.

"Trust me, I've searched and searched for her number. It wasn't on the call log on the house phone so the call must have been made on Richard's mobile. I've been through all of Mr Harrington's phone book. There's nothing."

There was a pause in the conversation. The old lady looked sick and sad.

"I can't just leave everything and go," said Luke, finally.

"What are you leaving, Luke?" Rachel asked. There was desperation in her voice now. "I know you're a teacher. But aren't you one of those temps?"

"Yeah, supply," said Luke.

"Well, don't you want a bit of adventure in your life, Luke? And don't you want to find out the truth too?" she asked.

"Of course I do," said Luke, a little upset with Rachel now. She was asking a lot of him.

"Anna needs to know her brother is dead. Uncle Fester won't find her, it's not in his interest. And I need to know what they talked about last Friday night. Don't you want to know why he killed himself, Luke?"

"Yes," said Luke.

"If you need money, I've got some savings," Rachel offered.

"No, it's not that. Truth is, I'm scared of flying. I'd have to drive," Luke said, a little embarrassed.

"I'd come with you if I was well enough and I didn't have to look after Mr Harrington. It's a toss-up at the moment, who's going to keel over first!"

There was another pause.

"Let me think about it, Rachel." Luke said, eventually. "How can we stay in contact?" he asked.

"You can write to me...here's my address." She handed Luke a piece of paper with her full name and a printed address. Obviously, Rachel had planned this all out!

"Thank you. I will write to you, whatever, I promise," said Luke.

"I better get back," said the old lady.

Rachel slowly got to her feet and they both walked back into the pub. "By the way, why do you call him Uncle Fester?" Luke asked as he held open the door for Rachel and felt the warmth of the pub on his face.

"The children nicknamed him - he has always had that bald head and those manic eyes." She laughed as they went their separate ways in the pub.

Luke was immediate seized upon by Josh. "Where have you been?"

"Smoking!" Luke replied, smiling.

"What!"

"Never mind." said Luke.

Luke circulated. It was a good wake. The place was buzzing and still packed. Richard's work-crowd were talking to the pub crowd and the cycling crowd and everyone was talking about Richard. Luke hoped that his wake would be half as well-attended but he knew it wouldn't. Richard meant so much to so many…and Luke was *his* best mate. He suddenly felt very proud.

He occasionally looked over to Uncle Fester. Rachel was sitting alone with a glass of water in front of her. Will was talking to a girl who worked at The Sunny but when he noticed Luke across the room he headed over. "Come on, I'll get you that beer. I'm on coke, I'm driving a drunk father back to London later. He will no doubt be snoring loud enough to wake the dead!" Will smiled. "Sorry, bit tactless, under the circumstances!" he said.

"You don't need to, you know. I haven't done those specs for you yet. But I will, I promise," said Luke.

"No worries, mate, I've already sold the bikes." Will beamed. "Got three and a half grand for the lot at a posh bike shop in London." And I'd have practically given them away if you hadn't tipped me off!"

Luke thought he'd still given them away, considering how much Richard had paid for them but he smiled back at Will who was clearly delighted. They reached the bar together and stood in line.

"Listen Will, did you happen to find Richard's phone in the house? It's just that it's got some photos I'd like on it," Luke lied.

"No, just his house phone. Rachel asked me too. But wouldn't the police have taken it?" he offered. "You know, looking for any last messages?"

"Yeah, I guess. I'll ask them," said Luke, feeling a little stupid for not immediately thinking about that himself.

After a while, people started to drift away from the pub. Uncle Fester, swaying perilously, was marshalled out by Will. And because he was so oblivious to all around him, Luke was able to study him more closely now. Rachel was right about the eyes, especially in his current state of drunkenness, they looked sinister. Rachel followed him out of the pub, giving Luke a tired smile as she left. It had been a long day for her and she still had a three-hour drive home with a drunken Uncle Fester. And many toilet stops, Luke imagined!

Luke went to sit around the large table with Josh and Alex - Dani had left earlier because she needed to relieve her parents who were on baby-sitting duty. Drew, another guy from the cycling club, was still there and a couple of other cyclists that Luke knew to chat to but not well. He was disappointed to see that Fran had gone. He'd been so preoccupied by Rachel that he'd completely forgotten about speaking to her again.

"So, did you cop off with the granny, then?" Alex said when Luke sat down.

"Fuck off, Alex, and go and get another round," Luke countered, laughing.

"What were you talking about for so long outside, then?" Alex asked, more seriously.

"Oh, she wanted to talk to me about Richard. She was his nanny when he was growing up. Then the house-keeper." Luke paused. "Richard's family are seriously minted."

"Did you see the car?" Josh exclaimed.

"Yeah, but I think they are also a thoroughly fucked up family," said Luke. "Was Richard just *normal* Richard when he was in last Sunday?" he asked, sounding alarmingly like Inspector Philips. "You sure he didn't seem depressed or upset?"

"No, as I said, he seemed just the same. Maybe a bit quieter but he was probably tired cos he'd been away and driven back Saturday. Why?" said Josh.

"It's just the old lady said he was really upset on Friday night. He spoke to his sister."

"Was she here today?"

"No, she lives in Italy. She doesn't know he's dead."

"Bloody hell!" said Alex.

"That's really what we were talking about. The old lady wants me to go and find her and tell her about her brother." Luke sighed deeply.

"Well, Italy's a big place!" said Alex.

"That's basically what I said…but we know she's in Rome. And I know what she looks like." Luke paused. "Well, what she looked like 20 odd years ago, anyway!"

"Is she fucking mad…why would you go on a wild goose chase to find a sister that obviously can't be arsed about him!" interrupted Alex.

"I must admit, I feel a bit like that…but then something tells me I should go. For Richard, like I feel I owe it to him." Luke paused. "But I'm scared of flying so…" he said sadly.

"I'll drive you!" Josh said. His tone was decisive. He'd been quiet during this exchange but he suddenly came to life.

"You can't, don't be stupid. What about Dani and the baby?" said Alex, sounding like a parent admonishing a child.

"Listen, it would be an adventure," said Josh, excitedly. "I haven't taken the new Audi for a proper drive yet, it'd be like those challenges they used to do on Top Gear!" Josh continued enthusiastically.

"But Dani!" said Luke.

"Let me have a word…she was talking about going to Lanzarote with her mum and dad anyhow and she knows I fucking hate lying about in the sun."

*

Luke must have walked home from the pub but when he woke in the morning he was still fully clothed and lying on top of the bed. The dog was at his side gently whimpering to go outside for his early morning ablutions.

Luke's head was banging and he had that horrible dryness in his mouth that comes after too much beer. He reluctantly followed Noah downstairs and opened the back door to let him out. He reached for the tablets, switched on the kettle and sat at the breakfast bar, head in hands. Luke started to recall the wake. It was strange because he expected the day to be very emotional as he grieved for his friend. And he imagined too that the funeral would have recalled that awful day when he said his final goodbye to Sarah. It had been difficult at the crematorium but only momentarily. The fact his day had been so full of conversation and incident had meant that he had not really had time to dwell on the grief. He was somehow relieved and guilty at the same time.

Luke might have allowed his mind to contemplate his life ahead at this point without Richard and Sarah and his loneliness. And his hopeless existence as a supply teacher and God's silence when he had expected an epiphany. This would have led to that inevitable downward spiral into paralysing anxiety and isolation and the dependence on pills and alcohol which followed Sarah's funeral. But this time it seemed different, Rachel's mission for Luke had intrigued him, he had to admit. And now Josh had offered to drive him! Maybe this was the epiphany he'd been waiting for at the reservoir. Despite his delicate condition, Luke felt excited.

He found his mobile phone. There were a number of missed calls and messages. *"Where are you?"* from Alex, obviously sent whilst he was outside with Rachel. *"Thinking of you. Xxxx"* from Emily. *"Hope it goes ok today."* from Sophie.

Luke texted Sophie back immediately, *"Are you free to talk?"* He didn't know whether she was working or not.

Sophie called back straight away.

"Hi, do you need me?" she asked, sounding concerned.

"Well, yeah, I needed to ask you something. Are you ok?"

"Fine. I was thinking about you yesterday," she said. "How was it? Pretty awful, I imagine."

"It was less awful than I expected, to be honest," Luke said, "It was a good wake, if you forgive the oxymoron!"

"What?"

"Nothing, just being silly. The Sunny was packed," said Luke.

"I'm pleased," she said. "What are your plans now?"

"Well that's partly why I rang. Can you ask your father if the police have Richard's phone? I need to get a number off it if I can."

"I'll ask him, he's upstairs I think," Sophie offered.

She was gone for a minute. Luke heard Sophie returning.

"No, they didn't find a phone, he didn't have it with him and it wasn't in the house or in his car," she said. "They'd also checked whether he'd left it at work." Sophie paused. "My father thinks he may have left it at his father's house the previous Saturday."

"I was talking to his father's house-keeper yesterday, he didn't leave it there." Luke paused for a response but went on when Sophie didn't speak. "You see, I need it so I can get his sister's number. The housekeeper has been searching for the number too and I'm sure she'd have found the phone and got the number had it been there."

"Well, I'm really not sure then. Maybe he threw it away or hid it before he killed himself," Sophie suggested.

“Why would he do that?” Luke said, surprised by Sophie’s suggestion.

“I don't know......something on it he wanted to take to his grave perhaps! I really don't know, Luke.” Sophie's voice was impatient and Luke could hear her father talking in the background.

“Ok, Sophie. Anyway, thanks for asking,” Luke said.

“I'll be in touch, I better go now,” Sophie replied in a half whisper. Clearly her father was getting impatient.

Luke put his phone down and drank his fizzy pain killer and then made himself coffee and cereal. First the glasses and now the phone! Inspector Philips could think what he liked, but something just wasn’t right. After a few minutes Luke started to feel a little more human. He decided to take Noah for a walk, Luke needed to think.

The day was spent pottering after the walk. He cleaned and hoovered the house and did some washing - he'd done little in the days since Richard's death.

When he returned from his walk, Luke wrote a letter to Rachel.

12 Avondale Rd

Darwen

BB5 1NY

2nd March

Dear Rachel,

It was nice to meet you yesterday. I'm writing this morning to say what I should have said yesterday. Since discovering Richard's body, I have felt strongly that his death was not suicide. I know that very few people share my view and automatically assume that some trauma or revelation led to Richard killing himself. But I am still convinced that the Richard I knew would not kill himself.

I've made a promise to myself this morning - if I get to speak to the sister and if she opens up about the phone call and if it turns out to be significant enough for Richard to do something totally out of character and take his own life then I will accept it -and I will be satisfied that at least I was prepared to seek justice for Richard if he had been murdered. And know that's a hell of a lot of 'ifs' but I must try to do something.

I had hoped that I could find Richard's phone for the sister's number but I spoke to Will Harrington (as I know you have) and the police and the phone seems to be missing. I will therefore have to go to Rome and try and find the sister to deliver the news of Richard's death – not for her or even for you, Rachel, but to satisfy my

own mind. I am hoping now that a friend will drive me. If not, I will have to consider the train.

In the meantime, is there anything more you can tell me about Anna that would help me in my search? Needles and haystacks come to mind at the moment! Hoping the ride back was not too awful with Uncle Fester!

Luke.

Luke copied out Rachel's address onto the envelope. Because he rarely sent letters there were no stamps in the house and he had to walk to the post office.

Luke now felt he needed to ring Josh and check whether his offer of driving to Italy was drunken bravado or genuine. The phone rang out and went to voicemail. But a few minutes later Josh rang back. He sounded hungover.

"Sorry mate, I was asleep when you rang."

"You not working then?" Luke asked.

"No, Lee's going solo today! How's *your* head?"

"I'm ok now, but I don't think I drank as much as you." Luke paused. "Can you remember our conversation about driving to Italy yesterday?" he asked, pulling one of those nervy faces as he did so.

"Yeah, yeah, I'm well up for that," Josh said, coming to life a little.

"You sure it wasn't just cos you were pissed. I'd understand if......"

"No, I want to do it. Be great." He paused. "I can't next week, though, we've got this big job in Knutsford."

"That's ok, but have you run it past Dani yet?" Luke asked.

"Yeah, yeah."

"You sure?"

"Yeah she's fine with it. We'll chat in the pub about it Sunday, yeah? When I can think straight."

"Ok, fine, see you Sunday. And thank you, Josh," said Luke, relieved, although not altogether convinced Josh has broached the subject with his wife yet. Yet he also knew that Josh clearly wanted to go and now that he had publicly offered to drive he would lose face in backing out.

Luke was now genuinely excited about the prospect of this adventure. The next task was to ring Emily and ask her whether Noah could stay. It shouldn't be a problem unless they, too, were away.

By the time he went to sleep that night Luke had sorted everything in his own mind. As Emily was working, he had spoken to Jon and it was arranged that Luke would drive over with Noah a week on Saturday. Luke has also been on Google Maps and worked out a suitable route to Italy and Rome. They'd get the ferry from Dover to Calais because Luke didn't fancy the Tunnel any more than flying. They'd take the route through France, then cut across to Brussels where they could have a night (Josh would love the beer!) then through Luxembourg and France again via Strasbourg before going through Switzerland and all the tunnels. After that, they'd drop down into Italy alongside Lake Como and on past Milan and Parma and Bologna and through Florence and Sienna and finally Rome. Luke reckoned they'd need another stop around Lake Como, it was beautiful round there. Luke knew the roads well, he'd been all over Europe with Sarah in the car. He loved a project and investigated good deals on hotels and ferry crossings and a route that avoided as many toll roads as possible.

His Saturday was unremarkable: dog walking, bank, supermarket shop, etc. He had a bottle of wine and was in bed by 8.30. He was looking forward to meeting up with Josh to talk about their Grand Tour the next day. Luke really couldn't stop thinking about it.

*

The pub was packed on Sunday. It was a lovely day in early March and people were taking advantage of the Spring-like conditions, walking up to the tower and round the woods. Luke had run with Noah earlier and he'd seen daffodils and snowdrops adding dashes of colour here and there. He remembered how Richard loved these first signs of spring and it made him sad again. Greg was in the pub with his children and so were Alex and Rebecca. Luke thanked Abbie for her fantastic spread at the wake, although he had to admit he ended up eating very little himself – he never did get to taste the wonderful-looking chicken dish! Abbie had started a Book of Condolence which was open on a table by the door of the pub. Luke wondered where the book would eventually end up – with Uncle Festa? If it *was* to be given to the family then it would more than likely be thrown into another black bin bag like so much of Richard's life.

Josh didn't arrive until 4pm and Luke was getting a bit edgy by then, fearing Josh had got cold feet. But he need not have worried, he and Dani had been to a christening. He'd just dropped Dani back at home and was desperate for a beer.

Josh said that Dani had booked the same week in Lanzarote with her mum and dad and the baby and was happy with the arrangement. Luke suspected she probably had little choice!

Of course, Greg had to have his say! He thought they were mad going on a 'wild goose chase halfway across Europe' and if they had that much money to waste then they could buy him a new bike! Luke wished that he'd arranged for Josh to come round to his house. But Alex was far more supportive of the venture and thought it would be great for both of them to get away for a week or so. Alex's word was pretty much law in The Sunnyhurst so Greg knew it was time to keep quiet. Luke was grateful to Alex - he'd been there with Rebecca when it was first muted at the funeral and clearly they had talked about it later.

When Greg drifted off to attend to his children, Luke, Josh and Alex opened a map of Europe that Luke had brought with him. They traced their fingers over Luke's provisional route which was essentially the shortest journey from Calais to Rome. The plan was that they would set off the next Sunday, early in the morning, getting the ferry at 4pm and hoping to be in Brussels for around 8pm. Luke had found a good deal at Hotel Pillows, a newly furbished boutique hotel in the centre of the old city and near all the bars and restaurants. Clearly Josh was setting the tone for the journey because he googled pubs in the centre of Brussels and within minutes had mapped out a pub crawl for the night. He decided that his starting point was Delirium, just across the road from the hotel.

Josh was also happy to go along with Luke's plan and head for Switzerland and then Lake Como in Italy after Brussels. Again, Luke had done some research and found a hotel in Como which was quite reasonable. The plan then was to complete the journey in one day to Rome. They didn't bother looking at hotels in Rome as Luke said they ought to wait to see if Rachel came up with any information about the whereabouts of the sister.

A discussion began between the lads on how to trace a missing person in a foreign city. Alex thought there must be an expat enclave somewhere in the city and that would be a good starting point. Luke had the old photograph he had rescued from Richard's bedroom wall but he knew it might not resemble Anna now - she might have put on a few stone with all the pasta, or she might have cut her hair short or dyed it pink for all he knew. Anything. Greg, who was now back at the table said Annabel might have moved out of the city to some remote village in the hills around Rome. He was really starting to annoy Luke. He hoped that Rachel came back with something tangible.

Luke offered to pay for petrol and road tolls and the ferry and they could then split the accommodation. But Josh wouldn't hear of it, everything was to be split 50/50 because after all, 'Richard was his mate too'. And anyway, this was Josh's dream holiday. A fast car and the open road .... and no nappies or sleepless nights for 7 days!

On Tuesday, Luke got a letter back from Rachel. As he opened it a cheque for £1000 dropped out.

Monday

Dear Luke,

Delighted to hear you have decided to go to Rome and find Anna. It does seem very strange about the phone going missing but in a way I'm glad you are going to be able to tell Anna face to face about her brother's death. I wouldn't want to hear news like that over a phone.

I've put a cheque in with the letter. Please put it into your bank account - I shall be angry if you don't! I've got nothing to spend it on or leave it to.

As far as having any clues to Anna's whereabouts, all I can say is that she told Richard she was still in Rome and I heard from her father once that when she was in London she had a child, a girl. By my reckoning she should be around 16 now. That might be a good starting point, I imagine.

I always promised myself I'd never get one of those cell phones but I went out and got one this morning so we can keep in touch. You can text me, it's much cheaper than phoning abroad. My number's 07846669225.

Good luck and keep in touch. By the way, when are you leaving?

Rachel xx

Sophie came round on Tuesday. She was apologetic.

"Sorry about the other day, dad seems to have a real problem with you!" she said. "As soon as he knew it was *you* asking questions he got angry again."

"I think it's a legitimate question to ask, don't you? About the phone?" Luke said.

"Oh, Luke, don't put me on the spot like this!" Sophie pleaded.

"But don't *you* think it's strange?" Luke pressed.

"No comment, Mr Adams!" Sophie laughed in an effort to diffuse the tension that was building between them. "Remember, I've got to live with my father after you've dropped me in it!"

"You know I'd never do that." Luke said, seriously. "Coffee?"

Luke walked into the kitchen and Sophie followed. "I'll just say my father and I have a different view on the matter! But I'm still in the force at the moment so I have to toe the line."

"What you mean - *at the moment!*" Luke said, as he filled the coffee maker.

"I'm planning on leaving later this year."

"Bloody Hell, how long have you been planning this?" Luke said, surprised.

"I've just decided, I'm not happy. I'd like to use my degree in psychology more. Anyway, it's been causing tension between me and my father." She smiled, sadly. "He's a grumpy old sod since mum died."

"Has this stuff over Richard's death had any influence on your decision?" Luke asked, cautiously, as they sat down at the bar in the kitchen.

"I'd be lying if I said it hadn't. But it's not just that…"

"So, what would you do?" asked Luke, sounding interested.

"I want to teach. I did some teaching of English abroad before I joined the police and after I left my job at the solicitors in Preston."

"So, were you a solicitor?"

"No, nothing so grand." Sophie laughed. "I was a solicitor's assistant, did all the ground work, I guess."

"Wow, you've done quite a bit in your relatively short life!" said Luke, impressed.

"Well, I *am* 36." I worked at the solicitors for nearly ten years. It was whilst I was married."

"Oh, I didn't know that either! I never liked to ask…."

"Oh yeah!" Sophie sounded like the memory still hurt. "Steve, that reporter from The Telegraph, he was our best man."

"Bloody hell, no wonder I sensed an awkwardness when you arrived that day!"

"He's ok, it wasn't his fault the marriage ended," Sophie said. "Mind you, I think my father makes him pay for what his mate did, sometimes!"

Luke did not want to ask any more. There was a brief silence before Luke went back to the earlier topic. "What would you teach, then?" he asked.

"Obviously I'd like to teach psychology and criminology. I've done both as part of my degree. I was thinking A Level maybe."

"You'd have to be in a big Sixth Form to teach them exclusively. You'd probably have to teach another subject too." Luke paused as he selected a pod for the coffee maker and inserted it. "What A levels did you do?" he asked as he got out the two mugs, put one in position and pressed the button on the coffee maker.

"Psychology, History and Business Studies…But I got a D in Business."

"Well History would be useful. You need to look into doing a teaching certificate…there are these ones you can do *whilst* you are teaching now."

"Where did you do yours?"

"Edge Hill, in Ormskirk."

"Ok, I was thinking of going to speak to someone. You know, sound them out. Would you come with me?" Sophie asked.

"I'd be glad to," Luke said, "but I'm going away next week."

"Anywhere nice?"

"Rome." Sophie looked pleasantly surprised initially although her expression changed as Luke explained. "I am looking for Richard's sister, Anna." He handed Sophie her coffee and started to prepare his own. "If I can't phone her then I will doorstep her."

"Oh, Luke, for God's Sake!" Sophie could not hide her frustration with Luke.

"I've got to…I haven't told you yet, have I? Richard phoned his sister on the Friday before he died."

"Does my father know?"

"I don't know. But she apparently told Richard something that upset him."

"So maybe my father's right after all, then!"

"Maybe, I need to find out what it was. And I've promised myself if it seems to be serious enough to have driven Richard to take his own life, I will let it go." Luke collected his coffee and sat down. "And at least I will feel I have done what I can for Richard," he said.

"But it is strange about the phone, isn't it? And the glasses?" Sophie said, unexpectedly.

"Well, well, PC Ronson! Are you taking the piss?" Luke's tone was playful but there was an edge to it.

"No, I was serious. And no footprints. Bloody hell, I shouldn't be saying this before the inquest!"

"What, none at all?"

"Well obviously some around but nothing they could identify as the shoes Richard had on. Mind you the ground was quite frozen." Sophie added.

"Would you like something to eat?" Luke asked.

"No, I'm on duty so I really ought to be getting back."

"I must say, I have nothing but praise for the force's 'after sales' service!" Luke said, smiling. "I wish to commend the excellent service - to whom do I speak?"

"That would be Detective Sergeant Philips, I believe!" Sophie replied, laughing.

"Of course it is! Maybe not, then!"

They both giggled like naughty children. Luke was flattered that Sophie seemed so comfortable talking to him. He still didn't really understand why she showed so much interest in him. At first, he thought it might be her father's prompting but that seemed far less likely now. He recalled the dream and then the kiss...but there was fifteen years between them, for God's sake! He wasn't Mick Jagger!

Maybe she just needed a father figure. After all, she seemed to have an uneasy relationship with her step-father. Yes, that sounded more plausible, Luke thought. But why him? He was an unlikely father figure. After all, he had no children of his own and despite dealing with other people's children all his working life, he never saw himself as particularly paternal.

Maybe she just enjoyed his friendship, like he was friends with Emily. But that was a different kind of friendship. And what about *that* kiss? Luke was confused. Could a man ever have *just* a friendship with a young, beautiful girl? Especially a lonely, vulnerable man like Luke. All Luke knew was he enjoyed seeing Sophie and she had this way of making him feel good about himself. Like Richard had done, and like Sarah.

They both finished their coffee in silence before Sophie spoke again. "Thanks for the coffee, Luke," Sophie said. "Your coffee is always excellent."

"No, thank you, Sophie. Thank you for everything," Luke said, looking into Sophie's eyes and noticing for the first time how incredibly blue they were.

"All part of the service, sir," she said with an embarrassed giggle. At that moment it took Luke all his self-control not to lean over and kiss the girl again as she stood in front of him.

"What is she thinking? What does she want?" Confused thoughts and feelings coursed through Luke's body. He had not felt like this for a long, long time.

"So, you really meant it when you said we couldn't have a relationship in case there was a murder trial. It wasn't just an excuse," Luke suddenly blurted.

Sophie was clearly a little taken aback. "Well, yes, it's a possibility. I just don't know, Luke." There was frustration in her voice. She paused then added, "But it wasn't an excuse, no."

"Ok."

"But what can I really do, Luke? I'm a very small cog, you know. If my father won't entertain the idea that it just might not be suicide, what chance do I stand convincing anyone else in the station?" Sophie was becoming frustrated.

"And, anyway," she said, "he'd be really upset if he found out I'd gone behind his back."

"Yes, I understand. I don't mean to put pressure on you," Luke said.

"And as you've said yourself, who in the world would have wanted to kill Richard? There's no-one with a motive, is there?"

"Well I've been thinking about this since the funeral," said Luke, excitedly. "What about the uncle? Maybe his son? Maybe even both of them!"

"Come on, Luke!"

"Well his sister has gone AWOL so Richard was the only beneficiary to his father's estate."

"And I guess with him dead then the estate might pass over to the brother," offered Sophie.

"Well, who else is there!" Luke gestured with open arms.

Sophie was warming to the topic now. She paused for a moment. "I'll have to speak to father - but I'm sure he must have considered this," she said, cautiously.

"Can't you just do some digging first?" Luke stopped when he saw Sophie's pained expression. "I'm sorry, I did say I wouldn't put you under pressure. The last thing I want to do is cause problems between you and your father."

"Ok, I will try to *discreetly* find out the whereabouts of the uncle and the son around the time of the murder."

Luke practically pounced on the word, "You said *murder*!"

"I mean Richard's death. Stop it!" Sophie struck Luke on the chest, playfully. Then she got out her notebook and a pen. "Now what were the names again?" she asked.

"The uncle's called Eric Harrington and his son is Will or William. They live in the Oxford area and the uncle has a shop in Woodstock. Sorry, that's all I know…but I guess I could get more from Rachel if you need it."

"Rachel?"

"Yeah, she the old house-keeper. She told me about the sister in Italy. Actually, she's the one who asked me to go and find her."

"Why doesn't she go herself?" Sophie sounded indignant.

"She's sick. Very sick."

"It's going to be difficult, you know." said Sophie after another pause. "I can't go wading in there and ask them their whereabouts on the night in question. Least not without permission and that's unlikely without something more concrete."

"Couldn't you contact the police over there and ask them to make some enquiries?" Luke suggested. "The uncle likes a drink. He might spend every Tuesday in his local, for example. I don't know how these things work but you must have ways of finding things out *before* you start asking suspects directly."

"I'll have to think about it." Sophie became serious. "But you are asking a lot, you know, Luke."

"But wouldn't you be failing in your duty as a police officer if a crime *has* taken place and you ignored it."

"Ok, Luke, don't preach, I said I would think about it." Sophie got up. "Listen, I really need to go now. When are you leaving?"

"Sunday."

"Ok, I will try and come over before you go."

And with that Sophie was gone. No hug this time. Clearly, thought Luke, Sophie felt under pressure and perhaps even quietly resented Luke's intrusion into police matters. But Luke didn't really care – he was convinced more than ever that Richard *had* been murdered and he felt that Sophie was slowly starting to feel the same – despite her father. Maybe this case would be the break she needed to come out from her father's shadow. Maybe he was doing *her* a favour

CHAPTER 7: THE GRAND TOUR BEGINS

The next few days flew by for Luke as he prepared for his excursion. Because Josh was working, he left all the preparation to Luke - like booking the ferry, sorting insurance, buying Euros. He called in on Frank and Brenda and told them about the trip and gave them his spare key. He also rang the agency and told them he was going to be away for 10 days. Who knew, he might feel better after his visit to Italy and anyhow he didn't want to burn his bridges with the agency completely.

Sophie came round again on Friday. This time she was in her civvies and Luke cooked her dinner. Well, at least he put a pizza in the oven which they ate with a cold lager. After a lot of thought she had decided to tell her father about Luke's 'theory'. She feared that her father might have immediately dismissed it and got angry but he was surprisingly open to her at least making some discreet enquiries if only to shut up "that interfering teacher" once and for all! He had even rung an old colleague who now worked for the Thames Valley Police and paved the way for his daughter to go down south and make some enquiries herself.

Luke was delighted – he felt that finally people were taking him seriously. And Sophie was clearly excited about being given this opportunity. Luke and Sophie promised to keep in touch and let each other know if they found out anything from their different lines of enquiry. Sophie reckoned it would be May at the earliest before the inquest so there was time to investigate the possibility that Richard had been murdered and even delay the inquest if they had sufficient evidence.

As they said goodbye, Luke and Sophie embraced warmly. Luke felt a little frustrated to be leaving Sophie because he really believed that things were just starting to happen in the case. But it was only for a week, he told himself.

Luke went over to Chester on the Saturday with Noah. Once again, Emily was working but he went for a quick beer with Jon.

"I keep saying to Emily that we must go to Rome." Jon said, when Luke told him about his planned trip. "Do you know Keats died in Rome? You can visit his house," he said with his usual enthusiasm for anything he regarded as cultural.

"I'm not going on a sight-seeing trip, Jon!" said Luke with a trace of indignation in his voice.

"Well, I hope you find this girl. It would be a bit of a bummer driving all that way and then finding she's gone on holiday! Or that she won't speak to you," said Jon.

Luke hadn't really thought about this, or he hadn't allowed himself to consider it. He must treat the whole thing first and foremost as an adventure, a distraction. Something he needed. He'd been cycling in France with Richard but other than that he'd not had a proper break for ages. And if, as he hoped, something more came from the trip - some answers - then this would be a bonus. Who knew, he might find something really helpful about Uncle Fester.

Luke went back with Jon just before setting off. He wanted to say goodbye to Noah. He was only going for a short time but he was going to miss him. He hoped Noah would miss him too, a little at least. But when Luke and Jon got back from the pub, Noah and Millie were lying beside each other, both fast asleep. They'd obviously tired each other out playing 'chase' around the house. Luke didn't wake him and left quietly.

*

Josh was very excited on Sunday morning. If he had any strong emotions about leaving his wife and child then he covered them up very well and to a point where Luke felt *he* needed to make a fuss. He hugged Dani and promised they'd be back soon and that he'd look after Josh as a father might look after a son. Dani and the baby were crying...but Josh was already a single man again.

As Josh drove down the M6, Luke started to wonder whether he'd been wise to so readily accept Josh's invitation. He was 29 and Luke was 51. Worlds apart. And Luke really did not know Josh that well. Of course, in the pub they could talk football or cycling in the company of other men. But the two of them together for a week or so - that was another thing altogether! Sophie had warned Luke on pain of death that he must not utter a word about his theory on the uncle and the pressure of keeping that secret after a few beers also weighed heavily on him.

Luke didn't know anything about cars. To him they were simply boxes on wheels to get you from A to B as efficiently as possible. He owned an old Skoda which was totally reliable but unremarkable in every respect. But Luke had to admit Josh's new black Audi Sportback was impressive and cool. It was clearly Josh's statement to the world that he was doing ok, a self-made man, although Dani had let it slip recently that his aunt had died and left him a little something that he had put towards the car. The car had the leather seats, the satnav, the parking sensors - the lot, in fact! It seemed to glide effortlessly down the motorway with little noise and Luke was surprised when he looked across at the busy panel in front of Josh to see they were cruising at a constant 100 mph. The motorway on a Sunday was quiet and they ate up the miles - Knutsford, Hilton Park, M5, M40, Banbury and then a first stop at Oxford Services for coffee.

"It's kind of appropriate we have stopped off here," Luke said as they drank their over-priced mochas and ate their calorific muffins. "This is where Richard was born. His father lives somewhere round here…and that awful uncle!" Josh seemed disinterested and bored. Travelling up and down motorways was very much a part of Josh's life but it was still unusual and a bit of an exciting novelty for Luke. How service stations had changed, Luke thought, since the days when you sat at plastic benches in soulless surroundings listening to James Last versions of last year's hits.

After Oxford, their journey slowed as they crawled round the M25. It was exciting at first watching the planes overhead, landing at Heathrow, but the next 50 miles to the M20 and the road to Dover dragged interminably. Josh had put Luke on the car insurance and asked him whether he minded having a stint behind the wheel.

They reached Dover by 3pm and were pretty much straight on the ferry and up to the large cafe bar on the back deck. They had a beer and sandwiches and watched Dover and England disappear behind them. And then like two teenagers on a school trip they went out onto the top deck and watched the French coast grow from a smudge to a coastline with towers and houses and finally people. They were in Calais.

And then they were off again. Josh back at the wheel, on the right side of the road gliding towards Brussels, their first destination. Unlike the wretched M25, the autoroutes were uncluttered and fast. They would be in Belgium in an hour, the satnav said. Josh couldn't wait to get to the hotel and then out on the lash. As the radio was now all in French they switched to their playlists which, of course, worked via Bluetooth in Josh's car. Finding some common ground in musical taste was harder than Luke had imagined because Josh had an unhealthy interest in the American Soft Rock of the 1980s, which Luke despised. Anyway, at least for this leg of the journey they compromised with Bruce Springsteen. Luke never felt superior in any aspect of life - except in his choice of music. His musical taste, he believed, was eclectic but discerning. He prided himself that he had not drifted into the middle of the road like so many men and women of his age. You'd never, ever find a download of Rod Stewart singing an old swing classic on Luke's playlists!

They played Springsteen tennis for the rest of the journey as they raced down the A5 at 140kph. Luke played 'Thunder Road'; Josh played 'Hungry Heart'. Luke played 'Racing in the Street'; Josh played 'Glory Days'. 30 - Love, Luke allowed himself a self-congratulatory smirk. Luke played 'If I Should Fall Behind'; Josh played 'Born to Run', a safe but unadventurous shot that clipped the net and just about won Josh the point. 30-15. When Josh played 'Dancing in the Dark', Luke played 'The River'. He felt it was an easy point - in his view 'Dancing in the Dark' was Springsteen's very worst moment! All that silly dancing with the girl from Friends. Luke said it was embarrassing.

Then Josh got bored (or ran out of songs he knew by The Boss). Anyway, they were about to queue for the toll and drive the 5k into the centre of Brussels.

It was just getting dark as they pulled up at The Hotel Pillows in Rouppeplein, part of the Old Quarter. They parked in the quaint little square just in front of the hotel and checked in. The hotel was stylish. Their room had bold, large print paper on the wall behind the beds and lots of, well, pillows! So many, in fact, it was hard to discern a bed under them. But the beds were very comfortable and after a long day Luke could have happily fallen asleep.

Josh had other ideas. He was showered, changed and ready for his first Belgian beer within 30 minutes. His short hair had dried almost immediately and he was on his way. He instructed Luke to meet him across the square at Delirium when he was ready.

Luke took his time, enjoying the room to himself for a few precious minutes. And he appreciated the rare splendour of it all. When he had showered and changed he had a quiet coffee in the bar downstairs and talked to the waiter - whose English was perfect - about their journey.

When Luke walked over to Delirium, Josh was at the bar on his second glass of beer. He has the beer menu in front of him: an English version, describing each beer and giving its strengths and prices. Josh was drinking Donker in one of those unusual glasses associated with Belgian beer and talking to the girl behind the bar. When he greeted Luke like a long, lost friend, Luke knew the beer had already had an effect. Luke decided to try the Delirium, the beer the bar was eponymously named after.

Apparently, the girl behind the bar called Elise had worked in a bar in Manchester before university. She'd taken a gap year and spent it improving her English. Now she was working her way through university in Brussels studying European Politics. Luke tried to talk to her about Brexit but he soon realized that Josh was bored and much more eager to swap drinking stories with Elise.

After one drink, Luke decided to walk to Grande Place. He'd seen the amazing buildings on photographs and had always wanted to go there himself. They were beautifully lit at night and there was an array of bars around the piazza.

Josh was happy just to stay in Delirium and flirt with the girl and get pissed. "I'm knackered pal, I'm really not bothered about seeing some old buildings," he said.

"Ok, well you stay here. I'm a big boy. I can find my own way," said Luke, quite relieved to be able to be by himself for a couple of hours.

"Elise says she'll make me a pizza. So, I'm set here," Josh said, smiling contently.

"Ok, I'll have a walk. See you later," said Luke.

Luke used his phone to direct him. He'd always enjoyed walking through a bustling city at night, especially if it was for the first time - you really had no idea what was round the next corner. The old quarter of Brussels was a delightful mess of new and old, the functional and the ridiculously ornate. It reminded him somehow of The Shambles in York on a bigger scale, somewhere Luke and Sarah had loved to wander round in their early days.

The narrow street suddenly opened onto a large piazza which was the famous Grande Place. It was a large expanse of cobbles, about the size of two football pitches. Around this stood, shoulder to shoulder, an array of the most elegant buildings Luke had ever seen. An enormous building dominated one side, it must have been the ancient town hall, Luke imagined. It had turrets and spires and every part of it was decked in exquisite and intricate detail, hewn out of limestone that had now weathered over time, making the whole structure look dark and serious and permanent.

The other buildings, although smaller, were no less impressive. They were narrow and of varying heights and appeared to be crammed together tightly, a bit like mates on a night out determined to get in on the commemorative photograph, to say "I was there too, you know!"

As Luke's eyes drifted down from the turrets and colourful tiled roofs of the buildings to street level, he became aware that each of these building had its own colourful bar or restaurant. And these in turn were fronted with tables and chairs that spilled out onto the cobbled square and were separated by posts and ropes. And each establishment had its own distinctive canopy. Everything coordinated beautifully - the canopies, the chairs, the table cloths...and the ropes that separated and defined them were in the same distinctive colours: deep reds, royal blues, gold and black.

Even though it was early March people sat outside, kept warm by overhead heaters. This new phenomena had transformed cafe society in the colder months and done wonders for business, Luke thought, as he began the almost impossible task of deciding which of these establishments would enjoy his patronage that evening. The smell of garlic and warm bread made him feel hungry.

He plumped for Le Corbeau and was ushered to a small table near the door by a young, friendly waiter. It was a good position as the heat from inside the bar gave extra warmth. He ordered a beer called Kriek which was dark, slightly fruity and very strong. The alcohol on his empty stomach took immediate effect and made Luke feel relaxed and content. He looked at the menu and decided upon the fish soup and pork and chorizo in a spicy ragu sauce with pasta. The couple next to him were eating it and it looked and smelt amazing. The fact that Luke was near the door and on the route from the kitchen meant that he had the constant attention of the waiter who recommended a special beer that he said was brewed only "one minute" away from them.

He looked at the empty chair across the table from him and he pictured Sarah sitting opposite as she had so often on evenings like this in Paris or Barcelona or San Tropez. She would have loved it here, Luke thought. And she'd probably have had the mussels and a plate of French fries; she would have had to slap Luke's hand every time he reached over and stole one. Oh, how Luke missed her, especially on nights like this!

Luke had enjoyed his evening. After eating he walked back to Delirium expecting to find Josh still there. But he wasn't and nor was Elise, the girl behind the bar. He went back to the hotel assuming Josh had returned early, he had said he was knackered. But Josh wasn't there either. Had he gone in search of Luke and they had missed each other, Luke wondered? Luke felt suddenly tired but he forced himself to stay awake because Josh hadn't taken his key card and Luke would need to get the door when he did return. Luke studied Monday's route on his iPad for a while and at the hotel they'd booked in Como. He passed an hour on the iPad, taking advantage of the free Wi-Fi. but he got to the point when he just couldn't keep his eyes open a moment longer so he turned off the iPad and he turned off the light. Josh would just have to wake him - he was obviously pissed somewhere in some late-night bar.

When Luke woke at 7am there was *still* no sign of Josh. He even checked outside his door in case his knocking had gone unheard and he'd collapsed there. Nothing. Luke got showered and dressed quickly and went down to the bar which doubled as reception. He tried to explain the situation to a waiter but her English was not good. He was hoping they could contact the local hospital but Luke was having little joy in making himself understood. The poor girl was confused and thought it was Luke who was sick. Fortunately, another guest who was having a coffee at the bar, managed to translate for her and she went for the manager immediately. She could see that Luke was becoming distressed.

At that moment Josh walked through the door of hotel. He was dishevelled but smiling.

"Where the bloody hell have you been? I'm just asking them to call the hospital," Luke, said, sounding much like he did when he was addressing a naughty student.

"Sorry, mate," he said casually, "I went back with Elise."

"You mean you slept with her!" Luke was indignant.

"Well, yes, actually. We went to a club and then we went back to hers. I hadn't got my key."

"I waited up to let you in!" said Luke tersely.

"Sorry. Have you had breakfast yet?" he asked.

"No, of course not, I've been worrying about you." Luke was angry.

"Well, I'm starving and we've paid for it, so let's eat," Josh said, leading the way into the bar area where they had set out breakfast. There was a trolley with cold salami and cheese, fruit, cereal and three fruit juices. A cooked breakfast was available if requested and Josh ordered the Full English, he hadn't eaten the previous night. Luke had cereal and fruit and coffee. Conversation was strained, Luke was disappointed with Josh and angry. First night away and he had betrayed his wife and Luke was amazed at how casual he was about the whole thing. Josh's only concern was for himself and his banging head.

"Listen, will you drive this morning?" he said as he was finishing his second coffee.

"Yeah, that's fine," Luke said, sighing, "I think you'd be still over the limit anyhow. How much did you drink?"

"No idea. But those beers are so fucking strong. It's like you are ok one minute and the next you are totally fucking wrecked!" Josh said. Luke sensed he was blaming his drunken state for his lack of judgement. Luke could see why women found him attractive. He worked out four or five times a week and he did a tough physical job too. Every part of him was defined - and his muscle-fit t-shirts were intended to show off Josh's physique.

Josh showered and changed whilst Luke studied the map. They were soon on the road again and heading for Strasbourg then Basle in Switzerland and Lucerne and then through the mountains to Lake Como and Italy. It was around 550 miles.

The first section around Luxembourg was dull. They talked about cycling and Le Tour. Josh said he wanted to come over in June and watch a mountain stage and then ride it himself the next day. Maybe the Col de la Colombière – he'd watched the stage last June on Le Tour and promised himself he'd have a go at it one day. He'd never driven abroad before or taken the ferry but now he knew how easy it all was he said he'd definitely bring the bike. He thought that Alex would be up for it too and he assumed that Luke would. Luke wasn't sure - being with Josh was not like being with Richard. Richard had been roughly the same age as Luke which helped. But Josh had a different mind-set too and spending time with Josh in the confined quarters of a car was frustrating Luke. The more they talked the more dogmatic Josh appeared to be. He could not – absolutely would not – entertain another point of view other than his own, whatever the topic. Luke found this understandable when it came to football and Josh's devotion to Liverpool. After all, you cannot truly be a fan and be non-partisan. But Josh applied this same myopia to religion and race, and to punishment and politics with great alacrity. And what frustrated Luke most was when Josh confidently voiced his dogma on issues he was entirely unqualified to discuss, like education.

Out of sheer devilment and boredom, Luke suddenly asked Josh to explain how he plastered a wall. He seemed deadly earnest, he asked about the preparation, the mix of the plaster, the finish, everything. He let Josh explain for ten minutes constantly interrupting him with sighs, shakes of the head and "What an absolute load of bollocks. Is that how you do it? Bloody hell, my dad was a plasterer and he'd run you out of town, you cowboy!"

Josh was totally taken in by this charade and seemed genuinely hurt. "Well, how did he do it then?"

"I don't know, but he certainly didn't do it *your* way!" Luke was enjoying himself now, it was kind of payback time for the previous evening. "Did you actually train at college?" he asked, incredulously.

But Luke could not maintain the pretence and when he suddenly started laughing Josh seemed confused. When it finally because apparent that Luke was mocking Josh's uninformed opinions he didn't like it and he sulked for the next thirty minutes.

Once Josh recovered his humour he insisted on playing musical tennis: one from me, one from you. Luke would play "Sally Cinnamon" by The Stone Roses (who, of course, were Manc and therefore shite!) and Josh would follow it with some fucking awful AC/DC song.

Dani rang Josh mid-morning. She was at the airport with the baby and her mum and dad and younger brother and they were about to board for Lanzarote. She sounded bright and clear on the car phone.

"Hi, love. Just thought I'd ring now cos you won't be able to reach me for four hours," she said. "Are you ok? Where are you now?"

Josh spoke to her in his usual relaxed manner. Told her he loved her and was missing her and the baby. He told her about his sore head from drinking too much. Luke agreed that the beer in Belgium was ridiculously strong and that it was just as well they were only staying one night. After the call Luke broached the subject of Elise.

"Don't you feel a bit shit talking to Dani after last night?" asked Luke. He had deliberately tried to use a casual tone that did not sound too judgmental.

"No, not really," said Josh, casually dismissing the suggestion, "what she doesn't know can't hurt her."

"But you know…and what if that Elise gets in touch or something?" Luke pressed.

"She won't. I didn't give her my number."

"So, you are not seeing her again?"

Josh laughed at the notion that he might ever see the girl again: "Don't be daft!"

"Do you do this often, then? I mean shag girls when you and Lee are working away?"

"Sometimes." Josh seemed disinterested in the conversation and played on his phone.

"Does Dani ever suspect you?"

"I don't know. I don't think so. We never talk about it," Josh replied. Luke could sense that he was getting frustrated.

"Do you think she would be unfaithful to you?" Luke asked, mischievously.

"Fuck, no!" Josh suddenly became more engaged.

"How could you be so sure?" Luke sensed he had touched a nerve.

"Well, she wouldn't, would she? She's happy with me." He paused as if contemplating the ridiculous notion for the first time. "And, anyway," he said, "who with? She doesn't see other men. Well, except for the guys in the pub!" Josh seemed genuinely astounded that his wife could even *think* about another man.

"But how would you feel if she *did*?"

"Well, she wouldn't...so..." Josh was rattled, he started drumming his fingers on the dashboard in time with his latest musical offering by Whitesnake.

There was an uneasy silence in the car for a few minutes. Luke thought it now wise to leave the subject of adultery and discuss the day ahead.

"We will need get some fuel soon? How do you feel about driving after that?" Luke asked.

"Sure, I'll just try and sleep off this head for half an hour then," said Josh, tersely.

With that, Josh pushed back and reclined the front passenger seat and closed his eyes. At least Luke could now play some decent music. He had an enjoyable forty-five minutes in the company of The Artic Monkeys. Josh might have a rubbish taste in music, but he had a great sound system in his car!

After a stop for fuel and coffee and a sandwich they headed for the Swiss border. The mountains on the horizon looked especially dramatic in early March with the snow against the blue sky. As they got closer to the border, the landscape changed. They drove through a series of tunnels near Lucerne and emerged into a world of mountains and lakes and snow. Lots of snow. Luke had driven this route once before with Sarah when they had stayed near Venice, but that had been in July. In March, it was so much more dramatic and beautiful. From the road you could see ski slopes and colourful alpine lodges. And, as the light started to fade, the Swiss mountains were speckled with a myriad of flickering lights. They stopped at an Aires de Service and took pictures on their phones. Josh sent one to Dani who was now in Lanzarote. She sent back a picture of a beach in the sunshine. Luke never ceased to be amazed by technology. It didn't seem *that* long ago when he had taken photos on his old SLR and sent them off for processing to be returned a week later (if he was lucky). And now a tiny device could share these moments thousands of miles apart and in a heartbeat! Luke recalled Hamlet: "What a piece of work is Man!" – with the mobile phone, the incredible car that could tear up the miles so effortlessly, those tunnels under the mountains they had passed through and that exquisite architecture in Brussels. And yet mankind also had this talent for fucking things up with alarming alacrity!

At around 6pm they reached Italy and Lake Como. They approached it from height and as they dropped down to the lake it felt like they were landing in a plane at night. The lake was a black hole surrounded by tiny lights.

Luke had booked Terzo Crotto in Cernobbio, on the northern side of Lake Como. The director Visconti had owned a family villa there that Luke was keen to see because he'd seen Death in Venice and The Damned and had once become quite obsessed with Visconti and Italian cinema, it was so cool and sexy. The hotel was ok, it was clean and the staff were friendly. And more importantly, it was away from the temptations of a city; Luke was determined to keep Josh close to him this time.

After they had booked into the hotel they went for a walk down the shore of the lake. The evening was much warmer than it had been in Brussels. They found Visconti's family pile quite easily and Josh took a photograph of Luke in front of it so he could send it Jon - he knew Jon would be impressed. Next door they discovered Lido Di Cernobbio, a most serendipitous find. The bar and restaurant were bustling even on a Monday night in March and there were even people still swimming in the pool which served as an amazing centre piece. It was lit from below and gave off a turquoise phosphorescence. On the wooden decking around the pool couples sat at intimate tables, each with a candle, drinking cocktails and looking out over the lake to the twinkling lights of Como town.

Luke and Josh chose to sit outside and were ushered to a table, it felt as if they had gate-crashed an exclusive party. They ordered bottles of Peroni and a big bowl of olives. Luke thought it very romantic.

"Buongiorno, Can I bring you the menu?" said a waitress as she passed Luke's table.

"Are we eating, Josh?" Luke asked.

"Yeah, thanks, and two more bottles please?" Josh was happy to sit there all evening watching the girls in the pool.

"What do you think all these people do?" mused Luke. "They can't *all* be on holiday, can they? At this time of the year?" As Luke took in his fellow guests he noticed that they were mostly young Italians, and mostly couples. There were two gay men on the table next to them talking intently as they shared a large cocktail. They looked over at the two Englishmen every now and then and giggled sporadically. Luke wondered how he and Josh appeared to these strangers, certainly an odd couple.

"Maybe they're all on the way to Rome to look for a needle in a haystack!" said Josh sarcastically, "By the way, what *are* we doing when you get there tomorrow?"

The young waitress brought the menus and laid them on the table with a smile: "They are in English, yes?" she said.

"Thank you," said Luke before responding to Josh's question, "She's married so I assume she's not going to be Annabel Harrington so it won't be straightforward. I thought I'd try and ask at any English speaking schools in Rome. She has a daughter apparently who's around 15 now. Actually, I Googled a couple of likely places whist I was waiting for you last night," Luke's tone was sarcastic.

"Bloody hell, it's a long shot! You don't even know her name," said Josh, ignoring any reference to the previous night.

"I know. I was hoping for more," said Luke, sighing. "If there are any questions I can always ring Rachel now, she has bought a phone. By the way, order what you like, this is on me tonight," said Luke, thinking about Rachel's generous cheque.

"Is Rachel that old girl at the funeral?"

"Yes. I think I'll have the vongole, what do you fancy?" said Luke.

"Well, the waitress actually." Josh laughed. "But I'll have a pizza, do you think they do ham and pineapple? It's not on the menu."

"That's because it's a proper Italian restaurant, you philistine!" said Luke impatiently. "Have something different, there's plenty of choice."

Josh studied the menu hard for a minute: "Ok, I'll have the margarita and some chips."

When the waitress came back they ordered the food and another beer. Luke had a green salad…he'd seen them on other tables and they looked lovely. It came with Parmesan shavings on top and they brought a selection of oils and balsamic to the table.

Luke was surprised, he was actually starting to enjoy Josh's company. As they ate, Josh asked Luke about his life with Sarah who he vaguely remembered he had met once at the pub although it was before he really knew Luke.

"Have you never had anyone else then? You know, since your wife?" Josh asked.

"I've been on a couple of dates. Women I've met through work. But nothing serious, no." Luke smiled. "I probably spent the evening talking about Sarah so……"

"You need to go on one of those dating sites…you know, like match.com. They link you up with someone your age, same interests."

"Yeah, maybe I ought to give it a try," said Luke, half-heartedly.

“After all you're in good shape for an old bugger and you've got your hair and teeth…Dani and her mum say you're cute!”

“That sounds so wrong, Josh,” said Luke, although he was quietly flattered.

“I'm just saying……”

“I know, and thank you,” said Luke, grateful for the compliment. “I will sign up for one of these dating things when this is all sorted. It’s not good to be alone.” Luke paused then said gloomily, “I just think I will never find anyone like Sarah again.”

“Well, you don't want another Sarah. You need someone *unlike* Sarah. As different as possible,” said Josh, sounding quite wise for a moment.

“I didn't really mean I was looking for a Sarah clone - just someone I could care about in the same way. I know I'll never find *that* again. I start thinking it's getting a bit easier without her, but then I start missing her again like hell. Like last night. And now this…” Luke gestured to all around him, “She'd have loved this……and it's almost like I cannot truly enjoy it without her. I feel it's wrong.”

Josh could tell Luke was getting emotional.

“I can enjoy this without Dani,” he said.

“But she's not dead!” Luke said bitterly. “You could always bring her here and you two could enjoy this together.” Luke had raised his voice and Josh thought it best to leave the subject.

After an awkward silence, Josh spoke: “Hey, let's go for a nightcap somewhere else before we turn in, should we?” he said.

“Where you thinking?” asked Luke.

“Just have a wander. It's a beautiful night.”

Luke feared that Josh was thinking about finding a bar or club where he could meet a girl again.

“Well I'd like to go to that hotel we passed on the way in. That one with the big balconies, it looked amazing.”

“Ok, let's walk up there, after,” said Josh.

They both agreed the food and the service had been excellent. And the location was simply amazing. Luke paid, leaving a generous tip and then they made their way along the side of the lake and through the small village of Cernobbio and then up a road which led to Casa Santo Stefano, the hotel Luke had noticed earlier.

“Wow! What a place!” said Luke. He and Josh felt immediately under-dressed. When they got inside, Luke asked whether the bar was open to non-residents. It wasn't clear whether the sophisticated older lady who greeted them understood him but she ushered them both into a large living room with big windows that looked out over the lake. The hotel's elevated position allowed them to look down on the lido and the bay and Visconti's house. There was a small bar on the opposite side and a few people drinking coffee and liqueurs. They'd obviously come from the restaurant in the adjacent room.

“We can't ask for lager here,” Luke whispered to Josh. But before he'd finished the sentence Josh had jumped in.

"Two pints of Peroni, love. And a couple of whisky chasers…"

"Sorry?" said the sophisticated lady, clearly confused.

"Beer? Grande?" said Josh with the accompanying gesture the English are always prone to use with the flat of their hands.

"Oh, Si! Sorry…" She made a gesture with two parallel flat hands to indicate small.

"Ok, four," said Josh and put up four fingers to illustrate, "and whisky…"

"Forget whisky, Josh!" Luke interrupted. "You're a bloody nightmare. I just want to crawl under a seat!" he said in a half whisper.

"Ok?" said the lady.

"Ok, thank you," said Luke, "thank you." Luke felt himself bow in supplication such was his embarrassment and awkwardness. The place had been silent before these noisy, drunken Englishmen had invaded and broken the peace. And no doubt, thought Luke, these people were paying shit-loads of euros for this kind of splendour - they would not be impressed. Luke scanned the room, but no one seemed at all phased by the intrusion…or maybe they were just too polite to show it.

Four glasses of lager arrived along with some little artisan chocolates on a plate. The lady said, "Gratuity," as she presented them. Luke noted that all the tables had them, but they were being eaten at the end of a meal with coffee or a liqueur.

"Excuse me, where are the toilets?" Josh's voice was unnecessarily loud.

"Pardon?" The lady was having problems again with Josh.

"Just back where you came in and then to the right," interrupted the man on the next table sensing the lady's dilemma. He smiled and gestured the route.

As Josh went off to find the toilet Luke felt he needed to apologise.

"I'm sorry," he said to the man, "we must be disturbing your evening."

He laughed, "It is not a problem, it was a bit too quiet, anyway!" The man had an Italian accent but spoke perfect English. He was sitting alone reading and drinking a coffee.

"We are staying at another hotel but this place looked so beautiful…"

"It *is* beautiful, and the staff are very friendly," he said. "Are you here for a holiday?"

"We are just passing through, actually. We drive to Rome tomorrow." The man seemed happy to talk so Luke went on to explain. "We are in search of a woman." Luke smiled ruthfully as he said it. "It's a long story but my friend died and we are trying to find his estranged sister to tell her."

At this point Josh came back from the toilet.

"I was just telling this gentleman about our little adventure," Luke said, trying to involve Josh.

"It's Thomas," interrupted the man, getting up briefly to shake Luke and Josh's hands.

"Hi, I'm Luke and this is Josh, we live between Manchester and Liverpool," Luke said. Geographically speaking this wasn't totally true but Luke had always said that when talking to strangers on holiday. It seemed a good touchstone.

Thomas smiled and sat back down. "So where are you going to start?" he asked, motioning for them to sit down on the sofa opposite him. "Do you know where this sister lives in Rome, yes?"

"No," said Luke, "no idea." The man smiled politely. "We were just talking about it earlier…it's not going to be easy." Luke suddenly felt very embarrassed, he wished he had not started the story. "We don't even know the sister's last name. I've just got an old picture of her and that's it really. I think she is married and that she has a daughter of around 15. So, I thought English schools might be a good starting point." Luke felt himself blushing under this intelligent man's gaze.

Luke tried to involve Josh in the conversation in an effort to change the subject: "Meet my driver!" he said, pointing at his friend whose eyes were slowly closing.

But the man seemed genuinely interested in Luke's adventure. He asked about the journey so far and Luke told him about the route and the night in Brussels (tactfully leaving out the story of Josh and Elise) and the planned route for the next day. They talked about the beauty of Lake Como and the surrounding area. Very soon Luke realised he was telling this stranger his whole story – discovering Richard's body, his doubts about his death and his meeting Rachel after the funeral. He even told Thomas about losing his wife and then joining the cycle club. Luke really didn't know why he had done it, maybe it was the drink, but there was something in this man's unassuming and quiet nature that invited confidence. Luke had just about finished his story when Thomas received a text from his wife who was now obviously wondering where her husband had got to. He got up to leave.

"Well, I hope you find this lady," he said. He pulled a card from his wallet. "I too work in education so if I can be of any help please let me know," he said, gesturing towards the card. He smiled and shook Luke's hand again.

"That is very kind," said Luke, putting the card in the back pocket of his jeans.

"I'm not in work this week, I'm on a holiday with my wife. That was her…" Thomas gestured towards his phone.

"What do you do in education?" Luke asked.

"Actually, I taught English," he said with a smile. "But now I teach at The University of Milan part time and do some work for the department of education. I studied in England for a while."

"Oh, where?" asked Luke.

"Oxford," he said, almost apologetically.

Luke smiled. "I too teach English. Well, I did……I've been doing more supply work recently…Stand-in teacher." Luke glanced over to Josh who was now asleep. "I better get my mate home. It's been nice to meet you."

As the Italian left the room, Luke caught the attention of the lady who had brought them drinks. He paid his bill and then gently woke up his sleeping friend who had hardly touched his two drinks. It was a long walk back to their hotel.

The next morning Josh was up and eager for breakfast at 7am, and they were on the road again by 8.30. The conversation flowed better and Luke and Josh decided to reintroduce music tennis in an effort to relieve the boredom as they passed through Milan and headed south. It was agreed that to make it a competitive game they had to decide on a specific artist as they had done with Bruce Springsteen. They picked The Beatles. Josh went first with 'Hey Jude', a safe bet, and Luke responded with 'Let it Be'. 15 all. Then Josh went left field with 'Taxman', if only because of The Jam riff. Luke won the point with 'Paperback Writer', similar but better. The next two points were tied: 'A Day in The Life/Long and Winding Road' which is basically Lennon versus McCartney, and then 'Yesterday' versus 'You've Got to Hide Your Love Away'. Josh surprised Luke with a killer point: 'Twist and Shout', the Beatles rocking out and the incredible Lennon vocal. Luke came back with 'When I Saw Her Standing There' but they both agreed that 'Twist and Shout' was the better song, even if, as Luke pointed out, Lennon and McCartney *didn't* write it!

The music was interrupted by a call from Lee asking Josh's advice about a job. Then Dani facetimed Josh whilst Luke held the phone. She was near the pool with the baby in the pram next to her. Josh talked enthusiastically about Lake Como and the lido. Dani pointed the phone at the baby so that it could see Josh's face. It looked singularly unimpressed. Dani and Josh both mouthed big kisses to each other before ending their conversation. Luke checked *his* phone. Nothing.

Josh had driven the first 200 miles but Luke had a stint after stopping at an Aires for fuel and coffee. Then they were back to music tennis with Take That and then a generic one with Motown songs. They were running out of musical common denominators. But soon they were driving through Tuscany in the hot sunshine. They saw the road signs for Florence, Sienna and San Gimignano but kept on driving. It was like walking down Darwen high street and passing Sir Elton John, Lionel Messi and the whole cast of Friends and just nonchalantly walking by on the other side. Both men had their eyes firmly fixed on their goal now: Rome.

Chapter 8: ROME.

But Luke and Josh didn't get to see Rome that Tuesday. In fact, Josh didn't get to see it at all! Whilst Josh drove, Luke had been scrolling through cheap accommodation in Rome and had found Camping Village Roma, a campsite just two miles north of the Vatican City. It seemed ridiculously cheap - 30 Euros a night for them both to rent a small lodge. The site had a pool, and there was a bar and restaurant. When he discovered there was availability, Luke made the reservation without even consulting Josh.

They arrived at Camping Village Roma at around 3pm. They both noticed how warm it was when they got out of the air-conditioned car, comfortable t-shirt weather. Josh made straight for the bar, it was in the centre of the pretty park, next to a large pool and surrounded by olive trees and those pink bushes they have in warm countries which seemed to flower all year. Luke booked in at reception and parked up next to the lodge and then he too headed for the bar. After a beer, Luke wanted to transfer his case and freshen up a bit but Josh persuaded him it could wait until they'd relaxed with a another drink so they sat outside and enjoyed what was left of the afternoon sunshine. Luke had expected the campsite to be quiet out of season but it was full of life; the waiter explained it was because of its close location to The Vatican City. 'The place was always full of young Catholics on pilgrimage at this time of the year,' he said. And there were nuns in full habit walking in the supermarket and seated around the pool eating ice-creams. Luke enjoyed incongruities like this, it made him chuckle.

They got talking to a couple of American girls who had just arrived back from The Vatican City. It seemed that they had made a week of it: visiting St Peters, going to mass, and just generally hanging round the place.

"We're on a kind of pilgrimage too," said Josh, "we've driven over from England to find a girl!"

They laughed. "Any girl?" said the more confident one.

"Well, no," Luke interrupted, "we are trying to find a woman to tell her that her brother has died. So, it's quite a serious, really."

"Oh, that's terrible. Isn't that the kind of thing the police usually do?" she said. "Well at least they do in America."

"The British police don't know where she is. And her family - or what remains of them - don't seem to care. So, it's left to us." Luke said, with an open armed gesture. "We were friends of her brother," he continued, in an effort to explain.

"Anyone fancy a beer?" said Josh, keen to lighten the mood.

If he had not witnessed Josh's predatory nature already, Luke would not have been concerned by this development. But he knew now how Josh thought. Two young naïve Catholic girls, looking for some profound spiritual experience…and Josh, who lived for the moment, for sensual pleasure. There was an inevitability about things, Luke thought to himself, gloomily.

"Don't you think we should have a look at the accommodation now?" Luke said out loud.

"Bloody hell, Luke, I've just driven 500 miles. Let's chill. I fancy those pizzas." Josh said, gesturing towards the hatch where the chef was throwing dough around for the entertainment of anyone who was interested enough to stop and watch.

“Ok, well I'll have another beer and share a pizza,” said Luke, reluctantly accepting defeat. “Then I must find out exactly where the International School is in the city. I think it's somewhere in the direction of the airport, wherever that it!” said Luke. “I’ll need to go to reception after.”

“Right sorted! So, what we all having, then?” asked Josh, looking at the menu. “I fancy the ham and pineapple…see, they do it here, Luke!” Josh beamed. “Should we get that and a pepperoni?” he asked no-one in particular. “If we get two big ones you can share them, girls. You haven't eaten, have you?” he asked without looking up.

“No, it's fine, we've got to do some washing soon,” said the quiet one.

“Oh, come on, you've time for some food first,” Josh said. “By the way, what are you two girls drinking?” He was halfway towards the bar as he asked, making it very difficult for the quiet girl to protest any further.

It was clear the girl who spoke first was keener to stay: “Can we have a bottle of Bud?” she asked.

Whilst Josh was ordering, the more talkative girl, who was called Stella, asked Luke more about their journey from England. She'd been to London during the Olympics and was keen to talk about how she had loved the city. They were both from small town mid-America and were clearly not used to cities like Rome and London.

The other girl retreated into herself. Maybe, thought Luke, she had the same concerns as he did!

They drank and ate and talked for a while before Luke excused himself and went back to reception to get a map and some information. But the man there didn’t know about schools in Rome. He didn't know about much, it seemed – he was from the north and had only just arrived for the season. Luke headed despondently back to the bar. Only Josh and Stella were there now.

"Are you coming to help me get the stuff out of the car?" Luke asked Josh. He used the tone that he adopted at school when he wanted to turn a question into an imperative.

"Bloody hell, you're an old woman sometimes. Can't you ever chill!" Josh was clearly miffed at the interruption. "Ok, I'll just finish my beer and come and help you unpack. Five minutes."

"It's T23, just down there," Luke said, impatiently waving his hand in the general direction.

"You unpack your stuff, I'll see you there." Josh said, smiling in the direction of Stella.

Luke realised it was futile to argue when Josh was showing off. He was never going to back down. Luke found their lodge easily, but it was not what he was expecting, not the quaint wooden structure you normally associate with the term 'lodge'. In fact, this could be more accurately described as a box…but a stylish box. Inside it had a feature wall with large zebras on it and it was painted in vivid green and white. On the large wall there was a big king size bed and, on the wall next to the door, a single bed. 'I wonder who will get the small one!' Luke thought.

To the left of the door was a large mirror with lights around it and a washbasin beneath, the kind of thing you might find in a theatre dressing room. There was a toilet behind that, and a large tiled wet room across from it. The box had no windows and the only natural light came from the sliding door that led out onto the small balcony. There was an avenue of these boxes, all exactly the same and all with the same balcony: no grass, no trees or shrubs. They were neat and ordered but soulless, like some Bauhaus throwback.

Luke unpacked his suitcase and rucksack. He hung up his clothes in the open wardrobe on the right side of the room and placed his shoes and the empty suitcase underneath, in the space provided. He'd had the foresight to bring an adapter, so he charged his phone. He noticed he had one new message, it was from Sophie:

"Hi, hope you enjoying your holiday (lol!) Have you found R's sister yet? Btw, was talking to someone at the stables today about the body in the woods. She said she was there late that Monday night cos her horse was sick – said she saw a white van parked at the end of the road next to the path to the woods! Going to Oxford next week. X"

Luke texted back: **"Have you told your father?"**

Luke didn't get an immediate reply. Sophie was probably working, he thought.

Josh didn't come back in 5 minutes as he had promised but arrived about 45 minutes later. He lay on the double bed and promptly fell asleep. Luke must have fallen asleep too because when he awoke Josh was showered and preening himself in the big mirror. He combed gel through his short hair and then ruffled and lifted it.

Josh's attitude to house-keeping was in marked contrast to Luke's - he had abandoned his suitcase in the middle of the room and clothes spilled out onto the floor as he searched for something clean to wear. He was now attempting to iron a t-shirt and jeans on a towel which he had spread out over a small table next to his bed. Sporadic curses came from him: clearly this was something that Dani would have done at home.

Luke would have been happy to lie on the bed and use the rest of the day to relax before starting the search for Annabel the next morning. He heard the message alert on his phone, it was Sophie again: **"He says it was probably a courting couple. X"**

Luke returned a kiss and then used his phone to search out the location of The International School in Rome. He thought this might be a good starting point. Of course, the daughter might be confidently bilingual and go to a mainstream Italian comprehensive or whatever their equivalent was here. But he had to start somewhere.

Josh had doused himself in aftershave and deodorant and was now dressed and restless to get out again. "I'm going for a beer, Ok?" he said. "I'll see you in the bar later, yeah?"

"Ok. Try and stay out of trouble and don't get too wrecked. Busy day tomorrow." Luke knew any advice was wasted but he felt he should offer it anyway.

Josh closed the door behind him with a smile, "Yes, dad!" he replied.

It was around 8pm by the time Luke had showered and changed and made his way down to the bar on the campsite. It was very different at night, the temperature had dropped so most people were inside the bar where the music was loud. Luke found Josh with Stella, but there was no friend with her.

"Hi," Luke half shouted above the sound of the music and the laughter of a large group of lads next to them. "Lager anyone?"

"Cheers, can Stella have a double rum and coke please?" Josh shouted.

Luke queued at the bar. "Where, did all these people come from?" he wondered. It was an ordinary Tuesday in March but it seemed more like high season! He looked over to Josh who was in close conversation with Stella. The loud music meant she needed to incline her head close to his so she could hear him. His words made her laugh. 'Bloody Hell!' thought Luke.

He took the drinks over and placed them on the table in front of the couple. They hardly seemed to notice him. Josh nodded in appreciation and Luke could see he was drunk. Luke decided to take his Moretti outside, he'd had the foresight to bring a jacket and he really could not stand the banging, anonymous racket that was spewing out of the large wall speakers in the busy bar. He had enjoyed the previous night in Como but this was not his scene at all, it made him feel old and boring. And, anyway, now he was in Rome, the immediacy of his mission was starting to weigh heavy upon him. He thought about Sophie's revelation of the white van and built a scenario around it. If Richard had been murdered then the killer may have done it elsewhere and brought his body down to the woods under the cloak of darkness. It was a short walk down a gravel path from where the van had been seen.

The more Luke thought about it the more anxious he became. Was no-one investigating this new development, for God's sake! Did Uncle Fester own a white van? Surely Sophie would consider that. It made Luke feel it was even more important that he did *his bit* and found the sister. But now he was this close to her, the prospect of finding her suddenly felt all the more remote. And there was Josh in the bar with some young girl, totally oblivious!

Luke couldn't finish his beer. He left it on a table and returned to his box. He was angry and anxious as he got changed into pyjamas and climbed into the single bed near the door, leaving the door unlocked. He switched off the light and lay in the dark, thinking.

He was still awake an hour later when Josh returned with Stella. He pretended to be asleep as they crept into the room whispering and giggling the way drunks do. In the darkness Josh tripped over his case and cursed loudly as he led the girl to his double bed.

Luke continued to feign sleep until he could stand the embarrassment no longer: "For God's sake, you two! Josh, give me the car keys?" Luke stood up pulling the quilt around him and switched on the light next to his bed. It blinded him for a second.

The couple were half naked and spread across the large bed, the girl pulled the duvet across herself and let out an indignant scream as though *Luke* was the unexpected intruder in this sordid drama.

"Give me the fucking keys!" Luke could use his voice effectively when he needed to. He'd had plenty of practice in school – without the expletives, of course! His shrill command startled a drunken Josh into action.

"They're in front of the mirror, you dick," said Josh laughing and motioning in the general direction.

Luke snatched up the keys. He didn't bother turning out the light but he left the box, slamming the door behind him. He stomped down the avenue and then gingerly across the gravel to the Audi. He pressed the button on the key and for a brief second the car lights lit up the dark corner of the car park. He climbed into the passenger seat, felt for the lever and reclined the seat, then he pulled the duvet over himself with a loud, angry sigh.

CHAPTER 9: ALONE AGAIN

Luke woke at 8am. He needed the loo. It was light and there were already site staff busying themselves, emptying bins and brushing paths. Luke couldn't simply relieve himself in the car park and there were no public toilets because each unit had their own facilities. He decided he would *have* to go back into the box.

He retraced the route he had taken in the night, opened the door and crept across to the toilet. The light was still on and he pulled the chain in the hope the noise would awaken Josh and Stella enough to cover themselves and avoid the embarrassment of last night. But it didn't. Luke had no option but to announce his presence.

"Can you two cover yourselves please?"

Stella opened her eyes and slowly became aware of Luke's presence standing at the end of the bed.

"Fucking hell!" she suddenly shouted at Luke as she became conscious of his presence in the room. "What the fuck are you doing, standing there, you pervert!" she screamed.

Luke was already tired and irritable and the girl's reaction enraged him. "If you don't get dressed and get out of this place in sixty seconds I shall call security," he shouted, mustering as much authority as he was able at such an early hour. "This place is booked in *my* name and you are trespassing."

"What the bloody hell is going on?" said Josh who had been woken by the commotion. "Why are you screaming at Stella, you mad bastard!" he shouted, pulling the quilt over himself and Stella.

"Why am I screaming? Fucking Hell, Josh!" Luke's voice always went up an octave when he shouted loudly and it made him sound quite feminine. There had been times at school when he had shouted at a child and they had laughed. Luke tried to adjust his pitch, he pointed at the girl in the bed: "I'm screaming because this fucking girl has just called me a pervert for having the audacity to use the toilet in *my* rented accommodation after spending an awful night sleeping in a car!" Luke ran out of words and a silence descended upon the room for a moment before Josh began laughing. He laughed long and loud and the girl started to laugh at Luke as well.

"Fucking Hell, Josh!" Luke said, with as much disappointment as he could muster. "Fucking Hell!" he said again. Josh continued to laugh.

Luke shook with anger now: "You *do* know he's married, love?" he said, gesturing towards Josh. "He has a pretty young wife at home *and* a baby. Was this part of your pilgrimage, yeah! Yeah?"

With that, Luke turned away from the bed and he stomped out of the lodge; he threw himself into the plastic chair on the balcony, folding his arms, like a young child mid-tantrum. The couple who were having breakfast on the adjacent balcony looked across anxiously.

From inside the lodge, Luke could hear Stella's tearful protests and the sound of movement. The news that Josh was married had clearly changed things. Within a minute she was at the door, dishevelled but fully dressed. She didn't acknowledge Luke as she marched indignantly past him and down the avenue.

Josh's face appeared at the door of the bungalow. He was wearing boxers now.

"Well, I hope you are proud of yourself!" he said to Luke, quietly spitting out the words.

"What!" said Luke, incredulously.

"Bloody upsetting a young girl. What is *wrong* with you?"

Luke wasn't going to continue this in full view of the neighbours. He stood up and pushed Josh back into the lodge and followed him in and then slid the door closed behind him. "Why did you come here, Josh?" he said quietly.

"What do you mean?" Josh was confused.

"Why did you come…why did you offer to drive to Rome with me? Was it just an opportunity for a fuck-fest, was it?" Luke paused. "Cos you haven't come for Richard, have you?"

Josh suddenly turned on Luke: "Richard fucking topped himself, and everyone accepts it but you," he shouted. "So why are we looking for 'answers' when the answer is as plain as the fucking nose on your face?" Josh made an angry gesture on 'answers' with his fingers. Sensing he now had the advantage, he continued as Luke fell back into the only chair in the box: "And why are we trying to find his fucking sister - she didn't give a shit about Richard when he was alive?" Josh paused. "You know why, don't you Luke, you want to turn this into some bloody murder mystery. You're not fucking

Sherlock Holmes – you're just some sad bastard who needs a bit of excitement in his dull fucking life!"

Josh was spent, he sat on the bed then threw himself back in a dramatic gesture, staring at the ceiling.

Slowly recovering, Luke roused himself from his seat, picked up Josh's car keys and dropped them onto his mid-drift: "Here," he said, "get into your expensive car and fuck off back to Darwen. You never know, you might be able to squeeze in a couple more shags between here and Calais!" Josh, sat up suddenly, shocked by the cold keys on his bare stomach. "Fuck you!" he shouted. And then again louder and with more emphasis: "Fuck you!" Luke fully expected Josh to rise up and strike him at this point…but instead he flung the keys violently against the wall of the lodge, the one opposite to where Luke was standing. Their impact made the flimsy walls of the little box shake. The neighbour suddenly appeared the other side of the glass door.

"Everything OK. Yes?" he shouted through the glass.

"Yes. Yes, this man's just leaving," Luke shouted back, "Thank you."

The man reluctantly disappeared and Josh immediately set to packing his case - throwing and stuffing his clothes into it with little interest in their condition. He disappeared into the wet room and returned with a body gel and a shampoo and scooped some euros off the small cupboard at the side of the bed where the car keys had been. These too were thrown into the case. Josh zipped up the case violently and jerked in upright. He scanned the lodge quickly, collected up his jacket, checking inside for his phone and wallet, then he picked up his case by the handle.

"What am I going to tell Dani?" Josh asked, avoiding Luke's gaze upon him.

"Tell her what you want," Luke said, dismissively.

"Are you going to…you know…?" Josh asked, his tone calmer now.

"I'm not going to deliberately hurt her, no. But whatever you decide to say make sure you don't make me out to be some weirdo or something…"

"I won't," said Josh, immediately.

With that, Josh stepped out of the lodge and into the gentle sunlight of early morning. Luke learnt back on his chair, stretched out his legs and stared at the ceiling. He listened to the Audi's powerful engine start up and slowly drive away across the gravel.

He hoped that Josh wouldn't change his mind and come back. He really didn't want to spend another moment with him. He'd never regarded Josh as a close friend, even before the trip, but now he had seen the Josh that few would recognise in The Sunnyhurst: a selfish opportunist that cared little for anything or anyone other than himself, it seemed. He thought about Josh's words. So that was what he really thought of him: *'a sad bastard!'*

These words played back in Luke's mind all day. Perhaps in his anger, Josh was just stating how everyone saw him, thought Luke. Perhaps he *was* just a sad bastard desperately trying to manufacture something more from Richard's suicide to fill the void within himself.

But after Luke had tidied the place, showered and changed he'd decided he must *not* dwell on what had happened that morning. Whatever others might or might not think about him, he was here for Richard…and nothing was going to deflect him now he was here. He must move quickly, find the sister, find answers then get home.

But it wasn't a good day for Luke. Firstly, he had no transport now. He really wouldn't have contemplated a campsite out of the city without transport but he'd paid upfront so he was stuck there. He had to get a slow bus into the city centre and then another one out to The International School which was in Municipio 15. It took him over two hours. And then, when he finally arrived, he felt silly. Why *would* they just give out information to a complete stranger in no official capacity! He should have known that from *his* experience in school. They were very polite and when Luke related his story the lady at reception did call for a member of the pastoral staff but she just couldn't help either. They suggested that if Luke were to obtain some authorisation from the family they could maybe look into it. They couldn't even confirm or deny they had a student there with a mother called Anna.

It was a long journey back to Camping Village Roma for Luke. He felt very alone again. He had reached a massive impasse already. If The International School who spoke good English had rejected his request, then what chance did he stand with the other schools in Rome? And there were hundreds of them too. What was he to do, simply give up and go home! And how would he get home now? The thought of flying immediately made him nervous, and the train across Europe would take ages…and it cost a packet! What an idiot he had been driving out to Rome with just a Christian name!

Luke decided to go back to his small box and think. When he changed buses in Rome he could see the familiar outline of the Pantheon in the distance but he was in no mood for sight-seeing. He called into a small supermarket and brought some wine, some plastic glasses and some cold meats and cheeses together with some salad and ready-made couscous. There were no cooking facilities in the lodge so he'd have to eat cold food. He certainly couldn't afford to keep eating and drinking out every night.

When he got back he decided to text Rachel and tell her he'd drawn a blank, in the hope she had some suggestions. She texted back immediately giving him encouragement. After all, she had even more resting on the outcome of all this and she was clearly desperate that Luke should not lose heart. She promised she would try and talk to Mr Harrington – he had fleeting moments of clarity – maybe he knew Anna's new surname. Rachel also promised to snoop around for any correspondence although she admitted she'd already looked long and hard.

He thought about going to the British Embassy in Rome and telling them his story. But he imagined he'd be confronted with the same response. He wasn't a member of the family and he had no official permissions for seeking out this woman. As Luke drank his wine he recalled Thomas, the sophisticated man he had met in Como. He'd only spoken to him for a short time at the hotel but he had been impressed with him and his offer to help had seemed genuine. He found the jeans he had been wearing the night in Como and retrieved the card Thomas had given him. It was a simple white card: *Thomas Calvi* and underneath *Ministerio de Educación.*

"Bloody Hell!" Luke said out loud.

Underneath, there was what looked like a mobile number and an email address. Luke decided to text. After all, Thomas could simply ignore it if he wanted.

"Hello, it's Luke. We met the other night in Casa Santo Stefano. You may recall I told you I was looking for my friend's sister in Rome. Her name is Anna (as I said I don't have a surname) and she has a daughter of around fifteen. I went to The International School today in Rome but understandably they are unable to tell me anything. I know this is a terrible imposition but I wonder if you have any contacts who would be able to tell you whether there was an English girl around that age with a mother called Annabel in any of the English speaking schools in Rome? So sorry to trouble you on holiday and please say if it's awkward for you. Luke Adams."

Luke was surprised when he got a text back almost immediately.

"Hello Luke. Yes, I remember our conversation in Como and I am content to find out what I can. I am presently at my home in Milan but I will be in my office tomorrow so I shall contact The International School in the morning. Thomas Calvi.

Luke felt a little more hopeful. Maybe between them, Rachel and Thomas would produce some lead he could follow up. But this was a day Luke would have liked to quickly forget - and, to cap it all, he hadn't bought any plastic plates and knives and forks and the shop on the campsite was now closed. He had to eat the food with his fingers out of their plastic containers. His body felt tense as if each event that day had twisted it a little tighter, the way his mother used to do with a sodden towel to wring it out. He'd taken his usual dose of Sertraline that morning but he needed more - a quick fix. He swallowed down a Valium with the last of the wine, switched off the light and pulled the duvet over himself.

The drug took immediate effect. The tightness in his neck and shoulders and gut slowly unravelled. But as he lay in the darkness of this anonymous box, 1500 miles away from home he knew the drugs and the alcohol were only masking his feelings, the way a paracetamol does a headache. Luke was fearful that his anxiety might start to consume him again. He was away from home and the security that represented and in a big city where he knew no-one, and he was stranded by his fear of flying. Luke was alone: No Sarah, no children that men of his age usually had to call on at times like this and no family to confide in. And now he was starting to believe he had no friends!

The more he thought, the more his anxiety fought against the numbing effect of the Valium. He must try to start thinking straight. He must try to be positive, to have a plan. He put one hand behind his neck as he'd been shown in his anxiety classes and the other on his forehead. He slowly started to calm. He forced out of his head the negative thoughts and put up a gate to keep them at bay. 'Now let's think positive,' he told himself. He thought about Sophie, this strange, unquantifiable new relationship that had grown out of death and he decided to text her: **"Starting to wonder why I ever thought it would be a good idea coming on this wild goose chase!"**

His phone rang almost immediately.

"What the matter, Luke? What happened?" Sophie sounded like she was just across the road.

"I feel stupid. More than stupid! Why on earth did I think I could find an Anna in a massive city life Rome. I don't even speak the language, for God's sake!" he said, his voice ringing with self-pity.

"Have you tried some schools then? You can't have tried…"

"I was knocked back at the first one," Luke interrupted, "no-one in their right mind is going to give out personal information to a complete stranger, especially these days. What was I thinking!"

"Well, I must admit…"

"Don't…! I know, I've been stupid."

There was a silence between Luke and Sophie for a matter of seconds but it seemed longer. Neither really knew what to say next.

"Do you want me to see what I can do this end?" Sophie said at last, "see whether we can get you something from the Italian police to say you are trying to find an estranged sister to inform her of her brother's death?"

"I'm not family, though."

"Well, I will have a try. I can explain your relationship with the deceased. And the fact that you are a teacher and had all the police checks, etc, to show you are not a risk."

"Thank you, Sophie. Bless you," Luke said, and he meant it. He'd reached out to Sophie in his hour of need and she was there for him, like she had been ever since she walked into his home on that awful Tuesday morning. Luke shuddered as he recalled it once again. "Actually, I'm still hoping to hear back from an Italian guy I met who is high up in education. He says he will make some enquiries in the schools to see whether he can locate the daughter."

"Well then, it's not all doom and gloom!" Sophie said, reassuringly. "Let's wait and see how that works out."

"Yes. I'm sorry, I just suddenly felt very alone. The guy that came with me has gone back to England." Luke suddenly felt embarrassed. "I shouldn't have troubled you."

"Don't be daft, it's no trouble. So why has your mate gone?"

"He needed to get back to his wife," Luke said. He felt a lie was easier than explaining. "Thank you, Sophie, you've cheered me up. I really don't know what I would have done without you."

"Don't put so much pressure on yourself. What's the worst that can happen – you don't find this woman? That old lady at the funeral should never have asked you? And this Anna clearly doesn't give a damn…"

"I know…I know…but I just thought I might find some answers about Richard's death." Luke interrupted, "I'm doing it for myself more than anyone."

"And I'm off to Oxford next week so I might have something to report myself. But please don't tell anyone – my father would get into such shit for sanctioning it!" Sophie added, earnestly, "it's totally unofficial. I'm officially on leave next week."

"Promise," Luke said, feeling far better. "Thank you Sophie, I'm sorry to have mithered."

"Don't be daft, you know you can ring or text anytime. We are mates. If I'm working I might not get back straight away. But I WILL get back."

"Thank you."

"Are you ok now?"

"Yeah, I'm ok."

Sophie made Luke promise he'd get back if he needed her help and he felt much better after talking to her. The situation wasn't as hopeless as he had thought earlier that day. There were options – both in Rome and in Oxford and surely one of these lines of enquiry would produce some answers.

Luke was woken the next morning by his phone ringing. He thought it was his alarm at first and tried to turn it off with a swipe as he usually did. But when that didn't work he realised it was an incoming call. It was 9.08 am.

"Hello," said Luke, groggily.

"Hello, I hope I didn't wake you," said the voice on the other end. He didn't recognise the foreign sounding accent. "I have spoken to The International School in Rome."

It was Thomas! "Oh, good, thank you." Luke was slowly coming round.

"Well, to be truthful it is not good news. They do not have a girl there with an English mother. Not a girl of 15 years. I asked about girls of 14 years to 16 years too. But there are none, and none left last year." Thomas paused to allow Luke to take in what he had said. "It appears they have very few English students or students with English parents. Mostly Chinese students now," he added.

"Ok, well, thank you for asking Thomas. And thank you for getting back so quickly. I really appreciate it," said Luke, finding it hard to disguise the disappointment in his voice.

"But let me keep trying," Thomas said in a more upbeat tone, as if the hopelessness in Luke's voice had galvanized him into further action. "There are plenty more schools in Rome! I have this morning just spoken to my friend in the Education Department in Rome. He will investigate for me."

Luke's tone changed. "Oh, that's great. Oh, thank you, Thomas, you have been so helpful. Thank you," he repeated. "By the way, I'm not sure whether it helps but the mother's maiden name was Harrington. Anna or Annabel Harrington."

"Ok," Thomas said. Luke could sense he was writing down this new information. Thomas repeated the name, "Harr…ring…ton. I will email this to my colleague. I will call you after my friend speaks to me. Goodbye."

"Thank you," said Luke once again, but the phone had gone dead already.

This wake-up call was just what Luke needed after the previous day. The kindness of this perfect stranger now took on a mystical quality in Luke's mind. If the roles had been reversed, he wondered, would *he* have gone to so much trouble for a person he had spoken to for a matter of minutes in a hotel bar!

Of course, the phone call had not really produced the result he required - he was pinning his hopes on The International School because it seemed the obvious place to find Annabel's daughter. But it nevertheless felt like fate had stepped in to reassure Luke he wasn't the sad, deluded creature he had been painted. After all, what had drawn them to that hotel in Como late on Tuesday evening other than Luke's instinct? And why had that nice Italian started speaking to them…a man who just happened to be in education? And from what he had achieved in a matter of an hour that morning, he was clearly a very influential man in education!

Luke started the day with renewed confidence. Thomas would help find Annabel for him – it was fate. He showered and dressed and walked across to the bar on the campsite where breakfast was served between 7am and 10am every day. He hadn't eaten much the previous day and he was hungry now.

At the bar he brought a token that allowed him to serve himself to a full cooked breakfast. The food had been laid out in the bar area which now had a very different atmosphere. There was no loud music now and the room was bright and fresh. He took the food onto the outdoor seating area and a waitress brought him a coffee. Luke sat in the morning sun and studied a map of the city he had picked up at the bar. It was one of those maps which labelled important landmarks in the city. Luke decided he would be a tourist for the day. He'd never been to Rome: he'd been all over Europe with Sarah and they'd always talked about going but it seemed just a little bit too far by car. Luke imagined it would take Thomas' contact in Rome a while to investigate whether there was a girl in their education system that had an English mother called Anna. And, anyway, he could contact Luke anywhere on his mobile.

He got the bus from outside the campsite and got off at The Vatican. From there it was a short walk into St Peters Square. It was still early morning and there were only a few people milling around but he was immediately set upon by a big lady selling *'A Unique Experience of St Peters'* which she said avoided queues. She promised you saw only the interesting bits like Michelangelo's famous ceiling with an expect guide.

"How much?" Luke asked.

"I can give you a discount. It's normally 40 Euros but I will do it for 30 because it's quiet."

Luke would have liked to see the Sistine Chapel but he wasn't that bothered about the other stuff. And he certainly had no intention of spending that kind of money. He politely declined but he knew he was never good at saying 'No' in an assertive enough manner when people had something to sell. The lady continued to hound him and practically pursued him out of Vatican City before he had chance to look round.

Luke had been brought up in a religious family. Church had been at the centre of everything, although *his* family were Anglicans, not Catholics. They called themselves Evangelicals, meaning they believed it was their duty to not only practice their faith but to *convert* the world to Christianity. Their faith, their path was the only true path to God and all others - especially the Catholics - were in error. *'They might be very sincere,'* his mother often said of other religions, *'but they are sincerely wrong!'* Luke tried to use the analogy of there being different roads into London, it just depended where you started out, but his mum wasn't having any of that! *'That's why we have missionaries and evangelists, dear. To show the right way!'*

Luke's family dealt in certainties and absolutes but when he went to university he started to ask why the family religion had to be the *only* way? He hadn't met many Muslims growing up in Lytham but now he saw how seriously they practiced their beliefs, how dedicated they were to prayer and fasting, how committed they were to good works and family. Why couldn't *their* way be just as valid? Or Hindus? Or Jews? Or *even* Catholics?

That was one reason he had drifted apart from his family. And they never really approved of Sarah because she was "spiritual" not religious, and the family would always emphasise the sibilance in the word when they used it: 'Sarah is spiritual, you know!' as if recalling the hissing of the snake in the Garden of Eden. 'Spiritual' was nowhere - it was vague and woolly, it was anti-Christian.

But the more Luke learnt the more he appreciated that Sarah being spiritual made far more sense than being religious. She believed in God, she prayed and read her bible when she wanted to and she would have probably called herself Christian if she had to be labelled. And if a faith was ever tested by fire then Sarah's faith certainly was. Luke had been so impressed with the way Sarah had faced her illness and inevitable death so stoically and how the faith within her had grown, outgrown that tumour. Luke had gone to pieces and it was Sarah who supported *him* and not the other way round. He still felt guilty about that. And in her final days there had been a radiance in her face. And in her eyes, her beautiful eyes, there was a new intensity as though they were looking out beyond the hospice walls, beyond Luke even, and into the very face of God.

As Sarah's faith in God grew Luke's took a real hit. Yet, three years on from Sarah's death on that sunny March morning in Rome, Luke's knew that faith was in his DNA, it was instinctive. He really wanted to believe there were reasons why things happened…like Sarah being taken away from him with so much of her life unlived. He wanted the assurance that Sarah lived on somewhere, somehow: that there was something beyond, something better. Luke felt like Thomas in that Caravaggio painting, the one Richard loved so much: "Lord, I believe, help my unbelief!" After all, Thomas got to see and touch the risen Christ and he *still* had his doubts.

But whatever faith was or wasn't, in Luke's mind, it had little to do with all this stuff in St Peters Square: the impressive columns, the expensive tours and the religious memorabilia in the shops on the wide avenue than ran towards the river and across the bridge into a far more secular world. Luke really couldn't see much difference between all this and any of those major football stadia around Europe where fans queue for hours for an opportunity to sit where Messi sat before a game at Camp Nou or lean over the hoardings and pick a blade off the hallowed turf!

So, Luke crossed the bridge by Hadrian's Tomb and made his way into the city and followed the blue street signs in the direction of The Pantheon. He'd always wanted to see that vast concrete ceiling. When he got inside and looked up it was bigger and more beautiful than he could have ever imagined. The ancient Romans were so bloody clever - perfect, symmetrical concrete in a time before Christ! He remembered how the ugly 1970's concrete in a school he taught at had deteriorated so badly that a whole block had to be pulled down and rebuilt.

Luke walked on towards the Trevi Fountain and caught himself staring intently at women who looked around Anna's age. Could they unknowingly be passing by each other? He couldn't stop every woman and ask, "Are you Richard's sister?" He pictured himself wearing a sandwich board: "STOP ME IF YOU ARE ANNA" and chuckled to himself.

After the Trevi Fountain, Luke sauntered towards the enormous and imposing, and far too showy, Victor Emmanuel Monument and found a cafe where he sat and people-watched and drank a beer. He decided he'd had enough of sightseeing, it was no fun alone and, anyhow, St Peters and thoughts of faith and doubt had distracted him. Maybe faith was like adrenaline, Luke thought: you got it when you needed it most and too much of it when you didn't need it was bad for you. But he had to admit his faith reservoir was pretty much empty at that moment: faith in a higher power, faith in friends, faith even in himself and his own sanity. As was always the way when he was anxious Luke's state of mind could change within minutes. He'd been so full of optimism after Thomas' call and now he was down and anxious and just wanted to get back to the relative security of his little box. He'd forgotten to take his pills that morning.

He got the bus back with no thought of what he would do for food or drink. There was a supermarket on the campsite but it wasn't well stocked. And he still had no plates or knives and forks. And he didn't even have the means of heating water for a coffee so there was no point in buying any. He bought a couple of bottles of water and some crisps. The route back from the supermarket passed by the bar and a few people were sitting outside drinking beer in the sunshine. He went in with his shopping and ordered a Moretti and sat outside near the pool. A solitary old man was swimming lengths. It had only just occurred to him that there was a total absence of children. All at school, of course!

Luke hated just sitting around normally. He'd always be walking Noah or running or cycling or pounding on a trainer at the gym. But inertia had set in now. He felt his life was on hold until he received news from Thomas. He ordered another beer, then another. The sun and the alcohol started to give him a headache so he was forced to go back to his box and take some pills with the water he'd bought. He lay on the bed and waited for the headache to pass.

Whilst he lay there Luke decided to text Rachel:

"Hello, Rachel. Bad news and good news. Good news - I've met someone who is being very helpful in my search for Anna. He's in education here and he's checked out The International School in Rome. No luck unfortunately! But he's now got his best man on the case looking into other schools in Rome. He's high up in education in Italy and he seems to have lots of contacts...so here's hoping!

Bad news - you might remember I told you I was traveling with a friend from Darwen in his car. Well, we've had a fallout and he's gone home so I'm stuck here for the time being, anyhow. I can't fly and I don't really want to get the train so it's a bit of a dilemma actually. Anyway, I'll let you know when I hear back from this guy. Let me know if you get anything out of Mr Harrington. Love, Luke X"

As usual with Rachel, he got a message straight back. She was adapting quickly to her new technology!

"Dear Luke, Sorry to hear your friend has deserted you. Quite sure you will be wishing you never met me right now! Anyway, I'm pleased to hear you have the help of this nice Italian man. I so hope something comes of it. I have tried talking to Mr Harrington but he's not good at the moment. But that sometime changes from day to

day. I've found nothing either. Feel I am letting you down this end. Sorry. Love, Rachel xxx

PS. I'm going to transfer another £1000 in a Santander Account for you in the morning. You can collect it at any branch as long as you have some ID with you. No arguments please!"

Luke texted back:

"Don't be silly, it's not your fault. And thank you. Luke xxxxx"

Luke walked back down to the bar after a rest decided to treat himself to some food at the restaurant. He'd just ordered a calzone pizza and another beer when his phone rang. It was the call he was waiting for. The name Thomas was on the screen. He felt immediately apprehensive.

"Hello," he said, tentatively.

"Hello Luke, it's Thomas speaking. I think I might have some news for you. I cannot tell you too much but I have found a school that may be able to help you."

"Oh, that sounds good." Luke's tone immediately changed.

"I hope so. Can I give you the name of a contact and an address?" asked Thomas.

"Yes please, I'm in the bar at the moment, I will need to get a pen and paper. Can you just hold for a moment, Thomas?" Luke said.

"Yes, of course."

Luke rushed inside to the bar. It was busy but he pushed past, "Sorry, could I have a pen, it's an emergency?" he asked, earnestly. The girl behind the bar immediately found him a pen and he tore apart a beer mat and rested it on the bar.

"Hello Thomas, I'm back," said Luke, now a little breathless.

"Ok, it's a Dr Harper, he's an American. Dr Harper," he repeated. "It's the Marymount Catholic School, Via di Villa Lauchli, Municiplio 15." Thomas spelt out the address very slowly. "The telephone number is +39065629201." Thomas stated each important detail in the same slow, clear manner. "I suggest you visit the school in person and speak to Dr Harper. He's the Principal," he added.

"Oh, thank you Thomas, thank you. You have been so helpful. I will call you and tell you the outcome. Thank you again, I cannot begin to……"

"Please, there is no need," Thomas interrupted, "I just hope that my help brings some resolution. But please understand that all the principal can do is make this lady aware of your request. The rest is up to her."

"Of course, of course. But thank you again."

"I just hope it is the lady you are looking for. Enjoy your drink!" Thomas said, warmly.

With that the phone went dead.

'Well, this must be fate, mustn't it!' exclaimed Luke inwardly. "Maybe even God intervening in human affairs!" He

was excited, like a child at Christmas. He wanted to go round every table and tell his news.

He texted Rachel as he ate his calzone and relayed the news. She rang back immediately.

"Oh, Luke, this is fantastic," she said, excitedly.

"I know," Luke said, "I can't believe Thomas got back so quickly. I was fully expecting this to take two or three days. Maybe more!"

"Are you going to go and see this Principal in the morning?" she asked.

"Yes, it seems like the school is in the same area as the International School I went to, so I'll get a bus into the city and a bus out to the school."

"Now you *will* stop at a Santander branch, won't you, to pick up the money?"

"Yes, I will Rachel, thank you. Are you sure?" asked Luke, relieved as he now expected to have to travel back on the train and the Eurostar and book an overnight cabin which was sure to be expensive.

"It's just sitting in a savings account. I was hoping to go on a cruise at some stage…but with Mr Harrington to care for and my health there's no chance of *that* now!"

"Ok, if you are sure. I'll be in touch as soon as I hear anything," Luke said, then added, "but remember Thomas warned me the school can only do so much. It's then up to Anna."

"I know, but this is a *real* break-through. Do you believe in fate, Luke?" she asked.

"You know, I was just thinking about it myself!" said Luke, enthusiastically.

They both laughed. Luke felt good about making this old lady happy.

After his pizza, Luke made his way back to his lodge. He planned to get to sleep early but he just couldn't settle…his mind was full of Anna. How would this thing work, he wondered? Would he have to write a letter that would be passed on to her? He hoped not. And what if she didn't want anything to do with anyone associated with Richard? It might be they had an enormous row that night over the phone…and the relationship had not been what you would call 'close' before that! Doubts started to push their way into Luke's mind, like gate crashers at a party he'd been looking forward to for ages.

He decided to try and take his mind off Anna by phoning Emily. She was pleased to hear from him.

"Luke!" she said excitedly, "Jon, it's Luke!" she shouted. "Are you in Rome? You sound like you are just down the road."

"Yeah, I'm still in Rome. I arrived the day before yesterday. I'm on a campsite about two miles from The Vatican."

"Bloody hell, sounds rough!"

Luke laughed, "No, it's quite nice, and I'm in this trendy box type thing. Sounds terrible but it's cheap and clean."

"So, have you spoken to that girl yet?" Emily asked.

"Not yet, but I've just got a strong lead today." Luke chuckled at the way he had phrased things. "Listen to me, Detective Adams!"

Emily laughed. "Well, you seem in good spirits," she said.

"I've been up and down…it's not been straightforward." Luke didn't want to go into the whole Josh thing over the phone. "Anyway, how's my dog?"

"Ah, he's absolutely lovely! Not a bit of trouble. Our Millie loves having him around. He's just in the other room, I think. I'll put him on the phone."

There was a moments silence whilst Emily went to find the dog.

"Here Noah, who is this?" Luke heard Emily saying.

"Are you being a good boy, Noah?" said Luke into the phone, speaking slowly and deliberately and feeling rather stupid. "I'm missing you, mate. Missing our little walks." Luke laughed, "I've been a right lazy bugger without you!"

The dog obviously recognised Luke's voice because it started barking. Noah hardly ever barked.

"He's standing up now and his tail is wagging, furiously," Emily said, speaking into the phone again. "He's so pleased to hear you."

"Ah, I'm filling up here, Emily. Bless him. Give him a big hug from me," Luke said. Except for the few days when he went to France with Richard, Luke and Noah were never apart. "I'll be home soon, mate, I promise," Luke shouted into his handset.

"So, when you coming home, then?" Emily asked, taking control of the phone.

"I'm hoping that I'll see this Anna in the next couple of days - so straight after that, I guess. Only problem is, I've no transport now. Josh, the guy who brought me in his car, has gone home."

Emily sounded surprised. "Why, you have a fall out or something?"

"Well, yeah," Luke replied, a little sheepishly.

"Why?"

"He was picking up women, and he pissed me off," Luke said.

"So…!" Emily sounded genuinely confused.

"Well, he's married with a little baby!" Luke said, indignantly.

"Bloody hell, Luke, what are you like!" Emily was laughing now but Luke could tell she was serious. "Why did you get involved? It's his life and if he wants to mess it up - like blokes do - then let him," she said.

Luke felt stupid. "Well, he just wasn't the person I expected him to be!" he said, defensively.

"You expect too much from people at times." Emily was serious. "Not everyone thinks like you, Luke."

"Apparently not," Luke said, gloomily.

"So how will you get home now?" Emily asked. "You know you hate flying."

"I don't know. I think I'm just going to have to dose up on Valium and fly…or get the train. I just wish they could anesthetise me and bundle me in the hold," he said, laughing. "Anyway, I'm not thinking about that *now*."

"Well take care, Luke, we worry about you," Emily said, like a mother would do to her child. "I just wish you hadn't fallen out with that friend," she added.

"I'll be fine, honest. I'll let you know when I'm coming back," Luke said, feeling he ought to reassure her. "Hopefully, Saturday or Sunday."

They said their goodbyes. And Luke said goodbye to Noah.

Luke woke a few times during the night. His mind was active, he had dreams about chasing this anonymous girl around the streets of Rome and just when he thought he'd cornered her she made her escape. It seemed, in this dumb show, that he was the evil pursuer and she the innocent unsuspecting victim.

Luke was awake by first light and there was little point remaining in bed. He dressed in his shorts and t-shirt and running shoes and jogged out of the campsite and down the arterial road towards the city. Luke thought how all cities seem to look much the same on the outskirts. He passed by small convenience stores where proprietors were assembling their displays of vegetables and fruit outside. And there were lauderettes, and dark narrow cafes with tatty posters and steamed up windows, and ubiquitous charity shops which all looked the same and sad abandoned shops with boardings or metal shutters covered in graffiti.

And then as Luke ran farther, the impressive dome of St Peters came into view and the familiar outline of the bridges and the city lay before him. Instead of crossing the bridge Luke ran along the embankment. Unlike The Thames, which is an integral part of the life of London and as photographed and pampered as any landmark, The Tiber is reduced to a supporting role, a mere sideshow in the life of the city. It seemed uncared for and untidy. Luke ran until he was level with the iconic structure of The Colosseum. He then turned and retraced his route back in fear of getting lost on this important of mornings. He followed the bend in the river with St Peters and the giant monument to Hadrian behind and then back up the road towards Aurelio and the campsite.

He was exhausted and very hot when he got back to his box. He sat outside sipping a bottle of water. When he had recovered sufficiently, he showered and changed and went to the bar for breakfast once more. The bus route was the same as when he made his fruitless journey to The International School the day Josh had left. But this time it was an American Catholic School. Why hadn't Luke thought of this? He knew Richard came from a strong Catholic family and it made sense that his sister would send her daughter to an English speaking Catholic school. Anyway, he told himself, his inquiry would have no doubt been met with the same response without Thomas' intervention.

The Marymount American School was in Municipio 15 on the edge of Park Dell'invioletella Borghese. It was a much grander affair than the other school he had visited. It's location next to the large park gave it a country feel, like Stonyhurst, a Catholic School in The Ribble Valley Luke had often walked around. The main building was in the Baroque

Italian style, like an affluent country house with balconies and columns and elaborate detail around each casement. The main entrance was large and ornate and the path leading up to it was lined with perfectly manicured bushes and trees.

Once inside, the main entrance opened into a large reception area with a desk opposite the door. Large statues and works of art were scattered around the room, students' work, Luke imagined. He smiled as he thought about the type of schools he had taught at recently on an altogether different scale. The young man behind the desk seemed to recognise Luke's name when he introduced himself, as though he had been already primed to expect a Mr Adams from England. He rang through to The Principal's office without asking Luke's business and was immediately given permission to show Luke through to a smaller room behind the main reception.

Luke sat in the room for a few minutes before an official looking lady came into the room and addressed him.

"Mr Adams, Dr Harper will see you now. Will you follow me please?"

"Thank you," said Luke. He'd ironed the only shirt he'd brought with him and he was wearing a pair of light chinos and his old suede boots. He suddenly felt self-conscious in this formal environment.

Luke was ushered into a large office that was dominated by the biggest desk he had ever seen. Behind it were four floor-to-ceiling windows which looked out onto an elegant quad with a fountain in the middle. Students were sitting around the quad reading books or chatting and drinking coffee.

Dr Harper was not behind his desk when Luke entered the room, he was sitting on a settee to the right of the door with a laptop on his knee. He put it down immediately when he saw Luke.

"Hello, Mike Harper," he said, extending his hand towards Luke, "I'm The Principal at Marymount. Would you like a coffee?"

"Thank you," said Luke appreciating the way in which Dr Harper had immediately put him at his ease, "if it's not too much trouble. It's been quite a long bus journey."

Dr Harper spoke into a device on his desk: "Rose, may we have two coffees please? Please sit down, Mr Adams. Are you staying in the city?" he asked. He had a distinctive North American Accent.

Luke was embarrassed and a little thrown by the question. "No, I'm actually staying at Camping Roma. It's two miles outside the city. Not far from The Vatican."

"Ok. Yes, I know the place. A lot of our students stay there when they first come over for interviews. It's popular with young people visiting St Peters too, I believe," he added.

"Yes, I've met a couple of Americans since I've been there." Luke paused. "This is most beautiful, Dr Harper," Luke said, taking in the surrounding with a gesture. He was grateful that The Principal had been so eager to make Luke feel relaxed and he wanted to repay him with a compliment.

The Principal smiled warmly. "Yes, it is. Every day I count my blessings, as the old song says! You're a teacher, are you not, Mr Adams?" he asked.

"Please it's Luke?" Luke said, smiling warmly at Dr Harper. "Yes, I teach around North West England, between Liverpool and Manchester."

"What's your subject?" the Principal asked.

"English."

"Excellent!" said the Principal. "I love The Brontë Sisters. And Wordsworth, of course…"

"Well, Howarth, where the Brontës lived, is only about 30 minutes from where I live. And the Lake District, perhaps 45 minutes. Wordworth's Cottage is in Grasmere, I've taken students there a few times," said Luke, now feeling quite relaxed.

"Wow!" said the principal who sounded genuinely impressed. "You know I say to my wife that when they finally give me my marching orders here we will have a long vacation in the UK. There's so many places I want to see."

Rose, the lady who had ushered Luke into the room, arrived with a tray of coffee and biscuits. She put it down on the principal's desk and handed out the coffee and a plate for biscuits. The principal took up position behind the desk and gestured to Luke to take a seat.

"Go on, have a biscuit," said Dr Harper when Rose had left the room, offering the selection. Luke took one. "Now, I've had this call from Tom Calvi. He says you are looking for an English lady who you believe now lives in Rome?"

"Yes, I've driven from my home in England to find her. Her brother, Richard, was a close friend of mine. But he died recently and she does not know." The principal nodded to say he already knew all this. "At the funeral," Luke went on, "I promised a very sick old lady who was the family nanny and house-keeper that I would try to make contact with Anna." Luke had prepared what he was going to say and he hoped the mention of the sick nanny might help influence the decision.

"Anna is the name of Richard's sister?" he asked.

"Yes, Annabel Harrington was her maiden name."

"And you believe she has a daughter?"

"Yes, who is around 15 years old." said Luke.

Dr Harper paused for a moment. "And the family nor the police have made any attempt to find this Annabel?" The principal seemed surprised.

"No, it seems not." Luke was afraid now that Dr Harper would go on to say it was *their* responsibility and he could only deal with them. But he merely shook his head in that gesture that suggests disapproval.

"Well, I imagine you assume by now that we *may* have a student with a British passport here that *might* well have a mother called Annabel." Dr Harper said this slowly and with the hint of a smile upon his face, deliberately emphasising the modal verbs as he spoke. Luke nodded.

"And you understand, as principal, that I have a responsibility to protect that student and respect her privacy and that of her family, yes?" Principal Harper stared intently at Luke as he spoke, watching his reaction.

"Yes, of course. Absolutely," said Luke, emphatically.

"Good." Dr Harper said, decisively. He got up from his seat. "Now this is what I propose. He pushed a piece of quality writing paper towards Luke along with a pen. "I'd like you to write down your name and telephone number." He paused, "I assume you have a mobile phone?"

Luke nodded.

"Ok. I will then give this to the mother and explain that you are a friend of Richard's who needs to talk to her. You do not want me to mention his death?"

"Well, I would prefer to tell her myself…"

"No, that's understandable," he said. "I'm sure you want to get this sorted out as quickly as possible so you can get back home to your family?"

Luke knew The Principal was fishing. "I have no children and unfortunately my wife died of cancer three years ago." Luke paused. "Frankly, I was a right mess at the time and I met Richard through a local cycling club and his friendship helped me so much. And now I want to try and do something for him."

"I will do what I can to help you, Luke," Dr Harper said, his tone friendly and reassuring. "Have you got time off school to come over here?"

"Well, I'm doing supply teaching," Luke thought he'd better rephrase it for clarification, "I'm a stand-in teacher at the moment. After my wife's death I had to give up full time."

Dr Harper nodded as if to say he understood. "Well, you've certainly got friends in high places!" he said, as if wanting to lighten the mood.

"Sorry?" Luke was confused.

"Your friend Thomas Calvi, he's the Chief Advisor on Education here."

"In Rome! I thought he was in Milan!"

"In Italy! He is chief advisor to the Italian Government and he is radically changing education in the country. He's a well-respected and busy man! In fact, this was the first time I have spoken to him." Principal Harper smiled, clearly he had been impressed. "And he dealt with your case personally. Well, with the help of The Education Department in Rome"

Luke smiled. He thought it was better not to explain to Dr Harper that he'd only spoken to Thomas for around eight minutes a few nights ago! The Principal personally escorted Luke back through the reception hall and to the main door of the school. Once again, he assured Luke he'd do all he could for him. The men shook hands warmly and then Luke walked back down the elegant avenue lined with trees and headed for the bus.

*

Luke wasn't usually one of those obsessives who constantly looked at his phone throughout the day. In fact, he often forgot to look at it at all. He would let the battery run down and leave it somewhere and then have to search to locate it. But that day he checked his phone constantly, like those Year 10 girls who so annoyed him in lessons. He looked at his texts and his missed calls, he checked the sound was on and that he hadn't inadvertently knocked the switch.

He'd hoped that Dr Harper had tried to make contact with this Annabel as soon as he left. But he had a big school to run and maybe some more pressing issue arose. Or maybe Annabel was not answering. Or maybe he'd spoken to her already and she was considering whether to call Luke or not. Luke tried to occupy himself. He didn't want to sit and drink all day in case she rang and arranged to meet that day. He wanted a clear head when he told her about Richard - and he knew his eyes betrayed him after two or three pints.

Luke went for a swim in the pool on the campsite, keeping his phone in full view. The feeling of sunshine on his back gave him a special joy after reading earlier that England was being battered by winds and rain. After getting showered and changed, Luke wandered out of the campsite and down the road and through a rather non-descript park. He ended up on a road of shops and coffee houses close to the main road into the city. Luke found a small but busy cafe where old men sat outside drinking espresso and smoking, and half-talking, half-arguing as they seemed to do in Italy. When Luke ordered in English they smiled at him and tempered their exuberance. Luke had ordered a grande espresso and he sat at the only free table, checking his phone. He even switched it on and off to ensure that it was working properly. Whilst he was drinking his coffee he sent a brief text to Rachel keeping her up to date with the latest developments. She thanked him for the update and reprimanded him for not finding a Santander to collect the money she had transferred.

After that, Luke walked back to the campsite and spent a couple of hours in his lodge. He was fast running out of clean clothes so he washed a pile in the campsite launderette and returned to collect the clothes before hanging them in what remained of the afternoon sun. He walked across to the bar and sat outside with another coffee and had a chat with a group of Chinese students who were there on a cultural visit. All this time Luke checked his phone.

At 6pm he decided that even if the sister rang that day there was little chance he'd be going to meet her that night so he had his first beer of the day at the bar. He could feel himself getting anxious again. In his mind, the reasons why Annabel would *not* want to see him now started to outweighed the reasons why she would.

He'd just ordered another beer and was sitting alone and morose outside the bar when his phone rang. After a day of watching it incessantly and listening out for the slightest noise, its ringing tone surprised him for a moment. He'd turned the volume to high and the sudden noise made others look around and it embarrassed him. He picked it up quickly.

"Hello, is that Luke Adams?" The voice on the other end was almost childlike.

"Yes, Hi, are you Annabel?" said Luke.

"Yes, sorry I didn't ring back sooner. Dr Harper left a message but I didn't notice until just now. I must have been in the gym when he rang."

"It's fine, I only saw him this morning……"

"So, you're a friend of Richard's, I hear. Dr Harper thinks you are a nice man and that I need to meet you."

"I'm hoping you will," Luke said, he wanted to close down the conversation as quickly as possible. He didn't want to tell Annabel lies but he certainly didn't want to tell her Richard was dead over the phone.

"Yes, of course I will meet you," she said brightly. "If you've come all this way then it's the least I can do!" Annabel paused. "Are you free tomorrow morning?"

"Yes, just tell me where and when?" Luke said, eagerly.

"The Spanish Steps at 10am?" Annabel's turned the statement into a question. It amused him that she automatically assumed everyone knew The Spanish Steps.

"Yes, fine."

"I live near the top."

"Yes, that's fine. 10am, top of the steps," Luke repeated back. "Thank you. And thank you for calling back."

"Why wouldn't I? I love my brother and I am concerned about him." Annabel sounded surprised. "I'll see you tomorrow."

And with that she was gone. Luke sensed the change in tone in Annabel's last statement. Her voice was warm and friendly but it had an edge to it. Luke was relieved that Annabel had finally got in touch but the relief now gave way to new concerns about what he would say when he met Annabel…and *where* he should say it. He'd gone along with her suggestion of meeting at the top of The Spanish Steps. Yet he couldn't tell Annabel about her brother on a busy pavement, could he! Luke reprimanded himself, like so often in his life, he just hadn't thought things through. He was always so fixated on the immediate concern he didn't think ahead.

Anyway, Luke told himself, he had to be thankful that fate, in the shape of Thomas, had stepped in and rescued him in Rome. He must trust now that things would work out in the morning. In the meantime, he would eat……and he had to then sort out a couple more days accommodation in the lodge, if they had availability. That was something else he hadn't thought about!

PART TWO

CHAPTER 10: ANNABEL

Luke could not remember the moment he fell in love with Annabel. But looking back on it, he probably fell in love with her the first moment he saw her standing at the top of the Spanish Steps waiting for him. Of course, it was a ridiculous notion - falling instantly in love with a complete stranger, falling in love with a woman with a teenage child, quite probably married and with, who knew, what other baggage; falling in love with a beautiful, confident, elegantly dressed woman who was so far out of Luke's league it was laughable!

By the time Luke had climbed the 138 steps from the fountain and Keats' house on the corner of the piazza, he was breathless. It was an unusually warm, sunny day for March, even for Rome, and Luke was perspiring and panting when he reached Annabel.

He recognised her straight away from the picture. Her face hadn't changed at all, she wasn't wearing as much make-up as he remembered and she didn't need to. Her honey blonde hair was tied into a pony tail and she was wearing a sleeveless linen dress with simple, flat sandals. A leather satchel was slung diagonally from her shoulder. Annabel was a study of understated sophistication.

She obviously recognised Luke too. Luke imagined it hadn't been too difficult to pick out the only Englishman as he reached the top of the steps with his pasty face and arms, and his perspiration.

"Hi, are you Luke?" she said, smiling.

"Yes, Hi," Luke said, breathlessly. "Bloody Hell, you didn't warn me there'd be *that* many steps!" he said, in an effort to relax them both. "I think I need oxygen!"

They shook hands. She was wearing a wedding ring he noticed.

"To be honest I hardly ever climb them. I drive up here, round that way." She waved her hand in the general direction of the road. "Should we go and have a coffee? There's a lovely little bar just a little down there." Again, she used her hands to indicate the general direction. Luke was relieved that she'd suggested somewhere they could sit down. He deliberately started small talk to buy himself time.

"I could do with a drink. Where I'm staying is only a couple of miles out of the city but it seems to take an age by bus," he said.

"Where's your hotel, then?"

"It's a campsite actually…"

Annabel started laughing. "Please tell me you're not sleeping in a tent!" she said.

"No, I've not done that since I was seventeen. It's a kind of lodge. But it's nice. And there's a pool and a bar," Luke added.

"So how long are you staying?" Annabel asked.

"Well I've just booked two more nights so I imagine I'll have to think about getting back, Monday."

When they got to the bar, Luke asked Annabel what she'd like to drink. The waiter clearly knew Annabel as he started to talk to her in a mix of Italian and broken English. She laughed as he launched into a long narrative. Luke felt a bit awkward standing with two coffees in his hand listening to a language he could not understand. Annabel soon became aware of this and backed away, taking her coffee from Luke as she did. Luke sat on a table near the back of the bar and Annabel followed in slow steps as she gradually released herself from the over-attentive Italian. The bar was quiet and the waiter had plenty of time to chat but Luke was impatient to talk to Annabel and wished he would leave her alone.

"I'm sorry," she said when she finally came to the table, "I could see you were getting impatient. So, let's talk..." she said with an open-handed gesture and a smile.

"Annabel, I'm sorry......" Luke paused and steeled himself for the next statement, "But I've come to tell you that Richard is dead."

"What?" Annabel stared at Luke, waiting for him to say something else, something that would somehow contradict his last statement. She let out one of those little laughs the way people do when they are told something so serious it is assumed to be some sick joke. "How?" she said, "I mean, are you sure? Was he sick?" Tears immediately started to fill up Annabel's eyes, eyes that had been dancing a matter of seconds before.

"He hung himself," Luke said, quietly. "Annabel, I'm so sorry......"

Annabel's silent tears gave way to loud sobs at this latest revelation and the tears ran down her face and into her mouth. The waiters in the bar stopped suddenly. They looked towards Annabel with concerned faces at this sudden transformation. Luke made a gesture to them that he was taking care of things and he moved from the seat opposite Annabel to the seat next to her. Although it felt awkward, he put his hand on her shoulder. Annabel's body shook with each sob.

Luke had expected a barrage of questions at this point but Annabel just sobbed. He handed Annabel the serviette to dab her tears and the waiter came over with extra ones then backed away. He resumed his position at the bar with the other waiter and started an earnest conversation, no doubt conjecturing about the news that had so suddenly changed Annabel's mood.

"Did he leave a note?" she asked in almost a whisper.

"No. Well, at least the police didn't find one," Luke said, quietly.

"So why did he do it?" Her question was followed by a fresh burst of loud sobbing. Her slender frame shook under Luke's hand.

"I don't know, I really don't know. It doesn't make sense to me." Luke paused. "I was hoping you might know of something......"

"I haven't seen him for ages," she said.

"The phone call?" Luke prompted, gently.

Annabel looked up for the first time since she'd received the news of her brother's death. Her eyes were red and tears ran down her face. It was a beautiful face, Luke thought, even in grief.

"We rowed," she said, finally. This statement was followed by fresh sobs, even louder and deeper than before.

"What did you row about?" Luke asked gently. "Tell me to mind my own business…"

"No, no……we rowed about father, actually. Richard thought I should come over and see him before he died." She stopped. "Is he……?"

"I think he's still alive." Luke paused. "He's very sick, though."

"You and Richard, were you partners?" she asked suddenly, as if the thought had just crossed her mind.

"No. We were just friends. I was married but my wife died. Richard was a good friend to me." Luke paused again as Annabel continued to sob. "Your brother was a *good* man," continued Luke, placing special emphasis on the adjective.

"Thank you," Annabel said. She smiled for the first time since she had heard the news and touched Luke's hand, the hand that was still on her shoulder. "Thank you for coming all this way to tell me in person. You must be so sad, too," Annabel said, kindly. "And losing your wife…what was her name?"

"Sarah. She died three years ago," said Luke.

"I'm sorry. She must have been young?"

"Yes, 43, actually. Cancer."

Annabel patted Luke's hand and paused for a moment in thought.

"Do you think Richard was sick?" she asked. "That's why he did it?"

"I don't know. I don't think so. He seemed very fit. He did Ironman," Luke announced.

"What?"

"It's a challenge where you run a marathon then swim across a lake and then cycle. You've got to be super fit to do it." Luke paused. "Anyway, I'm sure the inquest will say if there was anything wrong with him." Luke thought as he spoke that he must try to find out from Sophie whether the autopsy found anything like cancer.

Annabel started sobbing again. "Do you think our row could have made him kill himself?" She stared into Luke's face as she asked, searching for a reaction.

"No, of course not!" Luke said adamantly, although secretly he was eager to know what exactly had transpired that evening.

"*He* rang you, yes?" Luke asked.

"Yes, just out of the blue. It was a Friday night, I think, and Russ was back and he had some people round." She paused. "I'd tried ringing him quite a few times before but he never picked up. Then suddenly it was him on the phone ringing me."

Luke was processing this. He'd always believed that Annabel had turned her back on Richard, not the other way round.

"So, didn't you want to see your father?" he prompted.

"No…*No*!" she repeated, emphatically, as if she was surprised by Luke's question. "He was quite prepared to keep me away from my mother when *she* was dying." She suddenly stopped and stared intently at Luke. "You know, he wanted my mother to die thinking her children didn't care about her. He wanted to punish her."

"What for?" asked Luke, shaking his head.

"For having an affair years ago. He never forgave her. That's what Richard and I rowed about. I told him he had more cause to hate his father than I did." Annabel's tone was now bitter. "He thought he was adopted, you know?"

"Thought?" said Luke, surprised.

"Well, he wasn't. And that's what I told him." Annabel paused, waiting for Luke's judgement. "I was drunk…I know I shouldn't have told him, but I was so angry." She stared at Luke appealing to him, wanting him to say something to make it right. "I was *so* angry, like all the years it had been bubbling under and then in that moment it came to a head." Annabel paused. "It was not with Richard really, it was father."

"So Mr Harrington is Richard's real biological father?" Luke asked.

"No, but his mother, Ruth, was his *real* mother. As I said, she had an affair. My father threw her out when he found she was pregnant. And then after she'd had the baby he took her back." Annabel paused recalling the events as they had been told to her. "But they'd told everyone they couldn't have children so he made everyone believe that he and mother had adopted Richard." Annabel was wringing the serviette she held until it was a chord of tissue. "You know, he's never told Richard - he's let him believe all these years that his real mother killed herself years ago." Annabel was bitter again. "And he forbade my mother to tell Richard anything different. I think that's another reason why he kept us away when she was dying. He knew she'd want to tell us." Annabel paused and then said, defiantly, "Well, she told *me*. She didn't let the truth go to the grave with her!"

"How come you got to see her then?" Luke asked.

Annabel let out a bitter sigh. "I got a nasty letter from my auntie telling me how disgusting I was for abandoning my mother on her deathbed! I raced over to Oxford to this horrible nursing home he'd put her in. I was living in London at the time. She was very sick but she wanted me to know about Richard and her affair." Annabel paused. "She died that night, like she was holding on to speak to me."

"Bloody hell," Luke interjected.

"And then at the funeral, my father made out like it was all very sudden and he didn't know his wife was dying. It was crap, of course! I haven't seen him since the funeral. I hate him for what he did."

"So why didn't you tell Richard at the time? About his real mother?" Luke said as gently as he could.

"I couldn't, I just couldn't. I wanted to." Annabel paused. "I was going to…I got in the car and drove over to where he lived at the time. It was in Abingdon, he'd got his first job and had moved out and was sharing this flat with a guy from work." Annabel continued to play with the serviette. "You know, I sat in that car for an hour just watching him. But I just couldn't ruin his life, like that. He'd suffered enough with my father and he was just getting his life together. It would have broken his heart."

Annabel started to weep again. "Then just because I was angry and drunk I did just that – I broke his heart. And that's why he killed himself, isn't it?" With that Annabel broke into a new wave of sobbing. "I didn't want to hurt him, Luke, I really didn't," Annabel said appealing desperately to Luke who thirty minutes earlier had been a stranger to her. "I wanted to hurt father, not Richard!"

Luke removed his arm from Annabel's shoulder, he turned to face her and held both her hands in his hands. Then he looked directly into Annabel's face, forcing her to pay attention to him as he spoke: "Now, listen to me, Annabel," Luke began, "I do not believe Richard killed himself. And I am quite certain he would not have killed himself over what you told him." Luke paused and saw that he had Annabel's attention. "I'm sure he was probably upset by the news and angry with his father and maybe even with you a little," Luke continued, "but he was in his local pub on the Sunday after you spoke to him and *everyone* said he was ok. No different, everyone said." Luke tried to sound as reassuring as he possibly could. "So please, Annabel, get that thought out of your mind straight away. You are *not* responsible for Richard's death."

Annabel kissed Luke gently on his cheek. "Thank you, Luke, thank you," she said. "But what do you mean, you don't believe he killed himself?"

"Well, I just don't. Firstly, he took his Catholicism very seriously - he went to mass and confession. And he believed suicide is a mortal sin……"

Annabel suddenly started to laugh. Luke stopped talking, surprised by this sudden change. "Boy, the apple doesn't drop far from the tree, does it!" she said.

"What do you mean?"

"Well, mother was very religious!"

And you? asked Luke. "Are you religious?"

"Me?" A seriousness came over Annabel's face. "I used to…"

"Used to…?" Luke prompted.

"Well you know, life is complicated…things happen and…" Annabel seemed to be searching for words.

"I know what you mean," Luke said, trying to help her out. He imagined the sudden news about her brother had done nothing to enhance her belief in a benevolent creator.

Luke smiled in an effort to lighten the mood. "I've only known you for a matter of minutes and here I am asking you intimate questions about whether you believe in God. Sorry."

"It's ok, it is something I think about a lot," Annabel said, earnestly.

"Let's change the subject," Luke said, "I was just trying to reassure you that Richard and I did talk about suicide but he said that he couldn't understand anyone ever resorting to it." Luke paused then asked. "Did you know he suffered from anxiety and he took pills for it?"

"No, poor boy."

"Yeah, we had that in common. He'd read up on it a lot and he really helped me to cope better with my anxiety. That's how he saw it - something you had to accept and manage."

"Could his anxiety have just got too much?" Annabel asked.

"Well, as I said, he knew more about anxiety than anyone - including the doctors - and he always knew it would pass. That's what he always told me when I was bad." As Luke continued, Annabel stared at him intently. "And, as I said, he was in the pub Sunday. If Richard had been really bad that weekend after you spoke to him, he'd have been in his house alone trying to relax and waiting for the anxiety to pass."

After Luke had finished talking, Annabel released her hands from Luke's hands and picked up another serviette and dabbed her eyes. She attempted a watery smile. "Do you fancy a beer? I think I need one!" she said.

"Will they serve us at this time?" Luke asked.

"Of course, this is Italy!" Annabel exclaimed, good-humouredly. Luke was pleased that his words had made a difference to her mood. He went to the bar and ordered two beers. When he tried to pay the waiter waved him away.

"Thank you," Annabel said, when he returned.

"Don't thank me, thank the waiter," said Luke, gesturing over to him with his head.

Annabel smiled, warmly at the waiter. "Are you ok for time, by the way?" she asked.

"Yes, as long as you are," Luke said.

"I want you to talk to me about Richard," she said, suddenly becoming serious again. "Did he have a partner, do you know?"

"No. Nothing serious anyway. I saw him with a couple of girls…not at the same time, may I add!" Luke said, with a smile.

Annabel smiled too at Luke's attempt at humour. Luke told Annabel about how Richard worked for British Aerospace and how highly he was thought of there. Luke talked for the next hour about his friend. Annabel's eyes filled with tears at times, and, when they did, Luke would try and change the subject and ask Annabel about *her* life.

Annabel told Luke how she had come to Rome to work as a nanny for an English family. She lived with them for a while and Eva, her own daughter, became like a sister to the other children. But then she met Russ and she and Eva moved in with him when the family went back to England. He was part of the expat community and sold homes in Tuscany to other Brits wanting to 'live the dream'. He also had a few properties that he rented out too. After they were married he expanded the business into Provence. "He is always away," Annabel said. She told Luke that her daughter, Eva, was 'a bit of a handful' but lovely. Apparently, she'd gone AWOL a couple of times and she and Russ didn't get on at all. Russ wasn't Eva's real father, a fact that Eva was quick to remind Russ about whenever he 'interfered' in her life.

Eva's biological father was a struggling rock musician in London who had his fifteen minutes of fame in the '90s. Annabel was a wild child then, after the death of her mother and falling out with her father.

"I guess it was my rebellion, really," she said, "but Eva's father was a total waste of space. I knew that wasn't ever going to work."

"But you kept the baby?" Luke prompted.

"Yeah, my friends thought I was mad. It was bloody hard - Eva's father didn't have a regular income and so he didn't help at all with maintenance. In fact, he was spectacularly disinterested in every aspect of Eva!" Annabel added, bitterly. "So, yeah, it was hard. Having to work, doing all sorts of shit jobs and trying to bring up a baby. My friends in London were fantastic though."

Annabel went on to explain how Eva had now built up this romantic notion of her maverick 'rock and roll' father living somewhere in England. This frustrated Annabel and annoyed the hell out of her husband Russ, who had always supported Eva since Annabel and he had got together.

Now Annabel seemed to be living the dream in Rome - she told Luke about her house which sounded fantastic - but she also admitted to Luke that she was bored and lonely. She spoke a little Italian but didn't really have friends in Rome, except for an English lady she'd grown quite close to after her husband died. She found little in common with most of the expats, apart from the obvious fact they were all living in the same foreign city. Annabel chatted with some of the parents at The American School but they lived across the city from her, so she didn't see them often. When Russ was around they'd go out for meals. It frustrated Annabel that he spoke fluent Italian and picked up and then discarded friends at will. Their friends, she had to admit, were Russ' friends first and foremost.

But Annabel loved the city and she loved the lifestyle. She loved it most at the weekends when Eva was home and they could go shopping together and go for coffee and cakes in the dazzling choice of cafes and bars in the city.

Luke bought more drinks and he insisted on paying this time. The bar was filling up with customers as it was approaching dinner time. Annabel and Luke had bruschetta, she said they made the best bruschetta in Rome. Luke was impressed with the sweetness of the tomato and the perfect balance of the garlic, red onion, fresh chilli and olive oil.

"What are you doing for the rest of the day?" Annabel asked, after they'd finished their bruschetta.

"Well, I guess I'm going to get the bus back to the campsite." Luke hadn't given much thought to what he'd be doing after meeting Annabel. All he knew was that he didn't want to leave her. Not now, anyway.

"Would you like to come and see my house?" Annabel said, suddenly. "Eva will be back soon and I'd like you to meet her." She paused. "You know, she never met her uncle."

At that moment Luke's phone bleeped, he'd got a new text message. It was Rachel: *"How's it going?"* it said. Luke realized he had not even mentioned Rachel to Annabel.

"I'd forgotten to say. I met your old nanny, Rachel, at Richard's funeral. That's her texting," he said.

Annabel looked surprised. "Is she still alive?"

"Yes, but she's very sick. Actually, it was she who persuaded me to come and find you." Annabel looked surprised. "You see, she knew that Richard had rung you. He rang whilst he was at his father's. She was desperate for you to know that Richard had died because she knew none of his family would ever make an effort to find you." Luke paused. "*And* she wanted me to find out what you two had been talking about that night…because she knew after that conversation that Richard had clearly made up his mind he wasn't ever going to see his father again."

"Well, I assumed Rachel knew it all anyway," Annabel said, coldly, "she's always been very close to father!"

"I'm sure she didn't," Luke said. "I'll ask her, though."

Hi. With Annabel now. Told her about Richard. Obviously upset. She says they rowed about their father. Did you know that Richard was not adopted? Ruth was his real mother. She had an affair. x

You've found Anna. Fantastic! Please send her my love to her and tell her I think about her every day. Ruth was Richard's real mother!! I really didn't have a clue but it explains a lot! Is Anna sure?

Yes, her mother told her just before she died. She went to see her the day before she died. x

I really didn't know any of this. I never understood why she never came back to see me or her father. I should have tried to find out, but I just believed her father's version of events. I've been a fool - I thought Anna had deserted us all. Please tell her I'm so sorry. I didn't know, I promise I didn't. xx

Luke showed Annabel the text thread and then texted Rachel back to say he was going to see Annabel's house and he would be back in touch.

"I feel really bad now, if that's true," she said. "If she really didn't know, then she'd have been very confused and upset that I'd never been in touch. I always imagined my father and her shared everything. Including a bed!" Annabel spat out the words.

"You think!"

Annabel paused, her head down. "Oh, I don't know. I don't know for certain. Richard said so and I guess it makes sense - his revenge on mother." Annabel paused again. "I really don't *know* anything when it comes to my father."

Luke thought that if Richard had said it then it was probably true – he certainly wasn't one for mere gossip.

"So, she says she didn't even know I'd even *seen* mother?" Annabel continued. "My father didn't tell her."

"No, it seems not," said Luke. "If she's telling the truth. Of course if Richard was right about Rachel and your father, she might have a motive to lie. But then why send me looking for you?"

Annabel started to cry again.

"Hey, I thought you were going to show me your cool house. And your 'difficult' daughter!" Luke adopted a deliberately upbeat tone.

Annabel smiled again and once again dabbed her tears away. After Luke had paid for the dinner Annabel led the way to her home, retracing the way they had taken from the top of the steps. It was really warm now and the sky was cloudless and blue. The road back to the steps afforded an elevated view of the dome of St Peters and the river opened out ahead of them. Luke took in the vista, scouring it for recognisable landmarks he'd seen in films and pictures. This was so much the centre of civilisation in the western world. It had been the centre of everything, Luke thought to himself, as he walked alongside his beautiful new friend.

"Dr Harper said you were a teacher," Annabel said, suddenly, as they walked. "Secondary or Primary?"

"Secondary, I'm not good with young children. Mind, I've been starting to think I'm not so good with children. Full stop!" Luke replied.

"So, what's your subject?"

"English."

"You and Eva will get on famously," Annabel said, excitedly, "she adores English. In fact, she won't read anything that's *not* by an English writer, well a British writer! She was in a right sulk because she had to read The Great Gatsby! And in an American school! Outrageous!" Annabel laughed. "She's bloody hard work, my daughter!"

"Trust me, I've taught a lot like that….!"

"I bet you have! Mind you, I think Eva's a little angel at school. They always tell me she is…then again when you are paying the fees we are they will probably tell you anything!"

Luke and Annabel were back at the top of the steps now.

"Ok, it's just over there," she said pointing in a general direction again.

Luke tried to follow the direction of her hand. If he was correct, she was pointing in the direction of a group of very grand houses with large balconies that looked straight onto the iconic steps and down to the piazza below.

Annabel led Luke down a narrow street just off to the left where there was a long terrace of period houses on three floors, made of dark stone. Their front doors led straight onto the street and their windows on the ground floor were shuttered. The shutters on the upper floors were open and some of the windows had small balconies.

"Here we are," Annabel said, as she opened the door of the third house along the street.

The door opened into a world of white, modern and bright and a complete contrast to the traditional outside of the house. There was a large vestibule with a highly polished marble floor and doors on either side. It was dominated by an impressive staircase and Luke followed Anna up to what was obviously the main living area. Again, everything was white. Towards the front of the house, and the windows that looked onto the street, there were two living rooms, one with a small balcony and a large ornate fireplace which dominated the room. All the original features were still there - the intricately detailed coving, the picture rails, an enormous chandelier. But the room was made bright and contemporary and chic by the flecked white walls and the brilliant white woodwork. It was dominated by two long white settees, arranged at right angles. The dark wood flooring had been retained and a large white rug covered the central area. No place for a dog, thought Luke!

Annabel proudly showed the other living room to Luke. It was smaller and more intimate. This was clearly the room where Annabel relaxed in the evening with her husband and daughter. It was still light but not white, more of an ivory colour and the cushions and throws on the settees this time introduced colour: deep reds and gold. There was a large TV and sound system to the right of the room between the window and another original fireplace. The flooring was the same as the bigger room but it had a darker square of carpet in the centre.

The back of the house was open plan with a large combined kitchen and dining room and a tiled floor. The whole back wall had been removed and replaced with glass doors that concertinaed back so that the balcony became an extension of the room. The large balcony, in turn, looked out onto the Spanish Steps.

To the right of the room was a long table with enough settings for a large dinner party. Once again, everything was white but the wall adjacent to the table introduced some colour with three large paintings. They looked like Tuscan scenes done in a style reminiscent of Cézanne, Luke thought, where nature was captured in blocks of colour. But the colours, unlike Cezanne's palette, were orange and gold and deep red and blue, giving the space a bright, contemporary feel.

The left side of the room, the part immediately in front of them as they walked in from the hallway, was dominated by a white kitchen with a central island surrounded by high seats. Above this, was the centre-piece of the room, a large light made up of thousands of small shards of coloured glass and twisted silver. Unlike the front rooms this space was contemporary, like one of those Manhattan loft apartments Luke had seen in the glossy lifestyle magazines he flicked through at the dentist.

Annabel picked up two beers from the American-style fridge and opened them. She opened two of the glass panels and Luke followed her out onto the balcony, now bathed in afternoon sun.

"Well, bloody hell!" said Luke, with a gesture that took in everything.

"I know, I'm very lucky. Russ and I hit on a rich vein a few years back - lots of bankers from London." She laughed. "Probably getting out before the crash!"

"It's very impressive, Annabel," Luke said, seriously. "And it's so…" Luke searched for the word. "…it's so very tasteful."

"I'm glad you said that." Annabel beamed. "I designed everything."

"Wow, you *are* clever!"

Luke's leant over the glass panel at the end of the balcony and sipped his beer. His eyes followed the steps down to the piazza and the fountain at the foot of the steps with its turquoise water. Little figures were milling around and taking photographs. Luke could have poured beer onto the heads of tourists climbing the steps, he was that close. When he raised his eyes and looked ahead, the whole city lay before him - the Colosseum was to his left and as he panned across to the right he could see the dome of the Pantheon and the jumble of ancient towers and facades that he knew must have had enormous cultural significance. And behind all this was the now familiar sprawl of St Peters.

"Wow!" Luke said again. He stood in silence for a moment taking it all in. "Doesn't it phase you, people looking at you, like you're a film star?" he asked.

"Well they can't really see us once we sit down because this glass is frosted," Annabel said. "But I must admit I do get a little embarrassed." She smiled. "Russ loves it, though!"

"So, where's your husband then? Did you say Tuscany?" Luke asked.

"Tuscany or Provence, yeah. He has a girlfriend out there," Annabel added casually.

"I'm sorry, I shouldn't be asking you all these questions," said Luke, embarrassed by Annabel's candidness.

"No, it's fine. Really, it's fine." She smiled. "To be honest we get on far better now. And he needs to be over there with the business too."

"Well, I guess all this needs a lot of paying for!" Luke said, gesturing around him.

"Well, as I said we had this bumper few years and we bought it outright. We had to gut the place - it had been owned by an artist who lived on the top floor and used the rest of the building as his studio and storage. Those paintings in the kitchen are his work." Annabel fell into a cushioned seat and patted the one next to her. "Now come here and sit down," she said, "I want you to talk about Richard again."

"Well, what do you want to know?" Luke paused in thought: "He was a rather quiet, self-contained man, you know."

"He wasn't when he was younger." Annabel looked sad. "But Father was always snapping at him. And worse! Nothing was ever good enough." Annabel paused as she reflected. "Of course, it all makes sense thinking back. He was punishing Richard for his mother's betrayal, as he saw it."

"Yeah, he told me his father was horrible to him. Of course, he never understood why his father took such a dislike to him. He thought it was just because he was adopted and - well - when you came along, his *real* child…"

"And I was such a little bitch at times. Bloody hard work. Like Eva, I guess," Annabel said with a sigh, "and Richard tried so hard to please father…worked so hard at school, was the perfect son." She sighed. "And suddenly he just gave up. Like he'd given it his best shot."

"But I'm sure your mother loved you both."

"Oh yes, but when she showed Richard any affection father would be even nastier to him so she stopped, at least when he was around. And yet it was Richard who went to see the old bastard. He obviously didn't hold any grudges."

"He was just a lovely bloke. I've never heard him say a bad word about anyone." Luke smiled as he recalled Richard. "But he didn't give too much away, you know."

"It's not surprising is it! It was his way of protecting himself. Tuck everything in if you are being kicked," Annabel said, sadly.

"And when you get into that mindset it stays with you. I've taught kids like that," said Luke.

Annabel went back into the kitchen to get a couple more beers.

"Bloody hell, I'm going to be pissed on the bus home!" Luke said, although he didn't refuse the bottle that was offered him.

"Well, I'm in a mood for getting very drunk!" Annabel sipped from the bottle.

They sat and talked for another couple of hours. Luke told Annabel about Richard 's house in Darwen and how it had saddened him to see it after he had died. He remembered he'd brought along the picture of Richard and Annabel he'd rescued from Richard's wall. Annabel cried again when she saw it. Luke then brought out the more recent picture of himself and Richard in their cycle gear and that seemed to make Annabel cry even more.

And then Eva arrived home. Luke wondered where she'd been all day. It was Sunday so she hadn't been in school. "Hi, where are you?" she called out in a loud, sing-song and confident voice.

"Darling, I'm out here. Come and meet Luke?" Annabel shouted.

Eva looked like a younger version of her mother. Fair, slender, the same loose fitting clothes. She had a leather satchel on her back and a wire coming out of the bag to some earphones that were now dangling around her neck. Luke stood up to greet her.

"This is Luke, you remember I told you I was meeting Richard's friend from England today?" Annabel said.

"Oh yes, Hi." She smiled sweetly at Luke and did that little self-conscious wave that young girls tend to do.

Then Annabel took hold or Eva's hands, preparing her for an announcement: "He's told me your Uncle Richard's dead."

"Oh, no! I'm sorry mum," she said, pulling her mother towards her and hugging her. She didn't ask any questions. Luke couldn't decide whether Eva was just being sensitive or whether she really wasn't that interested. Yet why would she be interested? Her uncle was a stranger to her! Luke felt certain that Annabel was relieved Eva had not wanted more details.

"Hey, Luke's a teacher. He teaches English," Annabel said trying to include Luke again.

"I just love English," Eva said.

"Yes, your mum said. So, what are you reading at the moment?" Luke asked, trying to show some interest in the daughter.

"Oh, 'Tess' and 'Death of a Salesman' and some war poetry. But I'm reading 'Lady Chatterley's Lover' at home.

"You really do like English, don't you! Don't you find D H Lawrence a bit wordy?" asked Luke. "I always did."

"Well, he's a bit rude!" Eva said, laughing. "But that's probably why I chose it!"

"Did you know when it first came out it had to be sold in a brown paper bag in England? I think it still holds the record for the use of the F word!"

"What, more than Roddy Doyle in The Commitments!" Eva said, surprised.

"Bloody hell, you are a reader! I'm impressed! My GCSE students used to moan about reading 'Mice and Men' and that's tiny."

"I'm not surprised - bloody American rubbish!" she said, dismissively.

"Hey, I'm not having that - it's one of the most perfect books ever written. Have you read it?" said Luke with a smile on his face. He was enjoying talking to Eva.

"Well, no."

"Don't judge a book......" he said, good naturedly.

"Ok, ok I'll give it a go." Eva said with a little bow, as if to acknowledge Luke's superior knowledge on the subject. "It should only take me a lunch break, anyhow!"

Annabel followed the conversation like a net judge. She was quite obviously proud of her daughter and loved the fact she was talking to a grown up so confidently. When Russ was around she usually communicated in a series of grunts, she told Luke later that evening. Eva said she was going to make herself something to eat and then go and do some work.

Luke and Annabel spent the next hour sitting outside drinking a coffee that Eva had made them. Luke noticed how Annabel retreated into herself at times, something he would become quite used to. She had stopped crying but Luke knew she was grieving inside for her brother and who knew what else. Her beautiful blue eyes told their own story, and, although she raised a smile when he caught her eye, Luke knew she was in pain.

"I ought to be thinking about going?" Luke said, suspecting that Annabel would rather be alone.

"Please don't go yet," she said. "I'm sorry, I'm poor company, but I really don't want to be alone."

"You've had a terrible shock," Luke said, "it's probably just starting to hit you."

"Yes, I keep thinking about my last conversation with Richard. What was said, you know? I mean, other than what I've told you already."

"Can you remember anything else?" asked Luke.

"No, but as I said, I was drunk. Did he hang himself at home?"

Luke suddenly realised he'd not told Annabel the full story yet.

"There are some woods where he lived, he was found hanging in there." Luke paused. "Actually, it was me who found him."

"*You* found Richard?" Annabel said in horror.

"Yes, I was out jogging with my dog. I didn't realise at first that it was Richard."

"Oh God, that must have been awful! Oh, Luke, I'm *so* sorry. I didn't think for a moment…"

"Why would you? To be honest I didn't think to tell you either, until now."

They both retreated into their own private thoughts.

"Would you like something to eat?" Annabel said, suddenly breaking the silence.

"What have you got?" asked Luke.

"I was planning on a ready meal from the freezer. But I can make you something, I'm not a great cook but I can put some chicken in the oven. Or stir-fry some prawns. What do you fancy?" Annabel asked, looking in the large fridge and then the freezer next to it.

"Go and sit down and open a bottle of wine, I'll make something," said Luke, suddenly taking control.

"You're my guest, I can't expect you to cook…" Annabel protested.

"I like cooking. Now sit down!" Luke said, smiling.

Annabel obeyed. As Luke began, she opened a bottle of red wine and poured each of them a glass then she put on some Coldplay from her phone and which was linked via Bluetooth to the speakers in the kitchen. *Look at the stars, look how they shine for you.* Then she sat on one of the high stools watching Luke prepare the food. Luke found the prawns in the freezer and defrosted them in the microwave. He cut up onions, chilli and garlic from the fridge and gently cooked them in olive oil, adding smoked paprika and some fresh tomatoes. Soon the smell of the Mediterranean filled the kitchen. Luke added a little salt and went onto the balcony and cut some parsley he'd seen growing in a tub.

"While you're sitting there admiring me, why don't you put on a pan of pasta and grate some Parmesan?" he said to Annabel.

"What song do you want, next?" she asked.

"Can we have a bit of Elgar? It seems fitting somehow."

"Pomp and Circumstance?"

"Bloody hell, no! Nimrod please."

"Coming right up."

"So, are you one of these intellectuals who just listen to classical music? Like Inspector Morse?" Annabel asked.

"Not at all. I just thought with this classical setting and then Richard and all that…sorry."

"No, don't apologise, it's lovely. I didn't know it was called Nimrod, I didn't even know it was by Elgar but it's beautiful."

"I think so, yes," said Luke. They both went about their jobs in silence. Luke caught Annabel staring intently out of the window with fresh tears in her eyes. Luke imagined her looking out to a past life when she and her brother were children and when life was simple and happy and innocent.

After the sauce had cooked down and blended, Luke poured it into a bowl. He cleaned the pan with kitchen paper and poured more olive oil into it. When it was hot he threw in the prawns and some more chilli and a little salt and even more garlic. He squeezed lemon over the prawns and tossed them in the sizzling heat.

"Let me know when the pasta is ready, sous chef?" Luke said, to further lighten the mood he had created.

"You're good, aren't you!" Annabel said. "You know, I'm ashamed to admit it - but I've got this lovely kitchen packed with all the gadgets you could ever need and I hardly ever use it. I either get takeaway or ready meals most of the time," she said. "Can I hire you as my in-house chef?" she asked with a smile.

"Hey, you haven't tasted it yet!" Luke said, "I hope you like chilli!"

"The hotter the better," Annabel said. "I think we'll have it round here, is that ok? We will get a bit lost on that table," she said, gesturing towards the large formal table at the other side of the room.

"Of course," said Luke with a smile.

Annabel cut some bread and set out the table. Then she checked the pasta. "Ok chef, pasta al dente."

Luke drained the pasta, pouring a little of the pasta water into the sauce. He poured the sauce over the prawns and shook them vigorously over the heat. Then he poured the sauce and the prawns onto the pasta and brought it to the table with the grated parmesan cheese.

"Wow!" said Annabel. This looks lovely. She clinked glasses: "To New Friends!" she said.

"New Friends!" Luke repeated.

"Mmmmm, this is *really* good," Annabel said after taking a mouthful. She took another sip of wine.

"Thank you," Luke said, "I used to cook all the time with Sarah. But this is the first time I've cooked a proper meal for years." He paused. "There never seems any point when it's just me."

"I'm the same. I sometime try, but it's not as tasty as this."

"Does Russ cook?" Luke asked, wanting to find out more about their relationship.

"You're joking, aren't you! He likes to go out all the time."

"So, you don't entertain?"

"Sometimes but I do a simple dish, like a roast chicken and a salad."

Annabel and Luke swapped stories about Richard all evening and Eva made the odd appearance when she came down for a drink. Annabel talked of family holidays and Christmas in the Harrington house. She recalled stories from when they were very young - one of them would get into trouble and be grounded in their room and the other would smuggle up goodies. Richard was three years older than his sister but they were best of friends as children. The stories brought a tear or a smile to Annabel's eyes, often both. They finished the wine and the evening went quickly. Luke enjoyed hearing about his friend's life long before he knew him and Annabel appreciated his interest. He asked questions and encouraged her stories.

But Luke suddenly started to feel very sleepy. He'd drunk a lot during the day and he knew it was getting too late to think about the bus home. It would either have to be a taxi back, which would be expensive, or staying over. Annabel must have read his mind.

"Well, you can't go back now, you'll have to stay here," she said. No doubt she'd become aware that Luke's interjections were becoming less frequent and reduced to grunts rather than words.

"Is that ok, are you sure? I can get a taxi," said Luke.

"Don't be daft. We've plenty of room," Annabel said.

"If you don't mind."

"Come on, I'll show you your room, Sir," said Annabel, taking him by the hand and leading him down the stairs.

The room was tastefully decorated as Luke had expected. "I've promised to drop Eva at school in the morning, she's got to take some art stuff and she's embarrassed to take it on the bus. Fancy coming with us?" Annabel asked, just as Luke was closing the door.

"Yeah, sure," he said, immediately.

"Great. You've got a bathroom if you want to shower. And there are towels in there too." She kissed Luke on the cheek.

"Thank you, Annabel," he said.

"And if you're up before us, help yourself in the kitchen."

With that, she was gone. Luke took off his shoes, trousers and shirt and fell into bed in his boxers.

*

He woke at 6am to the sound of a text alert. It was Josh.

I'm in Lanzarote. Flew out to meet Dani after I got back. I told her I was missing her lots and you needed to stay

on in Rome. Hope you've found Richard's sister. See you later. Josh.

Luke allowed himself a smile but he didn't reply. Instead he texted Thomas, thanking him for all his help and telling him that he'd made contact with Annabel and spent the day with her. Thomas texted back immediately to say how delighted he was that things had worked out so well. **I only wished problems could be solved so successfully in Italian education!** he added.

Whilst he had the phone in his hand, Luke remembered he had promised to get back to Rachel. He wrote that it was too early to call but just to say he'd had a lovely day with Annabel and that he was actually staying over at her magnificent house. He said that Annabel was understandably upset about Richard but they'd had a lovely evening reminiscing about him. He told Rachel that Annabel was married to Russ, who was away at the moment, and she had a daughter, Eva, from a previous relationship, who seemed very nice. Luke said he didn't know his plans for the day but he'd ring when he could.

As he was fully awake, Luke put on the white dressing gown he found in the wardrobe and went up the stairs to the kitchen. He took a picture, showing the kitchen in the foreground with the balcony and the view across the city and sent it to Rachel with the text: **She's done quite well for herself, hasn't she!**

Luke made himself a coffee and sat on the high seat looking out over the balcony as the light came up. He Googled the weather in England, taking a childish pleasure in reading that high winds and rain were forecast for Monday.

Luke was soon joined by Annabel in a black dressing gown. She had removed what little make-up she was wearing the previous day but this did not diminish her beauty in any way. In fact, thought Luke, she was somehow even more beautiful as sleep had lent her skin a glow that made her look even more beautiful. She smelt fragrant as she passed by him on her way to the fridge for some fruit juice.

"Morning, Luke. Did you sleep well?" she asked.

"I did, very well. I'm amazed I'm not feeling rough this morning, actually. We drank a lot yesterday." Luke smiled. "You can drink, can't you! Bloody hell!" he said.

She laughed and came and sat by Luke as her kettle boiled.

"You're not telling me northern girls in England can't drink!"

"Well, yeah. But you're so petite and sophisticated. I didn't expect…"

"Didn't your wife drink then?" Annabel asked.

"She'd only have a couple usually. Occasionally she'd get totally pissed at a party or somewhere and then be really sick. She was a lightweight, to be honest." Luke laughed.

"What was she like?" Annabel asked.

Luke paused. "She had a really beautiful face: beautiful shape…and beautiful eyes, beautiful skin. Sorry, that's a lot of repetition!" Luke paused again, his eyes were dewy. "Her beauty was very natural. Like yours." Luke suddenly felt embarrassed by his own comparison. Annabel coyly accepted the compliment with a smile. "But her beauty was different.

She was darker than you and a different build. Not overweight, just a few more curves. And her hair was shorter too. She was quiet, unless you knew her but she had this way of making people feel totally at ease, even complete strangers. She always knew the right questions to ask to let them talk and she made them feel they were the most interesting, most important person in the room." Luke stopped, he hadn't meant to talk so long. "I must admit I'm awkward with strangers, but Sarah wasn't," he added.

"You weren't awkward with me yesterday," said Annabel.

"Thank you," said Luke, appreciating the compliment. "That's because I had something important to say. I would have been ordinarily. I'd have been wrought dumb, intimidated by your beauty and all this," Luke said, gesturing.

Annabel laughed.

"Stop it. You're being silly. You're a confident man, you know. The way you took charge of the meal last night." Annabel stopped, she seemed to be contemplating Luke closely. "And you can talk about feelings too. That's rare - it takes a certain type of confidence."

"Well, I think Sarah encouraged that. As I say, she was such an active listener, if you know what I mean. She gave me confidence." Luke paused for a moment and then changed focus. "And then Richard too, he was like Sarah. He was quiet and unassuming but he would listen intently to what you had to say and then respond with some little bit of wisdom. He could talk about his feelings too."

"I love it when you talk about him," Annabel said, smiling at Luke. Can I get you some toast?"

"Yes, thank you. I'll make you a coffee." Luke said. "I think I'll have another."

They both embarked on their designated tasks in silence for a moment.

"Was Richard into this Carpe Diem thing when he was younger?" Luke said, suddenly.

"What, 'Seize the Day!' No, I don't recall…"

"Well, maybe it was as he got older," said Luke, "he was very into trying to live in the moment. He kept quoting that John Lennon quote: 'Life is what happens whilst you are making plans for tomorrow.'"

"What a cool saying! I must remember that: Life is what happens whilst you are making plans for tomorrow," Annabel repeated.

"Yeah, he felt we should try to live in the present." Luke went on, "to celebrate life, even the dull bits like Monday mornings…" They both laughed. "Not that this is a typical Monday morning, not for me anyhow!"

"Me neither! I'm not usually getting philosophical this early on a Monday!" Annabel said, laughing.

"Yeah, he was always telling me to find the value and the beauty in the mundane as well as the spectacular," Luke continued. "We'd be on our bikes and it would be pissing down or blowing a gale and he'd be shouting over it to me, 'smell the hedge-row'. It was kind of shorthand for: *awaken your senses, take it in.*" Luke paused. "I remember one day we were cycling in The Lakes up 'The Struggle', they call it, and it is! And it was grey and drizzly and depressing. But we got to the top and got off our bikes and he just said, "Look! Look at that beauty! And it was like an epiphany - the low cloud hanging over the valley below us, the warm rain on our skin, the swollen stream running alongside us. And, because of the weather, the quietness…the unexpected quiet of the moment, like your soul whispering to you." Luke paused and became self-conscious. He laughed. "I'm sorry, I do go on…"

"No, I love it. I love it. Thank you. You know, I'm going to try to take his advice," she said. "I'm going to live in the moment." She stopped. "That's all that matters, right?"

"Well yeah, I guess," said Luke, rather taken aback by Annabel's sudden seriousness.

Annabel was lost for a moment in her own thoughts. Then she returned. "What are we doing today, Luke?"

"We?" Luke said, laughing at the sudden change in tone and Annabel's assumption that they would be spending the day together again.

"Yes, before you go home I'm going to make the very best of having you here! Why, you weren't planning anything else, were you?" Annabel looked bemused. "You weren't going back today?" she teased.

"I don't know what I was thinking to be honest," Luke said.

At that moment Eva appeared.

"Come on, mum! You're not even dressed yet. Remember, you're taking me!" Then she noticed Luke, "Good morning Luke. Like the look!" she said smiling and gesturing towards his dressing gown.

Luke wrapped the gown tighter round his chest, slightly embarrassed.

"Luke's coming with us too. Right, I better nip up and have a shower. Can I get you any of Russ' pants or anything? He's a different build but......"

"No, no," Luke interrupted, "I'll be fine," he said. "But I will have to go and get a change of clothes this morning sometime."

"Well we can drive there after we've dropped off Eva," said Annabel.

With that, she went up to her bedroom, leaving Luke and Eva alone in the kitchen.

"I hope you are ok about me coming with you?" he said to her. "I don't want to impose on that mother/daughter time!"

"Of course, it's ok. In fact, it usually ends in a row and me slamming the car door - with you there we will both be on our best behaviour! Just promise me you're not going like that!"

"I'll address it right away." Luke left the kitchen, laughing.

As soon as Luke was ready, the three of them walked down the narrow street to a communal garage where Annabel's car was parked. It was a Mini convertible and poor Eva was cramped in the back with the large case for her art. If Luke had not been with them she'd have automatically gone in the front and put the art across the double seat in the back, but Eva was good-humoured about it. Annabel remarked after she'd left that Eva would have complained all the way had it been Russ and not Luke in the front!

When they got to the American school, Luke thought it would be polite to call in and thank Dr Harper for his help in acting as the honest broker between himself and Annabel. He'd not only passed the message on but had given Luke something of a character reference according to Annabel. Luke was grateful.

And so Luke and Eva walked into the school together. Eva turned left on route to class and Luke stopped again at reception, introduced himself and asking whether he might have a very brief word with Principal Harper. It was a young lady at reception this time and after a brief phone conversation she led Luke to the now familiar waiting room. Dr Harper came out of his office to greet him.

"Come in, Luke, I'm just about to do assembly, but do come in! Success then?" he asked.

"Yes, very much." Luke paused. "I won't keep you, I know you're a busy man. I just wanted to say how grateful I am that you helped Annabel and I make contact. We had a nice day yesterday. And I've met Eva too. It's been lovely," he said.

"Good, good. That's excellent. And how did she take the news of her brother?" Dr Harper was routing through some papers as he spoke.

"She was upset, of course, but I think she appreciated finding out this way. We talked a lot about her brother," said Luke.

"So, what are your plans now?" Dr Harper asked. He had found what he had been looking for.

"I'm spending the day with Annabel then I'll have to think about the journey back, I guess," Luke said, with a short sigh.

"You don't fancy stopping a little longer, do you?" the Principal asked, "I'm desperate for an English teacher." He said it with a smile and it almost seemed like a throwaway comment but Luke could sense it was more than that. "I thought Mrs Blackmore would be back today but she has just rung in to say it will be at least another two weeks!"

"Well, I think I have to get back. But thanks for the offer," said Luke, awkwardly.

"Ok, well thanks for dropping by. Sorry, I can't give you more time," he said.

"No, I understand. Thank you, Dr Harper." And then just as Luke had turned to leave the room he turned back again. "Can I get back to you about the job?" Luke said. "Is it Literature or Language?" He paused. "You *were* serious?" he added.

"Yes. It's both, actually." Dr Harper said, warming to the topic now. "You know Macbeth, I guess? I know that's something that the 10th Grade Students need to be getting on with as soon as possible."

"Yes, I've taught it a lot. I'm just thinking about my dog…and accommodation. But I'll get back, I promise."

"Well thanks. If accommodation is a problem, there might be a spare room here. Anyway, let me know if you could give us a couple of weeks." Dr Harper scurried away in the opposite direction as Luke retracted his steps.

When he got back into the car with Annabel he told her about Dr Harper's offer. She thought it would be a great idea. In fact, she told him to ring back the Principal immediately and accept his offer before he offered it to someone else.

"But I must ring my friends who are looking after my dog first. It's only fair I run it by them. And then it depends on whether Dr Harper has accommodation for me," Luke said. "I can't travel in from the campsite every day."

"You can stay with us," Annabel said, excitedly, "and I'll get you put on the car insurance and you can give Eva a lift too. Sorted."

"I can't just burden you like this. It's not fair," Luke insisted. "And what would Russ say? And I don't even know whether it's full days yet."

"Russ will be fine. Just ring your friends about the dog and then ring Dr Harper and we will take it from there." Annabel paused before a thought struck her: "Hey, you'll be teaching Eva if you're doing Mrs Blackmore's classes! They've had some history teacher trying to muddle his way through recently, but I think some of the parents have started to complain."

Luke did as he was told. He spoke to Emily who said it was 'absolutely fine' about looking after Noah. She asked about progress and Luke gave Annabel the phone so she could introduce herself. After the call had finished, Luke explained that Emily had been Sarah's best friend. Annabel said she'd remembered visiting Chester when she was with Eva's father.

Luke rang Dr Harper who wasn't available but he rang back when Annabel and Luke were packing up at the campsite. He was delighted and relieved that Luke had agreed to his offer and asked whether he could start on the Wednesday. He could give him a full time-table. But Dr Harper said he would need to speak to someone for a reference and as proof he was still working in education and that Luke was who he said he was. This was simply due diligence, Dr Harper explained. Luke quite understood and gave the name and contact details of the agency in Preston. He also gave him Mrs Woods name, his old Head of Department, for a reference. He still saw Miss Wood occasionally and she'd always thought highly of Luke.

They had to leave the car at the gate of the campsite as it was not registered so they walked to the lodge, packed and then carried Luke's two bags back to the car and then returned the keys to reception.

"Did you get a taxi here from the airport?" Annabel asked.

"No, I came down with a friend by car, did I not say?"

"Oh, I didn't realise! I assumed you flew. You mean you drove all the way from England!" Annabel sounded impressed.

"I'm nervous about flying so a friend who knew Richard too offered to drive."

"So where is he now…has he gone back?" she asked.

Luke didn't want to get into the falling out. "Yeah, I think he was missing his wife, to be honest."

"Ah, that's sweet," Annabel said.

"What will you do, then? When you eventually go home…if you won't fly?" Annabel asked as they arranged Luke's stuff in the small boot of the Mini.

"I don't know." Luke really didn't want to think about it. "I guess I will just have to bite the bullet and fly," he said, grimly.

"Anyway, you don't have worry about it for a while now," Annabel said. She beamed at Luke before she put her key into the ignition. "Don't you think this is an exciting adventure…you could be in England now in the rain?"

"Yes and trying to teach a nightmare class that nobody wants!" said Luke.

"Well, you will be appreciated at Eva's school, I just know you will."

Luke smiled. They were soon driving back through Aurelio towards St Peters and the city.

"I'm still wondering whether I should ask Dr Harper if he can find me a room," said Luke. He would have liked nothing better than to stay with Annabel in her fantastic house in the centre of the city but he needed to feel that it would sit well with Russ. He wondered about their relationship. She hardly ever mentioned him and they hadn't been in contact at all whilst he'd been with Annabel.

"Listen, if it makes you feel better, I'll ring him later," Annabel said. There was a hint of impatience in her voice.

“Well, it would actually,” Luke said.

“OK. But today, we are going shopping for clothes. You can't wear that stuff at Eva’s school. We have a reputation to maintain!” Annabel laughed and gestured towards the two bags on the back seat.

“Ok, mum, whatever you say!” Luke teased.

When they got back, Luke ironed and changed his clothes. Annabel was right, his bags consisted of jeans, chinos, t-shirts and jumpers. Most of his clothes were at least five years old and had been chosen by Sarah.

They walked from the house down the steps and into the central shopping area. It was full of expensive names: Hugo Boss, Ralph Lauren, etc. Luke suggested they look in Zara, he thought he could forage in the menswear whilst Annabel looked at the ladies. But Annabel wasn't interested in ladies clothes, she was interested in finding clothes for Luke. Once they'd established that Luke was medium with 32” (or 48 continental) waist, she began selecting things, and, by the time she'd scoured every rail, Luke had around twenty items over his arm.

“Right, try that lot, and let me see them. I'll wait here for you here,” Annabel instructed. She sat on a sofa adjacent to the changing rooms and spoke in Italian to the girl assistant who smiled at Luke, knowingly.

Luke was pleasantly surprised that most of the clothes fitted him well. He was in reasonable shape still and Annabel had picked out dark colours that made him look sophisticated and stylish. She complimented him every time he appeared before her: “Oh, that really suits you, Luke,” and “Wow, who's this sexy man!”

They decided on eight items from Zara: a pair of dark blue trousers and the same in black, a couple of polo shirts, a thin dark grey v neck, two white shirts and a dark grey suit with a herringbone design. When it came to paying there was a heated discussion at the till as Annabel beat Luke to the card machine. Luke protested but Annabel was adamant that she was paying for Luke's new wardrobe.

"You are my new project, Luke," she said. "As my mum used to say: 'clothes maketh the man.'"

They walked across the street and Annabel picked out shoes: a pair of those pointy ones in light brown and a pair of black Chelsea boots. Then they went to an accessory shop where Annabel bought Luke socks and boxers and pyjamas. And then Annabel shepherded Luke to a large departmental store where there were lots of famous labels all under one roof. Annabel found him a light French Connection jacket and a pair of nice jeans. "They fit you nicely round the bum, those old ones just hang off you," she said.

"Now please," said Luke, "can we find somewhere to have a beer? I'm knackered!"

Annabel laughed. "Are you not pleased with our morning's work, though?" she asked, proffering the handful of bags she was carrying.

"I am, thank you. THANK YOU, you are so kind." Luke kissed Annabel on the cheek as they walked down the high street, like lovers would. Then he felt a little embarrassed by this untypical show of affection in public.

"Come on," Annabel said, "I'm going to take you to the best bar in Rome. She was now very much on the front foot. They walked in the direction of the Pantheon and the river to Campo de Fiori.

Luke followed Annabel into The Ristorante Campo de Fiori just off the busy square where market traders shouted good-humoured insults to each other. Franco greeted them, he spoke perfect English and made a fuss of Annabel who introduced Luke as "my new best friend." They ordered Peroni and had three starters between them instead of a main meal: the calamari, the prawns in chilli and garlic and an anti-pasta starter along with a green salad. After dinner, they looked round the bustling market. Luke bought some clams and pasta flour and bread for supper.

"Still living in the moment, then?" Luke asked, as they walked back.

"I am," Annabel said earnestly. "No other thoughts except for right here, right now!" she said impressively.

When they got home, Annabel phoned Russ as she had promised. She was very open about it: "Hello Russ, how are things?" she began, not waiting for his response. "Just calling to say Richard's friend from Darwen is here with me. Yes, how many other Richards do I know!" There was a pause. "Richard was found dead last week." There was a longer pause now. "Yes, suicide apparently. Yeah, I know." Luke could hear her husband talking but he could not make out the words. "Well, I'm upset, of course!" Annabel said, before another longer pause. "He's his mate, as I said." Annabel continued. "He came over to tell me!" There followed another long pause - Russ was obviously talking before Annabel interrupted him "Anyway, that doesn't matter at the moment. Luke's staying with us for a couple of weeks," she said. "Yeah. Yeah, I know." Annabel laughed awkwardly followed by another long pause. "Well, it's a long story, but he's teaching at Eva's school as a stand-in teacher." She laughed. "Yeah, I know. Yeah, Ok, I will. When you next in Rome?" Annabel asked. "Ok." she said. "Bye."

And that was it. "Sorted!" Annabel said, when she came off the phone. It all seemed strange to Luke, but he was relieved that Annabel had now told her husband.

When Eva came home that evening she said her class were all very excited about the news that a real Englishman was coming to teach them English. It was as if he had been out drinking with Shakespeare and walked through The English Lake District with Wordsworth. Luke was secretly delighted that Eva seemed so proud to be associated with this replacement teacher, Mr Adams.

"Well, at least we're going to finally learn something!" she said.

Luke had to model his new clothes for Eva and she applauded loudly when he appeared in each new combination.

Luke made some fresh pasta after the floor show. He mixed the three cups of the pasta flour with three eggs and a little olive oil and salt. Luke rolled it into a ball, put it in a plastic bag and left it in the fridge for an hour. He then rolled it flat and put it through the pasta maker he'd found in a cupboard, still in its box. When he'd made the linguine he hung it to dry on the glass around the balcony.

He fried some onions and garlic and chilli gently in some olive oil, and when it was ready he threw in the clams he'd bought and a glass of white wine. He covered the pan for three minutes, shaking it occasionally, and added a few little tomatoes and parsley - and right at the end a little butter and cream. When the home-made pasta had boiled for two minutes he drained it and threw that in with the clams and mixed it together before bringing it to the table and serving it with bread and Parmesan cheese. Again, Annabel was delighted and full of praise. She'd never had a man cook for her before. Eva loved it too: "It's even better than Campo di Fiori," she said.

After supper, Luke rang Rachel and handed the phone to Annabel so she could talk to her old nanny. Rachel was thankful to Luke for bringing Annabel back into her life. They had been able to make their peace and explain their misunderstandings. Annabel folded her arms around Luke, looked into his eyes and whispered 'thank you'. She kissed him on the mouth and Luke tasted her salty tears. It made him feel good about himself, the whole crazy adventure to Rome seemed worthwhile.

But Annabel had awakened in Luke feelings that frightened him. They *could not* be reciprocated – Annabel was married to Russ and she still wore his ring. Was he caught up in some kind of marital game? Or was it simply her need to express love in the absence of her husband, the right and proper object of her affection?

Dr Harper rang on the Tuesday morning to say he'd done the appropriate checks, and Miss Wood had been positively glowing in her phone reference. He was looking forward to seeing Luke the next day. The Principal had spoken to the Head of English and Luke would be teaching Macbeth to 10th Grade and Reading and Writing skills further down the school. Luke spent most of the day prepping on a laptop he borrowed from Eva, he'd downloaded the Macbeth text and highlighted important quotes in green. Eva had said they were up to Act 1, Scene 7, the Temptation Scene, when Mrs Blackmore went off sick.

After a light lunch on the balcony, Luke and Annabel walked around the city. Luke was surprised at how little of the culture Annabel had seen. They visited The Pantheon and Luke explained about the dome and Roman concrete. Annabel seemed more impressed that the Ancient Romans managed to move and lift enormous columns without cranes and JCBs. They sat outside in the sunshine and listened to a young man play some Vivaldi on a cello. It was beautiful and haunting. Luke quite enjoyed being a tourist with Annabel beside him.

Annabel decided that before he started work Luke needed a haircut and beard trim and she gave detailed and precise instructions to the barber, in a mix of gesture and simple Italian phrases. On the way back to Annabel's house they stopped at the piazza at the foot of the Spanish Steps near Keats' house, another expat who had come to Rome, in an effort to extend his tragically short life. Annabel took Luke's picture in front of the plaque on the wall to send to Miss Wood along with a 'Thank You' for the reference.

They called in a café in the piazza for a drink before climbing back up the steps. Annabel insisted on taking a photo of him on her phone. She had done a good job, they both agreed, when they studied the picture. Luke's new haircut and beard trim made him look younger, and together with the clothes that Annabel had bought he looked every bit the sophisticated Italian about town.

CHAPTER 11: THE AMERICAN SCHOOL.

Annabel couldn't have been more helpful. As promised, she put Luke on her insurance so that he could drive her car into work and this meant that he and Eva could travel together. He was made welcome at The American School by staff and students alike. The students were mainly children of well-heeled Americans working in the city of Rome and so different to students Luke has taught in the UK. In the UK, you were seen as a 'Keeno' if you wanted to work hard and showed any genuine enthusiasm for a subject. In fact, some regarded you as positively weird and you were often bullied for it. But in The American School that was the norm and the disengaged students were the outsiders. The students at The American School were extraordinarily respectful towards the staff, they greeted them with a 'Good afternoon, Mr Adams' and sat in reverent silence when Mr Adams spoke, hanging on his every word.

Eva's class were a special delight. They were grateful to The Englishman for helping navigate them through the obscure 16th Century language. And they engaged enthusiastically with the themes and the characters and seemed far more excepting of the language than their English counterparts. They wanted to discuss Lady Macbeth's influence on her husband and most were convinced that Macbeth would not have gone through with the murder if it had not been for her. Some of them, including Eva, who led the discussion, felt she sacrificed herself for her husband, whilst others felt she was just an angry and bitter woman, defying God for taking her baby from her.

Luke found it strange to see how the American culture with its strong religious mind-set made for a very different reading of the play than in England. Much closer, Luke guessed, to how an audience would have treated it at the time Shakespeare wrote it. They took the witches very seriously and were appalled that Macbeth could be seemingly so reckless in 'jumping the life to come'. And they were appalled at the scene where Lady Macbeth calls upon evil in a demonic parody of the Christian conversion ritual.

Eva and Luke carried on the lesson as they travelled home that night.

"So, I'm guessing *you* believe in fate?" Eva said, as soon as she got in the car.

"Well, yes, to a certain extent." Luke paused. "For example," he said, "if I hadn't happened to walk into a bar in Como on the way up here I'd have never met the nice man in education and I'd have never have found you or your mum."

"You may have found us another way, who knows," Eva countered.

"So, you don't believe in fate!" Luke countered.

"I'm not sure. I think you make your own luck…or bad luck!"

"Yes, I do too…to a certain extent. But it's a balance. That's what Shakespeare's saying - the witches and Macbeth's wife influence him. And if he hadn't been married to a woman like that, and if their baby hadn't died then maybe he wouldn't have killed the king and would have gone on to have a happy life and died in his bed at a ripe old age surrounded by his friends. But, at the end of the day, he made a bad choice so maybe it's a bit of both." Luke smiled. "Sorry, am I sounding like a teacher?"

"Well, I think we are all responsible for our own happiness," said Eva, firmly, ignoring Luke's attempt to lighten the mood.

"Oh, the brave idealism of youth!" Luke's voice betrayed a slightly bitter tone.

"Are you taking the piss, Mr Adams?" Eva asked.

"Well, my wife got breast cancer - an inherited gene because her mother had breast cancer. They both died of breast cancer." He looked across at Eva. "Neither had much choice in that!"

Eva went quiet. "I'm sorry, I didn't know that," she said.

"But I think you are right in many ways. We *are* responsible for our own happiness in terms of the things we can control. And sometimes I must admit I do nothing and allow circumstance to dictate. I need to be more…" Luke searched for a word, "…more Existential!"

"But then it's the pressure of doing the right thing - making the right decision, isn't it? *That* stops us from acting. I live in a lovely house and I have to admit I have a comfortable life and mum is fantastic. But I've got to make some choices about next year after I've finished Grade 10." Eva was intense and serious and Luke was impressed. He knew he would have never been able to articulate such things at a similar age.

"What are you thinking?" Luke asked.

"I'd like to go back to England, to London, and study. But mum would miss me terribly." Eva fixed her gaze on Luke as he drove. "She's lonely, you know?" she said.

"Is Russ away a lot?" Luke asked.

"Yes. Here's hardly ever here, which suits me fine. And I don't think mum's bothered about Russ anymore. It's not that," Eva said.

Luke wanted to ask more about the relationship but felt it was wrong to quiz Eva. He changed the subject and they talked about Eva's friends at school before they got back to the house and Annabel.

"How was your first day at school?" Annabel asked Luke.

Eva answered before Luke had chance, "Good. We had this new teacher in English," she said, smiling, "the girls said they thought he was quite cute. For an older man, that is!"

"But could he teach?" enquired Annabel, maintaining the little pretence.

"He could, actually. He was good," said Eva, smiling at Luke.

"Well, that's a relief!" said Annabel. "Did anyone comment on his nice suit and shoes…and his tie?"

"No-one, I'm sorry Annabel, your exquisite taste was wasted on them all," interjected Luke.

"Well, I think you look very handsome," she said. "I thought that we'd go out for something to eat. To celebrate."

"Only if you let me pay," said Luke, "as a thank-you for my new wardrobe."

"Ok, but we are going cheap and cheerful. What about that bar I took you to when we first met?"

They talked about England and the north during the meal. Annabel was keen to reminisce, and Eva was fascinated by all things English. Annabel told them how she'd been to Liverpool with Eva's dad when he played in club down Mathew Street, opposite where The Cavern used to be. Although Annabel was a little younger than Luke, they had liked the same music at the time and discovered they had both seen The Clash on the White Riot tour and pogoed in sweaty clubs until they nearly passed out with heat and exhaustion.

Eva was fascinated to learn about this part of her mother's life and how she talked so openly about Dave, Eva's father. Dave was a bass player in a band called The Barbed Wire of Auschwitz who went on tour with The Damned and were expected to go big, but it had never worked out. Annabel said it was probably down to the fact that they had a shit name and a singer that made Johnny Rotten sound like a choirboy! Eva laughed. A veil had been drawn over this part of her mother's life up but after a few beers - and with Luke to prompt her - Eva now saw a new side to her mother, a carefree, reckless side. She wished she could somehow be transported back in time to see her, the young Annabel before Rome and Russ.

Luke was enjoying the evening too. He ordered a mushroom risotto and Annabel had pasta parcels of butternut squash and ricotta cheese in a butter and sage sauce. Eva insisted on chicken and chips, as English as she could find in an Italian bar!

As they all walked home, arm in arm, the light was fading in the west and the city skyline was in silhouette and monochrome, except for the orange glow of the setting sun.

If Luke had been at home in England, he would be shut up inside alone, with wind and rain beating at his windows, anticipating another gruelling day on the supply circuit. But here he was in the warmth of a Roman night with a beautiful woman and her intelligent daughter and looking forward to another day teaching at the American School, where students were polite and appreciative.

Eva went to bed when they got home and Annabel and Luke had a nightcap. Luke had a whisky and Annabel a gin and tonic.

"So, what did you do today?" Luke asked Annabel. "I feel guilty depriving you of the car."

"I hardly ever use it, except for shopping and we can do that on Saturday together. Everywhere I go is within walking distance."

"So where *did* you go?" Luke persisted.

"Well, today I went to the gym in the morning and had a Zumba class and a swim."

"And then?"

"Are you checking up on me?" Annabel said, playfully.

"I'm interested!"

"Well, I went to see an old lady I visit quite a lot. She's an English expat. She's called Clara and she's quite frail. She lost her husband last year."

"That's very kind of you."

"I enjoy talking to her, hearing her stories about life in The Blitz when she lived in London."

"So, what did you do after that?"

"Bloody hell, this is turning into a full interrogation! Well, we just popped into Holy Trinity Spagnoli and then I went home and waited for you and Eva."

"Ok, now let's just rewind," Luke said, laughing, "you popped into Holy Trinity Spagnoli! I guess that's a church?"

"Yes."

"So why does a girl who says she's not religious, just pop into church on a Monday afternoon?" Luke asked, playfully.

"Clara wanted to go to confession and I took her. It's a beautiful church," Annabel said a little defensively.

"It's strange how different people express faith, isn't it? Sarah was a strong believer but she never felt she needed to go to church." Luke smiled as he remembered his wife. "She certainly wasn't into all that confession stuff!" he said.

"Did my brother go to church then?" Annabel asked.

"Yes, he went to mass most Sundays, I think."

"Catholics tend to get drawn to a specific place," Annabel said, "it's probably because the sacraments are so important. I'm guessing Sarah wasn't Catholic then?" Annabel said.

"No." Luke didn't want to elaborate on what Sarah thought of the Catholic idea of using confession as a license to do anything you want.

"Have you done all the confession stuff, then?" Luke asked.

"In the past, yes."

"Was your father not religious?" asked Luke.

"No, not at all - I think it pissed him off mum when mum went to church. Sometimes I think she did it as an act of defiance."

"I went to church lots when I was young, Church of England. But I haven't been for a long time," Luke offered.

When Annabel didn't reply Luke continued: "I wish I could be more like Sarah was," he said. "I admired her so much for never questioning why she had cancer, never getting bitter. She just had this inner certainty. I sometimes wonder whether she had doubts sometimes but she never expressed them because she wanted to be strong for me."

"She sounds like an amazing person," said Annabel.

"She was," said Luke. "Don't get me wrong, she wasn't a saint, or anything. She had a temper sometimes and she could get wound up by really little things." Luke paused. "But, yes, she was amazing."

"You know I'm so glad you found me," Annabel said suddenly and seriously. As she sat next to Luke she leant into him. She placed her forefinger on his brow and then traced down over his nose and through his moustache, lingering there a little to brush each side and then onto his lips, gentle exploring them from side to side. Luke moved back self-consciously and made some banal reciprocal comment about how he was glad he'd found her and Eva too. She seemed slightly put out by this. But what did she expect, Luke asked himself? She was still married to Russ! And he was God-knows where paying for this fantastic lifestyle. It wasn't right to betray him like this even if he had a girlfriend in Tuscany or wherever! And Luke remembered how angry and indignant he'd been with Josh for betraying his wedding vows. He would be the worst kind of hypocrite to give into to passion like this.

"Why do you still wear the ring?" Luke asked, motioning towards her wedding finger.

Annabel smiled. "I've taken it off a few times, I can assure you. And I've thrown it at Russ more times than I can remember." She paused in reflection: "I know what you are thinking, Luke, but it's just there out of habit now. And it keeps the Italian men at bay!"

"I'm really confused about your relationship with your husband," Luke said.

"There isn't a relationship anymore, Luke. It's just business now," Annabel said, tersely. Her eyes were sad. There was a distance between them now and Luke felt that a lovely evening had turned sour. He heard Emily admonishing him and his silly scruples: *'Lighten up, Luke!'* he heard her say.

But Luke made his excuses of being 'really tired' and retired to his room. He lay on his back in the dark with his hands behind his head thinking about Annabel. He thought about how she looked under those loose-fitting clothes. Her breasts and her nipples that he'd seen delicately pronounced underneath her t-shirt. And then his eyes drifted down along her flat stomach, which he had noticed previously had a piercing. In his imagination she was lifting her top over her head…He stopped himself.

"What is happening to me?" he exclaimed, audibly. He'd not had any interest in women since Sarah and now he'd fantasised about two women in the space of a month. He really didn't know what that moment in the middle of the night with Sophie had been about – but he'd been vulnerable and let his passion take over…and then he'd been rejected and made rather a fool of himself. He certainly wasn't going to make the same mistake with Annabel!

Luke was far too tired and drunk for any further analysis of the evening and very soon he succumbed to sleep.

*

The next two days at The American School were better than Luke could have ever expected. Luke thrived on receiving a little positive feedback and Dr Harper was gushing when he stopped Luke in the corridor

"Mr Morris says he's delighted with the way you've fitted into the department. He was in and out during your 7th Grade lesson and he said the children were engaged and making real progress. And I've heard some great reports from 10th Grade too," the principal said.

Luke had been doing creative writing with 9th Grade and some war poetry with the younger children. At his best, Luke was interesting and resourceful and he was good at putting the poems in context and talking about the poets, focusing on the human stories and showing video clips. He told the story of Wilfred Owen and his mental breakdown which they referred to as 'shell-shock' then, and his determination to go back to the front and be with his men…and then being shot dead by a sniper's bullet the day before Armistice. When children were engaged and interested to learn, they could not have had a better teacher than Mr Adams.

On Thursday evening Annabel made coq au vin with roasted Mediterranean vegetables and after the meal Eva brought out a guitar to show Luke. Her mother had bought it her because she was always singing around the house and Annabel thought she had a real musical talent. But Eva soon got frustrated with it and lost interest. To Eva and her mother's pleasant surprise Luke tuned the guitar and started to strum.

"Come on then?" Annabel said, "let's hear a song?"

Luke played 'Here Comes the Sun' as it allowed him to show off a little on the guitar - he was self-conscious about his voice which was weak.

"More! More! More!" the girls chanted in unison when Luke had finished, so he played 'Subterranean Homesick Blues', a good choice for those who are not strong singers because you can half rap the lyrics. After that, Luke taught Eva the simple chords then sat behind her and pulled her fingers over the frets until the strings rang rather than producing that discordant sound you get when a chord is not formed properly. Now the guitar was in tune, Eva suddenly felt much more confident - and even after Luke and Annabel had gone to bed she was still practicing a series of simple chords Luke had drawn out for her on a serviette. Annabel was delighted to see Luke and her daughter getting on so well and any little tension at the end of the previous evening was now completely forgotten.

On Friday Luke and Eva drove home in animated conversation about Macbeth. Eva had no sympathy for him although Luke insisted that she must understand that he too is suffering. It wouldn't be tragedy without it.

But as they arrived in the house Eva and Luke noticed a golf bag in the vestibule. They both stopped.

"Oh God!" Eva said, "he's here!"

CHAPTER 12: RUSS RETURNS.

Russ was friendly enough. He wanted to take them all out for a meal but Luke had offered to cook on Friday after school and Annabel had bought the ingredients, so they stayed in. Annabel and Russ sat in the kitchen and drank and watched Luke prepare food. Although perfectly affable, Luke noticed Annabel and Russ rarely spoke directly to one another and neither really instigated a conversation…Luke had to do that. He had promised to cook koftas and a Moroccan theme and he mixed the ingredients in a bowl and shaped them for the BBQ and then made a salad and some couscous.

By the time it as all ready, Russ was drunk. He was tall and ripped, apparently he'd played rugby to quite a high standard when he was in his twenties. Luke nodded and feigned interest in Russ' over-long anecdotes at the dinner table as he name-dropped famous rugby players he counted as his friends and looked disappointed when there was no hint of recognition on Luke's face. Of course, Luke tried to engage and said he'd heard of Will Carling and the bloke who scored all the kicks in that World Cup.

Russ enjoyed the food and was generous in his compliments. "This is bloody fantastic!" he said to Luke when he was offered more. "Annabel told me you were a good cook, but wow!"

"Thanks. Well, I've got to make myself useful whilst I'm here," said Luke noting as he spoke that Russ and Annabel had obviously been discussing him at some stage. "By the way," Luke added, "thanks for letting me stay."

"No problem at all," Russ said, and he genuinely seemed pleased to have Luke around the house. "My shout tomorrow. I can't cook but I can at least take you all out. Mind you, it'll be hard to beat this!"

Eva stayed in her room all evening and when the food was ready Annabel delivered it to her on a tray as though she were confined to bed. They ate around the window end of the large table and afterwards Luke helped Annabel tidy up the kitchen whilst Russ lay on the settee in the smaller front room, drinking whisky and flicking through channels.

"I know I said we could drive to the coast tomorrow. But I'm going to have to see what Russ has planned first. I can't very well just leave him," Annabel said as she packed the dishwasher.

"That's fine," Luke said. "I've got some planning to do. And I may just have a wander after that."

"I'm sorry, I was looking forward…"

"Don't worry, we can go some other time," Luke said gently. "Listen, you and Russ haven't seen each other, you need some space. I'll keep a low profile."

"Thank you," Annabel said. She looked tired.

"I'll get to bed now, I've had an eventful week," Luke said as he threw a tea-towel playfully at Annabel. It raised a smile.

"Thank you, Luke," she said again, "and thank you for that lovely meal. You are so clever, you know."

"I'll see you in the morning," Luke instinctively put his fingers to his lips in the gesture of blowing a kiss and Annabel mirrored his action. "Goodnight, Russ, I'm off to bed," Luke shouted as he made for the stairs. There was no reply.

Luke walked down the elegant stairway to his room and got straight into bed. He put his phone on charge as usual. He thought he should at least text Sophie sometime soon and tell her his latest news about the job and Annabel. But not now, he decided.

He wanted to lie there and try to make sense of Annabel and Russ and their marriage. He was relieved that nothing had happened between Annabel and himself on the previous evening, yet there seemed no intimacy, no affection, between the married couple, the relationship seemed empty of *any* emotion. Or was it they were conscious of Luke's presence, he wondered? Would they now be making love, he wondered? Luke knew he had no right to be jealous and resentful of Russ, but he was. He tried to push these thoughts out of his mind as he turned off the light.

Luke was always an early riser and he was surprised to find Russ already in the kitchen at 7am making himself coffee. Apparently, he'd arranged a game of golf with some friends. Luke felt a little awkward and ended up thanking Russ again for allowing him to stay and offering to find accommodation if it was a problem. Russ assured him it was not.

"I'm just grateful that you came all this way to tell Annabel about her brother and that you went to all the trouble of finding her," Russ said.

"Well, I needed to clear some things up in my own mind as well," Luke said, smiling.

"To be honest, I'm pleased for Annabel - I've not seen her as happy in a long time. And Eva too – she really likes you." He paused and a sadness came over him suddenly: "I'm sure you know we've never had the best relationship. Bad timing, I think!" Luke decided he quite liked Russ. He was warm and open and not what he had expected somehow. He imagined he'd have been a bit older and one of those hard-headed businessmen you see with younger, beautiful women. But Russ looked young for his age and was in good shape and he could perfectly understand why Annabel had fallen in love with him. Russ said, it was only a flying visit as he was driving to France in the morning. He was in talks with a French company in the same field who were quite interested in his business.

As soon as Russ had left, Annabel came down in her pyjamas.

"So, what are you planning this morning, then?" she asked.

"I thought I'd go for a jog, those trousers are pinching a little," said Luke, thinking about Russ and his perfect physique.

"Why don't you come with me to the gym? I've got a free pass that I haven't used. It's meant to attract new members," Annabel offered. "I heard Russ leave - has he gone to play golf?"

"Yeah. And yeah, that would be nice. Can I have a swim there, too?"

"Of course," said Annabel, "they've a fantastic pool."

At that moment Eva came down: "So, what were you rowing about this time?" Her tone was one of exasperation.

Annabel looked embarrassed and sighed. "Him being him - doing things without any consultation. Do you know, he's swapped the Porsche for a hatch back!" Annabel suddenly became aware of Luke's presence and how her complaint must have sounded: "To be honest, I'm not bothered what car he has. It's just that I'd like to be kept informed!"

"I don't understand why you are so surprised anymore!" said Eva, her arms folded aggressively.

"Please Eva, don't start!" Annabel sighed again. "It doesn't help when you ignore him like you do."

"It's because of *this* shit!" Eva interrupted.

"Eva!" Annabel said, reproachfully.

"Well, we have a nice time without him, don't we?" She paused, hoping for a response: "Well, *don't* we?" Her mother nodded and a sadness had come over her. "And then he's home for a night...and there's conflict!" Eva raised her voice, she was becoming upset. Luke felt he ought to help Annabel.

"He probably feels that turning up in a Porsche sends the wrong message to the clients, especially in these difficult times. You know: 'I'm gonna rip you off to pay for my expensive lifestyle!' type thing."

"Well that's what he said, actually." Annabel smiled at Luke gratefully. "But it would be nice to be consulted first!"

"Come on, let's have a coffee and then go to the gym," said Luke, "are you coming Eva?" Before waiting for a reply he addressed Annabel: "By the way did I tell you, Eva was my prize student yesterday? She's a clever girl, your daughter!" he said.

"I know she is!" said Annabel.

Eva smiled: "You are so full of shit, Mr Adams! I just googled Tragedy."

"You explained the idea of the tragic hero far better than I could…and then all that stuff about Aristotle! I was proud of you." Luke beamed at Eva.

"Thanks," Eva found it hard to hide her delight at the compliment. "I'm off to drama club so you two can burn off a few calories for me too."

"Ok love. You're in for tea, aren't you?" Annabel asked.

Eva hesitated. "No, I'm staying at Jenny's. Is that ok?"

"Well, Russ is taking us out for a meal to Antonio's. You like it there," her mother said, forcing a smile.

"Mum!" Eva said, as if to say you know the situation.

"Come on, you can chat about Shakespeare to Luke," Annabel pleaded, good humouredly.

"I will think about it," Eva said. She went to make herself some toast and Annabel mouthed 'Result' to Luke and smiled.

Luke and Annabel walked to the gym and spent forty-five minutes on the treadmill and the bikes and then around the same in the pool. Afterwards, Luke brought up the subject of her husband. "Russ tells me he's driving to France tomorrow," he said as he returned to the table with two fresh orange juices.

"Is he? Well, I've no idea what he's doing," her tone seemed disinterested and impatient at the same time. "I suppose you can see for yourself, Luke, that Russ and I live separate lives." She paused. "But Eva is wrong to suggest we row all the time because we don't. Not as much as we once did." She stopped. "I've grown to accept how things are with Russ."

"Do you still love him?" Luke hadn't meant to be so direct. "Sorry, that was…"

"I still care about him, but, no, I cannot say I love him." Annabel went on, ignoring Luke's protest. "In fact it's probably my fault because I drifted away from him first. I know Eva seems perfectly charming with you, but it *has* been difficult for Russ." She paused as if trying to recall when she stopped loving Russ. "You lose track of when it all started going wrong and who did what, who said what…but lots of things have been said. Too many to unsay." Annabel played with her glass. "And now he has *his* life and I have mine." Annabel went quiet after she had explained, withdrawing into herself like she did on the first day after Luke had delivered the news about Richard.

"So, what are you going to do?" Luke asked, finally.

"I don't know, Luke, I really don't know." Annabel stared into Luke's eyes. "I bet you're thinking I'm an ungrateful bitch - with my fantastic house and daughter at private school, etc, etc. But I helped him build the business…"

Luke interrupted her, "Hey, you really don't have to explain yourself to me."

"Russ says because of the economy here the value of the house has fallen - but when things pick up a bit we will sell it and make a clean break."

"Would you stay in Rome?" Luke asked. "You have a very comfortable life here."

"Oh, it's not as comfortable as it seems." Annabel said, "Anyway Eva wants to go back to England."

"Yes, she told me."

"I'm amazed how quickly she's taken to you. I was thinking about that when I was in bed last night," Annabel said. As she spoke she reached over and touched Luke's hand.

"So, what are we doing for the rest of the day, then?" Luke asked, suddenly changing the subject. "Will Russ be out all day?"

"I don't know. But it's a bit too late to drive to the coast now."

They went home and Luke made some homemade tomato soup. He put in plenty of onion, chilli, paprika and garlic and a tea spoon of sugar and salt at the end just before he blended it. It was tasty and warming and Russ had some when he returned at 2pm. He said he had to go through some paper-work in preparation for his meeting the next day, so he stayed in all afternoon.

Luke and Annabel had a walk through the city and ended up in Piazza Navona sitting outside a bar people-watching. Luke was starting to get used to the city and the noisy exchanges of the locals who seemed to get animated over the most mundane of things. Two men with bikes and dressed in lycra stopped at the same bar and were discussing their machines. Of course, Luke had no idea what they were saying but the gear system and bottom bracket on the older man's bike seemed to be the topic of conversation. It was then compared to the younger man's gears. The men pointed at their bottom brackets and gestured and shouted in equal measure before finally sitting down with their beer, clearly exhausted from discussing with such exuberance the relative merits or demerits of each other's cogs and chains. Annabel picked up enough words to give some sort of commentary and they both giggled at the unexpected drama.

Annabel was wearing jeans and a simple long-sleeved black top which was backless with woven detail. Her hair was combed back off her face and tied into a pony tail. As usual her make-up was understated, allowing her skin colour and bone structure to show off her natural beauty. Luke had worked out that she must be around forty-five but she looked younger. She was beautiful and self-effacing and fantastic company and Luke was proud to be seen out with her.

They walked back to the house, through the Piazza di Spagna where they playfully splashed each other in the fountain and then up the Spanish Steps to the house. Russ was sitting on the balcony sipping a beer with empty bottles around him. He'd watched them climb the steps, giggling and seeming so comfortable in each other's company. Luke was embarrassed. Maybe their marriage was unusual but he knew how he would have felt if the roles had been reversed.

"I'm going to have a rest, if you don't mind," Luke said, leaving the married couple alone together in the kitchen. He went downstairs and locked the door to his room and lay on the bed and heard them talking above. He would ask the school about the possibility of staying there for the rest of his time in Rome when he got into work on Monday. This situation was unfair on Russ. It was unfair on Annabel too because he would be going back to England soon. And it was unfair on Luke, himself, he was becoming emotionally attached to a girl who was another man's wife.

Luke was tired from his exertions in the gym and drinking at dinner time and promptly fell asleep. He must have been very tired because it was 6pm when he was woken by a knocking on his door. It was Eva who was back from her friend's and now dressed and ready to go out for the promised meal. Apparently, they were eating early because Russ needed to be off prompt in the morning. Luke washed and changed and went upstairs, Annabel and Eva were chatting in the kitchen whilst Russ sat in the smaller living room watching golf.

They all walked down the steps and across Piazza Di Spagna to a restaurant down a side streets to the right of the piazza. The staff greeted Russ and Annabel warmly. Russ was made especially welcome with warms hugs and hand slaps and he was able to converse with the staff in fluent Italian. In fact, Russ seemed to know everyone - the maitre d', the waiters and the owner, Antonio, who suddenly appeared 10 minutes after their arrival.

Russ spent very little time with Annabel and his step daughter during the meal and Annabel, Eva and Luke chatted together about Shakespeare. Luke recalled watching plays in Stratford and visiting Ann Hathaway's Cottage and Shakespeare's birthplace. Luke described the place to Eva using all his descriptive prowess to bring the historic town to life. Eva loved to talk about England and Luke suggested she should come over and stay with him so he could show her Liverpool and Stratford…and London, the place that really excited her. They talked about Macbeth, Annabel remembered it from school so was able to join in the conversation although her recollections were a bit hazy. Eva told her mother how the class had a lively discussion in Friday's lesson about ambition. Luke had posited the question: "How far would you go to get what you wanted?" And some of the responses from the American boys had quite shocked Eva. It seemed that Shakespeare's themes were as relevant now as ever. Eva, Luke and Annabel all agreed they were on the opposite end of the spectrum and decidedly unambitious, especially if it meant trampling on others to achieve it! If they'd been Macbeth, they decided, they would have taken the promotion and looked forward to the enhanced pension. "After all, who wants it all!" said Eva. "What do you do with your life then?" They decided in his absence, because he was at the bar chatting, that Russ would probably be the most ambitious but even he liked being popular more than being powerful.

They got back quite early, Russ was drunk again; he was morose on the walk home and went straight up the stairs to bed as soon as he got in. The girls and Luke sat on the balcony and drank coffee and Eva insisted on another guitar lesson. Eva was impressed by the way Luke knew how to play well-known riffs and chord sequences. He taught Eva 'Here Comes the Sun' and then 'Feels Like Teen Spirit' by slowing down the finger-work and then placing the guitar in Eva's hands and standing behind her, pulling her fingers onto the relevant strings and frets like he had done the previous evening. Eva cried out in pain as Luke bent her fingers around the neck of the guitar, but she was a fast learner and her mother applauded loudly when she got it right. Eva had a sweet voice too and was able to sing the songs she played. And Eva was already doing them her way, Luke noticed; she took the spirit of the song and made it hers.

"Aren't you glad Luke came to find us?" Annabel said to Eva as she finished clapping. She was intoxicated by the night and the alcohol.

Eva who had not been drinking stopped playing. "He's ok, you know!" Her face was happy and serious at the same time. Annabel leaned across and hugged her daughter and Luke together, and Luke felt Eva pull him closer to her. The tenderness and intimacy of the moment threatened to overwhelm him. He had not experienced such feelings since Sarah's death. All the aching loneliness and hurt seemed to be written out by this one precious moment where he felt he belonged again, he felt loved again. A tear rolled down Luke's cheek and he made no effort to disguise it or wipe it away. Annabel noticed it and smiled sweetly.

"Thank you," Luke said, getting up from his seat, "thank you and goodnight to my favourite girls!" As Luke said this, he did one of those ironic bows before turning and heading through the kitchen down the stairs and into his bedroom.

Luke undressed, cleaned his teeth and put on his pyjama bottoms. He got into bed still thinking about the evening. Thinking about Annabel, willing her to come to him. And then after what must have been around ten minutes of waiting and willing, as if she had heard Luke's unspoken supplication, there was a gentle knock on the door: Annabel was standing there in front of him, like an impossible dream. And there was an intensity about her as she pushed Luke gently backwards into the room and shut the door behind her without speaking. They stood together behind the closed door and kissed. This wasn't a kiss like before, this time her mouth was open, it mirrored his and the kiss was deep and passionate. Luke put his left hand at the base of her back and pulled her closer, allowing her to feel his cock against her.

"Where's Eva?" he said, pulling away from Annabel for a second.

"In bed."

"Russ?"

"In bed."

Annabel pushed Luke the short distance from the door to the bed and they fell, entangled together, she on top of him. They kissed passionately, he placed his hand between her legs and she reached down, unbuttoned his pyjamas and pulled on Luke's erect cock. Luke's hand found the warmth and wetness of Annabel's desire. He drew her long dress up and she raised her arms to allow him to slip it over her head. And there she was, naked before him. Despite living in the sun for years her skin was as white as alabaster and her breasts were small and firm. In a single, smooth action Luke pulled her around so that he was now on top of her. Annabel gasped excitedly as she suddenly felt him inside her.

Luke tried not to rush things like a teenager but he was excited by the strength of Annabel's feelings and passion, and her sighs only served to arouse him further. They tore into each other in a desperate struggle as if these were their last moments on earth. Luke knew sex could be awkward and uncomfortable, with the lovers seemingly dancing to different tunes. But this was different, Luke felt in control of his body. He felt, for once, he was the lover he'd always wanted to be.

But even at that moment he knew it was she - confident and experienced enough to marry passion with technique - that made him feel this way. They stared into each other's eyes, understanding everything: their fears, their loneliness, the unspoken sadness of life. And every part of Annabel engaged with every part of Luke until that final, unstoppable moment of joy. Pure, unmitigated joy.

Sated, the lovers lay side by side on top of the bed. Once his breathing had returned to something approaching normality, Luke turned to Annabel and kissed her gently on the forehead. And then the words that never really capture what has passed between lovers at that moment: "Bloody Hell!" he said.

Annabel smiled: "Yeah, Bloody Hell!"

Luke smiled back but said nothing more, he ran his fingers gently down Annabel's nose and across her lips. She was beautiful.

"I ought to get back upstairs, I don't want trouble," she said.

"Are you going back to *his* bed?" Luke asked.

"No," she said emphatically, "we don't sleep in the same *room*!" She laughed: "Did you really think we slept together!"

"Well, I wasn't sure," Luke said, embarrassed.

Annabel stood up and adjusted her clothes, checked her hair in the mirror momentarily with a Hollywood gesture and then she backed towards the door. She blew Luke a kiss, mouthed "Wow!" and slipped out of the door quietly.

Luke understood she had to go but he desperately wanted her to stay. He wanted to hold her and hear her breathing and feel her breath on his face. He turned into the pillow that just moments ago Annabel had been lying on and smelt her perfume. He wanted to cherish this moment, to commit to memory every little thing about the whole day: the gym in the morning; the bar in the Piazza Navona, and the two funny Italians and their bikes, the walk home, the meal and the coffee on the balcony with Annabel and Eva and the guitar and the group hug. And then this: a beautiful, sexy woman coming to his bed. Luke knew he should be feeling guilty, he remembered how he'd exploded with Josh less than a week before, and yet he was feeling so alive, so bloody pleased with himself……and so in love

CHAPTER 13: AN ABUNDANCE OF LIGHT

Everything about the next month was perfect. Luke was enjoying teaching more than he had ever done. His anxiety seemed like a distant memory although he was sure to take his tablets every day; he had arranged to get his prescription from a chemist in Rome. He'd learnt through bitter experience that often the worst, most debilitating attack came when you were the most relaxed and least expecting it. But Luke did have a renewed confidence in himself and when he looked in the mirror he saw a confident middle-aged man finally at peace with himself. And why shouldn't he be! He lived in a beautiful city where the sun seemed to shine all the time, in an amazing house with a fantastic location. And above all he was in love with Annabel and she was in love with him. For the first time since Sarah got sick, Luke could say he was truly happy.

But it wouldn't have been Luke if he hadn't woken up on the Sunday after making love to Annabel full of guilt and fear. He had made love to another man's wife. Ok, maybe Annabel and Russ had a marriage in name only, maybe she really didn't love him anymore and maybe they never slept together, but they were still man and wife and he could sense how hurt Russ had been to see he and Annabel so intimate and comfortable on the steps the day before.

And then there was the fear, the fear that the sex had ruined everything, that Annabel would be full of remorse that morning and retreat into herself. Maybe, in the cold light of day Annabel would have to admit to herself Luke just didn't match up to the younger, more athletic man she was married to. Maybe, Annabel just wanted to get her husband's attention……and what better way than fucking a relative stranger in his own home? Luke didn't really believe any of the above, but he did fear that Annabel did not feel like he did, how could she!

And so, Luke showered and dressed slowly that Sunday morning. His euphoria of the previous night had evaporated. He wondered too whether Russ would be still at home, he really hoped he wouldn't have to face him.

On the way to the kitchen, Annabel called him: "Hi," she shouted in a sing-song voice. She was lying on the settee in the large living room. "I was worried you'd snuck out during the night. That I'd frightened you away," she added with a smile.

"Oh Hi, I didn't expect to find you in here," Luke said.

"I was waiting for you. Come here?" she said, holding both arms aloft as an invitation for Luke to embrace her.

"Where's everyone?" Luke said.

"Russ has gone. Eva's still in bed."

Luke felt reassured and smiled. He bent down and allowed Annabel to pull him towards her. He lay in her arms on the large settee.

"Are you ok?" Annabel asked, smiling at Luke.

"Mmmm" he said.

"Sure?"

"Yes, aren't you?" said Luke, a little concern was evident in his voice.

"Oh, Yes!" Annabel said, as she pulled him tighter.

"No regrets?" he asked.

"None!" she said. She seemed surprised by Luke's question. She pushed him away momentarily, "Why, have you?"

"No, I just thought…"

"Don't be silly. I loved it. Didn't you?"

"I did." Luke sat up a little so that he could look Annabel directly in the face. He wanted to say more but he didn't. "So, what have we planned today?" he asked instead.

"Eva's got work to do so I thought you and me could drive to the sea today. Would you like that?"

"I'd love to," said Luke. "Have you had any breakfast?"

"I had a yoghurt, but I'll have another coffee if you're making one, you sexy man!" She tickled Luke playfully. He got off the settee and playfully hit her with a pillow until she playfully pleaded for mercy.

Annabel followed Luke into the kitchen. As he faced the work surface to make the coffee she put her arms around his waist and kissed the back of his neck. "You make me feel like a young girl again," she said.

Luke turned with a coffee in each hand and kissed her on the mouth, a gentle kiss. The sun was already up and the balcony was bathed in light. "Should we?" he said, gesturing towards the large glass doors.

They sat in the early morning sun and discussed their plans for the day. They decided to drive to Ostia, the closest beach to Rome on the Tyrrhenian Sea.

Luke watched Annabel preparing for the day. She was wearing a light summer dress with a large pattern and simple sandals, like she had on the day Luke first saw her at the top of the steps. A small leather bag was slung casually across her and it hung down just below her waist. A casual observer would assume that Annabel wore no make-up and indeed Luke had thought this at first. But she wore a light lipstick and a little make-up around the eyes to emphasise the shape and blueness of them and some subtle foundation, carefully applied, to accentuate the shape of her face. Annabel's hair was also understated and might even be described by those who knew no better to be a little uncared for. But this was Annabel's look and Annabel's charm. Luke recalled the first picture he saw of her with her brother - physically, she had changed very little but then her natural beauty had been hidden behind extravagant colours and manicured hair. Here now was a woman in her prime, thought Luke, a real head-turner who understood perfectly, that in matters of beauty, less is most certainly more. Luke went back to the bedroom and returned five minutes later in a different shirt and shorts and with a little gel in his hair.

When they got to Ostia it seemed most of Rome had had the same idea. Luke found it hard to believe it was only April - the beach and the lidos and the promenade were vibrant. Men played games of volleyball and families strolled the promenade. It was still only 11am and people were already swimming and splashing in the sea.

Annabel and Luke strolled the beach and held hands for the first time like a proper couple. Luke took off his shoes and felt the sand on his feet, something he'd loved to do as a child walking across the sands at Abersoch in North Wales where he used to go with his family. He pictured that bay as he walked and imagined the scene was probably a very different right now. It prompted Annabel and Luke to talk about family holidays. It turned out they had both gone to St Ives in Cornwall as children. Annabel's father had rented a cottage next to Porthmeor Beach which sounded idyllic. Luke had stayed with his parents in a caravan in a muddy field without proper toilets, he recalled. They laughed at the contrast.

Of course, Annabel could not mention her childhood without talking about Richard again. He was very much the sporty type even then and spent the holiday mastering the surf. Annabel said how much the girls loved him with his lean body and his tan. Annabel became coy as she remembered it was on that holiday that she lost her virginity to a surfer boy, a friend of Richard's. They would have parties on the beach as the sun went down and light a fire and drink warm lager and one thing led to another. Luke imagined he was probably sitting in the muddy field miles away from the action, playing Snap with his mum and dad and sipping cocoa!

The talk of Richard made Luke feel uncomfortable. He'd not really thought about him for a week. And this had been his whole purpose for coming to Rome! Had he instinctively accepted that the news about his mother had been a strong enough reason to kill himself? Or was it more honest to admit he was having too much of a good time to think about his dead friend and whether he might - or might not - have killed himself.

"I know it's not really a suitable topic for a day like this, but can you imagine anyone killing your brother?" Luke asked, suddenly.

"Boy," Annabel took a sharp intake of breath, "where did *that* come from!"

"Well, we *were* talking about Richard," Luke said, "like I said before, I cannot believe he took his life…"

Annabel sighed again. "I know it might sound uncaring, but I really don't want to think about how Richard died at the moment. I know that might sound rather callous but I am quite good at pushing bad things to the back of my mind. I've had to do that quite a bit. It's my survival strategy."

"No, I understand," Luke said, "I wish I had been a bit better at that in the past."

"But I hope you don't think I don't care about Richard. I think about him every day and it breaks my heart that he is dead…and that I could have somehow been responsible."

"I'm sorry, I shouldn't have brought this up again. Especially on a beautiful day like this…And after last night. I'm sorry." Luke kissed Annabel. "And for the record, you are *not* responsible. Ok?"

Annabel smiled a sad smile and Luke felt guilty. But he promised himself that when he had a moment alone he would ring Sophie for an update.

In the meantime, Luke was enjoying the warmth of the sun on his face and the sand between his toes. Without any words, Luke stopped for a moment and he pulled Annabel towards him and kissed her passionately. Annabel closed her eyes and returned her kiss with passion and pulled him closer to her. When Luke finally released for a second, Annabel kissed him again, making him feel reassured that she felt what he felt. Their eyes met in a precious moment of shared understanding.

As they walked back towards the bars and restaurants they were stopped by two parents from the American school who recognised Annabel. When Annabel introduced Luke as the new English teacher they were excited to meet him, their daughter had come home full of news of Mr Adams from England. Annabel held his hand more tightly and stroked it with her thumb as they spoke. She was proud of Luke.

They found a bar at the Lido and ordered beer and mussels with frites and dipped their bread into the creamy, garlicky sauce and fed each other, like Luke would once do with Sarah.

"You do know I'm kind of falling in love with you, Mr Adams," said Annabel as she offered him another piece of bread.

Luke smiled, he leaned across to kiss Annabel. "And I'm kind of falling in love with you too, Mrs… Gosh, I've just realised I don't know your surname! Isn't it crazy! Remind me, how long have I known you?" he said, laughing.

Annabel laughed too. "Sumner. Annabel Sumner," she said, "I so wanted to come back to you this morning but Russ was still around," she said, in a half whisper.

"I do feel bad about Russ," Luke said, "did he know?"

"I don't know. But he's always been discreet about *his* relationships so I'm kind of trying to do the same."

"Relationships? Plural?"

"There had been a few before the current one." Annabel had become serious.

"How do you know?"

"It's just no big secret," she said, dismissively. "Anyway, I don't want to talk about Russ on a lovely day like this."

"So, what you fancy after this?" Luke asked.

"I thought you might like to go to Ostia Antica, the old Roman town, it's on the way back," Annabel said.

"Yeah, sounds nice. You like old ruins then!" Luke asked, playfully.

"Stop it!" Annabel said, hitting Luke around the head with the menu.

They took a couple of selfies at the table with the beer and mussels in the foreground and the sea behind them. Annabel sent one to Eva and Luke sent it to Rachel.

Ostia Antica was the old port of Rome but was now two miles away from the sea. Luke had seen Roman ruins in England, but these were so much more complete with intricate mosaics, an amphitheatre and columns and streets. But like in Rome itself, the Italians made no attempt to beautify the setting. A little money spent having the grass cut and pulling up the weeds would not have been extravagant, Luke thought. They needed to draft in The National Trust!

Annabel found it fascinating, she was more interested in the little things that revealed something of domestic life at the time like the perfectly preserved toilets and the early attempts at central heating. She hadn't visited the place before despite living in Rome for over ten years. In fact, she hadn't seemed to have visited much until Luke arrived!

But as the day went on Annabel started to withdraw into herself again.

"You're very quiet." Luke said after a while.

"I'm just tired," said Annabel. "You've worn me out!" she laughed.

"Is that all, you sure?" pressed Luke.

"I've had a lovely day, I just don't want it to end. And you're back at work tomorrow." She paused and looked over at Luke as he drove. "Then what happens after the work finishes and Mrs Blackmore returns?"

Luke had been having the same thoughts all day, especially since they'd said they were falling in love with each other. It was just his luck to find the perfect woman - 1500 miles away!

"Now that you've found me, I'm scared of losing you," she said.

"Me too," said Luke. He wanted to put his arms around her. They were entering the city and the road was busy so he pulled onto a shopping forecourt. "What are we going to do, sweetheart?" he said. He pulled Annabel towards him as they sat side by side in the car with the bulky handbrake between them. It was more of an exclamation than a question.

"I don't know," she said. "I'm stuck here at the moment with Eva and…"

"I know," Luke interrupted. Then he paused before going on. "Listen, Annabel, there's not much for me in England now so I'd be happy to stay…If you want me to, that is. I don't want to impose……"

"Don't be so silly," Annabel interrupted. "I'd absolutely *love* you to stay. Eva would too," she added, enthusiastically.

"What about work though, you know when Mrs Blackmore comes back?" Luke asked.

"I'd bet they'd find you something. They seem very impressed. Anyway, there's always other teaching jobs in the city for a brilliant English teacher."

"I'll speak to Dr Harper tomorrow, I think," said Luke as Annabel leant over and kissed him, "but I need to sort things out with the house and Noah. I'd only intended leaving him for a week!"

"Why don't we go and collect him?" Annabel said.

"When? How? I'd need to arrange a doggy passport and all sorts of injections!" said Luke, although he was quietly delighted that Annabel had suggested it. "No, it's too complicated. Anyway, it will be too hot for him in the summer."

"Well, we can sort it all out if you really want. It's up to you," she offered. "You, me and Eva could drive over in the summer holidays."

"Thank you," he kissed Annabel and smiled. "I'll think about it."

Luke started the car again and normal conversation was resumed. Annabel and Luke were giggly and excited by the time they reached home.

Annabel opened a bottle of wine as Luke prepared a salad and Eva joined them for a while in the kitchen and had some food. Later when Eva went to bed, Annabel came to Luke's room again and they made love. They fell asleep together and in the morning Eva brought two coffees to Luke's room. She didn't seem to be at all fazed to learn that her mother and her teacher were now sleeping together.

The next day at school Luke took the opportunity to speak to the principal at dinner time. He said he was meaning to speak with Luke anyhow because Mrs Blackmore's health was not improving and he suspected she was looking for early retirement. The principal said he had been delighted with the way Luke had fitted into the school and the difference he had made. He offered Luke work until the end of the school year with a strong chance of a position beyond that if he wanted it. He'd have to apply for a work permit but the principal didn't think that would be a problem, especially with his friend, Thomas. Luke thanked the principal and immediately rang Annabel with the news. She was delighted. And when Luke told Eva at the end of the school day she gave him an enthusiastic hug in the school car park.

When he got home, Luke spoke to Jon in Chester and explained the situation and the fact he would not be home before the summer. If it had been Emily who had answered the phone, he would probably told her about Annabel and falling in love but he felt a little awkward saying such things to her husband, especially over the phone. He just said he was enjoying the new job and had been asked to stay on. Jon assured Luke that Noah was very content and there was absolutely no problem with him staying there as long as Luke needed.

Luke realised that he should get someone to check on the house so he rang Alex later that evening.

"Bloody hell, I thought you were dead!" Alex said when he heard Luke's voice.

"No, very much alive," said Luke. "How are things in Darwen?" he asked.

"Ok, I guess. I was in the pub yesterday. It was busy cos it was quite a nice day. Hear that Josh abandoned you 'cos he got homesick. The wuss!" Alex said, laughing.

"Yeah, well, it took me a while to find Richard's sister so I think he couldn't wait," Luke lied.

"So, you found her, then?" said Alex.

"Yes, I'm living at her house actually. That's why I rang. I've got this teaching job until summer and I can't get back," Luke said. "Don't suppose you could check the house?" he asked tentatively. "Next door has a key."

"Yeah, sure, no prob. So, when you planning coming back? Guess you'll have to fly, after all!" Alex laughed. "Are you trying to build up the courage?"

"Yeah," said Luke, sharing the joke. "But if you could check it would put my mind at rest."

"What's she like then, this sister?" Alex continued.

"She's nice," Luke said. "Yeah."

"And have you found out anything…you know, about Richard killing himself and that?" Alex pressed.

"A bit. Listen, we'll catch up when I get back. Ok?" said Luke. "And send my love to Rebecca."

Luke could sense that Alex wanted more - but Luke closed down the conversation. He was now waiting for Sophie and her investigation into the fat uncle and his son but he'd promised Sophie he would say nothing at this stage to anyone. If *that* proved fruitless then Luke had already accepted that despite his mood on the Sunday in the pub Richard must have found his sister's revelation too much to bear and killed himself. Not that he could ever say that to Annabel, of course.

Later that evening Luke got a text from Rachel. She sent her thanks for the photograph and said how beautiful Annabel was and how happy and well they both looked. She went on to say that she and Mr Harrington were now in a nursing home close to the centre of Oxford because she'd had a bit of a turn and Uncle Fester – who was now very much in charge - had decided she couldn't look after the old man any longer. Luke sent a text back that Annabel dictated, assuring Rachel they were both thinking about her and hoped that she was listening to advice and allowing others to look after her now, after a lifetime serving others.

Luke enjoyed his journeys into work with Eva. He'd finally found someone who genuinely appreciated his playlists. Eva was receptive and eager to learn, she trusted Luke's musical taste and would persevere with songs and artists that Luke recommended, even if she didn't get it immediately. Luke introduced her to Joni Mitchell and Dylan, Leonard Cohen and Springsteen. And Eva would investigate further and introduce other songs by the same artists and play them to Luke a few days later. Like Luke, she understood that the best songwriters were the poets of today. They'd have an American morning followed by a British return trip with Oasis and The Bunnymen, The Arctic Monkey, Elvis Costello and Radiohead…and The Beatles, there was always The Beatles! Luke teased Eva that she should really be listening to The Stones given her London-centric world view, but she adored John Lennon and that was that!

Annabel could see how Eva had flourished since Luke had come into their lives and it delighted her. Russ had tried his best with Eva in the early days, but the two were very different and, anyway, Russ had caught Eva at a difficult age. Luke and Eva, however, chimed together from the first with their common interest in music and literature. Annabel didn't regard herself as cultured despite her middle-class upbringing: *'How do you know that? How has all this passed me by?'* she kept asking. Luke couldn't answer her question on either count, it seemed that you were either born with that particular antennae or you weren't!

And then late in April, Luke got a text from Sophie. "Hello stranger," it said, "Still alive?" Luke felt immediately guilty, Sophie had been there for him when he needed her but now he was all loved-up with Annabel he had not really given her much thought. And *he* had set her off on this murder conspiracy and then just left her to it. He decided to ring her instead of texting so he made an excuse to go out to the shop for ingredients and made the call in a bar just off the Piazza di Spagna.

"Hi, can you hear me?" his tone was immediately apologetic. "Really sorry I've not been in touch. Been so full-on since we last spoke."

"So, you've found Annabel, then?" Sophie's tone was distant and disapproving.

"Yeah, I've found Annabel. And her daughter Eva. And Russ, the husband."

"So, she's not a Harrington then?"

"No, she's Annabel Sumner."

"Ok, so you having a good time, yeah?" Sophie's question had an edge to it.

"Well, I've got a job at Eva's school - just till the end of the summer." There was little response. "Are you ok?"

"Well actually, no!" Sophie paused. "You went over there on this mission and you even started to make me believe you were serious. But now you don't seem to give a damn about Richard!"

"That's unfair, Sophie." But even as he said it, Luke knew Sophie was right. He's been so seduced by Rome and the attention he had hardly given a thought to Richard.

"Annabel told Richard he was not the adopted child he thought he was. His adopted mother was his real mother," Luke said.

"And…?"

"Well, it's a bit of a shock, isn't it?"

"So, Detective Adams is now thinking case over!" Sophie said bitterly, echoing Luke's own words about her father.

"I don't know," Luke said. He was uncomfortable now. He really hadn't expected this reaction from Sophie.

"You haven't bothered to *know*," Sophie continued. "You haven't even bothered to ask about my trip to Oxford, have you?"

"Actually, I was just about to!" Luke said, now adopting the same hurt tone.

There was a pause. When Sophie spoke again she had calmed a little. "Still, it would have been nice if you had got in touch with me first," she said.

"Yes, I know, I'm sorry," Luke said, "I wasn't sure when you were going to Oxford and I didn't just want to text and I didn't want to ring when Annabel was around." As he said it, he realised he hadn't even mentioned Sophie to Annabel.

"Why? Is she not interested what happened with her brother?"

"I think she accepts he took his life. Let's be honest, she really didn't know him anymore," he said. "So, what happened in Oxford?" Luke asked.

"Well, if you are interested, the local police knew Eric Harrington pretty well. Lots of dodgy schemes. All quite low-level stuff. Bit of an Arthur Daley…but without the charm!" Sophie said.

"Yeah, I got that impression at the funeral."

"I really didn't like the guy," Sophie said.

"So, you actually got to *see* him then?" said Luke, warming to the subject.

"Yes, I met this detective at Thames Valley – he's been trying to nab him for a while. He's got a dodgy antique shop where he passes off worthless crap for big money to American tourists and he owns some property for rent in the city. *And* he's supposed to be a nightmare landlord. His son is his enforcer and if you can't pay or he wants you out it gets nasty. When I told Frazer - the detective at Thames Valley - the story he thought this Eric would do pretty much anything for money…especially big money. He thought there might be something to your theory."

"Wow!" Luke was excited. "So, what did you do?"

"I called on him. Frazer said it would be better if I went alone. If he went too it might put him on his guard. I just door-stepped him really, said I was compiling information on Richard for the coroner." Luke could tell Sophie was keen to tell her story. "Of course, he was happy to tell me what he really thought of Richard - he really painted a negative picture of him. Mad, bad and dangerous to know, type thing!"

Luke was angry. "That's absolutely not true! And coming from him!" he shouted down the phone.

"Listen, I know Richard wasn't like that. It's not just because of what *you* said but even my father said that no-one had a bad word to say about him. So, this ridiculous character assignation attempt made me even more suspicious. I desperately wanted to ask where he was on the night Richard died but I knew I couldn't. When I asked about Richard's father's estate and what would happen now that Richard was dead, Eric Harrington seemed to be especially awkward. He closed down the conversation quickly saying he didn't want to think about his brother dying." Sophie paused for a moment to get breath. "Honestly Luke, I think he did it…or he got someone to do it."

"Bloody Hell. So what next?" Luke could feel himself shaking as he held his phone to his ear.

"Well, just before I left I said that I would need to talk to Will, his son. He said he was out of the country and got really defensive. Said 'what the bloody hell did I want to talk to his son for, he didn't know bloody Richard?' He got all arsy after that and said next time I wanted to speak to him or his son, I needed to inform him three days in advance so he could invite his solicitor." Sophie laughed. "I think I got him rattled. Anyway, after that, I went to the local pub like you suggested. They all knew him and Will, but no-one would say anything. Like they were all scared. Just said he and his son lived alone in their big house since the wife scarpered."

Luke was delighted that someone was now taking him seriously. He was also pleased that he could also reassure Annabel that she truly wasn't to blame for her brother's death. But before Sophie hung up she reminded Luke that he couldn't mention anything to anyone…especially a member of the family. She said her father had been back to the coroner, saying he wanted to delay the inquest on the grounds of further enquiries.

"So, are you going to interview the uncle formally? Like under caution?" Luke asked eagerly.

"Ooh, listen to you!" Sophie laughed. "I'm going to see the coroner first." Sophie was serious again. "There was something about the condition of Richard's body that I want to ask him about."

"What?"

"I'm sorry, Luke it wouldn't be right…"

"Ok, I understand," Luke interrupted. "Bloody Hell!"

"I've got some mug shots of the uncle and his son from Thames Valley and I've passed them round the station and asked the coppers to subtly show them around in Darwen. If we could get an ID around that Tuesday then that *would be* a result."

"Bloody hell, Sophie, I'm impressed!"

"I'm feeling good about this, Luke, I really am!" Sophie said. Her mood had changed completely now since the opening of the conversation.

"What about all that talk of leaving the force?" Luke asked, mischievously.

"Well, let's see how this goes first!"

Luke apologised again for his prolonged absence and promised to call Sophie later in the week for an update.

Luke finished his beer and picked up a few ingredients at a delicatessen. He was still buzzing as he walked back to the house. 'Act normal!' he told himself.

"Where have you *been*?" Annabel asked, good humouredly.

"Sorry, couldn't resist a beer in the piazza. It's so beautiful at this time of the day."

"You should have texted, I'd have joined you." Annabel was clearly a little disappointed.

"Let me cook. I've brought a nice bottle of red back," Luke said, keen to diffuse the situation.

Luke cooked spaghetti with tuna and some sweet tomatoes but his head was full of Sophie and Oxford. He was excited and felt the confidence of knowing that despite nearly everyone else immediately assuming Richard had killed himself he had seemed to have been proved right in his conviction. Maybe it really was fate that took him up that path after all. Yet even as he stood at the kitchen worksurface chopping tomatoes, his buoyant mood was undone by feelings of guilt. How had he forgotten about his friend so quickly! Thank God *Sophie* had persevered when he had lost interest. Maybe she was part of fate too!

Over the meal he was tempted to ask Annabel about her uncle but he feared it might produce more questions than answers. No, he must sit tight and wait for Sophie.

*

"Why don't we drive down to Florence this weekend," Annabel said, on Wednesday evening as they made their evening meal. "Have you been there, Luke?"

"No, I'd love to. But what about Eva?" Luke asked.

"I'll speak to her. We can offer to take her too. But I think she will want to stay at her friends."

"Ok, it's fine either way," said Luke.

Annabel kissed Luke over the pan he was transporting from the dishwasher to the cupboard. "Let's chill on the settee with a coffee and have a look for nice place to stay after we've cleared up," she said.

They found a hotel in the centre of Florence called Grand Hotel Minerva with views of the famous cathedral dome. Eva arranged for her friend to stay over, and they'd decided to invite a few friends from school on the Saturday night. Annabel was a little concerned about this but after promises had been made and conditions explained she felt a little more comfortable with the prospect. This was the first time that Eva had been left alone and Annabel was understandably nervous. In Annabel's mind, Eva had her father's genes and the potential to be wild and reckless.

Luke and Annabel set off early on Saturday for Florence and reached the city by eleven o'clock. Being central, the hotel provided a fantastic base to explore the city and after checking in and freshening up they headed for the Piazza della Signoria. Luke explained to Annabel that this place was where it all began, that Florence was synonymous with The Renaissance, the rebirth of Roman and Greek culture after the dark Medieval period. "It was here," Luke said, waving his arms around like an enthusiastic guide, "that the flame was first lit!" As he said it, Luke pictured the look on Emily's face

- he would not have got away with such an indulgence in Chester!

They headed for Galleria dell'Accademia to see Michaelagelo's David, and then the Uffizi Gallery to the paintings of Raphael and Caravaggio. When Luke told Annabel of her brother's enthusiasm for the Renaissance painter, she started to take a special interest in him. And whilst Luke prattled about the dramatic lighting and the artist's use of colour Annabel was far more interested in the narrative that lay behind. She was particularly drawn to Rubens' painting of Christ on the Cross.

Luke wandered around the gallery, viewing other painting but when he returned Annabel was still staring intently at the Rubens, transfixed.

"Why do you like this one so much?" Luke asked.

"It's the two crosses either side," she said, "you know, I'd almost forgotten about the two thieves who were crucified with Christ. You normally see a single cross."

"They used to say in Sunday School that they represented the two different responses to Christ," said Luke.

"What do you mean?" Annabel was studying the painting.

"See the one on the right?" Luke pointed towards the picture. That's the look of forgiveness," he said.

"And I guess the other poor man is damned, he appears pretty miserable."

"Well, I think I would up there! He's the one who mocked Jesus." Luke said.

"It makes sense now," Annabel said. "Thank you, you do know a lot, don't you?" She kissed Luke gently on the cheek and slipped her arm through his.

"I knew all those hours in Sunday school would come in handy one day!" said Luke, gently pulling Annabel away from the picture. "Now, come on, I need a coffee?" he said, now good humouredly dragging Annabel out of the room.

Annabel stopped him as they got outside the room and kissed him. "Thank you." she said.

"What for?"

"For bringing me here. Do you not feel *anything* when you look at these pictures?" she asked, earnestly. Annabel was looking hard into Luke's eyes, hoping for some shared existential moment, but Luke turned away.

"I prayed so hard that Sarah would get well." Luke said, suddenly becoming serious. "I prayed that the treatment would work." He paused. "She was a good person, Annabel. And so young, so full of life!" he said.

Annabel took Luke in her arms and embraced him as they stood in the busy gallery.

"Now let's get a drink?" said Luke after he had recovered a little. Annabel got a paper handkerchief from out of her bag and dabbed a tear running down Luke's left cheek.

"There," she said, "I'm here to look after you now." Luke smiled and linked arms with Annabel, marching her towards the exit. The bright Florentine sunshine found them as they left the gallery.

"Forget a coffee, I need beer now!" Luke said, regaining his humour.

They retraced their route towards a bar they'd noticed on the walk to the galleries, where they had a couple of beers and a fish soup with artisan bread. Luke had been complaining that his feet were hurting with all the walking. He was wearing the formal leather shoes Annabel had bought him in Rome and he needed something more comfortable.

They found a departmental store and Luke bought some more casual shoes, similar to his trusty desert boots. They looked good with his jeans and he arranged with the assistant to put his old shoes in the bag so that he could wear the new ones immediately.

Before they left the store, Annabel pulled him over to the clothes section. Luke had started to combine his new clothes with the older shirts and t-shirts he'd brought over from England and Annabel complained they were far too bright and garish. She persuaded him to try on a dark blue polo shirt which Annabel said looked classy with the jeans and the new boots. She insisted on buying it for him, along with another t-shirt she had picked out.

When it came to paying Annabel slipped her card into the machine, like she had done in Rome. But it was declined this time. Annabel was confused and embarrassed but Luke quickly produced his card and sorted out the transaction.

"Oh God, I'm so sorry, Luke! How embarrassing!" she said.

"It doesn't matter. I should be paying for my own clothes anyhow. After all, I give you nothing for staying at yours."

"I offered to buy them," she said, visibly upset, "you paid for the trip. I don't know why it was declined."

"Maybe Russ has seen the statement for your last shopping trip," said Luke playfully. "I must admit I wouldn't be too chuffed, having to pay for another man's smalls!"

"No, the statement comes to me. He pays the standing order. I'll ring him later," she said, angrily.

"Then you'll have to explain about being in Florence. Just leave it, Annabel. It's not a problem. And Florence is *my* treat," Luke said. "After all, I haven't cashed that money Rachel sent over yet."

"But I didn't intend you to pay *everything*: hotel, food, galleries, everything. It was *my* idea."

"Please don't worry, I'm loving it here with you. And, anyway, I haven't been on holiday for years, so please let me pay?" said Luke, kissing Annabel on the forehead.

"You sure? I still feel so bad," she said.

"Not another word." Luke put his finger across Annabel's lips. She stopped protesting. "Fancy a walk down to the river?" suggested Luke.

The afternoon sun was warm, too warm for a jacket or jumper. The river Arno was prettier than The Tiber and they walked alongside it before crossing the famous Ponte Vecchio bridge into the Palazzo Pitti, an impressive and commanding building with manicured gardens. It provided fantastic views of the city and the iconic Brunelleschi Dome. The beautiful Tuscan hills surrounded the city on every side like a scarf of green. Annabel stood admiring the view and Luke stood behind her, his arms around her waist and his head to the left of hers.

Luke and Annabel walked back across the Ponte Vecchio and browsed the shops there which sold overpriced jewellery and souvenirs. Then they made their way back to the hotel and swam in the outside pool in the late afternoon sun. They made love when they went back to their room and then fell asleep for an hour before showering and dressing for the evening. It was dusk before they walked back into the centre and the Duomo was dramatically lit against the darkening sky and the Piazza della Signorio was a feast of light and colour with its quaint restaurants and the bars. And being Saturday, the city was buzzing with families and couples: looking in windows, taking photographs, or looking for food and drink. Even the street performers seemed synonymous with the place playing classical music on bowed instruments: Luke wondered whether the city elders had banished all electric guitars and their tinny amplifiers to some student backwater on the outskirts of the city for fear that they might somehow blight this cultural paradise.

Luke and Annabel found a bar on the edge of the piazza and ordered beers. The intention was to go back to the hotel for a meal later as they'd booked half board.

But during the meal Russ called Annabel. Obviously, the issue with the credit card had been eating away at her and she had texted Russ. She'd clearly been expecting a text message and was flustered when she had to take Russ' call at the table.

Russ said he couldn't understand why the card had been declined and was apologetic. But when she explained she was in Florence for a short break with Luke he started to question her.

"Eva is fine alone. She's not a child anymore." Annabel laughed uncomfortably. But clearly Russ was wanting to pursue the point.

"What could happen to her, Russ?" Annabel asked, impatiently.

"Ok, I'm sorry, I guess I should have told you. Anyway, we are back tomorrow sometime." There followed a silence whilst Russ questioned Annabel. "Because we fancied a break! I haven't been out of the city for ages, Russ!" she said. This was followed by another silence. "Yes, as I said, I'm sorry."

Russ had obviously hung up after that because Annabel did not have chance to say goodbye.

"He's worried about Eva," Annabel said, wearily, when she put the phone down.

"From what I know of her, I honestly don't think she would do anything silly. She's mature." Luke said, in an effort to reassure Annabel.

"He seems more worried about her being alone and vulnerable if people know I am away. I suppose he has a point." Annabel sighed. "He said I should have informed him and he would have come over"

"Like he informs *you* over things!" Luke could not hide his frustration. "I think he's trying to make you feel guilty because you are here with me!" Luke said.

"I don't think it's that!" Annabel said, trying to close down the conversation.

"Well, I do, and in my mind it's not fair - you said he's had lots of women. He lives his own life and does exactly what he wants it seems," Luke was getting angry.

"Please, Luke, let's drop it. Can you get me another drink?" Annabel said.

"Are you sure you are not still in love with him?" Luke's question shot out involuntarily.

"What?" Annabel said, taken aback.

"You sure you are not using me, Annabel? Trying to get his attention?" Luke said, sulkily.

"No, don't be stupid. I told you I loved you!" Annabel was clearly hurt. "I've only ever said that twice in my life. Now please shut up," she said, hoping to finally put an end to the conversation.

"You seem remarkably tolerant with him, Annabel. Why do you need to appease him all the time - shouldn't it be *he* apologizing to you? He's with another woman and their baby, for God's sake!" Luke was indignant.

"I don't need this, Luke. You are ruining a lovely day," Annabel said, suddenly. She glared at him over the table. "Are you going to stop this *now* or am I going to walk back to the hotel, alone?" Annabel's tone was becoming impatient.

"Please yourself!" Luke said, casually.

Annabel got up from the table and left Luke with his empty glass. He was aware that his row with Annabel had become something of a floor show. He felt embarrassed and self-conscious. Luke paid for the drinks at the bar and left soon after Annabel.

But Luke was quite determined he was not going to follow Annabel lamely back to the hotel. He went in search of another bar and found one below street level and not the type the typical tourist would be drawn to. He sat at the long American style bar feeling that he should be ordering a bourbon but he settled for a bottled beer. A band played Country songs in the corner of the bar. How appropriate, he thought: he'd just had his first row with Annabel. Was he right, he wondered? Was she still in love with Russ and just trying to get her husband's attention? He'd seen it happen to a colleague who fell hopelessly in love with a married woman. He could see what was happening and felt sorry for the poor man caught up in a hopeless love triangle. But *he* didn't see what was happening until it had broken his heart. It was often like that, Luke thought. But Luke was not going to be that naive he was going to address this issue. He walked back to the hotel with purpose in his step.

But when he let himself into the room Annabel completely disarmed him. She had not changed out of the dress she had been wearing and she was sitting on the bed and facing the door as Luke opened it. He could tell that she had been crying. Annabel got up from the bed and walked over to Luke and placed her arms round his neck.

"I love you, you stupid, stupid man. How can I make you understand? I don't love Russ, I love *you*!"

"But…" Luke was about to protest.

"Shhhh please," interrupted Annabel, placing a finger over his mouth. He noticed immediately that she had taken off her wedding ring, there was an indentation where it had sat. "I just don't want to hurt him. I know he's not really happy - he didn't want the baby and business is much tougher than it used to be. And now I feel guilty that I'm having such a perfect time with you." Annabel smiled. "You should be flattered," she said. She kissed Luke when she sensed his manner was softening towards her. She leant back and stared into his eyes, "Luke, since you arrived I've had the most perfect time. I feel alive again. I feel good about myself again. Please believe me!" she said. "You might have thought when you first saw me that I had it all…but I was unhappy, more unhappy than you could ever know." Annabel stopped for a moment. "And, yes, I was angry with Russ. But you've changed *everything*." Annabel kissed Luke gently on the lips again. He could taste the salt of her tears.

Luke paused before he spoke. "Do you think we can still have that table we booked?" he said.

"You're going to have to let me clean up this face." Annabel said, pointing to it.

"Ok, you've got five minutes or you're having a kebab from that dodgy takeaway on the main road!" said Luke. He couldn't stay angry with Annabel for long.

Annabel smiled and kissed him again. A hard kiss. "I do love you, you know?" she said again. She walked into the bathroom to wash her face but she still carried on talking to Luke. "Have I told you how timid and helpless you looked when I saw you at the top of the steps. I just wanted to put my arms around you there and then!"

They had a lovely meal: sea bass and vegetables with a rich hollandaise sauce followed by cheese and biscuits. After that they went out into the town again and back to the bar where Luke had gone in protest earlier. It was now very different to the bar he had left earlier. It was full and noisy. Beer was cheap and this attracted local students rather than the tourists who felt more comfortable at street level in the glitzy bars and restaurants. An intense young man with a battered guitar covered in stickers was playing 'The Eve of Destruction' at the back of the bar.

When Luke disappearing to the toilet, Annabel got talking to a young couple from Milan who were studying at the university. He was doing Architecture and she Education. Annabel introduced Luke when he returned. They talked about schools in Italy when they learnt that Luke was a teacher. It seemed they had many of the same problems that Luke had experienced in England. Of course, Luke couldn't resist mentioning how his friend Thomas Calvi was planning big changes to the education system.

The young couple asked how Luke and Annabel had met. They had assumed in England. But Luke began telling the story about the body in the woods and Inspector Philips and his daughter Sophie, who was also a police officer who had supported Luke in the days after the discovery. Then he talked about his journey all the way to the Spanish Steps and falling in love with Annabel. The young couple were fascinated. As Luke recounted and recalled he started to appreciate what an incredible adventure he'd been on since that morning in early February. He hadn't mentioned anything of Sophie to Annabel up to this point but on the way back to the hotel she asked Luke about her.

"So, you never told me about Sophie!" Annabel said, mischievously.

"Didn't I!" Luke said, vaguely.

"No, so come on, tell me more?" she teased.

"There's no more!" Luke was smiling and feeling uncomfortable.

"Why was she Sophie to you and not PC Whatever?"

"She told me to call her Sophie," Luke said, a little defensively.

"Did you fancy her?" Annabel asked.

"No, don't be daft. She's a police officer," Luke said, "and a *young* police officer!"

"So, are you still reporting back to PC Whatshername?"

"No," Luke lied.

"So, what's her opinion, then?"

"On what?"

"Don't act dumb - on Richard's death?"

"Well, her father's the investigating officer and he thinks it's a tragic suicide, so I guess she feels the same," said Luke, once again lying.

"Well, I can't believe that you've forgot to mention her till now!" Annabel was clearly hurt. She retreated into herself again and Luke felt awkward. He hated lying to anyone, let alone Annabel. But he had promised Sophie not to mention anything to a member of the family – not that it would have mattered, Luke felt. Now he had to maintain this lie. They walked back to the hotel in silence.

"I'm sorry I didn't tell you about Sophie, sweetheart," Luke said when they got back to their room. "To be honest I've been so totally obsessed with you since I first set eyes on you, I've not given her a thought." he said. And until the recent phone conversation, Luke would have honestly meant it.

Luke and Annabel had been drinking for most of the day and they collapsed, fully clothed, onto the bed and immediately fell asleep. Luke woke at 3am with a dry mouth and a horrible head. He took some tablets and drank three glasses of water in an attempt to rehydrate himself. He felt wretched and he knew Annabel would feel the same when she awoke. He took off her shoes and put a cover over her. Then he undressed and got back into bed next to Annabel and listened to her gentle breathing.

Luke lay awake and thought about the eventful day. Florence had been all he'd hoped but the day had been marred by the call from Russ and then by him carelessly mentioning Sophie. If he had been sober he would have been more careful. Luke felt there were still things he didn't know about Russ and Annabel; for a moment he wondered whether he had given his heart away too quickly and that he would live to regret it. And yet as he looked over at the sleeping Annabel his doubts and fears evaporated into the warm Tuscan night. He only had to look at Annabel to believe, like Peter walking on the water.

When she finally awoke, Annabel seemed miraculously unaffected by the previous night. So unaffected, indeed, that she was quite determined to make use of the hotel gym before breakfast. Luke was feeling fragile but he did ten minutes on the bike and then had a swim in the pool. After a few lengths he had another of those 'pinch yourself' moments as he looked over the iconic skyline of Florence on this warm Sunday morning in early May.

Luke and Annabel walked back into the city and to the cathedral after breakfast. The Brunelleschi Dome seemed to eclipse the cathedral in reputation and artistic status and Luke felt this was unfair. Of course, the dome was a thing of beauty and a landmark achievement at the time that paved the way for cathedrals all over Europe. But Luke had not been expecting the beauty of the bell tower and the front facade carved out of pink marble as delicate as icing. Luke thought about the men whose life's work would have been carving this hard stone with simple chisels and mallets. These anonymous craftsmen would never enjoy the accolades that rained down upon Brunelleschi or Michelangelo like holy water. And yet in their way they were just as talented. Did they understand what they were creating, their place in history, Luke wondered. Maybe they even regarded their labours as their own personal pass to heaven? Or was it simply a day job - beer money?

Luke recognised the modern zeitgeist was one of cynicism when it came to religious belief. The poor souls who still believe are painted as weak-minded, unintellectual, deluded. And yet Christianity in Europe had inspired some of the most incredible achievements of the human endeavour. Were all these brilliant minds and artisans living and working under the same delusion!

When he discussed it with Annabel on the way back to Rome she said she really didn't know. "It's probably a delusion," she said, "but it's a very *beautiful* delusion. It was for me."

"I think you still believe despite what you said on that first day together," Luke said to Annabel. "You were captivated by that painting of the crucifixion yesterday."

"Well it certainly made me see things a bit differently," Annabel said. "You love talking about God, don't you, Luke? If anyone in this relationship is the closet believer, I think it's you!"

"When life is as good as it is now, it's quite easy to believe…but I guess faith is belief in the hard times. That's when I'm a bit flaky!" Luke said, smiling.

*

Eva was glad to see them when they got back. She said that Russ had been in touch apparently concerned about her. "He said he'd drive back if I needed him. Of course, he knew I'd say I didn't!" Eva paused for emphasis, "Shame he couldn't have been like that for the last ten years!"

"Now Eva. It wasn't all one way, was it?" Annabel said. "So, no wild parties?"

"It was just me and Francesca in the end. And a bottle of prosecco. Mind you, we did have a bit of a boogie on the balcony at 2am!"

"What time did Francesca go?"

"Around midday, she had homework. By the way, Mr Adams, when are you going to mark those essays on The Temptation scene?" Eva asked, playfully.

"Bloody hell, I better do them tonight. I bloody *hate* marking!" Luke got a beer out of the fridge, mumbling to himself.

*

The next couple of weeks flew by. Luke and Annabel would go running in the evening before a meal. Annabel had her membership at the gym but Luke much preferred exploring the city: the river and the parks and the maze of streets and the piazzas. They'd suddenly discover a new one with its own bars and its own little church or religious statue. Luke tried to make a mental note of its location so that he could visit it again and stop for a beer and have a leisurely look round with Annabel, although he invariably forgot the location and got totally lost on a second visit.

Annabel loved to watch Luke making his own pasta. Ricotta and spinach ravioli in a spicy tomato sauce became a popular meal but sometimes Luke shaped the pasta into linguine which they had with prawns or tuna or meatballs in a spicy tomato sauce.

Annabel took Clara to church two mornings a week and then they called in somewhere and had coffee before Annabel took her home. Her husband had been a British diplomat in Rome for years and they had had lots of friends in the city. He had helped Italy's transition after the war and after Mussolini and they'd met royalty and Churchill and other world leaders. Clara recalled a gala in Rome when she and her husband had invited the young and beautiful Princess Diana and Prince Charles. But now the parties had stopped and her British friends had either died or returned to England, and the Italians she mixed with when her husband was alive had all disappeared. She was quite alone but for Annabel - without her she would not have been able to get to communion and confession.

Luke had texted Rachel a couple of times asking how she was getting on in her new home but he got no reply. This was not like her and it concerned him. He mentioned it to Annabel who suggested he got in touch with Will as he still had his number. Of course, Luke couldn't tell Annabel that Will may now be a murder suspect but he took her advice.

He tried to sound as matter-of-fact as possible: **"Hi, it's Luke, we met in Darwen, I'm Richard's friend. Just wondering whether you have any news about Rachel, the lady you brought to the funeral? I've tried to keep in touch with her through text but heard nothing back recently. I know she's in a home now with Mr Harrington. But a little concerned as I know she wasn't well. Sorry to trouble you."**

To Luke's surprise he got a text back almost immediately: **"Sorry to say Rachel died the week before last. I think she ended up with pneumonia. I've been in France so don't know any more details. Will."**

Annabel was talking to Eva in her bedroom when Luke told her the news and she started to cry. "I feel kind of a fraud getting upset like this," she said. "After all, I've not seen her for years, I've not given her much of a thought to be honest." Luke put his arms around her. "Poor woman, she gave her life to my father. And for what?" Annabel said.

"She must have died very soon after we sent that picture of us," said Luke. "She was so delighted that I found you. And you and she made your peace too." Luke smiled.

"You know, I feel good about it, and so should you." Luke kissed Annabel tenderly on the forehead. Eva hugged her mother and then Luke went back down to the kitchen. He'd been preparing food when he received the message from Will.

*

The contact with Will reminded Luke that he must ring Sophie to see whether she had made any progress. He was surprised and a little guilty that he even needed a prompt. How quickly had life in Rome reoccupied his mind since that initial shock and excitement of Sophie's phone call!

Luke texted Sophie: "Are you able to talk?" in a free period at work. When she immediately texted "Yes" he Facetimed her.

"Hi, just thought I'd call in for an update," he said. "Any progress?"

"Bloody back to square one!"

"What do you mean?" Luke asked.

"The uncle was out of the country in February," Sophie said, gloomily.

"How do you know?"

"Well, I decided we had enough to open an enquiry on Richard's death so we formally interviewed Eric, with his solicitor, and he said he was in France at the time. He was able to provide evidence that he flew out of Heathrow to Charles de Gaulle on the 1st February and didn't return until the 8th February."

"What about Will, then?"

"Eric says he went to meet him. Will had driven over apparently."

"Yeah, he told me he goes over to buy antiques from markets for his father's shop."

"Well I'm going to check up on him because if anyone murdered Richard it seems more likely to be him, especially if he does the heavy stuff in the relationship," Sophie said.

Luke was impressed that Sophie still wasn't prepared to give up on the idea that Richard had been murdered. "I'm sorry the Eric thing led to nothing," he said.

"Well there's still the son, and whatever comes of that, we are now treating it as a murder enquiry." She paused when Luke seemed surprised. "Remember, I said that I wanted to talk to the coroner?

Luke nodded.

"Even he has doubts about the condition of the body. It's not consistent with a hanging."

"What do you mean?"

"The neck suffered a lot of trauma. I looked at photos of a body after hanging. The rope doesn't usually rupture the skin in that manner. I know it was a thin rope but even so…" Sophie paused. "We don't need to talk details, Luke."

"I want you to tell me?" Luke insisted.

"Well, if the initial drop did not kill Richard, then he slowly asphyxiated and that may have caused the trauma. It's horrible to think about, I know," Sophie said apologetically. "But the coroner *now* thinks that the length of the drop – if indeed he did hang himself - would have broken the neck immediately."

"So, he wouldn't normally expect to see the rope eating into the flesh in that manner?" Luke was surprisingly calm and unemotional.

"Not usually…and the neck *was* broken, so he didn't seem to die of strangulation, which might have caused the trauma to the neck. But then coroner says the trauma might have happened *after* death because the rope was so thin and strong." Annabel was talking slowly the way people do when they are being cautious. "But it wasn't as if he was a heavy dead weight," she added.

"Did the coroner pass on these doubts to your father, then?" Luke asked.

"Yes."

"Brilliant!" Luke said, angrily.

"Don't be too hard on him, Luke. There's a lot of pride there."

"That's no excuse! If he wasn't your father, I'd put in a complaint now."

"Please Luke. I've trusted you in being so open," Sophie pleaded. "This is changing my relationship with him quite a bit. But I'm impressed with the way he is accepting things. Accepting he might have been wrong - that's a big deal for him."

"So, what's the plan now?"

"Well let's remember, my father still could be right - Richard might have killed himself," Sophie said.

"Ok, I will accept that. I was starting to believe it myself but…"

Sophie interrupted: "Anyway, they are doing a sweep of all UK ports and airports to track Will's movements in and out of the country in early February.

"And if you find he was in France, then what?"

"Well, I suppose we must consider a third party might have killed Richard. A friend, someone on the payroll of the family - even a hitman!"

"You're really not going to let this go, are you Sophie!" Luke said. There was a warmth in his voice again. "I'm very impressed!"

"Well, *I'm* knackered! I'm doing all this *on top* of my day job. I'm not a detective, you know?"

"You seem like a bloody good one to me!" Luke said.

"Thanks. To be honest, this has made me think about applying. And I guess I've got you to thank for that. If you hadn't been so bloody persistent!" Sophie laughed for the first time in the conversation.

Sophie asked about Rome and Luke's job at the school, and Luke told her about Annabel and the amazing house and the talented daughter and the absent Russ and the strange relationship. After the call he felt a bit guilty about discussing Annabel's private life. Luke had, however, omitted telling Sophie that he and Annabel were lovers - he sensed that she somehow disapproved of Annabel for abandoning her family. And, of course, Luke still did not know what Sophie's feelings were towards him.

That week Luke and Annabel went to the Roman Globe, a replica of the one on the South Bank in London which in turn is a replica of Shakespeare's Globe of 1599. The travelling company's repertoire included some plays in original Elizabethan English and Luke, Annabel and Eva watched 'Romeo and Juliet'.

"It just makes more sense here," said Luke, as they walked across the park after the performance in the warm evening sun, "you know, with the heat, and people chatting in Italian all around you…and all that gesturing. I love the way the Italians treat every conversation like it's going to be their last!"

"Did Shakespeare come to Italy, then?" asked Annabel.

"I don't think so, he just read a lot…it's incredible to think - what a leap in imagination it must have been for the writer……and for the audience at the time too. Words were everything…no TV or photographs - just words and a vivid imagination. Now, even if you haven't been to a place, you've seen pictures or seen it on TV or something - it doesn't demand as much imagination anymore."

"I got lost a bit at times," said Eva, "I'm glad I'd seen the film first. All that Mercutio stuff was really weird!"

"I know, I always try and gloss over the Queen Mab speech when I teach it. Then I pray they don't get asked a question about it in the exam." Luke laughed. "Who said they didn't have psychedelic drugs in those days!"

"Have you always liked books and plays and things?' Annabel asked Luke as they sat and waited for their drinks at a small bar on the edge of the park.

'Well, yes. We didn't have a TV at home. Not until I was about seventeen, anyway."

"Bloody hell, you poor bastard!" Eva said, dramatically.

"Why?" asked Annabel, sympathetically.

Luke became a little embarrassed: "My parents used to think TV was a corrupting influence." He laughed. "And I imagine they thought I was easily corruptible!"

"What by Muffin the Mule!" exclaimed Annabel. Both girls laughed although Luke imagined Eva didn't really understand the incongruity.

"Ok, well maybe not that," said Luke, a little defensively. "But 'Bouquet of Barbed Wire' was a bit racy. And 'Play for Today' had its moments too. I remember my friends coming into school and telling me all about seeing naked women on TV." Luke smiled. "I was very jealous!"

So, when had your parents seen sex on TV if they didn't own one?

"Oh, they left all the watching to Mary Whitehouse - she was this prim and proper old lady with flowery dresses and enormous glasses and she selflessly sat through all the filth on TV and film…and then gave graphic descriptions of what she'd seen and warned everyone they'd be going straight to hell if they even caught a glimpse of this Godless nonsense!" Luke paused. "I wonder where she is now?" he added, mischievously.

The girls laughed. Of course, the reference had meant nothing to them but Luke was funny when he was on one of his rants.

"And, to be fair, I think they also felt TV would distract me and my brother from our work too," Luke went on, as if to try and justify his parents' stance a little.

"I didn't know you had a brother." Annabel said, surprised.

"We are not close at all," Luke said. "To be honest, I sometimes forget."

"Another thing we have in common - estranged brother, estranged father, dead mother."

"But you haven't got a pain-in-the-arse daughter, have you?" Eva said, laughing.

"Sadly not." Luke said. His sudden change in tone drove all humour from the moment. "I wish Sarah and I could have had children."

"Well, you've got *me* now," Eva said. "She leant over the table and hugged Luke. There was a pause whilst Luke recovered. "So, what happened when you got into school and everyone was talking about what they'd seen on TV?" asked Eva, steering them all back to the original conversation.

"Well, I just stayed quiet. But I made up for it by reading. I read everything I could about football - I developed this encyclopaedic knowledge to make up for it. And I listened to the radio too - football commentaries and Radio Luxembourg."

"But didn't you get bored with books?" Eva asked.

"No, never. I loved them. Do you remember those Ladybird books?" Luke addressed his question to Annabel who nodded in recognition. "I loved the history ones. I remember 'Warwick, The Kingmaker'. I used to stare at the pictures, especially the picture of Warwick lying dead on the battle field in his armour. It was just a drawing of course but it was so dramatic. And then I would read Enid Blyton."

"Oh, I *loved* Enid Blyton!" said Annabel now able to contribute. "I must have read 'Malory Towers' over and over…and I loved 'The Naughtiest Girl in the School'."

"Well I was more into The Famous Five - the Find-Outers. I loved a good mystery." Luke allowed himself an internal grin - he was becoming a real-life find-outer now!

The drinks arrived, Eva said she was hungry, so they ordered some garlic bread and olives.

"Then I progressed to Agatha Christie." Luke was warming to the subject, "Mum and dad insisted on lights-out at eight but I'd lie reading under the duvet with a torch until late. My granny didn't like me having second-hand books so she'd take me into town on a Saturday and buy me a book - sometimes two. And batteries for my torch! It was our little secret."

"Why couldn't you have second hand books?" Annabel asked incredulously. "You had a weird childhood, Luke!"

"Well, they spread germs. People could have been sick or gone to the toilet and not washed their hands. Anything!" said Luke, laughing.

"You know, I don't think I've met anyone quite like you," Annabel said, as Luke paused. But she said it as a compliment. She seized both his hands and stared into Luke's face. You are so......" she searched for the appropriate adjective.

"Strange?" offered Luke.

"No. I was looking for a nicer word." Annabel thought hard: "So *different*...so refreshingly different. You are like someone from a different time almost. You're not a blokey bloke, are you?"

The girls laughed, and Luke feigned a protest.

"But I like that about him, he's interesting," interrupted Eva, "it's like he's from a time when men dressed in ruffles and bowed to women and kissed their hands and all that. But he's kind of cool too...he looks younger than the dads at school...and he's into good music and everything.

"Ah thanks, Eva. That's nice...I think!" Luke said, assuming a perplexed smile.

The breads and olives arrived and Luke ordered another round of drinks. Annabel still held Luke's hand in hers across the table and the waiter had to find room for the plates around the outstretched hands.

"You are what I've been searching for all my life, Luke," Annabel said, suddenly staring intently into his face. "I didn't know it was until that first day I met you. But I knew when I invited you back that I wasn't going to let you go. There was *no way* you were ever going back to England. Least not without me!"

"Thanks mum, so where was *I* in all this?" said Eva, feigning hurt.

"Well of course I'd never ever do anything without you, sweetheart. But I just knew you'd love him too," Annabel said smiling and playing with her daughter's hair.

Luke smiled too. "I felt *exactly* the same! I thought this is mad, I'm here to tell this woman that her brother's dead…and I'm falling in love with her…and she's married and beautiful and I must be crazy!" he said.

"And then I got home," added Eva, "and I thought, 'this is weird, mum's just learnt her brother's dead and she's very upset and everything…but she's also *so* happy!' It was like a different *you* when I returned that evening."

"Didn't you feel kind of resentful?" said Luke. "I mean, Russ had brought you up."

"Russ is a stranger to me. I don't know him and he doesn't know me," Eva said. "We never came out together like this, did we mum?"

"No, and we didn't go out as a couple either, not just him and me. If we went out it was always with others. He'd be either talking golf or rugby with the guys or flirting with girls." Annabel laughed. "Either way, he wasn't talking to me!"

Night was falling over the city as they walked back to the car arm in arm, Luke in the middle. Annabel drove back to the house as she'd only had a small beer. Eva went straight upstairs to her room after thanking her mother and Luke with a hug.

Annabel pulled Luke into the large living room mischievously. It was dark except for the luminescent haze of the city seeping through the glass doors that led onto the balcony. Annabel opened the doors and motioned to Luke to follow her. The night was warm and still. Luke had not been out on this balcony before; it provided an altogether different view into Italian domestic life, like a scene from 'Rear Window', one of Luke's all-time favourite films. But unlike Manhattan, the buildings were much older and there were no sky scrapers. And, except for the ubiquitous satellite dishes, Luke imagined that this aspect of the city had not changed much since Keats struggled up the Spanish Steps two hundred years before.

Annabel stood leaning over the balcony rail, the little street below was deserted as were the balconies around them and across from them. Luke stood behind Annabel and as she learnt over the rail she teasingly pushed back into him. She turned and they exchanged a glance that made each feel the other's anticipation. Luke reached down and pulled on Annabel's panties sliding them down so they rested at the top of her legs. He undid the buttons on his trousers, reached inside his boxer shorts for his excited cock and pushed into Annabel and the balcony, in one continuous movement, breathing in the night's warm air.

A few minutes later the lovers fell back into the room and onto the light, soft rug, breathless and sated. "We're like two horny teenagers!" Annabel whispered in the darkness. "What would your mother say?" she teased. "You sure it was Enid Blyton under the duvet with your torch!"

"Please don't mention my mother at a moment like this!" Luke said, laughing and still breathing hard from his exertion.

Annabel undid the buttons of Luke's shirt and kissed his chest and his neck. She kissed him hard on the mouth. "I love you so much," she said.

CHAPTER 14: THE DINNER GUESTS

Sophie went very quiet for the next week. Luke texted but there was no reply. He even tried calling her but the phone went to voicemail: 'She's probably busy or she doesn't want to disappoint me with *another* dead end!' Luke thought to himself. But, in fact, Luke and Annabel were far more concerned about Russ.

Luke didn't claim to know Russ. He'd been back for the flying visit in March, when Luke had first arrived, but he was out playing golf or talking to locals in the bar when they went for a meal and Luke had seen very little of him. But, even so, there was no doubt in Luke's mind that when he returned for a second time Russ had changed.

Annabel said Russ had always liked a drink. He had since his days playing rugby - it kind of went with the territory. But now he was drinking copious amounts of beer pretty much from first thing in the morning, and towards afternoon he was mixing this with gin and tonics and glasses of red wine and *'God knows what else!'* Annabel said. But he wasn't a happy drunk – he was morose and preoccupied. He'd changed physically too. Since his last visit, around two and a half months earlier, he'd lost weight and his athletic frame had become wiry and his face gaunt. His designer jeans and shirts hung from him instead of defining and accentuating his once well-honed physique.

Russ had arrived late on the Friday and had drunk beer and watched TV and then gone to bed. The next day he appeared in the kitchen mid-morning after Annabel and Luke had been jogging. Luke had made some soup but Russ wasn't interested. He had an espresso but was soon back on the beer and watching TV in the smaller living room. Life carried on around him as it would have any Saturday. Eva was becoming very proficient on the guitar now and learning new songs daily. She sat on the balcony quietly strumming with her mother and Luke as her audience. She seemed to be working her way through The Beatles catalogue but Luke was delighted how she made each song her own - like her namesake Eva Cassidy had done before her tragically early death.

'What was eating into Russ?' Luke wondered. *'Why was he so withdrawn and preoccupied?'* "Was he sick?" he asked Annabel. "People don't usually drink as much as he did and actually *lose* weight!" Annabel offered an open hand gesture and shook her head.

Russ announced around midday that he'd invited round his two new business partners for a meal, much to the annoyance of Annabel who once again had not been consulted. They were keen to see the house and the family, he said. As neither he nor Annabel cooked to any reasonable standard Russ wondered whether Luke would make something Italian. They were from the south of the country, the other side of Naples.

Luke felt he owed Russ, and anyway he enjoyed showing off his cooking skills. He decided on making kebabs on the BBQ with some pork he had bought from the excellent butcher near the top of the steps. He marinated the pork in olive oil, lemon, crushed garlic, chilli and fennel seeds and fresh thyme, and he added salt and a little paprika. When it had marinated it for two hours, he put the meat on skewers mixed with the vegetables that Annabel had neatly cut. These would be cooked in front of the guests as they drank on the balcony. Next, he made an insalata of courgettes, fennel, onion and peppers along with a mixture of herbs and finished off with white wine vinegar. Eva was getting very good now at making home-made pasta linguine which she hung to dry around the balcony. This was then cooked and mixed with a homemade green pesto sauce. Luke also made a green salad and a spicy hot tomato sauce and some homemade flat bread. For sweet, Luke made a medley of sorbets with mascarpone - lemon, strawberry and a tangy blueberry - which he serves up in tiny glasses with some ginger biscuits. The whole concept of the meal was that guests could help themselves, making it more relaxed than a formal dinner party. Annabel said she hated formal parties, especially with Russ' friends.

When the guests arrived at 7:30, the two men immediately made Luke and the girls feel uncomfortable. It was very clear that Russ was now consorting with the underbelly of Italian life. Although superficially polite, these men carried menace in their speech and their appearance. After the briefest of introductions, Russ ushered them into the large front room and the door was closed firmly behind them. Luke, who was still prepping in the kitchen opposite, could hear that it was the guests who did most of the talking and not Russ. In fact, talk seemed to be dominated by the older man, called Edoardo, a portly bruiser with heavy gold rings and those light-sensitive lenses that stayed permanently dark and made him look sinister. The younger man Matteo was handsome, dark and dressed in a well-cut black suit and white shirt. He was quieter and more sullen than the older man. Russ asked Eva to serve drinks to the guests and this became a full-time occupation given their rate of consumption. But every time Eva entered the room with a tray of newly prepared gin and tonics and whisky and cokes, all conversation stopped abruptly. "I don't like those men," Eva said, as she returned to the kitchen with yet another tray of empty glasses. "Where did he find them, gangster.com?"

When they all eventually emerged from the living room, Russ, who had been morose all day, was now unnaturally buoyant and excitable "Was it the alcohol or whatever they had been taking in the front room, or was it he had made some sort of deal?" Luke wondered. Anyway, Russ went out of his way to thank Luke and the girls for their hard work in preparing the food. He'd heard Eva's singing and insisted she give an impromptu performance before the meal. Eva protested at first but when she realized it was futile she sang a Beatles song 'Eleanor Rigby'. Paired down to a plaintive voice and a sparse guitar, it took on a new dramatic tone. Eva had the courage to adapt some of the original phrasing too which made Luke consider the lyrics in a manner he had not done before. It was quite brilliant. Eva's voice was pure, but it had an edge to it and her guitar playing had improved significantly in the short time since Luke had shown her those few basic chords. The two guests and Russ applauded politely. Annabel hugged her daughter over the guitar when it had finished.

"We are going to have to get you a better guitar," she said.

Then Eva played a song she had written herself. This came as a surprise to Luke and Annabel, it was loosely based on Lady Macbeth and the loss of her baby, told from her point of view. It was beautiful and literate and deliberately ambiguous. The minute it had finished Luke wanted to hear it again.

The meal was appreciated by everyone and the Italian visitors were especially impressed that an Englishman could cook so well. After copious amounts of wine and beer the men had relaxed. They talked football with Luke. Russ - with little interest in the subject - retreated into the background. And even when Annabel tried to change topic to a story of first setting up the business in an effort to include him, Russ just smiled benignly.

But after the visitors had finally staggered from the house and into a taxi, Russ, for a brief moment, became the animated force Luke had seen in the bar off the piazza, the night Annabel came to him. He embraced Luke: "You were a star, Luke, thank you. Thank you," he said, slurring his words. "We managed to pull it off. Thank you. And thank you, Annabel." Russ hugged his wife too. "And where is Eva, she was amazing?" He swung round in his drunken state to search for her.

"She went to bed ages ago, Russ!" Annabel said.

"Of course. And that is where I shall now go," he said, pointing in a general direction the way a drunk man does.

"Bloody hell, I thought I was drunk!" said Annabel, kissing Luke. Together, they switched off lights and blew out candles before Annabel took Luke's hand to lead him to bed.

Russ didn't surface on the Sunday morning. Luke and Annabel had been for a swim at the gym and were sitting outside with Eva when Russ finally appeared in his boxer shorts, revealing the shocking extent of his weight loss. He took some pain-killers and then sank into a chair with a bottle of cold beer. It was immediately clear he had returned to his morose state.

"What you planning to do today, Russ?" Annabel asked.

"I need to go and see Edoardo and Matteo," he said.

"Are you back for dinner?" Annabel asked.

"I'm not sure, don't do anything specially for me, mate," he said, addressing Luke.

It certainly wasn't Luke's place to ask whether Russ was ok: was there something he needed to talk about? Why was he having so many meetings with these strange men? And why was he permanently 'out of it', as Eva had described him? Yet Luke *was* a little surprised that Annabel seemed so indifferent. Did she *really* not care anymore?

Russ was smoking on the balcony when Luke next went into the kitchen. Looking out across the city, yet not really looking at anything in particular. Again, he was lost in his own thoughts and to Luke he seemed a man in his own private hell. Luke could not simply ignore him.

"Are you ok, Russ?" he asked.

The question made him jump. He obviously hadn't noticed Luke walk onto the balcony.

"Bloody Hell, mate, where did you come from!" he said.

"Sorry, I didn't mean to sneak up on you. I could see you were deep in thought," Luke said.

Russ threw his cigarette butt onto the decking and stubbed it out with the heel of his shoe. He bent down and picked it up and then flicked it over the glass partition. He massaged his forehead with his fingers.

"It's business," he said, "it's really not as easy as it used to be. And a couple of bad investments too." Russ paused:

"You haven't got the odd couple of mill lying about, have you?" he said, sarcastically.

"Sorry," Luke said, maintaining the pretence, "If you'd only asked me last week…"

Russ smiled. "Listen mate, you look after Annabel, will you? I can see you make her happy." He paused. "I fucked things up there good and proper."

"You guys had good times, though. She told me all about you two building up the business…living the high life." Luke wanted to make Russ feel better.

"Yeah, we did. We did!" he said, and for the first time in the conversation a warmth came into his eyes. He suddenly shook Luke's hand. "You are a good man," he said, "I can see that." Russ paused. "Now it's time to face Brothers Grimm again so I will see you later, yeah?"

"Are they brothers?" Luke asked, surprised.

"No idea," Russ said, "but they *are* grim!" He allowed himself a bitter laugh and left with his hands in his cream linen jacket pockets and his head down.

Luke returned to the kitchen and unpacked the dishwasher - something he had intended to do before he saw Russ on the balcony. Annabel joined him in the kitchen soon afterwards but Luke didn't say anything about his conversation with her husband. He had some marking to do so he spent the rest of the morning sitting in the balcony reading some short stories a lower school group had written for him. Luke gave Annabel his bank card and pin and she drove to the supermarket and returned an hour later laden with bags. Luke - always eager to find something to distract him when he was marking - helped her put the shopping away.

Then they lay on the couch in the smaller living room and watched back-to-back episodes of a British crime drama that Luke had introduced to Annabel; although neither admitted it, they were both waiting for Russ' return. Annabel was unusually quiet and kept getting up to do little jobs, then she made a coffee that she didn't drink, then she checked on Eva. Finally, she asked Luke whether he could pause the programme because she just couldn't concentrate. She went to sit on the balcony alone.

*

When Russ *did* return it was late afternoon and he announced he was driving straight back to Tuscany. He was 'out of it' again and Annabel suggested he wait until the morning before he made the journey. But Russ was adamant. He hurriedly packed, thanked everyone again for their help the previous night and left.

Although Annabel and Luke were concerned about a drunken Russ driving to Tuscany, there was a palpable sense of relief in the house as soon as he had gone. Eva reappeared, Luke opened a bottle of wine and Annabel finally started to relax.

Chapter 15: The Leap of Faith.

It was the next morning whilst driving into school that Luke received the text from Sophie: **"We need to meet today – I'm in Rome. Don't tell ANYONE about this text and please delete. Sophie."**

Eva was with him and he had to make some lame excuse to her about a reminder from a colleague that he'd promised to help later with some planning for the next academic year. The excuse turned out be quite useful as he could then ask Eva if she could make her own way home after school instead of waiting for him. When Luke got to school he returned Sophie's text: **"Meet me outside the Pantheon at 5pm. What's it about?"** Sophie didn't return a text.

Luke could not think about anything else all day. What was it all about? Why was Sophie in Rome? Why had she not said she was coming? Why the mysterious and abrupt text? By the time the final bell of the day sounded Luke was in an anxious state. He hadn't eaten his dinner and he was conscious of sweating in front of his classes, he'd turned up the air-conditioning until the students started complaining they were cold. His instinct was to drive into the city immediately the class was dismissed but he knew he had to wait for Eva to catch her bus and be out of the way. From the staffroom, he watched it leave the front of the school and then he half ran for his car.

Of course, the traffic into the city was bad and parking a nightmare. Then he had to walk three blocks to reach The Pantheon, his breathing was laboured and he was sweating. It reminded him of the first time he met Annabel at the top of the Spanish Steps.

When he finally arrived at The Pantheon he immediately saw Sophie sitting on a bench. She was dressed in linen trousers, sandals and a t-shirt and she was wearing large sunglasses. She looked very different to how he remembered her - after all, he had really only seen her in uniform and winter casuals until now. But Sophie blended effortlessly into the chic style of the city. With her dark hair and olive skin, she could have easily been mistaken for a local.

"Hi you," Luke said, somewhat nervously. From the curt tone of the texts he feared another reprimand. Maybe she was angry with him for setting her off on this wild goose chase in the first place. Maybe Uncle Fester had made an official compliant and Luke had effectively ruined her career. But Luke's fears we immediately eased the moment she saw him.

"Hi, you too, don't you look well!" she said, embracing him.

"Well this is a surprise!" Luke said. "I've been on tenterhooks all day."

"Yeah sorry about the cloak and dagger stuff but you'll understand when I tell you," Sophie said.

"Let's find somewhere to get a drink?" Luke suggested. "I know a café just two minutes away." He had already decided to take Sophie to a place he had not been to with Annabel and that he was unlikely to go to in the future. It was a small unassuming cafe frequented by the local older men who would drink espressos and smoke.

"Go and find a quiet seat at the back," Luke instructed, "I will order the coffee, I know what you drink by now!"

Sophie heard Luke order in Italian and was impressed. She smiled at him when he returned with the coffees and two bagels. "Thank you," she said, "you look so different. Rome obviously agrees with you!" she said, admiringly.

"Thank you. Now, come on, what's all this about?" Luke said in a business-like manner.

"Well, here goes…" Sophie took a deep intake of breath. "You know the last time we spoke I told you I was in contact with UK customs and Will's movements?"

Luke nodded.

"Well, it came to nothing. Will took the Dover to Calais ferry on the twenty-ninth of January and didn't return until the tenth of February," Sophie said, casually.

"Bloody Hell, are they certain?"

"Yes, quite certain. Anyway, that doesn't matter *now*," Sophie said, waving away Luke's concerns impatiently. "So, I was at a dead end. I was still convinced that Richard had been murdered - but the two people who had a real motive were both out of the country when Richard died. I went home that night depressed and I was just about to text you when my father walked into the house. I told him about it and I honestly expected him saying 'I told you so!' But he didn't. His golden rule in murder cases is always 'look for a motive before you look for the killer'. I was still harping on about the bloody uncle and thinking about an accomplice. He said it was rare that killers involve a third party - it's too risky. 'Who else would have motive?' he said. 'What about the sister?'"

Luke started laughing. "Was that his ONLY contribution? Bloody Hell!"

Sophie suddenly went serious. "Why are you laughing? She *does* have a motive."

"She doesn't!" Luke almost shouted across the table in his indignation. "She hasn't seen her father in years - she's out of the will, Richard told her."

"But did he?" Sophie asked calmly, "You've only got *her* word for that?"

"She wouldn't kill her brother. If you met her you'd understand. She's incapable of harming anyone, let alone her own brother!" Luke was angry and animated by now. To the locals in the bar it must have seemed that this English couple were having a domestic.

"Is there something between you and her, Luke?" Sophie asked.

"Yes!" Luke said, defiantly.

"Bloody hell, Luke!"

"What do you mean, 'Bloody Hell, Luke!' I can see who I want to see, you know. I'm widowed and she and Russ live separate lives!"

"I know. It's just that it would be less awkward if you weren't emotionally involved."

"Annabel did *not* kill her brother, Sophie! What's all this about, anyhow?" Luke said, in an aggressive whisper. "Are you jealous of her?"

Sophie averted her gaze, concentrating on the wall behind Luke. Her eyes were sad. "Do you know how arrogant that sounded, Luke!" she said.

There was a moment's silence. "I'm sorry, I know you are just doing your job and I want you to." Luke sighed. "But I'd stake my life on Annabel being innocent."

"Hear me out, Luke. Just calm down a minute and hear me out. Ok?"

"Ok." Luke said, begrudgingly.

Sophie composed herself again. "I went back to UK Customs and discovered that Russel Sumner was on the Calais to Dover ferry on the 2nd February and he returned on the 4th February."

Luke laughed again. "Well he was probably on business! He does up property in France and Italy and sells it to the Brits."

"Has he told you he's recently come back from England?"

"No, but…"

"Well don't you think that's strange considering you *are* from England?" interrupted Sophie.

"I don't see much of him. He lives in Tuscany with his girlfriend and his baby," said Luke, whilst admitting to himself that Sophie was right, it was strange he hadn't mentioned it.

"I know a lot about Russel Sumner," Sophie said. "Remember that white van that my friend saw near the woods on the night of Richard's death?"

Luke nodded.

"Well, we discovered that Russel Sumner left his car in Calais and hired a white VW van from Avis in Canterbury. He then drove north and ended up in Darwen."

"How do you *know* he drove north to Darwen?"

"He's been caught on various cameras."

"Oh God!" Luke said, starting to understand the significance of what Sophie was telling him. "Oh God!" he repeated.

Luke was more subdued now, allowing Sophie to continue: "We've tracked the white van on motorway cameras and it's on security camera on Darwen High Street, the A666, on Monday 10th February."

"Fucking hell."

"I know this is probably not what you were wanting to hear, Luke." Sophie said, gently. "Of course, that doesn't automatically mean that Russel killed Richard but…" She paused and stared hard at Luke, who was now learning forward and breathing heavily like a boxer between rounds. "We are still hoping that someone will ID him in Darwen on the Tuesday," Sophie continued.

"How will they know what he looks like?" Luke asked.

"I've lifted a photo from his website."

Luke held his hand over his mouth. Then an awful thought occurred to him and his heart raced and his stomach tightened. "Was she with him?" he asked, breathlessly.

"No, Anna didn't leave the country," Sophie said, immediately, as if she was expecting the question.

"Thank God!"

Sophie stretched out her hand and placed it on his hand: "But Luke," she said, "we cannot discount she had something to do with this."

"This is a nightmare!" cried Luke, suddenly getting up from his seat. "I just want to get the next flight home!"

"Don't be silly, you cannot do that." Sophie said, firmly. "And, anyhow, you may well be right, Annabel might be completely unaware of all this. Russel might have acted totally alone. He's got serious money problems, you know?"

"Yes, he was telling me yesterday."

"Luke, if you disappear now it will raise suspicion," Sophie said, gently guiding Luke back into his seat. "We've got to sort an extradition order for Russel, that's what I'm doing at the moment. Then we can arrest him and interview him."

"When?" Luke interrupted.

"As soon as we can. But it's complicated, you will need to be patient."

"This is awful!" Luke said.

Luke and Sophie sat in the café in silence for the next few moments whilst Luke took in the enormity of what he had just learnt. He felt his whole world was once again crashing down around him. His first instinct was to resent Sophie for coming into his sunny new world and turning it upside down. But Sophie was just doing her job - something he had urged her to do all along. It wasn't *her* fault that it hadn't all been neatly resolved with the arrest and conviction of Uncle Fester, was it!

Sophie broke the silence first: "You must not say a thing to anyone at the moment, Luke." Luke tried protest that he understood this, but she continued: "And you *must* act as normal as possible so as not to arouse suspicion. I've really taken a risk in telling you at this stage. The local plod didn't want me to speak to you but…"

"So, you've spoken to the police here. They know all about Russ?"

"Of course, they invited me over. You cannot go barging into situations like this." Sophie looked at her watch. "And speaking of the local police, I need to go now, I've got a meeting."

"Before you go, please reassure me that you don't think Annabel has anything to do with this," Luke pleaded. "They practically live separate lives, he's hardly ever in Rome."

"I wish I could, Luke, I really do." Sophie reached over and put her hands over Luke's shaking hands on the café table. "We just don't know at the moment. I'm sorry."

Tears welled in Luke's eyes. Tears of frustration and anger and fear and self-pity. Why as soon as he was happy did life always do this to him! There was nothing Sophie could say or do to make things better and she reluctantly left Luke alone in the café with his thoughts and his cold coffee. He really did not want to go back to Annabel and the house, but he knew that he must.

*

"Are you sure you are ok?" Annabel said at the end of dinner. "You haven't eaten much, and you've hardly said a word."

"I'm ok, just tired, I think. I need an early night," Luke said, without daring to make eye contact with Annabel.

"It's probably all that cooking you had to do Saturday. It's so much pressure, cooking for strangers. Russ really shouldn't have expected…"

"It was fine. Really." Luke interrupted.

"I love you so much, Luke." Annabel said, suddenly. "I don't know what I'd do now if anything happened to you!" She walked round to where Luke was seated and put both her arms around him as he sat. Luke shivered. "I just want it to be me and you and Eva."

In that moment, Annabel was so vulnerable and earnest; it disarmed Luke completely. "I love you too." Luke said, and he meant it. He meant it more in that moment than ever. Tears welled in his eyes.

"Oh sweetheart," she said putting her arms around him, "you are really not yourself. You get to bed and I will tidy up."

Luke lay on the bed he and Annabel had shared in the basement ever since the first night they slept together. Although it was not as large as Annabel's room and did not enjoy the views over the city, Luke did not want to move into the main bedroom on the top floor, especially with the thought of Russ sleeping in the next room when he returned. Luke could now hear Annabel above him as she packed the dishwasher and cleaned the surfaces. He was hoping he would be asleep when she finally came to bed.

But Luke had little chance of sleep. His head was full of scorpions. He thought it strange how in genuine moments of crisis he would reach for some literary allusion to explain his condition. He regarded poeticising personal suffering as pretentious when others did it. It seemed to diminish it in his mind, making it indulgent and superficial. But he had done it when Sarah was dying and he was doing it again now. Maybe only Shakespeare could give him the language to explain his feelings in moments of crisis.

He started to compartmentalise things. He wasn't upset that suspicion had now fallen on Russ, if Russ was guilty then that was ok. This is what he wanted, wasn't it, to find Richard's killer? To find justice for Richard. And if it had not been for him pushing and prompting Sophie and asking annoying questions then Russ would have got away with it. Luke thought back to that image of Richard hanging in the woods. He shuddered. In his mind's eye, he saw Russ standing on that bench beneath the tree, hauling Richard's lifeless body up and throwing the thin rope over the branch with one hand as he held Richard in the other. Russ the big prop forward versus Richard the tiny cyclist was captured in freeze frame in Luke's head. Luke wondered *where* Russ had killed Richard. Had he drugged him first? No, the autopsy would have picked up that. He must have caught him by surprise?

Scenarios invaded Luke's mind, one followed another. He was starting to panic. His was started racing. He sat up in bed and tried to catch his breath. 'Stop over-thinking!' he told himself. He wasn't a detective, it was not his job to second guess *how* Russ had murdered Richard.

'Think on the positives!' Luke told himself. Sophie had said that Annabel had not been in Darwen or indeed the country at the time of Richard's death. That was something. And yet did she know what her husband was planning to do? Maybe they planned it together. She might have even persuaded him to do it. After all, there *had* been a row between the brother and sister just before Richard's death. Who knew what really transpired that evening? Maybe Annabel was the prime mover in all this – the Lady Macbeth to a weak and desperate man. "Oh God!" he thought. *'Oh God! How can I possibly face her, sleep in the same bed as someone who might have consigned her own brother to a frightful death!'*

Luke switched on the bedside lamp and for the first time since meeting Annabel, he took two Diazepam from his toilet bag and swallowed them down without water. He rarely took two at once, even in his worst moments. His doctor had warned him once it was dangerous, but at that moment Luke really did not care.

He had just switched off the light again when the door opened gently. He watched a silhouette of Annabel undressing in the semi darkness before sliding into bed beside him. She kissed him gently on the forehead.

"Good night. God Bless," she said.

*

Luke woke suddenly and looked at his watch. It was 6am. He roused himself and left the bedroom as quietly as Annabel had entered it a few hours earlier. He climbed the staircase and walked through the kitchen towards the soft light of early morning. The Roman skyline was as beautiful as ever. He slid the door open and immediately heard the sounds of early morning - the Mediterranean bird that sounds like a cricket, the distant sound of traffic. The day was already warm and Luke wiped beads of dew from a chair and sat down in his boxer shorts. 'How could death and betrayal and chaos enter a world as beautiful and ordered as this?' he wondered. 'How could he feel so unhappy in this perfect environment?'

"Good morning? Are you feeling better?" Luke turned to see Annabel behind him. She was still naked and knowingly leaning against the window with her arms behind her revealing a body that wars were fought over, that men died for. "Come back to bed, sweetheart?" she said. "It's too early," she said.

Luke took her hand through the kitchen, down the staircase and into the bedroom. Before he reached the bed, he was fully aroused and determined to fuck her. Nothing would stop him. He might be fucking Lady Macbeth but at that moment it didn't matter. He pushed her onto the bed, pulled her over, took his cock in his hand and entered her from behind. She gasped at the unexpected violence of the moment. This wasn't the Luke she was used to; it excited her.

"Mmmmm, I must have been a *very* naughty girl!" Annabel said, turning her head to him and giggling.

"What?" Luke said, stopping suddenly.

"Go on, I like it, Mr Adams!" she teased.

Luke withdrew as quickly as he had entered. He fell onto the bed next to Annabel and stared at the ceiling. When a confused Annabel looked over to him she could see tears running down the side of Luke's face.

"I'm sorry. I'm sorry," she repeated, stroking his brow and kissing his fore-head. "I was playing, I was just playing," she said, "I thought you would like it." When Luke didn't reply, Annabel become worried: "What's the matter, Luke? What's wrong, sweetheart?"

Luke sat up and he wiped the tears with the back of his wrists.

"I need to have a shower and get ready for work," he said, decisively.

"You sure you are ok for school?"

"I'll be fine. I'm sorry," Luke said, as he walked towards the bathroom.

Annabel sat on the bed for a moment trying to make sense of what had just happened. She was a little frightened. "I will make some coffee," she shouted above the sound of the shower. She put on her dressing gown and left the room.

As he showered Luke chastised himself. He had promised Sophie he would 'act normal' and here he was a few hours later threatening the whole investigation. 'Pull yourself together, you idiot!' he said audibly. He dried and dressed and brushed his hair and went up the stairs to the kitchen. He smiled sheepishly at Annabel. "I'm sorry," he said. "I suddenly thought about Sarah."

"You need to talk about it?" Annabel asked gently.

"Not now," Luke said. "Is Eva up yet?" he asked, changing the subject.

Eva and Luke drove to school in relative silence that morning. She played on her phone whilst Luke thought. He decided he was going to text Sophie the minute he got to school and arrange to meet again.

Hi S, can we meet? Same café?

What time?

11?

k.

Luke spoke to the secretary in the front office who arranged cover. He lied about a toothache and said he'd made an emergency appointment at the dentist for eleven.

The first lesson was with a lower school class in the library followed by Eva's literature group - Macbeth was 'losing it' at the banquet but Lady Macbeth was still calm and composed at this stage in the play and covering for her husband. As soon as the bell went for break Luke ran to the car and drove into the city. When he arrived at the coffee shop the man who had served him the day before smirked knowingly and motioned towards Sophie who was sitting in the same seat. Clearly, he assumed they were having an affair. Luke waved at Sophie and ordered two coffees and then sat down next to her.

"Any news?" he asked.

"I only saw you yesterday, give us chance!" Sophie said.

"I'm not coping with this at all well," Luke said, although there was little need. "How long must this pretence go on?" he asked.

"I really don't know, Luke…only a day or two, hopefully," said Sophie. "Not long."

"What was your meeting all about?" Luke asked.

Sophie started to stir her coffee. "You know I can't tell you that!"

"Well, why did you tell me *anything* at this stage then!" Luke asked, angrily. "I'd rather be in blissful ignorance than *this*." Luke had raised his voice and the men at the bar looked in his direction.

"Luke, calm down," Sophie said. "I thought you deserved to know what was going on. And I knew you'd be upset if I suddenly turned up and arrested Annabel without any warning."

"Are you going to?" asked Luke.

"I don't know yet." Sophie paused. "What I *can* say after my meeting yesterday is that we are more interested in Russel at the moment. He's in a lot of trouble." Luke was waiting for more. "He has been keeping bad company," Sophie added.

"Yes, I think I might have met them!" Luke said.

Sophie was interested: "Why, have they been to the house?"

"I cooked for two of Russ' business partners on Saturday evening." Luke said, dramatically gesturing quotation marks as he said 'business partners'.

"They are mafia from Naples," Sophie whispered.

"*Fucking hell, Sophie*, I'm getting really frightened," Luke said, a little too loud. "I'm just a simple English teacher. I need to go home."

"Shhh! You can't. Not yet, anyway." Sophie was assertive. "And what about Annabel and her daughter, you can't just abandon them!"

"But what if Annabel is in on it too!"

"I'm less inclined to believe that now…with this new stuff."

"Really?" said Luke, his tone changing for the first time since he had sat down.

"I think Russel is a desperate man. He clearly needed money. Maybe he owed these mafia guys. The Italian police think he's been living this double life for a while. And we do know he and his wife have lived separate lives for some time." Sophie paused for emphasis: "But we cannot say for certain at this stage, Luke. So, don't go thinking Annabel's totally in the clear."

"I won't," Luke said, "but thank you, that does make me feel a bit better." He smiled a little. "Well, about Annabel, I do, the mafia frighten me…"

"They won't be interested in you, Luke. Don't worry." Sophie interrupted.

"You think?"

"I'm quite sure. Now try and chill out and please don't say a word."

"So, what's the plan now?" Luke asked.

"I think Russel is back in Tuscany with his girlfriend. The local police will pick him up and bring him to Rome so I can question him here." Sophie stopped. "I really shouldn't be telling you all this!"

"I'll feel happier when that happens, I tell you!"

"Just be patient, Luke. It's going to be sorted soon. Mind you, I'm going to the Colosseum today, so I hope it's not *too* soon!"

Luke went back to school in a more relaxed mood. The school was closing the next day for its summer break so he allowed his classes to watch films, a tradition in the English school system which had not seemed to have crossed the channel. This gave Luke time to think about Annabel. He was relieved that the Italian police and Sophie seemed to be of the same mind that Annabel was probably unaware of her husband killing her brother. But Luke still had nagging questions. How did Russ know about the money? And how did he know where to find Richard?

Luke tried to satisfy himself with answers. He remembered Russ had been at the house the night of the phone call. He would have surely asked Annabel what it had been about. And Russ was clearly a resourceful man who could have found Richard without the help of his wife.

By the time Luke got back to the house that evening he felt exhausted. Annabel greeted him warmly. She had made pizza from scratch and asked Luke to choose a topping. "Artichokes," he said flippantly, secure in the knowledge that Annabel would not have them in the house. They both laughed, and it broke the ice a little. They decided on anchovy pizza in the end with a nice green salad and a bottle of red wine.

But conversation was strained. Annabel tried to bring up what had happened earlier that morning but Luke closed down the conversation. He didn't want to have to tell more lies about Sarah – it sullied her memory to be used in such a way.

Annabel was conscious that Luke was constantly checking his phone that evening and it started to make her suspicious. It was she who decided to go to bed early that evening.

The next day was the last day at school and Eva was out with friends at an end-of-term party that evening. She travelled in with Luke as usual but Luke drove home alone. Again, all day his thoughts were on Russ and Annabel and the whole damn mess. He even imagined at one point he was being followed home by a big dark Mercedes.

When he got in the house Annabel was dressed for going out. "Come on, we are eating out tonight to celebrate the holidays. We can have a few drinks first. It's my treat."

Luke really wasn't in the mood for going out but he showered and changed and very soon he and Annabel were walking down the Spanish Steps to a bar on the piazza. He drank beer and she had pink gin. Luke drank it quickly in an effort to relax a little and ordered another. Despite Annabel's protests he insisted on paying. He didn't want to risk Annabel's card being rejected again.

Annabel suggested another bar off the piazza. This was livelier but still conversation between Luke and Annabel was strained. Since they had met silences had never been a problem, this was something that had impressed Annabel from the very start. But now they sat like strangers.

"Do you really love me, Luke?" Annabel asked suddenly after another awkward silence.

"Yes. Yes, I do," Luke said.

"Because if you are getting bored of me, or you've seen someone else, I'd just as soon know." She stopped as if waiting for some kind of positive response, but none was forthcoming. "I'm a straightforward girl," she said at last, "I love you, Luke, I really do. I've surprised myself at how much I love you and how quickly I've fallen in love with you. You know, I'd be prepared to give all this up and come and live with you in England if that's what's troubling you."

"No, it's not Rome," Luke said, "I love it here. I love teaching here. Everything!" said Luke, and he meant it.

"So, what is it Luke? Is it me?" Annabel pleaded.

"No, you are lovely and beautiful. Everything a man could ever want," Luke said.

"Then what's the matter, Luke?" There was a desperation in Annabel's voice and tears came into her eyes. Her voice had become shrill and she nearly shouted the question over the table.

"Please Annabel, just give me time," Luke said. "I told you yesterday, it's Sarah. I suddenly feel guilty about Sarah."

"But wouldn't Sarah want you to find love again?" Annabel asked, gently.

"I know, it's silly. I'm sorry. I'm sure it will pass. It just doesn't seem right that I'm so happy and she's, well..." Luke was growing into his part now. He felt wretched using Sarah in this way again but what choice did he have!

"Doesn't Sarah's death at such a tragically young age show us all that we have to seize the moment and whatever happiness comes our way?" Annabel asked. "Remember what you told me about Richard?"

"You are right, of course, it's just that......" said Luke, still protesting.

Annabel took hold of both Luke's hands over the table and stared into his face. "Listen, you silly boy, I'm crazy about you. And I love what you've done for Eva too. We have a fantastic future together, I just know we have." She paused, expecting Luke to respond in kind. "But if you need time," she went on, "I'll give you as much time as you need. I won't rush you. Just as long as I can be certain you love me too. Ok?"

"Thank you." Luke squeezed her hands in his. Tears came to his eyes. *'I love this woman!'* he exclaimed to himself! "I don't deserve you," he said out-loud and he meant it. He hadn't prayed since Sarah's death but he prayed at that moment: "Please God, if you are there, *show* me that Annabel is innocent!"

They walked back to the house holding hands. If faith was an act of will then he would *will* himself to have faith in Annabel. For the first time in his life he would take a leap of faith and not look back. Wasn't faith about belief without waiting for absolute proof? And were not your instincts your guide in moments like this? Luke's instinct said that this was a good woman, an honest, good woman who – despite her grand life and her grand house – had suffered like he had suffered and was still suffering now. They must face whatever lay ahead together. Luke would not leave himself stranded in a state of nothingness like he had before but commit to whatever was on the other side. 'I believe,' he prayed, 'help my unbelief!'

And there it was, Luke's epiphany. He glanced across at Annabel and he *knew*. He didn't need to wait for the interviews or Russ' confession or the inquest. He knew there and then that Annabel was *innocent*.

CHAPTER 16: THE CLOSENESS OF DEATH

To anyone observing from outside, the next couple days would have seemed very normal for Annabel and Luke. Now Luke had finished work, the couple spent the Thursday together – they went to the gym, did some shopping and then leisurely cooked and ate on the balcony. On Friday they walked down the steps and into the Piazza again and sat outside at a bar and shared a bottle of wine. But all the time Luke's thoughts were elsewhere – he was feeling guilty and awkward, knowing as he did, that investigations were underway across Europe to gather sufficient evidence to extradite and eventually convict Russ, and yet he was unable to tell Annabel, to prepare Annabel. However much he tried, Luke could not ignore the undeniable fact that Russ had killed Richard and the awful truth was about to come out. Luke imagined the knock on the door somewhere in Tuscany – Russ being escorted from the house, head-bowed and handcuffed, like he had seen on so many news reports. And then the tsunami of media in Italy and England descending on Annabel, hungry for exclusives…desperate for exclusives. Bloody hell, the story had everything! Poor Annabel – her life would never, ever be the same again.

*

Annabel usually took Clara, the elderly expat, to church on a Friday. But when she phoned to arrange, as she always did, the maid told her that Clara had been sick and would not be able to go to church. Assuming it was a flu bug, which seemed rife in the city at the time, Annabel thought little more about it until the maid rang back to say that Clara had asked to see her. It was late in the day by then so Annabel decided to visit Clara the next morning and she asked Luke to go with him.

"I'd like you to meet her," Annabel said, "she's forever asking about you. It will cheer her up to finally meet you."

So, on Saturday morning Annabel drove to Clara's large house in Aventino, an exclusive area in the city. The maid who answered the door was clearly relieved. She ushered Annabel and Luke into the large front room and closed the door behind them as she explained in her broken English how she had found Clara on the Thursday in the garden. She had fallen, and it wasn't clear whether she had tripped or collapsed. The doctor wondered whether she had suffered a stroke – apparently, he had wanted to send Clara to hospital for observations, but Clara was adamant that she would stay at home. She was just tired, she said. Clara was upstairs in bed – where she'd been since Thursday – and showing no sign of getting better. The maid was so concerned she had called the doctor again who had visited first thing that morning and taken bloods. He had promised to return later that day.

Annabel and Luke listened in solemn silence as the maid explained all this. She had worked for Clara and her husband ever since they had arrived in the city and she was clearly greatly attached to the old lady. Her husband Antonio also worked for Clara as the gardener and odd-job man. As she spoke she started to weep – this and her broken English made it difficult at times to understand her. Annabel had never been upstairs in the house before but when she asked whether she could see Clara the maid welcomed the suggestion. She led the way up the grand stair-case – Annabel followed the maid and Luke followed them both. He felt awkward about being shown into a stranger's bedroom.

The room was at the front of the house and the maid pushed the two large doors open in a single, decisive action. The room was grand and ornate with large burnished gold furniture and wall hangings. It reminded Luke of those grand rooms at Chatsworth that were now relics of a long-forgotten era. On the left wall and opposite the curtained window was an enormous four poster bed and in it lay the tiny frame of the old lady. Everything in the bed was white: the bedsheets, the old lady's nightdress – even the hair on the old lady's white shrunken head that lay sleeping on a large white pillow.

"Madam?" the maid said, gently caressing Clara's hand lying on top of the bed clothes. "Madam?" she said again. "You have visitors, Annabel has come to see you."

The old lady opened her eyes slowly and smiled in recognition when she saw Annabel. She tried to sit up and the maid arranged the pillows for her.

"I shall get tea, yes?" the maid said to Annabel. "Madam, tea?"

"Yes, thank you, Maria, that would be nice," the old lady said.

Annabel sat on the edge of the bed and took Clara's hand in her hand.

"So, what have you been doing, you naughty girl?" she asked in mock indignation.

The old lady smiled weakly. "I was cutting some flowers for the table," she said.

"And then what?" Annabel prompted.

"Oh, I don't know!" the old lady said, dismissively. "The next I knew I was inside on the couch with Antonio…and poor Maria wailing over me." She smiled again weakly. "They are so dramatic these Italians!" she added mischievously in an attempt to diffuse the seriousness of the moment.

"Well the doctor thinks you've had a stroke." Annabel said, not allowing Clara to dismiss the situation so readily. "You really don't look well, Clara."

Clara's gaze shifted to Luke, noticing his presence for the first time.

"Hello, I'm Luke," he said, not that it was really necessary to introduce himself.

"Of course, you are!" The old lady's face lit up. She looked up to Annabel. "I approve," she said.

"I've heard a lot about you, Clara," said Luke. "Annabel speaks very fondly about you. You've had quite a life!" he continued.

The old lady's face turned suddenly sad as if Luke had reminded her of times she would never enjoy again.

"Are you feeling any better?" Luke asked, hastily.

"I'm just very tired," she said, "but I'm not in pain. In fact, I can't seem to feel anything down this side," she said, gesturing towards her left side.

"Have you told the doctor?" interrupted Annabel. "You should be in hospital, Clara."

"I'm happy here," she said, decisively, "I've got Maria and Antonio."

At that moment an elderly man came in with a tray of drinks and a few home-made biscuits.

"Oh, thank you," said Annabel, getting up from the bed. "Luke, this is Antonio, Maria's husband."

The man put the tray down on the dresser and acknowledged the visitors with a faint bow of the head. "You wish me to…?" he said, gesturing towards the tray.

"No, no, I will be mother," Annabel interrupted.

With that, Antonio bowed again and left the room, closing the doors behind him.

"Antonio's such a sweetheart," Clara said when he had left the room. He walked round to the church yesterday and asked the priest to come and see me.

"Have you always been religious, Clara?" Luke asked, in an attempt to make conversation.

She smiled. "No, I've got Annabel to thank for that. She told me about this beautiful church she went to where the priest spoke English."

"Oh!" said Luke, confused, "I thought it was *you* who had encouraged Annabel to go to church!"

"Oh no," said Clara, smiling again. "I used to go to church as a child in St Johns Wood but when we got married Hugo wasn't interested and I just got out of the habit…but when I met Annabel she kept asking me."

At that moment Maria came into the room announcing the doctor had returned so Annabel and Luke hurriedly left the bedroom and went back down into the large front living room. After around thirty minutes the doctor came down and explained the prognosis, first in Italian and then in English for Annabel and Luke. The blood tests had revealed that Clara was dying, it was not a stroke as first thought but advanced Leukaemia. Clara knew she was dying.

As the doctor spoke Annabel's phone rang. She ignored it, but it rang again. Then Luke's phone rang. It was Eva – probably wanting a lift somewhere, Annabel guessed, 'And at a time like this!'

After the doctor had left, Annabel rang Eva back. She was very upset because Russ' Italian friends had returned and were now ensconced in the front room. 'Waiting for Russ', they said. Annabel was torn – it wasn't fair to leave Eva with two men but she desperately wanted to see Clara again, especially now that she knew the truth about the illness. She explained to Maria who told her she must go home immediately and she would explain to Clara who she knew would understand. Annabel and Luke left with Annabel promising she would return the next day.

When Luke and Annabel finally got back to the house they were greeted by a frightened Eva standing at the open front door, looking out for them. "I'm scared, mummy!" she said. She'd clearly been holding back tears but she now broke down as she clung to her mother.

Luke walked ahead of Annabel into the large living room where the two Italians had ensconced themselves. "What do you want?" Luke said, in his most authoritative teacher's voice. The underlying menace of the men last week had been masked by a thin veneer of general politeness. But now all pretence had gone.

"Where's Russ?" Edoardo, the older man, spoke directly to Annabel completely ignoring Luke's protest.

"I've no idea," Annabel said, curtly.

"Call him now!" Edoardo demanded. Meanwhile Matteo, the younger of the two, was walking round the room picking up ornaments, inspecting them and then putting them down. He was full of threat and menace like some cameo gangster.

"Why are you speaking to Mrs Sumner in this manner?" Luke asked. "Whatever your issue with Russ, it's nothing to do with her," said Luke, gesturing towards Annabel. He was feeling frightened but trying to assert himself. "Now if you don't leave the house immediately, I am going to call the police."

The older man looked at the younger man momentarily – a weary, knowing look but not the look of a man who was in any way intimidated by Luke's assertive tone or mention of the police.

"I think, sir, you should stay out of this," Edoardo said, his tone was strangely courteous. "Please allow us to speak with Ms Sumner alone."

"I will *not* abandon Ms Sumner to you," Luke shouted, summoning up as much courage as he could muster. "*And* I think I know more than you imagine. Now, I ask again, will you leave the house…or am I to call the police?"

Annabel was surprised at Luke's calm authority and it suddenly gave her the confidence to speak. "Could you please leave my home immediately…you are frightening my daughter." And as if to illustrate her point Annabel drew Eva towards her.

As Annabel spoke the younger of the two men, who had now positioned himself near the door to the room, effectively cutting off any means of escape, calmly and very deliberately picked up a large vase that stood on an ornate cabinet near the door. He examined it briefly and then in a sudden, single action hurled the vase towards the large mirror that hung over the fireplace. The impact of the breaking vase and glass reverberated around the sparse room like an explosion. As a deliberately provocative action designed to emphasise the seriousness and intent of these men, it certainly worked. There followed a moment of shocked silence interrupted only by the sound of a large piece of glass falling from the mirror onto the stone hearth, breaking as it did. Annabel and Eva screamed in unison and clung to each other like poor souls cast adrift in a raging tumult. Luke tried to calm Annabel by placing his hand gently on her shoulder. His other hand reached for his phone.

When Annabel and Eva screams had subsided a little, Edoardo spoke again. "Please understand Ms Sumner that it's over now," he said, in the same calm manner which seemed so much at odds with the violent actions of his partner, "this is not your home anymore. This is *our* home now." He smiled, benignly. "Now you must call your husband. You must tell him we need to talk to him."

"What do you mean, this is *your* house?" screamed Annabel, confronting the man now face to face whilst still holding on to her distraught daughter.

In her fury Annabel had unintentionally sprayed spittle into the man's face. He pulled a handkerchief from his jacket pocket and wiped away the spittle in an exaggerated gesture. "Speak to your husband, Ms Sumner," he said. "We will go now but we *shall* return." And then he repeated: "Speak to your husband, Ms Sumner."

With that, the older man left the room and Matteo followed – but he backed towards the door, staring intently at the terrified mother and daughter. A smirk spread over his usually dour face and he used his right hand to mime a pistol, which pointed at Annabel's head before he too finally disappeared from the room. The front door slammed and the house fell silent.

A silence existed for nearly thirty seconds as time stood still to catch its breath. Annabel suddenly broke the silence: *"Oh my God! Oh my God!"* she wailed, *"What's happening?"* she cried out. "I'm scared Luke! I'm really scared!" Eva hugged her mother but was weeping herself.

Luke was already speaking into his phone. "Sophie, thank God," he said, "it's Luke, we've just had the two mafia men round." Luke raised his palm gesturing to Annabel and Eva for quiet but there was really no need – the intrigue of Luke's intervention caused both to listen. "They were wanting Russ." Luke explained. "Ok," he said after a longer pause. "Hello, yes, I'm Luke Adams." Luke said, in a more formal voice. "Yes, she is here with me. And her daughter, yes." There was another pause. "No, he's not here yet." Luke said, followed by an even longer pause "Ok. Ok, right," Luke said, finally.

Luke motioned towards Annabel and nodded: "Yes, she has. Of course, there's no guarantee he will pick up!" A pause. "Ok. Yes. Yes. Thank you, inspector." Luke pressed his screen to end the call.

"What's going on, Luke?" Annabel said, just as soon as the call had ended.

"I need you to ring Russ. Tell him what's happened and tell him you need him back here *now*," said Luke.

"Is that the Sophie you talked about?"

"Yes."

"Why did you call her?"

"Please, Annabel, just call Russ. I will explain later."

"Why is everyone telling me what to do at the moment!" Annabel shouted again, sitting down on the sofa with her head in her hands. She was silent for a moment. "How long have you been talking to the police, Luke?" she said, impatiently.

"Since Sophie asked me to meet here last week." Luke said, calmly.

"So why didn't you tell me?" Annabel said, bitterly.

"Can I explain it all later, Annabel?" Luke repeated. "I am just trying to help you now. Please trust me. Call Russ and tell him to get back here now."

"But he's in Tuscany! It's at least two hours……!"

"He's not," Luke said, impatiently.

"How do you…"

"Please Annabel, just do it!" Luke was becoming impatient with Annabel.

The urgency of Luke's imperative sparked Annabel into action. She sulkily retrieved her phone from the kitchen, and as she returned to the living room she was scrolling to find Russ' number. She stabbed at the screen. At first it seemed that Russ would not answer. "He's not…" she started to say, and then: "Russ, those men have been round, the ones from last Saturday, they were horrible. Where are you?" Annabel spoke in a torrent of words. Then there was a pause. "In your *car*! Where?" Annabel shouted into the phone. "Well, you need to come back, *quickly*. You need to sort this out, Russ! They say this is *their* house!" A pause. "What do they mean, then?" Annabel demanded. Luke could hear Russ' voice trying to pacify his wife on the other end of the phone. "Ok, well hurry up." Annabel pressed the screen and put the phone down and fell back into the large couch. Her head was bowed for a second or two and the stillness re-entered the room. Eva was now calm. She sat beside her and put her arm round her mother who was now sobbing quietly. After all the frenetic activity and conversation of the previous ten minutes it seemed cathartic to Luke.

"You know what this is about!" Annabel said, finally breaking the silence. "You *knew* Russ wasn't in Tuscany." Annabel's tone was bitter and accusatory and it surprised Luke.

"Annabel please just trust me. I can't tell you anything," he said. "You'll understand why later. Please trust me." Annabel started to sob again. Quietly at first. But every sob seemed to give momentum to the next and grew louder and deeper and her body shook under the sheer force of them. "I'm scared," she said.

Luke walked to where she was sitting on the coach. He stood opposite her and then crouched to Annabel's eye-level, the way he had done many times with children in distress at school. "Now listen to me, Annabel," he said, "I cannot tell you much but you and Eva are *not* in danger. This place is being watched by the local police, they won't let *any* harm come to you and Eva, I promise." He paused, then said decisively, "Now let's just wait."

Annabel seemed to calm a little.

"Eva, could you go and make us a drink please?" Luke said. Eva, who had been both impressed and surprised with the way that Luke had handled the situation since the men had left, nodded and without saying anything got up and went to the kitchen.

Luke took the opportunity to speak to Annabel about what the man had said. "Who owns this house?" he asked, taking Eva's place next to Annabel.

"We do!" she said. "I mean, Russ and I."

"Have you a mortgage on it?"

"No, Russ brought it outright, like I said. He got it cheap. And then he spent nearly five hundred grand doing it up like this." As she said this, Annabel instinctively looked around, catching sight of the broken vase and the shattered mirror.

"So, did he get a loan or mortgage for the alterations?" Luke pressed.

"No, I told you," she said impatiently, "we'd had a bumper year selling properties and Russ paid cash for everything. He was very proud." Annabel paused for breath, "So why do you think that Edoardo says it's his?" she asked.

"I don't know." Luke paused. "Did you know that Russ was having money problems?" he said, gently.

"He told me he was sorting it. How do you know?"

"It's just little things," Luke said, "like downgrading the car and your credit card. Did you ever resolve that, by the way?"

"No," Annabel said, with a sigh.

Eva entered the room with the tray of hot drinks. "Anyway," said Luke, "you can ask him when he gets back. He should be here soon." Luke smiled at Eva. "Thank you, sweetheart, you're a star!"

*

"What's keeping him, Luke? How long did it take us to drive from Florence to Rome?" Annabel asked. They had all moved into the smaller living room now. Annabel tried to stay seated and Eva held her but she got to her feet whenever she heard a car engine in the immediate vicinity of the house.

"About two hours," said Luke. "But we don't know where he's coming from. It could be north of Florence. And the traffic may be bad," said Luke, who was now starting to get concerned himself that Russ had done a runner.

"Even so, he should be here." Annabel could hardly suppress her tears. "I'm so scared of those men coming back. But I don't want to go out without talking to him. I need to know what the truth is about this place." Annabel paused. "I could have lost everything, Luke." Annabel's voice broke again as she uttered the words.

"Come on, let's try to think positive," said Luke. "I'll make us another drink."

"Luke, I'm sick of bloody coffee…" Annabel said, angrily.

Russ' day began in Tuscany with his Italian girlfriend, Alessia, and their baby. There had been a knock on the door. It was very early and they were all still in bed. Russ came down the wooden stairs of the little stone cottage, situated just outside the picturesque Tuscan village of Marti, west of Florence. He was bare chested and in jogging pants and muttering to himself about 'how fucking ridiculous that anyone should call at such an hour on a Saturday!'

When he opened the door he was surprised to see Vincenzo and another man standing outside in uniform. Vincenzo was the local police officer and he lived in the village. Russ and Alessia had been out drinking with Vincenzo and his wife and regarded them as friends. But this morning Russ could sense Vincenzo's awkwardness. "I'm sorry, Russ," he said, in his broken English. "I'm sure it is a misunderstanding but we have to arrest you. There's been an extradition order from England on suspicion of a serious crime." Vincenzo was reading from a charge sheet.

"What?" said Russ, incredulously. "You must have made a mistake, Vincenzo. Please go back to your office and check again."

"What's the matter?" Alessia said, standing at the top of the stairs in her pyjamas.

"Vincenzo's come to arrest me!" Russ said, laughing in an exaggerated fashion.

"I'm sorry, Alessia, I'm sure he'll be back before dinner!" Vincenzo called up the stairs. "Can we come in please? It's a bit embarrassing..." Vincenzo gestured to the house next door.

"Yes, of course, of course," said Russ, ushering them both into the front room. "Alessia, will make you a coffee whilst I get washed and changed. Ok?" he shouted up the stairs. "It's not your fault Vincenzo," Russ said, "it's just a mistake."

The two Italian policemen sat down on the sofa and Russ went into the kitchen behind the small living room to switch on the coffee-maker to allow the water to warm up. He then switched on the TV for the officers, the Sky Channel was showing a rerun of a European game between Barcelona and Inter Milan.

When Russ got upstairs, Alessia was putting on her jeans. Her face was serious and frightened. She said nothing but hugged Russ for a moment. Then she carried on changing and tidying her hair and cleaning her teeth before heading downstairs and into the kitchen.

Russ got dressed quickly and stuffed a few items into a rucksack. He picked up his phone and the car keys he had managed to slip into his jogging pants whilst the officers watched the TV. Russ opened the balcony doors in the bedroom, moved quietly onto the balcony and stealthily climbed over the rail, down the adjacent wastewater pipe and onto the pavement at the back of the house. From there, Russ crept round to the front of the house. Being sure to keep low and under the eye-line of the windows, he made his way to the far side of the police car. Kneeling, he let the air out of the back tyre. When this was completed, Russ repeated the process on the far front tyre by removing the cap and pressing the metal pin at the centre of the valve with the end of his car key. It was frustratingly slow but Russ knew it needed to be done properly if he was to make his escape.

When he was satisfied that both wheels on the far side of the police car were flat, Russ retraced his steps, still bent low. He opened the door on his own car, the door furthest away from the house which was the driver's side. He did this with a key so as not to engage the bleep that signalled the door was open. Russ threw his rucksack into the passenger seat and started the car, simultaneously thrusting it into reverse and accelerating backwards out of the drive, causing a loud screeching noise. Then he was into first and straight ahead down the quiet country road. As he changed through the gears he saw Vincenzo and his partner in his rear-view mirror racing out of the front door of the house and towards their car with Alessia following. Russ allowed himself a brief smirk.

Russ drove to Rome using the minor roads. He knew the route well because in the early days of setting up the business in Tuscany he could not afford to pay toll prices and so he would weave his way across the country on minor roads past vines that seem to stretch as far as the eye could see.

Russ didn't really have a plan, but he needed to be away from Tuscany and the fear of police custody and the almost inevitable prospect of extradition and a trial in England followed by, God knows, how many years in prison. And what when he eventually got out as an old man? He had nothing now. Nothing. He drove towards Rome, towards another danger, but he knew he must.

He had reached the outskirts of Rome before Annabel rang and delivered the frantic news about the gangsters. He'd half expected it. If they touched Annabel, he swore to himself, he'd have another murder on his hands! It was like a pincer movement - on one side, the police; on the other the gangsters wanting their pound of flesh…and much, much more!

He thought back to the days when he had started the business. When he and Annabel were young and hungry. She was always brilliant with the British punters, she could charm far more out of them than they had ever intended. And how the business took off in the early 2000s! It was like taking candy from a baby. Properties in Tuscany were cheap, bloody cheap. But the ones the Brits went for - the old farm houses with a few olive trees - were also very dated and not at all the style these middle-class investment bankers were used to. So, Russ bought them by the shed load and spent a few bob ripping everything out, painting them neutral colours and fitting flat pack kitchens and bathrooms. He did a good job, mind - surprising what you can do with a bit of paint and imagination. And then, bingo, they sold them on to the eager punters with more money than sense. Russ and Annabel worked bloody hard and did a lot of the labouring themselves in the early days.

And he and Annabel lived the life. Oh, how they did! Out every night. Eva was a bloody nuisance but he paid for a nanny so she stayed over most of the time. Actually, Russ had a little fling with her, he remembered.

And then they saw this property on the market near The Spanish Steps in Rome. It was in a right state but the artist who owned it was desperate for money, he had a serious coke habit. And when Russ offered him cash, literally euros in a big suitcase, he couldn't resist. Russ learnt he'd blown it all on booze and drugs and was found dead in some hostel a couple of years later. Anyway, Russ had got himself one hell of a house. And you couldn't have a better position. People would take him seriously now, all those Oxbridge twats he sold to. And his public school mates back in England who never fucking let him forget he was the scholarship boy! In fact, he paid for one to come over just so he could report back. And he shagged his missus before they left.

But then he expanded into Provence. Big mistake! The bloody French were a nightmare to work with, so much fucking red tape. You just couldn't cut corners or do deals with cash in the same way. And there were less punters after the fucking crash. In fact, they started backing out of deals after the contract was done and dusted. He made fucking sure they paid a penalty, though. Too fucking right!

He concentrated mainly on Tuscany after the crash. Plus, he'd met this Italian bird. Annabel was good for her age, no denying it, but she'd got boring and religious and this girl was young and exciting. But then she went and got bloody pregnant, didn't she, and she was determined to keep it. She thought they were going to get married and play happy fucking families.

Alessia knew about Annabel, of course. But Russ had told her about the nightmare daughter and that it was just a business relationship now, which was more or less true. He said he couldn't divorce her yet. It was a bit embarrassing really, he'd had to borrow money against the house in Rome and if they divorced he'd have to come clean about it. She'd be devastated to find out she had nothing! He just couldn't do that to her.

As things began to slide, Russ was drinking and taking shit loads of coke instead of grafting! Lots going out, fuck all coming in. It was simple arithmetic. He had to sell the four properties in Tuscany to settle his debts in Provence because the French bastards wanted to lock him up for fraud…and they were still after him for more! Another thing he couldn't tell Annabel. He'd even borrowed against the house he was living in, the one left to Alessia by her family! He bought a couple of shitty, cheap places in Tuscany but he hadn't got the funds or the energy to do them up properly and he had to sell them at a loss. Was it the recession or had he just lost his touch!

And then his biggest gamble, he borrowed against the house in Rome. Again! And it didn't even belong to him! But he convinced these guys from down south he met in a bar that he was some sort of high-flying entrepreneur and they had wanted to get into a legit business as a kind of front for their 'day job'. Russ still had the lifestyle and the car and the house and the wife…and he could move round Europe without attracting suspicion. But after they'd handed over the euros, Russ went AWOL for weeks along with their investment. Then they started getting nervous and asking Russ for his house deeds and taking his Porsche as security. Russ kept spinning them any old shit just to buy time till something came up. But now they were threatening him and turning up at his house in Rome and getting him to run 'errands' for them. It was all getting quite scary, he had to admit!

Russ had never been interested in Annabel's family. Or his own for that matter. But these were desperate times and Annabel had always said her father was loaded. The old Russ had got on just fine without having to go cap in hand to family…and it would have been a total waste of time with his fucking bunch of losers. But Annabel's father? Well, it was worth a punt! And Russ had carried her all these years - she'd come with nothing. In olden times women came with dowries, for fuck's sake! And her bloody brother was going to get it all. Annabel had always said that - and it hadn't really bothered Russ. Until now, that was.

Russ recalled the night he sat Annabel down and told her the truth. Well, his version of truth: "We've got problems." Annabel couldn't believe it, because whenever she asked about the business Russ fed her the same old line, 'we're holding our own'. She was angry, 'why hadn't he told her before?' Then she was upset, he'd never seen her so upset. When she'd calmed down a little, she suggested she come back and work with him, like old times, but Russ knew it was far too late for that. No, Russ' rare and untypical moment of honesty was merely to prepare the ground: "You must go visit your father," he said. "Make your peace with him." Russ had done a bit of research, posing as one of those cold callers who prey on the old, persuading them to release capital from their homes. He spoke to a housekeeper who said Mr Harrington wouldn't be interested as he was very sick. That was all he needed to know. The timing was perfect!

But Annabel was having none of it. There was no way, she said, she would ever speak to him again. Russ pushed and pushed, he tried everything. But she was determined. She'd rather live on the street than go cap in hand to her father. It was bollocks, of course, she wouldn't last a minute on the street. She loved her comfortable life. Her little trips to church and her respectable friends. And she loved Rome.

And just about when he had given up all hope, there was a phone call one Friday evening and it was the brother. He said the old man was dying. But in a moment of clarity he'd begged the brother to contact his sister. He wanted to see her one last time. The brother said he had promised he would try his best - he pleaded with Annabel. Annabel was drunk and angry. "Was this the same father who had tried to deprive his dying wife of seeing her children?" Russ liked an argument and this was a humdinger!

"Am I even in his will, Richard?" she asked suddenly, after what seemed like an eternity wading through the fucked-up family history.

Clearly the brother was thrown by the directness of the question but Russ knew exactly what Annabel was thinking. There was a lot of prevarication but the he finally admitted everything went to him. And Russ knew, then and there, whatever happened, they couldn't change that. Not with the father's Alzheimer's. Fuck!

He guessed the brother must have said something along the lines of "What did you expect!" because Annabel came out fighting: "You little fool, you fucking little fool," she shouted, "you weren't adopted, Ruth was your mother too. She'd had an affair," And then my sweet, innocent wife started enjoying herself: "And that fucking dying old man - the one you are so desperate to help now - stopped your mother telling you the truth all these years. And he's now leaving you everything out of guilt, not love. He's never loved you Richard!"

The brother was devastated, of course. Apparently, he said he never wanted to see or hear from the family again. Apparently, he wouldn't touch his father's money, and he'd give it all to the church - his mother would approve of that and his father would hate it. The phone went dead - along with Annabel's last hope of family money.

Russ wouldn't call himself a principled man. He certainly didn't believe that people were held accountable for their actions. He didn't believe in heaven and hell or karma, and shit like that! He believed in the survival of the fittest. He'd lied and he'd cheated and he'd stolen, but he'd never before taken a life. But he, Russ, was the king of the animals. He'd do anything to survive. Anything.

He was so fucking clever about it. He drove to Calais, left the car there and took the ferry and hired a van at the other side. Not from Dover, just in case. And then he drove to Darwen, bloody shithole! He waited till it was dark then parked his van behind the brother's house, he'd found his address on the internet. Then he called on him, introducing himself as Annabel's husband. Had all the pictures so it looked kosher. He'd brought some wine with him - strong Italian wine - and he asked rather cheekily if he could stay over. You see, he didn't know the area and he'd driven twenty-four hours solid. He'd heard the row on the Saturday and he'd been so upset for them both. He just wanted to be the peacemaker, the bridge between them if he could. You see, it was all very sad, but Annabel was dying.

Fucking brother bought the whole story, like taking candy…. 'Of course, he could stay the night'. They opened a bottle of wine that Russ had in his rucksack - along with the rope he would use to strangle Richard later. Then Russ opened another bottle and watched Richard get more and more drunk as they swapped stories about Annabel. Russ made most of them up - but who would ever know!

And then around midnight Richard's eyes started going. He hadn't realised it, but he'd drunk nearly two bottles of strong red wine on his own. Russ had been so charming and it had been such a shock, the news of his sister. Russ crept up to the toilet with his rucksack and when he came down Richard was well away. He snuck up from behind the sofa, and dropped the noose over, like you'd put a lead on a dog. Easy. Richard was only fully awake when the rope was tight around his neck with Russ standing over him at the other side of the sofa, and by then it was too late. Russ knew he had to do it quickly, he didn't want Richard thrashing about and getting bruises on his body. He didn't want his hands to scratch round his neck, the tell-tale signs of a homicide. But Russ had the element of surprise and he was sober too and much taller and bigger than Richard. It should have been easier than it was, but the puny cyclist put up a real fight and the rope was thin and cut into his neck more than Russ had expected. All quite messy. In all the excitement, the phone got smashed, that wasn't in plan. But with one sudden violent wrench the fight was finally over. Then there was the clearing up, checking for blood on the sofa and the carpet, cleaning surfaces, placing the wine glass and the phone in the rucksack. He bundled Richard's body inside one of his canvas bike bags - Russ was having to improvise now.

Russ checked the coast was clear, then it was out of the back door and into the van with the bag, through the deserted golf club and up the lane to the stables - he'd rekeyed it that afternoon - parking the car just before the tarmac finished. He'd bought two pieces of rolled plastic at the same B & Q as the rope in Canterbury. He rolled them down in front of him as he carried Richard's body to the tree he had in mind for him. Clever. The bike bag had carrying handles and a long strap that went over his shoulder, it had been a lucky find! 'Thank God he's not a fat bastard!' Russ thought, as he started to sweat. It was bloody hard work carrying a dead weight, and it was made even harder because Russ had to keep putting it down and picking it up to reposition the plastic sheets. Mind, he was pleased to note that the ground was hard from the cold of a February night so the plods wouldn't be expecting footprints.

But the hardest part was fastening one end of the rope around the thick branch. Russ needed to hold the body whilst reaching up to tie the knot. Russ' arms ached and beads of sweat ran into his eyes as he stood precariously on the flimsy bench under the tree. The bench, they'd assume, Richard had launched himself off.

When the job was done Russ stepped back to check his work, the way a craftsman might. It seemed convincing. He retraced his steps using the rolled plastic again and then into the car, a three-point turn - careful not to put the wheels on the verge - and then off. Straight down the track, past the stables. The light was on now and there was a car outside. SHIT! He drove past as quietly as possible, trying hard not to rev the engine. Before he knew it, he was out of the town on the M65, then the M6 and well on his way. He threw Richard's phone hard onto the road and saw it disintegrate.

That had been early February and Russ was still waiting. He scoured the internet for news of the old man's death… but fucking nothing! And then Shakespeare had turned up - and now he and Annabel were playing happy fucking families and that silly bitch Eva was swanning around like butter wouldn't melt.

But Shakespeare was the least of Russ' worries, he could handle him. He'd tried desperately to find someone to invest in the business but when they looked at the figures they were out of Rome like shit off a shovel. So what choice did he have when the loan sharks from the south offered to help him out. And bloody hell, talk of sharks! Coming on like Joe Pesci, frightening the wife! Bloody frightening him too! Russ had to admit he'd underestimated these guys - they were dangerous…and they had dangerous friends. How was he to know they were the fucking Italian mafia…he thought all that shit was in Sicily!

Anyway, Russ was always one step ahead of the game. He had this half decent forgery of the house deed. It wouldn't stand up to close scrutiny, but long enough to get The Brothers Grimm off his back if they were hanging about.

Russ decided he'd wait for dark and sneak back into the house. The Italian plod were sure to be around but he could sneak in the house from The Steps and climb over the balcony. And with the stuff in the safe he could start something in Bulgaria or wherever - just anywhere that didn't extradite. He'd wait for it to get dark and slip in when the coast was clear.

He parked in a quiet side street not far from the top of the steps. He must have dozed off because he was suddenly aware of a gentle tap on the side window. Russ turned. A silencer was pointed straight at him. Phutt. Russ slumped back in his seat, a perfect red hole in the centre of his forehead and a little trickle of blood which ran down his nose through his designer stubble and collected around his lips, red and glossy like lipstick.

Annabel decided she must do something to relieve the tension of the waiting. She went down to the bedroom below - the one she shared with Luke - to freshen up and change, leaving Luke in the living room. She was undressed when she heard the sudden and insistent knock on the door. "Oh God, it's them back!" Annabel cried up to Luke.

"Don't be daft, it will be Russ," Luke shouted back.

"He's got a key, he doesn't knock," shouted Annabel, desperately trying to pull a t-shirt over her head.

"Trust me, we are being watched by the local police. I'll get it," Luke shouted, as he sprinted down the stairs. He pulled the bedroom door closed, leaving Annabel to finish dressing and then opened the front door. Luke was greeted by two Italian policemen and Sophie.

"Oh, hello," he said, a little taken aback by Sophie's presence.

The Italian officer spoke first. "Mr Adams, I am Inspector Gian Greco and this is my Assistant, Marco Benini. You know PC Ronson, I think?"

"Yes, I do," Luke said, acknowledging her with a smile.

"Is Madam Sumner here?" asked Inspector Greco.

At that moment Annabel opened the bedroom door next to where they were all standing. She looked embarrassed but greeted the officers warmly, clearly relieved it was the police and not the men returning as she had feared.

"Good afternoon, Madam," said the inspector, bowing slightly as a mark of respect. His manner was very formal but calm. "I am Inspector Gian Greco and this is my Assistant, Marco Benini …and PC Ronson from England."

"Please, come upstairs." Annabel said. The officers followed her up the impressive staircase and into the living room which still remained as the men had left it.

"Madam Sumner you are married to Mr Russel Sumner, yes?" Inspector Greco said, looking around the room at the damage.

"Well, yes…" Annabel said, a little embarrassed.

"I show you a photograph for identification, madam?" The officer produced a piece of A4 from his top pocket, unfolded it and gave it to Annabel. It was Russ' website picture. "Is that Mr Russel Sumner?" the inspector asked.

"Yes," said Annabel, returning it to the inspector.

"I have something very important to tell you, Madam Sumner." The inspector paused for a moment to steal himself before continuing: "Mr Sumner was found in his car about thirty minutes ago. He is dead, madam."

"Oh God!" Annabel cried. Eva clutched her mother to her. "Oh God!" Annabel cried again. She put her hands to her face and her mouth remained open, as if frozen.

"Was it......was it an accident?" she said at last, her voice close to breaking.

"No, Madam Sumner, your husband has been shot." There was a hint of drama in Greco's voice.

"Oh God! Oh My God! Oh God." Each utterance grew in volume and intensity. "Where?" she asked.

"Close to this house, madam," the inspector said.

"Oh God!" Annabel's body shook and her face twisted in despair. She swayed unnaturally and Luke, fearing she might faint, shepherded her towards the couch. But she resisted him, pushing Luke away from her. "Was it those men? The men who were here today?" she asked, bitterly, looking around the room and at the damage to illustrate their presence.

"We do not know, madam. We are even now investigating." The inspector paused. "Madam, we were waiting to arrest Mr Sumner."

"Arrest him! Arrest him for what?" Annabel said, incredulously. She looked punch drunk and each new revelation unsteadied her a little more. She fell back into the large sofa, her small frame seemed dwarfed by it.

Luke suddenly spoke. "Can I now explain to Annabel what *I* know. Obviously, I didn't know Mr Sumner had been killed but I did know about the rest." Luke was watching Annabel closely as he spoke. "I promised PC Ronson that I wouldn't tell *anyone* because I might have put all our lives in danger. But now Annabel can hear it, I would rather it came from me," he said, looking from one officer to the other.

Inspector Greco and Sophie looked at one another and nodded. Annabel sat forward, staring absently in front of her. Luke remained standing and Eva sat next to her mother and put her arm round her. Luke started to explain from the beginning - how he had found it hard to accept his friend Richard had killed himself, his meeting Rachel and his journey to Rome to find Annabel and tell her about her brother's death and to try and find answers. He talked about his suspicions of the uncle and Will, the son, and Sophie's enquiries back in England. He reminded Annabel of their conversation about the phone call when they first met and how this had made him wonder whether he had been wrong, and that his friend *had* probably killed himself after all. Then Luke went on to explain about Sophie's sudden appearance in Rome and the revelation that Russ had taken the ferry to England and driven to Darwen in February. Luke admitted that he wouldn't believe it at first but soon the sheer weight of evidence persuaded him of the truth. Russ had killed Richard. Throughout his testimony Luke watched Annabel, her face was inscrutable and emotionless. When Luke had finished he sat down across from Annabel, giving Sophie the cue to take up the story.

Sophie explained that she had been in contact with customs about Eric Harrington and his son Will Harrington and that when it drew a blank she decided to enquire about Russel and Annabel as they were the only others who could have benefitted from Richard's death. Russel's name, she said, came up immediately - he'd taken the Calais to Dover ferry on the Monday before Richard's body was found in Sunnyhurst Woods. Sophie explained how Russel had got a taxi from the port to Canterbury where he'd hired a car and driven down the M40 and M6 to Darwen. How - after a reconnaissance of the area during the day - Russel had parked his white van at the back of Richard's house and gained entry by some pretext.

That Russel had somehow over-powered Richard and strangled him in his home and then taken his body into the woods, and how he'd then made the murder look like suicide by hanging the body from a tree before driving back to Dover and returning to mainland Europe the next day. Annabel began to weep silently during Sophie's graphic account; child became mother as Eva pulled her mother's hair back from her face, stroking it, wiping away her mother's tears with the sleeve of her jumper. Assistant Benini brought in some coffees on a tray just as Sophie finished talking.

Inspector Greco then began his account. He'd received new evidence the previous evening from England - there had now been a positive identification of Mr Russel Sumner in Darwen the day Richard was murdered. And the same make and model of van that Mr Sumner had rented was seen behind Richard's house on the night in question by a neighbour putting out his bin. The same van had been caught on camera on the M6 motorway in the early on Tuesday morning. This new evidence had been enough for the authorities in Rome to grant an extradition order, and local police had been sent to arrest Mr Sumner that morning in Tuscany. The inspector became a little embarrassed when he explained that Mr Sumner had managed to evade arrest. Luke had presented his account in an understated, almost apologetic manner, but Inspector Greco's delivery was animated and dramatic, like Poirot. The inspector's clipped English made the comparison with the little Belgium detective even more apt in Luke's mind.

"Madam Sumner, now that you have heard these accounts," he said, "are you satisfied to come to the Carabinieri and make statement?" Inspector Greco asked.

"Yes," Annabel said in a half-whisper, nodding her head. All strength seemed to have left her. She had stopped weeping during the inspector's account although silent tears still ran down her face.

"And after that I do not think it wise for you to stay here tonight." Inspector Greco paused to gauge Annabel's reaction before going on. "This house must be sold. We know that the house was…how do you say…? Garanzia?" He paused, searching for words before Sophie intervened.

"This house now belongs to the building society," she said. "Around a year ago, Mr Sumner borrowed money against the house, using it as security."

"Did you know this situation, Mrs Sumner?" Greco asked.

Annabel shook her head. "When those men came they said this house belonged to them!" she said.

"Madam, this is very complicated, please understand." Greco added, "Mr Sumner had *many* debts…"

"Well what will I do?" Annabel suddenly became animated and interrupted the inspector. "I literally have nowhere to live!" she cried out. Annabel brushed aside her daughter and stood up from her position on the sofa. "This house was in joint names, you know?" she cried out.

"Yes, but it seems that Mr Sumner… er, copy your signature," the inspector said gently, as if he was talking to a child now.

Luke had watched helplessly as Annabel's life fell apart in such a sudden and public manner. She'd learnt her husband was dead and that he was a murderer…he'd murdered *her* own brother. And just as it seemed it could hardly get worse, she'd now learnt that she had lost *everything*. When Luke suddenly spoke again and broke the awful silence, it surprised everyone in the room. His tone seemed oddly upbeat and excited and his new sense of authority surprised even him.

"You can come back to England. You and Eva can come and live with me? It's not a big house like this but it's nice and it's got three bedrooms." He paused to assess Annabel's reaction. "I know Darwen's not Rome but the people are friendly…"

Annabel suddenly laughed at the ridiculousness of the notion, "We couldn't just…"

"Why not?" Luke interrupted jovially, "You said the other day…"

"I know, but it's not fair on you," she said.

"I would love nothing better," Luke said.

"And what about Eva?" Annabel pointed to her daughter.

"I'd love it!" Eva almost shouted. "You know what I think about England." She jumped up from the sofa with excitement.

Annabel turned to Eva. "But what about your schooling and all that?"

"Mum, what's more important right now?" Eva replied, decisively. "Anyway, they *do* have schools in England!"

"But a new educational system? And it won't be like The American School!" continued Annabel, trying to make sure that Eva understood the implications of such a decision.

"Mum, I'll manage, I promise," Eva said, "and anyway, I don't think we have much choice, do we!"

"And if you don't like it we can always come back to Italy when things have calmed down," Luke said. "I can sell up in England."

"I think you should listen to Mr Adams," Inspector Greco added. "Madam, I very much hope the men who killed Mr Sumner will not want to kill you but I think you must leave Rome now."

Luke was surprised at the inspector's candidness, he didn't know whether it was his limited English or a deliberate attempt to frighten Annabel into action. The initial excitement that Luke's offer had generated in the room had started to wane with the reminder of Russ' murder, quite probably by the same men who had been in the house that very morning. The closeness of death weighed heavily upon them all.

"Have you all got passports?" asked Assistant Benini, in an effort to distract Annabel.

"Yes," they said in unison.

"Good," said Greco. "Now first you must accompany me to the Carabinieri where PC Ronson, who is the British investigator, will interview you." He looked at Sophie who nodded. "Do you understand, Madam?"

"Yes," she said.

"You will be interviewed under caution, Mrs Sumner," said Sophie. Luke had never seen Sophie so serious. "Do you require a solicitor, Mrs Sumner?" she asked.

"Whatever for? Of course not!" Annabel said indignantly, turning to Sophie. "Can Luke stay with me?"

"I'm sorry, Mrs Sumner, but I must speak to you alone if you do not require a solicitor." Sophie said in the same serious tone.

Annabel nodded.

Luke attempted to lighten the mood: "So you *are* coming back with me to England, madam?" he asked Annabel, mimicking Greco's term of address.

"Yes, thank you," Annabel said, trying her best to raise a tired smile. "Thank you," she repeated, putting an arm around Eva. Within a matter of minutes, Annabel had been through the whole spectrum of emotions.

"What are we going to do with all *this*?" Annabel suddenly said, looking around her, and addressing no-one in particular.

"Madam, you must leave everything excepting your clothes, yes? You can collect them later but now we drive to the Carabinieri?' said the inspector, "After that, I will send officers to help you," he said.

When they arrived at the Carabinieri, Annabel was immediately taken away by Sophie and Inspector Greco. Luke and Eva were shown to a sparse waiting area with an inquiry desk and plastic chairs along two walls. It seemed to be the main thoroughfare for the local police and the general public. For all its culture and stunning architecture, Rome's main police station was remarkably prosaic.

Luke was aware that Eva had hardly spoken since the revelations. Whatever her issues with Russ, she had just learnt that the main male presence in her life was dead, killed in the most dramatic of circumstances. Luke had been standing as Annabel left but he now sat next to Eva and put his arm over her shoulder. She had sat down as soon as she had entered the room and folded her arms and rested her head on her chest, but now she leaned into Luke.

"Is it ok to say, I haven't the foggiest idea what to say to you right now… other than thank you for swinging the England thing?"

"No probs, brov," Eva said, with a little smile. "Probably not the way I imagined it, but I knew I would go home someday."

"Do you want to talk about your father?"

"There's little I can tell you - musician, lives in London, bit of loser, according to my mother who is obviously a great judge of character!" Eva said, flippantly, deliberately misunderstanding Luke's question.

"Thanks!"

"You know what I mean," she said, smiling at Luke. It was a weary smile. "Sorry, but I'm not going to cry any tears over Russ. Never really liked him…and obviously our relationship has not really improved much since I learnt he killed my uncle!"

Luke smiled: "You know, Eva, you have a good line in irony!"

"Trust a bloody English teacher to analyse language at a time like this!" she said. "Have you any cash with you?"

"A little. You want a coffee?" Luke asked.

"No, I need chocolate."

Luke counted out the coins in his pocket and gave them to Eva. "That will get you four euros of chocolate. Ok?"

"Ok," Eva said. "Thank you."

*

When Annabel finally returned to the waiting room with Sophie, she looked very tired and she had clearly been crying again. But Luke was reassured to see that she smiled warmly at him. Luke assumed the interview had gone quite well.

"Sweetheart," he said, embracing Annabel. Eva stood up and Luke put his arms around the two of them. "You've had the worst possible day, girls, and I cannot imagine how you are feeling at the moment - *but* we will get through this together, I promise," Luke said. "I promise."

No words came from Annabel and Luke's display of affection made her cry again. Her body shook as he held her.

Greco interrupted them with a gentle cough. "I'm sorry but we must now take statements from you Madam Sumner and you Mr Adams. I'm sorry," he repeated. "Regarding the visit of the men…"

The statements took another hour to complete. Luke finished first and as he made his way back to the waiting area he saw Sophie who was just leaving.

"So, are you finished here now?" he asked, feeling a little awkward.

"Finished here, yes. Off to Tuscany in the morning to see the girlfriend."

"So, you are certain he did it?

"As certain as anyone can be. Greco's just given me a sample of his DNA so we can try and match it up - mind, there's not much left in Richard's house now. But there's the rope and Richard's clothing."

"Anyway, I guess there's not going to be a trial now… with Russ dead," Luke said.

"No, but all the same I want to do a thorough job for the inquest…and for Richard."

"Thank you," Luke said as emphatically as he could. "*Thank you, Sophie.*"

Sophie seemed a little embarrassed by Luke's show of emotion and there followed an awkward silence.

"So, you finished with Annabel?" Luke asked, tentatively.

"Well, we shall need to speak to her again once she's in England. But we know where to find her!" Sophie said.

"Do you really need to speak to her again? Can't you just let her alone now, Sophie? After all she's been though, I want England to feel like a sanctuary for her."

"Sorry, Luke, it's procedure." Sophie's tone was suddenly cold and professional. "I've obviously got to check out her story with the girlfriend and then I'll have Annabel back in again."

"Bloody hell, that sounds ominous!" said Luke, a little offended by Sophie's tone.

Sophie deliberately ignored Luke's comment. "Just be careful, Luke, remember Annabel comes from a very different world to us. All this stuff with the mafia…"

"That's Russ, not her!" Luke interrupted.

"Let's hope so!"

"You really don't like her, do you?" said Luke, sounding hurt. "I'm really sorry you didn't get your day in the sun but that's not Annabel's fault!"

"What do you mean?" Sophie asked, looking confused.

"You didn't get to bring Russ home in hand-cuffs."

Sophie took a loud intake of breath and shook her head. She was angry and hurt: "Fuck you, Luke!" she said, deliberately averting her gaze. "God, you really don't understand, do you!"

At that moment Annabel came back into the waiting area.

She smiled at Sophie. "Are we going to find a hotel, Luke?" she asked.

"Yes, and then we need to think about getting a flight," Luke said to Annabel, although his eyes were still fixed on Sophie.

"Are you coming with us?" Annabel asked Sophie.

"No, I'm getting the train to Tuscany," Sophie replied.

"Well, let's get going then, Annabel?" Luke said, as Sophie walked towards the main door. Both of them watched her as she crossed the road outside the building and turn right before disappearing into the darkness of the night.

"You ok?" Luke said, touching Annabel's arm.

Annabel nodded and smiled weakly. "I've had better days," she said.

At that moment Inspector Greco appeared again. He was excited. "Sorventindete Capo, the Chief Policeman, is coming to the Carabiniera tonight," he said impressively, like he was announcing a prize fighter. He wanted to speak to Annabel and the whole Carabiniera was on high alert; it wasn't often they were visited by this important man.

"Must we stay? You can see Annabel is exhausted." Luke said.

"You must. It is very important," said Greco. "*There is a development.*"

CHAPTER 17: GOING HOME

After another thirty-minute wait, news came through that the senior policeman had just arrived and would see Luke and Annabel in his office along with Inspector Greco. Eva was asked to wait outside and Luke and Annabel were ushered into a plush office that looked out high above the city. Sorventindete Capo sat at his desk with the dark city skyline behind him. His was a small, wiry man who he smelt of cigarettes and strong cologne. Luke noticed that the white shirt under his tunic was creased, no doubt he had been called out suddenly. It would probably account for the air of impatience he gave off. The large desk was empty save for a single sheet of A4 paper.

Capo nodded at Annabel and Luke and motioned for them to sit down. He spoke quickly and aggressively in Italian to Greco who nodded constantly. After he had spoken, Greco relayed the latest developments to Annabel and Luke. It had now been established, he said, that the Ndrangheta from Calabria had killed Mr Russel Sumner and they were eager to take full responsibility for it. They had let it be known via social media that this was punishment for stealing money and insulting the Cosa Nostra.

Greco went on to explain that there had been various attempts recently to challenge these big players in the Italian mafia. They were separate from the Sicilian Mafioso and not as well known outside Italy but, nevertheless, a powerful force within Italy itself. This killing was a clear message to all who underestimated them.

The chief lent forward and talked animatedly again to Inspector Greco. Inspector Greco responded by nodding his head and the occasional "Si, Si." After the chief had finished Inspector Greco turned to Annabel and translated.

"We have not heard directly from Ndrangheta, but we believe now that Mr Sumner was a courier for them," he said.

"Drugs, you mean!" Annabel exclaimed.

"Yes, last week we learn he delivered cocaine to Lyon for Ndrangheta. The money was exchanged but there was a problem…with the weight." Greco paused. "It was too…how you say…light?" Greco paused to allow Annabel to digest this new information.

"So, they assume that Russ had taken some of the cocaine?" Luke said.

"Yes, yes," the chief said, obviously understanding Luke's English.

"This is very embarrassing for Ndrangheta," Greco went on, "for their reputation. Reputation is everything."

The chief gave a weary sigh and signalled for Greco to continue. "This is taken very seriously by the mafia, Madam Sumner. The Ndrangheta must show their contacts in Lyon too that they have taken the matter very seriously."

"I fear, you, Madam…and Miss Sumner may be in danger," Sorventindete Capo warned, speaking English for the first time. "You must leave Rome immediately. You understand?"

"I don't know anything about the money!" Annabel cried out. "And I don't know about any drugs either!" She was trembling now. Luke put his arm around her.

Inspector Greco spoke again: "You knew, you did not know … it will make little difference to The Padrino, I fear. Your husband, Madam Sumner, has insulted him personally."

"In these cases the mafia punish first and then retrieve," the chief added. Did your husband use cocaine, Mrs Sumner?" It was clear that the Capo could speak English when he wanted.

"I do not know, we lived separate lives." Annabel said.

The chief let out an impatient gasp. "But he visited your house in Rome, yes?" said the chief.

Luke wanted to help Annabel: "He rarely came. Since I have been living there in March he has only visited twice."

The Sorventindete Capo nodded at Luke to show he understood his point.

"So, Madam, you have never seen him use cocaine?"

"Once or twice maybe."

"Thank you, madam." Capo smirked, celebrating a minor victory in establishing that Russel may well have taken the drugs for himself.

And as if to reiterate Greco said, "A quantity of cocaine was found in a rucksack we found in the car."

Once again Sorventindete Capo bombarded the inspector with an Italian onslaught. Luke wondered why he did not simply speak in English to them, he was clearly capable.

When he had finished Greco spoke again: "As for the money, the Ndrangheta believe they own your house - but we understand that it now belongs to the societa edile…to Santander. When Ndrangheta learn, they will be very angry.

Very angry, madam!" Greco paused as the chief passed him the A4 paper.

"Mr Sumner had many debts and has no money to reimburse Ndrangheta," he said, looking down at the paper.

"Madam Sumner, have you any money? Now please you must be truthful, madam, did Mr Sumner give you *any* money or items of value?" Sorventindete Capo asked.

"No," said Annabel, her voice was weak and hardly audible. "He paid all the bills and my credit card. That's all I had," Annabel insisted.

"Yes, there is a balance of 6000 euros." Greco said, looking down at the paper he was now holding. "And Mr Sumner had other cards, his full debt on credit cards - nearly 50,000 euro."

"I ask you again, do you have any assets, madam?"

"No."

"Or do you know of any assets that Mr Sumner might have?" The Superintendent pressed.

"No. There's the car, but I think that's rented. He had a couple of houses in Tuscany - I think he sold them recently. You will need to ask Alessia," Annabel said, impatiently.

"Is that the girl he lived with?" Greco asked.

Annabel nodded.

"We shall, Madam Sumner." Greco said, "She too may be in danger."

"Have you got police looking after her?" asked Luke, suddenly remembering that Sophie would be visiting her in the morning.

"Yes, someone has stayed with her since we informed her about Mr Sumner," Greco said.

The Superintendent looked like he had the weight of the world on his shoulders. Once again, he spoke to Greco in Italian but a little calmer this time. And, once again, Greco relayed what had been said: "If what you tell us is true madam, Sorventindete Capo wants to try to help you." Greco looked at his boss who now put his head back, inviting Greco to go on speaking for him. "He likes to maintain dialogue with Ndrangheta. He will try to convince them, yes, that it would not be in their interest to punish you, madam, or your daughter, yes." He paused again. "But he says once again, madam, you must leave the city."

Annabel nodded to show she understood.

"Mr Adams, did you at any time discuss where you live in England with these men?" Greco asked.

"*No*!" Luke paused and thought hard. "No, we talked about England but not about where I lived, I'm quite certain." Luke said.

"Good. I am hoping Mr Sumner did not." Inspector Greco turned his attention to Annabel again. "We shall transport you to a hotel tonight. Tomorrow, we shall take you to collect personal items, yes. Take only some clothes, shoes, photographs if you wish, passport, yes? Please leave everything else, yes?"

Annabel nodded again.

"We shall escort all of you to Milan Aeroporto and you shall fly to London." His tone was serious and emphatic. "We have a reservation. Ok?"

Annabel turned to Luke who nodded. "Yes, ok," he said, "I'll be ok."

Annabel seemed mollified by what Greco had told her. Her demeanour was now calmer, almost neutral. She had retreated so far into herself it was as if she wasn't there.

Sorventindete Capo got to his feet, signalling the meeting was over. He nodded to Sergeant Greco who in turn ushered Luke and Annabel out of the room.

"You are very honoured." Sergeant Greco said, as he escorted Annabel and Luke down the corridor to where Eva was waiting. "If you were Italian you would not have this attention."

"What do you mean?" asked Luke.

"How do you say…you would be thrown to the wolves, yes?" the inspector said with a smirk. "But you, my friend, have our protection!" he said shaking his finger to emphasise the point. "One Englishman has died in our city, that is enough. Bad for tourists!" he said, smiling.

They joined Eva outside who was full of concern. "Not now," Annabel said as she started to ask questions.

The three were driven in an unmarked car to an anonymous hotel in an anonymous part of the city. Another car followed behind. Once they had stopped, two officers directed them into the hotel and through the lobby, straight into the lift and then to a room on the top floor. The room contained a double and a single bed and a view of a car park. It had all the charm of a hotel Luke once stopped at a stag night in Blackpool.

All three were exhausted and although there were many things to speak about the conversation focused on the immediate concerns of sleeping arrangements. Annabel and Eva stripped down to their underwear and got straight into the double bed. Luke lay on the single bed, still fully dressed. He immediately switched out the light.

"Did Greco ask you what those men looked like?" Annabel said, suddenly, in the darkness.

"No, he just asked about what they said," Luke replied.

"Well, how are they expected to find them, find whoever killed Russ?"

"I doubt very much that anyone will ever be charged with Russ' murder, Annabel," Luke said, wearily. "Now try and get some sleep."

"Why, what do you mean?" Annabel switched on the bedside light and sat up in bed.

"Annabel, you heard Greco, he said Sorventindete Capo likes to have dialogue with the mafia. I guess it goes something like: *'You leave the wife and daughter and girlfriend alone and we turn a blind eye to who killed Mr Sumner. Capiche?"*

"You think?"

"I'm certain!" Luke said. "Now can we please go to sleep?"

Annabel turned out the light. "Thank you, Luke," she said.

"It's always a pleasure. But just be very careful with your packing tomorrow, yeah? If in doubt, leave it out!" Luke said. "Now get to sleep, sweetheart, Eva's snoring already."

*

Luke was woken early by a persistent but gentle knocking. At first, he was disorientated and it took a few seconds for him to get his bearings and remember why he was in this strange room. He went to the door.

"Hello," he said.

"You must come now, please," a voice said, from the other side of the door.

"Ok, ten minutes. Thank you," returned Luke. Annabel was slowly rousing, she had been wakened too by the knocking. "Wake Eva, we need to be out in ten minutes." Luke had an urgency in his voice.

They opened the hotel door ten minutes later. Two policemen were waiting for them and ushered them into the lift, then through the reception area and out into a large black Mercedes people carrier, like one of those Luke had seen delivering film stars to and from The Oscars. It contained a driver and two other policemen with automatic rifles in their laps. One sat next to the driver, the other in the back with

Luke, Annabel and Eva. After the door was closed, the policeman in the back smiled and handed over a Macdonald's bag containing breakfast muffins and cartons of orange juice. The three of them had not eaten since breakfast the previous day and Luke and Eva ate their food quickly. Annabel pinched at her muffin with little interest.

"You have your key, yes?" the policeman asked Annabel as she stared absently through the window.

"Yes," she said.

"Good."

"Are we going straight there?" Luke asked.

"Yes, we go straight," the officer replied, gesturing with his forefinger.

The party sat in silence and it wasn't long before they arrived at the top of the steps and parked on the little road, the road Luke had walked down that first day with Annabel. He hadn't looked at his watch or phone but he knew it was early. The light had not yet come up and there was still a chill in the air as the Mercedes' door slid open. The officer took the key from Annabel with a "Please?" and led the way. Luke turned to see another black Mercedes carrier pull up behind and park across the full width of the road, blocking it off. He noticed there was a police car blocking the road in front of them too. Four uniformed officers emerged wearing flak jackets and carrying sub-machine guns. Four sets of eyes scoured the immediate vicinity whilst the officers who had been in the Mercedes ushered the party into the house. Annabel grasped Eva close to her as she walked through the now open door.

They returned to the vestibule by the front door twenty minutes later with three suitcases, one piece of hand luggage each, and a guitar - all the officers would permit. It hadn't been difficult for Luke, he'd travelled light and had acquired a few new clothes, but that was all. But he felt keenly for Annabel – it was like she had just packed for the rest of her life, in twenty minutes. He imagined the choices she had had to make from her extensive - and expensive - wardrobe. Whilst an officer checked the bags, Annabel walked back up the stairs and Luke followed her into the kitchen. She paused for a second, staring out onto the balcony as the first light of day broke through the darkness: it was sad and mysterious and beautiful, like Annabel. When she became aware of Luke's gaze upon her she forced a smile and then slowly closed the blinds on the large doors. "I must check the other rooms," she said. Her tone seemed strangely light as if she were discarding a mere trifle, but Luke understood the deep emotions coursing through her small frame. She was walking away from a world that yesterday had seemed so secure, so certain. Eva and Luke filled the Mercedes, allowing Annabel the time to say her farewell to each room in turn.

When Annabel finally reappeared in the vestibule, the officer motioned with his hand for her to lead the way out of the house. The officers followed Annabel, Eva and then Luke and an officer locked the door and put the key in his pocket.

"Do you have another key, Madam?" he asked, as they stepped into the carrier.

"I've left them on the table in the kitchen," Annabel replied.

The officer nodded. He closed the door of the Mercedes and the car was manoeuvred out of the street. At the same time the four officers with automatic weapons climbed back into the second carrier, its headlights shone bright in the darkness and lit up the narrow street.

The city had not yet wakened and within minutes they were across the bridge and past St Peters, and then on down the road through Auriela, near Camping Roma. The second black Mercedes followed closely. There was silence in the carrier, the policeman in the back did not speak and nor did Luke and Annabel. Even when they merged onto the autoroute and were waved through the barrier they did not speak. Eva was asleep, her head on her mother's shoulder with Annabel's arm around her. Luke sat opposite Annabel and when he caught her eye he mouthed, "I love you."

"I love you too," Annabel mouthed back, but her eyes showed no sign of the life. A shell of a women sat in front of him that used to be Annabel.

"It's going to be alright," Luke wanted to say, *"I'm going to watch over you and keep you safe and make you happy again…I promise, it's going to be ok,"* Luke wanted to say.

EPILOGUE

Annabel understood what Luke was thinking. Luke was a good man. These last few months had been the happiest of her life. And it was because of Luke. And if things had been different she would have been happy to grow old with him in England, of course she would. Get a part-time job, help in the community, go walking with the dog. But this could never be: the very thing that had brought them together would eventually, inevitably tear them apart. She so wished she had met Luke before this…and yet without <u>*this*</u> *they would have never met in the first place.*

"What a fucking paradox!" she said to herself, as she fondled the pearls in her pocket. The safe was at the back of a fitted cupboard that could only be accessed when all the drawers in the cabinet had been removed and the false back had been slid away. It was as if Russ had always been expecting a day like this. She'd had to act quickly whilst Luke and Eva were packing the Mercedes and waiting for her. Some of her jewellery was missing - Russ must have raided the safe on an earlier visit - but the pearls alone would fetch enough to get the best legal advice if there was to be a fight for her father's estate. Her father owed her that at least…and now Richard was dead she would inherit everything, she was determined about that.

Annabel shuddered when she thought about what she would have to do with the pearls inside the public toilet at the airport, but there were just some things you had to do if you wanted it all. And Annabel still wanted it all: she wanted Luke, she wanted Eva to be happy, but more than anything she wanted to be…'comfortable' again, that word Luke had used. Comfortable like before Russ had dropped the bombshell. Now she hadn't a penny to her name, not enough to buy a sandwich, she was totally reliant on Luke and it wasn't fair: it wasn't fair on Luke…and it wasn't fair on her.

And now she was being taken to Richard's town, fate's final sick joke. She imagined the dark wood and the hanging man, his lifeless stare would never leave her - even if God had left her. But she had always known that. It couldn't all have been for nothing, could it?

THE END

Andrew Lewis lives in Darwen, Lancashire, with Amanda. He is a teacher of English and *A Light Deficiency* is his first novel.

Made in the USA
Middletown, DE
30 September 2021